PROTECTING Braden

Custos Securities Series
Book 2
By
Luna David

Protecting Braden
Custos Securities Series Book 2
Copyright © 2016 and 2018 by Luna David
ALL RIGHTS RESERVED

Cover by Kellie Dennis at Book Cover by Design
Custos Securities Series emblem designed by Kellie Dennis, property of Luna David.
Edited by Jessica McKenna at http://liteditor.com/
Editing by Miranda Vescio at V8 Editing and Proofreading
Proofreading by Allison Holzapfel at Allison's Author Services
Interior Design by Morningstar Ashley at Designs by Morningstar
Interior Design and Formatting by Flawless Touch Formatting

The unauthorized reproduction or distribution of this copyrighted work is illegal. No part of this book may be reproduced or transmitted in any form or by any means, including electronic or mechanical means, including photocopying, recording, or by any information storage and retrieval systems, without express written permission from the author, Luna David, author.luna.david@gmail.com. The only exception is in the case of brief quotations embodied in reviews.

This book is a work of fiction. While references may be made to actual places and events, the names, characters, places, and incidents either are products of the author's imagination or are used fictitiously. Any resemblance to actual persons, living or dead, events, or locales is entirely coincidental.
Licensed material is being used for illustrative purposes only and any person depicted in the licensed material is a model.

Warnings

Intended for an adult audience. Contains explicit sexual content, violence, and elements of BDSM. **HEA ending, no cliffhanger.**
Trigger warning: physical assault and recollections of past sexual assault.

Trademark

Luna David acknowledges the trademark status of the following trademarks mentioned in this work of fiction:

iPad, Google, Walmart, Honda, Green Berets, SEALs, Special Forces, Imitrex, Pretty Woman, Ray LaMontagne's "Hold You in My Arms", Velcro, Fleshlight, Kindle, MH-47G Chinook Helicopter, Fort Carson, Lers Ros, Peet's Coffee, St. Regis Hotel, Starry Night

Dedication

To my readers, for loving my guys as much as I do. Thank you for being patient and in some cases, not so patient, while waiting for Braden and Z's happy ever after.

Once more, to my husband.... forever and always. Your constant support means the world to me. Again, I've failed in my assignment of picking your chosen title for my second book, *A Submariner's Tale: Long, Hard, and Full of Seaman*. It was a close call, but in the end, I had to go with *Protecting Braden*.

Chapter 1

BRADEN

Braden's brain came back online slowly, almost like an old computer that took forever to boot, running through its programs, one by one. The very first thing he noticed was he felt as if he was weighed down by something. He couldn't move his arms or legs. He tried lifting his head and got even more frustrated. His head, his ribs, his wrist, all of it fucking hurt. Not being able to move yet feeling so much pain filled him with a sense of foreboding he couldn't fully comprehend. Everything seemed fuzzy, muddled. He forced himself to calm down and tried to use his other senses to figure out what was going on.

He breathed in through his nose, trying his best to smell something, anything, but realized there was something stuck in his nose that felt strange and uncomfortable. He couldn't smell much, but there were some lingering, familiar scents, though nothing he could put his finger on, irritating him. He kept trying, but nothing came to him, so he moved on.

Braden listened carefully and tried to pick up on any sounds, any clue; where he was, who he was with, how long he'd been out, what had happened. He still wasn't getting enough input from his senses to answer those questions So, he quieted his mind, stopped the jumbled, panicked thoughts, and tried to quiet his breathing. There it was, music playing softly in the background.

A song ended, another began; both he was very familiar with. His heart picked up speed. That was good, right? Wasn't that good? He couldn't answer that, but those two songs, by different artists, came one right after the other on his long "Baking" playlist. The first stirrings of hope bloomed.

He wasn't about to give up now that he'd recognized something, so he tried little things like moving his fingers, his toes, his lips, his eyelids, even his nose. Then he tried everything all over again, found it was working and figured some movement was better than none. His whole body felt weighed down, and he sincerely hoped a blanket was what gave him that feeling.

Again, he tried to move his hand and flex his fingers but found them caught by something and tightened his grip, trying to use it as a catalyst to keep going. Something, someone, next to him shifted. His heart rate ratcheted up, and he couldn't figure out why someone being in the bed with him would freak him out, but it did. He concentrated on his eyes. Squeezing them tighter, he moved them around and tried to open them. He couldn't. Frustration filled him again and he shook his head or tried to. He let out a soft moan and startled himself when he heard it. Once again, he tried to open his eyes, and this time, he was somewhat successful, but everything was cast in shadow. His eyes felt tired, and they drooped shut again, but he forced them back open.

He looked at the ceiling. He lowered his eyes and looked at the wall in front of him. It was green with a TV mounted on it, so he knew he wasn't at home. He looked to his right and saw a curtain hanging from the ceiling, pulled halfway shut, blocking a door, and knew right away he was in a hospital. He moaned, scared all over again. How did he get here? What had happened to him?

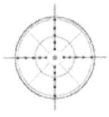

Cade

Cade had finally succumbed to exhaustion. As he took stock, he realized he must have been asleep for several hours because he felt much better, both mentally and physically. Remnants of a wonderful dream still flitting through his mind, he had no idea what had awoken him until he felt movement beside him. He heard Braden moan, and his eyes sprang open. His heartbeat quickened when he saw Braden was awake and looking around confused. He was so surprised his breath caught, and he only managed to whisper Braden's name. When Braden finally turned his gorgeous green eyes on him, they were somewhat dazed. At first, he looked confused then Cade saw realization dawn, and with it came abject sadness and guilt. Fuck. He shook his head and moved to clasp Braden's face in his hands. Before he could utter a word, Braden had tears running unchecked down his face.

"I'm sorry, I'm sorry, I'm so sorry," he whispered, brokenly, over and over again.

"Shhh. Braden, no. Baby, stop, you have nothing to be sorry for. Shhh." Cade moved closer to Braden, wanting desperately to take him in his arms. Shudders wracked Braden's body, and there was such sorrow there Cade did his best to wrap himself around Braden protectively, being careful of his injuries. Braden struggled to turn toward him, and Cade tried to stop him. "Sweetheart don't move. You've got a lot of injuries, and I don't want you hurting yourself. Let me call the doctor. You've been in a diabetic coma for two days."

Braden shook his head. "Not yet. Wait, please. Not yet."

Cade acquiesced and continued to hold Braden, whispering to him, telling him he was going to be all right. Braden's sobs finally ebbed, and they lay in each other's arms. Braden placed his hand over Cade's which was cupping his cheek. Tears were still leaking steadily from his eyes as they looked at each other, Cade's eyes moist as well.

"I'm sorry, I wasn't thinking, I just reacted. In my head, I had to save you guys from Eric, and I went, I just left. Like my default setting was to do what he said, and I couldn't see any other way. As soon as I got in the car, I knew I'd made a mistake, but he sped off, and I didn't have a chance to get away."

"You're here now, Braden, and you won't make the same mistake twice. We can talk about everything later, but now, please, let me call the nurse. I can see you're in pain. I can raise the head of the bed, so you aren't flat on your back."

Braden nodded, and Cade got the bed in a comfortable position for him. When he pressed the call button, a nurse's voice came through the intercom, and Cade told her Braden was awake. She said the doctor was at nurse's station, and she would notify him.

Braden looked fearful and Cade reassured him. "You're all right, you're going to be just fine. I love you, Braden. I love you so damn much."

Braden whispered, "I love you, too," just as a doctor and a nurse walked through the door, flipping on the overhead lights. The doctor walked up to Braden, who was cringing a bit, and smiled.

"Hello, Braden, I'm Dr. Himmel." He reached out to shake Braden's hand. "Glad to see the best scone maker in San Francisco is awake. You gave us quite a scare, young man. How are you feeling?"

Braden explained he felt nauseous and was experiencing pain pretty much all over. Dr. Himmel used a penlight to check Braden's pupils, causing him to jerk his head back and moan. The doctor raised his eyebrows. "Braden, what is it?"

"The light shining in my eyes is like daggers to my skull, and the overheads aren't much better."

Cade sat up fully and Braden reached out and placed his casted hand on Cade's leg, silently asking him not to leave. Before the doctor could inquire, Cade looked at Braden. "I'm not going anywhere, Bray. Is it a migraine?"

Braden closed his eyes and took stock of how he felt. The doctor asked the nurse to turn off the overhead lights. "Do you get migraines often?"

"Migraines with aura, mostly when I'm under stress and my insulin has been off. Yeah, I'm feeling like that's part of what's going on with me right now." He reached up and gingerly touched where his head had been injured and winced. "The rest is centered right here, where he slammed my head against the car window."

Cade growled, curling his hands into fists, and Braden rubbed his casted wrist along Cade's thigh to calm him. Dr. Himmel gave them both a sympathetic look. "What medications do you usually take for your migraines?"

"Imitrex."

Dr. Himmel nodded. "Okay, good. That's safe for you to take right now. How is the pain from your other injuries?"

"Not good. I'm feeling pretty awful."

"That doesn't surprise me. You were held captive without your insulin for over twenty-four hours and severely beaten by your kidnapper. It's going to take your body some time to heal. I'm going to have Samantha here draw some blood and take your blood pressure. Let me ask a few more questions then we'll run a few tests. In the meantime, I'll place the order for Imitrex and other pain meds."

Cade caressed Braden's arm. "Baby, do you still have your contacts in? If you've been wearing them since Eric abducted you, they're probably shot and contributing to your pain."

Braden blinked his gritty eyes and nodded. His dexterity wasn't what it should have been, so it took him several tries, but a few grumbled expletives later, he pinched the offending lenses out of his eyes, handed them to Cade, and fell back against the bed, strangely exhausted.

Cade kissed him softly on the crown of his head. "I think I asked Maya to bring your glasses. Let me see if she did."

Cade got off the bed, tossed the contacts, and dug into the bag on the reclining chair beside them. He came up with Braden's glasses case, took them out and handed them over. He could tell the pain hadn't lessened when Braden winced again and rubbed at his temples. Cade got back onto the bed with him and they waited for the doctor.

Dr. Himmel continued to tap in his updates on the iPad then looked up. "Do you have any specific concerns besides those we're going to alleviate with the meds?"

"When I was first waking up, I felt like I was weighed down. I couldn't move. I tried my arms, my legs, my head, my entire body. Now I can move everything, it's just painful. Is there a reason for that?"

"That's a common feeling coming out of a coma, especially if you've been through some physical trauma. Essentially, your brain was having a tough time getting signals to your body. So now that your brain is basically back online, the signals your brain sends to the rest of your body are working. When you were comatose, those signals weren't getting through. Does that make sense?"

Braden nodded. "Do I need to worry about it happening again, not being able to move? And I know this is probably a stupid question, but am I in danger of going back into a coma?"

Dr. Himmel smiled. "No questions about your health are stupid. You shouldn't have any further issues, and you're not in danger of lapsing back into a coma. You were in a coma because you hadn't gotten your insulin, and you stayed in a coma longer than you would have, I believe, as a result of your other injuries. I think your body just needed a little more time. Is there anything else?"

Braden blushed. "Yeah, when can I get all the tubes out?" He gently touched the tube that was coming out of his nose. "I'm fine with this thing, if I'm still getting meds and fluids that way, but can I have the others taken out?"

"Do you feel like you can walk?"

Cade couldn't keep himself from interjecting. "If he can't walk himself, I'll carry him. Please have everything removed as he's asked."

Dr. Himmel smiled patiently. "We'll send a nurse in to get the catheters, but I'd like to keep the Nasogastric tube in place. We can remove it in the morning and then start you on some simple, easy to digest foods as we monitor your glucose levels. I'll evaluate the test results once the lab issues them to me, and I'll be back in a few hours to check on your meds and everything else. We're glad you're back with us, Braden. Cade has been worried, and you've had a lot of family and friends here to visit. I'll see you in a bit."

The doctor went out the door, but the nurse stayed for several minutes doing what she needed to do to get the tests underway. She smiled and patted Braden on the arm. "I'll be your main nurse while you're here. You can call me Sam. Let me get this blood sample to the lab, and I'll be back in a bit."

When another nurse came in to remove the catheters, Cade asked if Braden wanted to have some privacy, but regretted it immediately. He hated the stark fear that leapt into Braden's eyes at the thought of him leaving.

Sam came back with several syringes, which she injected into Braden's NG, telling them the meds should ease his pain fairly quickly. She patted Braden on the arm and left them alone. Cade turned all the remaining lights off and lowered the bed when he saw Braden fading. "Do you want to change positions and try your side?"

When Braden nodded, Cade helped move him to the far side of the bed, rolling him onto his right side to avoid aggravating his injuries. "Would you be more comfortable holding onto some pillows? I can sit in the chair next to you."

Braden shook his head and reached his hand toward Cade. "Mmm-mm. Please."

Cade lowered himself gently onto the bed. Braden lifted his head, and Cade slid his arm under it. Braden snuggled up next to him, gently placing his leg over Cade's and leaning his head on his chest. Holding Braden in his arms made him feel whole. He vowed to never again take being with Braden for granted.

Braden started to apologize for needing him, so Cade kissed him on the head and shushed him. "No more apologizing. We have time to talk about everything later. Right now, I need to do my job and take care of you. You're exhausted and in pain, so I need you to sleep for me, okay? I'm going to wait until tomorrow morning to call Nana and Maya. I know they'd head over here no matter the hour, but I think you need some time to rest."

Cade heard Braden sigh and felt him nod against his chest. His smaller body began to slowly relax against Cade's own, and he knew from the way Braden's grip loosened he was sleeping. Cade kissed Braden's head again and rubbed his wide palm soothingly up and down Braden's back. This moment felt like a culmination of everything he'd been hoping and, if he was honest, praying for since the moment Braden had been taken from him. He was so grateful everything he needed in the world was sleeping in his arms.

Sam came in to check on Braden. After checking his monitor, she glanced up and caught Cade's eyes. "The drugs kick in?"

"Yeah, hopefully he sleeps the rest of the night."

Nodding, she walked toward the bed, lifted the call button cord, and wrapped it around the railing on the side of the bed. "If you need anything, don't hesitate to push it." She patted Cade on the shoulder and smiled warmly at Braden.

As she turned to walk out, Cade whispered, "Thank you, Sam."

Cade woke up around eight-thirty a.m. and was surprised he'd slept that late, until he realized Braden was still asleep, cuddled up next to him. Sam had come in the middle of the night to administer a second dose of all meds to allow Braden to sleep as peacefully as possible. He'd had a rough night of pain and bad dreams, waking several times in a panic, only being reassured by Cade's presence, his voice, and his touch.

He lay there for a while, listening to Braden breathing, feeling so thankful he had him back in his arms. Careful not to wake him, Cade reached for his phone which was charging next to the bed and texted his business partner and best friend.

Cade: Braden out of coma. Let Maya, Nana, S & J know. Give us at least an hour before you head over and keep visitors to u 3 today.

Cooper: Thank fuck. See you in a bit.

Cade was about to respond when he felt Braden shift and let out a low moan. He rubbed his hand lightly through Braden's hair and felt him flinch away from his touch and whimper. Frowning, he whispered soothing words which seemed to calm him immediately, and he dropped back to sleep. Cade gave it a few minutes before lifting his phone again and texting.

Cade: Will be a rough day. Text when u arrive. Might need to keep people out.

Cooper: Will do. They're going to want to know, is he going to be okay?

Cade: Eventually.

Cooper: I want at this guy.

Cade: Get in line.

He messaged his family and let them know Braden was awake, but it would be best to wait another day to come to the hospital. He set his phone aside and rested a little while longer, not wanting to let Braden go.

Before he realized it, nearly an hour had passed. Cade needed to use the bathroom and knew he didn't have much time before Braden woke up and the ladies showed up with Cooper. He slowly extricated himself from underneath Braden, placing a couple of pillows strategically so Braden wouldn't think he was alone. The fact he didn't wake him up was testament to the meds they'd administered and the exhaustion that must still be weighing him down.

He quickly used the toilet, remembering he had a change of clothes. He checked on Braden to be sure he was still sleeping, took a quick shower, changed his clothes, and brushed his teeth. As he was walking out of the bathroom, his cell vibrated, notifying him of an incoming text. Making sure Braden was still asleep, he checked his phone and went to the door to head off Cooper and the ladies.

He walked through the door and saw them coming down the hall. Approaching them, he gave each of them a hug. "He's still sleeping. The meds they gave him last night knocked him out."

Maya's brow furrowed in confusion. "He woke up last night?"

Cade glanced down at Maya and nodded. "He did, yeah."

Her face crumpled, and his heart clenched at her pain. "But, why didn't you call us?"

He reached out and rubbed her shoulders, drawing her into his side and gave her a one-armed hug. "I know you'd have liked to be here, but he woke up last evening, disoriented and panicked, and when he realized what happened, he completely broke down. He was in a lot of pain from his injuries and he had a huge migraine. He wasn't in a good place and frankly, visitors were the last thing on our minds."

She nodded in understanding, but he could still see she was frustrated. She held herself rigid, unwilling to put her arm around him yet. He sighed and glanced over at Cooper and Nana, willing them to understand. "He needed rest and he's struggling right now. I'm only out here because he's asleep. He's scared out of his mind and having bad dreams, and so far, I've been able to soothe him."

Maya's whole body sagged at that admission and she finally relented, leaning her head against his side and wrapping her arm around his waist. He went still in her grasp when he heard Braden called out for him then again, much louder, panicked. Cade turned and ran, tossing back to them over his shoulder, "I'll let you know when it's okay for you to come in."

It was still fairly dark in the room as he'd kept the curtains drawn and the lights off. Braden was in a full-blown panic, sitting up, looking around frantically, having thrown off his covers as if he was going to get out of bed. Cade sat on the edge of the bed and captured Braden's face in his hands. "I'm here, Bray. I'm here."

Braden's body was shaking violently, and Cade cursed himself for having left him even for a second. He wouldn't make that mistake again. He gathered him gently in his arms, rocking him. Braden gripped him hard. "You were gone," He released a shaky breath. "Don't... Please, just don't leave."

Knowing he'd put Braden through such panic killed him. "Baby, I'm not going anywhere. I'm right here. You're with me, you're safe."

Braden's eyes were still filled with fear. "I'm sorry, I just can't be away from you right now."

"You have nothing to be sorry about. I'm the one who's sorry, I shouldn't have stepped out. I didn't leave you; I won't ever leave you, Bray. I was just outside the door speaking with Maya and Nana. They came to see you. I thought you were sleeping soundly, and I didn't want to wake you."

Cade moved the bed into a sitting position, gathered Braden onto his lap, and continued to hold him. Braden curled up, tucked his head underneath Cade's chin, and fidgeted with the cast on his left hand. "I panicked. I just remember it seemed like every time I woke up there, he beat me. Every time I wake up now, I feel like he's going to be there. I knew, in my head, you were here somewhere, but I kept thinking he would show up instead."

Cade's jaw clenched, and his arms tightened around him. "Fuck, Braden, I'm so sorry we didn't find you faster. I failed you when you needed me most."

Braden shook his head, crying silently. "No, don't you see? I failed you! I made it impossible. I left behind all the things that would have helped you find me. I wasn't thinking clearly. All I could think about was the fact you were all in danger. How could I have gone with him? I *chose* to go with him!"

"Braden, we have time to go through all that later, but for right now, I know you're still hurting. I know your migraine is still bothering you and you probably need some more meds. Let me call the nurse."

Braden shook his head again. "Can you help me take a shower?"

"Braden, you're exhausted, let's do that later."

Braden's body shuddered. "I can't. I have to do it now. I can't have him on me. He touched me, Zavier. I have to get clean. I feel filthy."

Cade stopped caressing Braden, his whole body stilled with tension. "Braden, did he… The doctors said he didn't…" His hands curled into fists and he let out a choppy breath. "I'm gonna fuckin' kill him."

Braden realized what Cade was referring to and finally looked up at him, but Cade's eyes were squeezed shut. Braden raised his hand to softly touch his face which had him popping his anguished eyes open and looking down at him. He shook his head, his voice much stronger. "No. No, nothing like that. I was either passed out or in a coma, which I think is the only reason he didn't. I just still feel him touching me, and I'm sure I smell awful. I just want to feel clean and wash the experience off of me. Will you help me?"

"Of course. There's a seat in there too. Let me call the nurse, so they can detach the NG and cover up your cast to keep it dry."

Sam came in, removed the NG, and brought a long plastic glove to cover Braden's cast. She helped them remove all his bandages, said it was all right for them to wash the areas with soap and she'd come back in half an hour with more meds. Cade locked them in the bathroom and slowly removed their clothing. He turned on the shower and had Braden sit under the hot spray, letting the water soothe his tired body. He washed and conditioned Braden's hair then helped clean the rest of him quickly but thoroughly.

He got Braden into some fresh clothes, and already, he could tell Braden felt more like himself. He smiled as he took the remote control and lowered the head of the bed just a bit. Sam came back in, this time with pain meds in pill form Braden tossed back. He was getting drowsy but insisted on seeing Nana and Maya, so Cade texted Cooper they were ready.

It was only a minute later when all three of them appeared, clearly anxious to see him. Cade moved off the bed to give everyone more room to see Braden, but the panicked noise Braden made as he reached out to Cade, brought Cade back immediately to his side. He tucked his arm behind Braden and could only feel sadness when Braden drew his legs up and curled into his side, seeking protection and sending a signal to everyone he wasn't ready to be touched.

Maya set down two coffee cups and a bag containing breakfast for them. Braden, uninterested in food and throat hurting from the NG tube removal, passed on breakfast and watched as Cade ate both meals and drank both coffees one handed, his other still tucked around him. Braden chatted a little, but it was mostly the ladies that kept the conversation going. Cade could tell Braden wasn't tracking, he was so exhausted.

Cooper got his attention by lifting a bag. He pointed to the corner sink where he'd placed the sandwich cooler. Cade nodded his thanks Braden wouldn't have to be subjected to hospital food.

After they'd visited a little while longer and could see for themselves Braden would eventually be all right, they made to leave. Nana slowly reached out to touch Braden on the back of his hand. Cade could feel Braden's body stiffen as he braced for the contact, subjecting himself to it for Nana's sake. He turned his hand over to clasp hers for a brief moment. Her tears fell silently as she whispered her love for him and told him she'd see him soon as she headed for the door with Cooper. Braden pulled his arms in tight to his chest behind the cover of his raised knees, clearly unable to be touched again by anyone other than Cade. Maya smiled sadly at him and moved around to the other side of the bed, hugged Cade tightly and whispered, "I'm sorry about earlier. I was being selfish. You did the right thing for Braden. Thank you."

Cade shook his head. "Don't worry about it, Maya. I think we're all under a lot of stress. Come see him tomorrow."

She kissed him on the cheek, patted the bed beside Braden's leg and left. Cade watched her walk into the hallway and saw Cooper hugging Nana then welcoming Maya into their embrace. He knew it was going to be a struggle for them to stay away and give Braden some space, but he knew they'd do it, nonetheless.

A nurse passed by them and entered Braden's room. She checked on him, and using a glucometer, tested his blood. Nodding her head, she showed Braden the results. Cade saw Braden relax and knew the results must be close to normal. The nurse drew insulin into a syringe and passed it to Braden who injected and passed it back.

When the nurse left, Cade leaned over and kissed the top of Braden's head, his hair still damp from the shower. "How about you rest for a bit? I'll be right here with you. I might get up after you fall asleep to get some work done on my laptop, but I won't leave the room."

Braden nodded, but Cade could tell he was struggling with something. "Do you think they're mad at me?"

Cade's brows drew together perplexed. "Who, Bray?"

Braden looked down at his hands, back up into Cade's eyes, and then down again. "Nana and Maya. I didn't… I don't feel comfortable being touched right now by anyone but you. I don't even know why. I just don't want them to be upset. It's probably stupid… I just…."

Cade clasped Braden's chin and raised it up so Braden had to look at him. "None of what you're feeling is stupid. You've been traumatized, Braden. Everyone deals with it differently. Right now, you don't want me to leave your side, and you don't want to be touched by anyone but me. Do you think those of us who love you most are going to fault you for being affected by what happened to you? All we want to do is help you, and right now, I want you to switch off your thoughts for a bit, relax, and get some rest all right?"

Braden looked more at ease when he nodded this time. He settled back and used the remote to lower the bed. He turned on his right side and hugged a pillow while Cade settled behind him, wrapping his arm around Braden's upper chest and clasping his hand in his. Braden sighed and snuggled back into him. "I'm sorry I'm feeling so unsteady and scared. Thank you for being patient."

Cade kissed the back of Braden's head. "Considering all the shit you've been through in the last several days, you're coping remarkably well. Please, baby, close your eyes and rest."

Braden went to sleep almost immediately and didn't stir when Cade got up to sit in the recliner next to the bed. He settled in, his laptop on the lowered rolling table, and got to work.

He'd been in California for several weeks now. Between managing this case and spending every waking minute with Braden, he'd neglected much of what he was usually in charge of for Custos. Cooper was picking up a lot of his slack, not to mention Olivia, who was keeping everything office management related running like clockwork. And then there was Micah, managing caseload allocation and anything else they usually would have overseen themselves.

He worked for several hours, purposely avoiding searching for updates on Eric even though he was damn curious if anything else had been found or if he was still in the wind. He caught up on emails and checked on the latest batch of After Action Reviews uploaded to their private server. On the last day of every month, Cade and Cooper would gather the guardians for a monthly meeting to review their closed cases. He wasn't physically there, but wanted to ensure he was up to date on all the AARs that had come in. He sent Micah a quick email asking how the team meeting had gone and decided he'd played enough catch up.

He was just shutting down his laptop when Braden started to wake with a bad dream. He got in bed and gathered Braden in his arms, talking to him in a soothing voice, settling him right down. They both fell asleep feeling comfort from the other. Several hours later, Sam came in. She apologized for waking them and asked if Braden would like a little late lunch, but Cade assured her they had food brought in. On her way out the door, she told them the doctor would be in a little later to check on him. She smiled widely when she mentioned he may be able to leave if his blood sugar remained stable, especially since Braden was used to managing it at home.

Cade loved the sound of getting Braden out of the hospital. He didn't know what to expect, as Braden had literally just come out of a coma the night before, but if they were going to release him, Cade couldn't be happier. When Sam left, he helped Braden to the bathroom and left him to his business while he went to see what Cooper had brought to eat. Inside the bag, a couple place settings sat atop a thermal heater bag and a cooler was tucked underneath. He placed the food on the rolling table and helped Braden back into bed.

Braden's face settled into a beautiful smile as he leaned in and smelled their lunch. Cade grinned at his obvious happiness and asked what put the smile on his face. Braden told him it was his Nana's eggplant lasagna. Cade couldn't imagine when Nana had baked it, but he supposed he'd given them enough time that morning. As he set about plating their meal, he listened to Braden as he talked all about his favorite dish. He used to love regular lasagna, but when he was diagnosed with T1D, he explained, his nana had started to get creative in order to give him some of his past favorites in low carb versions. This was one of the ones he loved best.

They ate in relative quiet, and the no longer hot but still warm lasagna tasted amazing. The cooler also held small side salads and Nana's homemade peach tea with agave nectar. Braden ate as much as he could then passed the remainder to Cade, who tossed it all back with relish. He checked the cooler again to see what else was there and found two large salads with veggies, chicken breast slices, shredded cheese, strawberries, and some almonds. They were set for dinner as well.

Chapter 2

CADE

Cade cleaned up their mess from lunch. When he glanced over to see how Braden was doing, he saw him hunched over and looking at his hands; a sure sign he didn't like what he had to say but was going to force himself to spit it out, regardless. Cade waited patiently, crossing the room toward him and sitting on the edge of the bed. He tipped Braden's chin up with his finger so their eyes met and realized Braden's skin had lost its color. Cade moved himself more fully onto the bed, facing Braden. "Talk to me."

Braden looked down at his hands again and sighed. "I know Eric is a master manipulator. I know that, I do, but god, it's hard not to let some of his poison in and fester in here and here." He knocked his cast against his head then over his heart. "He just kept hammering home the fact that a man like you would never stay happy with a man like me."

Cade opened his mouth to tell Braden just what he'd like to do to Eric for spouting such bullshit, but Braden reached over and squeezed his leg. "Let me finish, please. He said I needed to realize I didn't have much to offer a man like you."

Braden glanced at Cade's clenched fists but continued with a shake of his head. "A man who has fought in a war with Special Forces, has a successful business with his family, and started his own security company is pretty likely to get bored with someone like me. Any way you look at it,

Zavier, I'm a homebody. At the end of the day, I just want to bake and come home. I can't offer you what you're eventually going to want because I'm not a thrill seeker."

Anger was building in Cade, and the more Braden spoke, the more Cade felt his legendary control slip away. Braden finally looked up again, and Cade asked him flat out if he was done. When all Cade got in response was a wide-eyed, affirmative nod, he spoke with the deep grit of someone who had lost all patience. "We're going to have this conversation once, Braden. Once, then we're never going to talk about this again. I'm only dignifying all of that with an answer because I see it's tied you in knots, and I won't belittle your feelings and act like they don't matter. So, once and done, do you understand?"

Braden met his eyes, looking a little like he regretted bringing it up, but nodded that he agreed and even managed a timid yes. Cade took a deep breath and let it out. "Braden, he said all that because he knew it would get to you and he wants you for himself. He doesn't know what type of person I am, but you do."

Cade reached and clasped Braden's hand in his. "Being near you makes me feel alive like I've never felt before. My heart rate spikes and my breathing quickens when I know I'll be close enough to touch you. But you're also my peace, my calm. No matter what chaos is surrounding me, I know I can come home to you, and that makes me feel at ease."

Braden looked up, his features pained. "It's just that--"

Cade squeezed his hand. "No. Listen to me, Braden. Hear me. When I told my family what you meant to me, my exact words were, 'he's become my everything.' It took one sentence and the look on my face for them to accept it as the truth and to bring you a gift to welcome you to the family."

Cade saw raw emotion slide over Braden's face. He leaned over and pulled the watch from his bag and handed it to Braden. "That's an Imperator McCade Watch which only our immediate family wears. They wanted you to have it because you're mine. It's as simple as that. I can't have you second guessing me. You're going to be my husband one day, and a father to our children. I see all that with you." Cade gently squeezed Braden's shoulders. "Why won't you believe me? What else do I need to say for you to put the same faith in me?"

Braden eyes teared. "Nothing." He looked down, blinking the tears out of his eyes so he could see the gleaming watch in his hand and whispered, brokenly, "Nothing. Zavier, it's so beautiful. You can't possibly imagine what it means to me."

He climbed onto Cade's lap, wrapped his legs around his waist, and hugged him for dear life, ignoring the twinge of pain from his bruised ribs. "You don't have to say anything more. You've said everything. I needed your words in my head, pushing his out. I'm so sorry I doubted you. I know you love me, and I *do* have faith in you. You're my everything too, Z."

Just then, Sam walked in the room and quickly shut the door behind her. She smiled widely, obviously enjoying watching them and not embarrassed in the slightest upon catching them in a compromising position. "Okay, I probably shouldn't think this situation is so hot, but you guys are really sexy together. Umm…" She tapped her finger to her lips. "Oh, yeah. So, I just came in to check your glucose levels, but I also wanted you to know there's a cop out there, asking if you've come out of your coma. I didn't know if you wanted to talk to him yet, so I wanted to warn you."

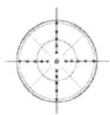

Braden

They thanked her, and Braden reluctantly crawled off Cade and back onto the bed. Sam checked Braden's levels and gave him an insulin dose. When she left, Cade leaned forward and kissed Braden softly on the lips. "I don't think we're ready for you to talk to the cops yet, so I'm going to tell him you're asleep right now and he can come back tomorrow. Are you okay with that?"

Braden nodded, feeling relieved. "Yeah. I don't really want to rehash everything with a stranger right now when I haven't even talked to you about it yet. And I'm exhausted again and would like to rest until the doctor gets here."

"Will you be all right if I step out of the room to talk to him? If you yell, I'll be able to hear you. I won't go far, Braden, and the door won't be out of my sight."

As much as Braden didn't want Cade to see it, he knew his fear came through. He figured if he was going to get over his panic at being left alone, he needed to start now. "I'll be fine, since I know you're leaving and won't be far."

Cade left immediately, and Braden kept his speeding heart and panicked reaction at being alone to himself. He distracted himself by looking at the watch that was still clutched in his hand. He watched the minutes tick by and felt a small measure of calm by focusing on that, rather than the emptiness of the room. Cade was back in less than five minutes. He sat down beside Braden on the bed and admitted Detective Miller was frustrated, but he understood he wasn't going to make it past Cade to get to Braden. He'd left with a promise to return in the morning. The doctor was only a minute or two behind Cade and entered with a smile on his face. "Braden, your glucose levels look great. How is your migraine?"

"The pain is gone, but the hangover still has me exhausted and weak."

Dr. Himmel made a sound of sympathy. "Just when you think the worst of it is over, it drags on and on, doesn't it? I'm sorry about that. Is it all right with you if I check your other injuries while I'm here?"

Braden tensed, still feeling raw at the thought of anyone other than Cade touching him, but he braced himself and gave a reluctant nod. Dr. Himmel stepped closer and did a thorough exam. "Other than recovering from your injuries and getting more rest for your migraine, I'd say you're pretty darn healthy considering you were in a coma last night. Yesterday, while you were still out, we did several brain scans to check for any damage as a result of the diabetic coma. We'd like to do the same scans now that you're awake to be sure there is no permanent damage prior to sending you home. I've scheduled the scans, and your first one is in about an hour and a half. Maybe you can get some rest beforehand. Do you have any questions?"

Braden tensed and placed his hand on Cade's thigh. "You think I have brain damage?"

Dr. Himmel shook his head. "I don't, Braden. You seem to have recovered from the ordeal, but it's best for us to double check to be sure there's nothing we missed that could cause any issues down the road. I feel confident after your external injuries heal, you'll be as good as new, but I wouldn't be doing my job if I didn't dot all the I's and cross all the T's. Any further questions?"

Braden cleared his throat. "Can Zavier come with me?"

Dr. Himmel gave Braden a kind smile and nodded. "Of course. As he's your protection detail, it's permitted, though he'll have to be with the technicians while you're in the scanning bays."

Braden, feeling uncertain, glanced over at Cade, who tucked his arm behind him and kissed the top of his head. "I'll be there with you."

Braden felt Cade rest his head against the top of his to lend his support and strength. He sighed and nodded, "All right. Thank you."

Dr. Himmel smiled down at him and said his goodbyes. Braden settled back, curling into Cade he fell asleep, his mind and body tired. Only waking when Sam came over an hour later to wheel him to the first of several brain scans.

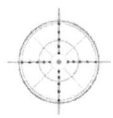

Cade

It was several hours later, the scans having been completed and nurses having come and gone for continued blood tests and injections, when they settled down to eat their dinner. They were both tense, waiting for the scan results, so neither of them were feeling particularly chatty. When they were done eating, Cade was cleaning up the mess from dinner when Dr. Himmel made an appearance. Braden tensed immediately and reached for Cade who sat beside him, taking his hand, and together, they waited for the doctor to share his findings.

Dr. Himmel brought up the scan results on his iPad and smiled. "So, Braden, how do you feel about going home tomorrow morning?"

Braden's shoulders sagged in relief and he grinned up at Cade who was beaming down at him. "Very agreeable."

Dr. Himmel chuckled. "I figured as much. Your scans are clear of any permanent damage that could have been caused by the diabetic coma or the concussion. I think you were brought in just in time, and as much as it doesn't feel like it, things could have gone much worse. Since it's already late in the day, I'd like to keep you for observation overnight so we can monitor your glucose and check your injuries one more time before you leave."

Dr. Himmel tapped a few things into Braden's file then glanced back up, meeting Braden's gaze. "With the coma and the concussion, I want you to take it easy and rest for five or six days, more if you experience any dizziness, headaches, or confusion. Your body is recuperating from quite an ordeal and the more you take care of yourself and rest, the better you'll be. Cade mentioned you're a serious runner, but I want you to wait at least ten days from your release date before you start back up with walking first, but again, only if you've had no symptoms. Stretching is okay to keep yourself limber, but don't start back with the yoga or pilates until you begin the walking. Do you have any questions?"

Frustrated, Braden asked, "I can't work for five days?"

Dr. Himmel was about to respond when Cade cut in. "Six."

He frowned. "I've had a concussion before. I went to work a few days later. It's not that big a deal."

Dr. Himmel raised a brow. "Braden, a brain injury is a big deal. Tell me, how did you feel, working eight hours on your feet, two days after that?"

Braden huffed. "I felt awful, but that's not the point. It's not that simple. I can't put the café out like that. I don't have anyone trained, and we would take too big a hit."

Braden clenched his hands into fists and only realized it when Cade clasped them gently in his, gently unfurling his fingers, and entwining theirs together. "The only day the café was closed was the day you left. Do you think Nana would hear of it closing when she could lend a hand?"

Braden's jaw dropped. "She... What?"

Cade smiled at him. "She's having a blast, baby. Maya is making sure she's taking plenty of breaks and is even helping her out when needed."

Braden's gaped, in shock. "Maya's in my kitchen?"

Cade nodded. "When it's needed, so Nana doesn't get overtired. But more often than not, Nana's just fine and shooing everyone out."

Dr. Himmel cleared his throat. "Sounds like you've got the help you need while you recuperate. So, let me bring up my final point then leave you to rest. You've been through quite an ordeal, mentally and emotionally. I have the contact information for a great psychologist who helps people who are suffering from trauma and PTSD which I'll include in your discharge papers. You can think about whether or not you want to talk to someone, but I can assure you, he's very good at what he does and is someone I trust implicitly. Now, can I get your word you'll give yourself time to rest?"

Braden sighed, knowing there was no way around it with Cade watching him like a hawk. He murmured an affirmative and Cade proved just how right Braden was when he responded gruffly, "I'll make sure of it, Doc."

"Good. I probably won't see you again, unless you need something, and in that case, the nurses can page me. Braden, my wife and I will be in next weekend to have some scones and coffee. It was an honor to meet the talent behind those wonderful pastries of yours. Take care of yourselves."

They all shook hands and the doctor left. Braden watched as Cade texted Cooper to come pick them up the next morning. He relaxed while Cade packed their bags to save them time the next day. They went to bed early and both had a fitful sleep when his nightmares plagued him several times.

By the time they were ready to go early the next morning, Sam was coming in the door with a smile on her face and some paperwork, including instructions for his care. "It's been great helping you both. Dr. Himmel said I need to get myself to your bakery, Braden, so I intend to do just that. Good luck with everything. Someone is bringing up a wheelchair, and you'll be escorted to the exit."

On her way out, she nearly bumped into Cooper and they all saw her blush and heard her mutter as she walked out the door. "Jesus, does every single one of you need to be so damn sexy?"

Cooper smiled, unfazed, as he sauntered in the room. "Well, I am rather good looking."

He grinned and looked at Cade when he snorted in reaction to his best friend's quip. "You're an ass."

Cade picked up their bags. Slung the strap of the duffle over his shoulder and handed the other to Cooper to do the same. An orderly came in with the wheelchair, and Braden sat in it, doing his best not to grumble and act ungrateful. Braden was glad to see Cade take the lead so he could keep him in sight and not get uneasy and panic. Cooper took up the rear, watching their six. Once they got to the car, they helped him in and Cade sat with him in the back while Cooper took the wheel.

According to Cooper, Maya freshened up his place and stocked his fridge and pantry. He knew he had a lot of people to thank, when all was said and done. When they rolled up, Cade helped him out of the backseat and both Maya and Nana came out and rushed to Braden's side, careful not to touch him but offering their assistance. Braden, at war with himself, finally relented and clasped both their hands to take the help they offered in getting him inside.

He was dizzy and in pain, and still uneasy with anyone putting their hands on him, but he knew he needed to take the step toward accepting help and allowing others to touch him. In the end, he knew it would help him move forward even if it was hard to keep a lid on the panic he was feeling. As he headed inside, he couldn't help but glance back. Cade kept watch on the surrounding area, and Cooper headed toward them, bringing the bags in. Braden settled onto the couch in his favorite spot in the corner of the sectional, amidst the many throw pillows. Nana and Maya bracketed him there, both seemingly reluctant to relinquish his hands.

When Cade headed down the hall to their bedroom, Braden braced himself while the panic slid through his veins, leaving ice in its wake. Maya called out to Cade and he turned. As soon as Cade's eyes met Braden's, shame quickly followed the ice, and he looked down at his lap. Cade dropped the bags, walked back toward him, and crouched down at the back of the sofa, clasping Braden's head in his hand. "Hey, I'm here. I was just going to put the bags in our room and unpack, but I can do it later."

"No, I'm fine, I'm sorry. It's so stupid. I'm being so irrational. We're in my own house for fuck's sake! Not to mention, I brought this on myself. I start to panic, and I can't seem to stop it, but I need to get over it."

Cade walked around the sofa and took the spot Maya vacated for him. He pulled Braden close. "It's not stupid, Braden, and it's not irrational. Your body is having a physiological response that is out of your control. You didn't bring this on yourself. You were trying to keep everyone you love safe. We'll deal with it together; do you understand me? It will pass when you're ready, and until then, I'll be here."

Maya came back from their bedroom several minutes later, smiling sadly at him, still wrapped tightly in Cade's arms. "Your stuff is unpacked. I need to get back over to the café. Do you guys need anything?"

Cade looked up and smiled. "Thanks, Maya. The doctor wants Braden to be off his feet and resting for several days, so help at the café would be appreciated."

Maya winked. "I'm pretty sure Nana would love to continue to help us. Don't worry about a thing, Bray. We're here for you."

Braden nodded, feeling frustrated. He watched Maya leave and sighed. "Z, I can probably..."

Cade looked at him with pleading eyes. "Braden, don't make me push you on this. You're exhausted and you need some recovery time. Please, baby."

Braden really looked at Cade for the first time and realized how exhausted he was. It wasn't just him going through all of this, it was Cade as well, and he needed to keep that in mind. Especially when it seemed like Cade could get through anything and everything so easily. If he looked closely, he could see what the last several days had done to him, so he readily agreed. "Okay, you're right. I'll get some rest," and thought, *you'll get some rest with me.*

Cade nodded. "Do you want to go to bed for a while?"

He shook his head. "No, I've had enough of beds for a bit. Can we just relax on the sofa, and maybe watch a movie or something?"

"Yeah, I'd love that."

Nana, still holding onto Braden's hand, brought it up to rub against her cheek before finally letting it go. She leaned over and gave Cade a hug. "I'm so grateful for you. Thank you for bringing him home to us. I'm gonna head back over to the café and get some work done. I'll be cooking dinner tonight, so don't worry about that."

Cade squeezed her hand before releasing her. He grabbed the remotes, turned on the TV, and they picked something to watch. They cuddled together, and in no time at all, Braden was out. Cade pulled Braden's Imperator watch from his pocket. He went to his bag, drew out his mini tool kit, removed several links from the watch, then placed it on the nightstand to give to Braden later. He went back to the sofa, relieved his absence wasn't noticed, and snuggled Braden back into him then he dropped out as well. They rested for several hours, only waking when they heard Nana in the kitchen cooking dinner.

The rest of the night went smoothly, and Braden seemed content spending time with Nana. She told them at dinner she was planning on staying until Braden was comfortable working for a full week. She said she didn't mind at all and it was fun getting back into the kitchen to bake for others. Cade was just grateful Braden had someone that was as good in the kitchen as he was so the café didn't suffer.

After getting ready for bed, Braden settled in next to Cade. "Did you guys find Eric?"

Cade tensed. He'd hoped the subject wouldn't come up so soon. "I don't think so."

Braden's eyes popped. "You don't know?"

Cade shook his head. "I handed it off to Cooper. I wanted to track him down myself and kill him, Braden. You were in a damn coma for fuck's sake. But I couldn't concentrate on anything but you. I told Cooper to handle it and not to talk to me about it until I said otherwise. The last I heard is he's in the wind. Dropped you off, hopped on a bus to the mall, where he threw his phone away we'd finally been able to trace, probably got a new phone, and stole another car. We can ask Cooper what's going on with the investigation tomorrow. But I need to know if you want to press charges this time."

Braden looked up at him with such terror in his eyes Cade held him closer still. "It's your choice, Braden. I won't pressure you at all. We've lined up a lot of evidence against him. When you were brought in, his DNA was on you. I checked if your rape kit was still in the hospital records and it was. They won't release it to anyone but the police if charges are filed. I don't know if you still have your video, but if you do, that's irrefutable evidence you were raped by him. I didn't want anyone searching in your computer for that, so I don't know if you still have it, but if you do, he will go away for a very long time. Rape and attempted murder with this much evidence are hard to get out of without a long prison sentence."

Braden released a shaky breath. "I just don't know if I'm strong enough to go through that, to testify, to have my name dragged through the mud and everything out in public. He was a public figure—everyone will want to know."

Cade tightened his hold. "No pressure. I'm leaving it up to you. I want you to know that with all of the evidence and the lawyers I would hire on your behalf, he would be going to prison for a very long time."

Braden shook his head. "But we can't even find him."

"If the cops were looking for him for rape and attempted murder, that means his face would be plastered all over the news and a lot more people would be looking for him, which means he would most likely be caught much faster."

Braden curled into Cade. "But that means my face would be plastered all over the news as well."

Cade snuggled him closer. "We'd do our best to avoid that. The names of victims of sexual assault are usually kept quiet, but I'm not going to lie, Braden, it's possible. I'd like you to think about it. Right now it's time to get some rest. Tomorrow we'll need to talk about what happened while you were with him, and we'll need to have Detective Miller come by to get your statement. He'll want to know if you're willing to press charges. If you don't know by that time, we can put off that decision, but you'll still have to talk to him. I'd also like you to meet my family, but if tomorrow seems like it's too soon, we can push that off another day, I'll leave it up to you."

Braden took a deep breath and let it out slowly. "I've really fucked up so much by going with him. I don't know what came over me. He texted me, and it was so unexpected I seized up and found myself back in that place where I did whatever he wanted. His threats loomed so big, I couldn't see around them to you."

"Braden, don't do this to yourself. You were scared to death for your loved ones. I understand. But you have to promise me to never do something like that again. I don't care how scared you are for others, you have to think of yourself too. You come to me if something like this happens. We'll deal with it together."

Braden nodded. "I promise, never again. I knew I made a mistake immediately."

Cade kissed Braden's head. "Let's talk more tomorrow, all right? We're both tired, and I think we could use a full night's rest."

They settled in and Cade listened to Braden's breathing until it was even and deep. Once he was sure Braden was out, he followed him into sleep.

Chapter 3

BRADEN

Braden was being kicked repeatedly in the ribs, stomach, and head. He felt like it would never stop. He did his best to cover himself, to roll into a fetal position and wait it out, but the blows just kept coming. Suddenly, Eric climbed on top of him, pushed his legs down, and straddled his chest, his knees on Braden's arms to keep him immobile. He growled, "I'm going to fucking kill you!" He reached down, gripped Braden's neck, and started squeezing.

Braden thrashed, kicked out, tried to scream but couldn't. He felt a hand on his shoulder and shrugged it off, sat up in a rush, and clutched at his throat, gasping for breath. He felt strong arms wrap around him from behind and he huffed out a "no" and tried to get away, but it was the steady, deep voice that stopped his frantic movements. He'd know that voice anywhere. It kept repeating the same thing, over and over. "I've got you. You're safe, baby. I'm here. You're safe."

"Zavier. Oh god, Z." He realized he truly was safe, and he broke down. Sobs wracked his small frame, and he gave up trying to keep them in. He felt himself being shifted, pulled onto Cade's lap, and enveloped in strong arms. He was being rocked, soothed, whispered to, and caressed. There were no demands to calm down, to be quiet, or to be strong. There were only reassurances he was safe and Cade was with him. And though it took a while, that was the only thing that calmed him.

After a long stretch of just sitting in Cade's lap trying to calm the shaking that had taken over his body, he slowly looked up into Cade's anguished eyes. Braden lifted his palm and caressed Cade's face, hooked his hand behind Cade's head, and pulled his mouth down to meet his own. They kissed, slowly, softly, no heat, just love. Braden pulled back and met his eyes again. "Thank you for making me feel safe. I love you, Z, so much it's an ache I feel in my chest, a warmth in my veins."

"I love you too, baby. You're safe with me, always. Can I get you anything? Do you think you can get back to sleep?"

Braden knew what he wanted, what he needed, but felt too embarrassed to ask. However, he also knew Cade would never suggest it at a time like this, so if he wanted it, he'd have to ask for it. He slowly sat up on Cade's lap, switched positions, and straddled him. He hugged him around the neck, his cheek pressing against Cade's. He felt Cade's chest expand as he took in a deep breath and wrapped his long arms around Braden's back, pulling him flush to his body, but not too tight. Gentle, always so very gentle with him.

Braden relaxed his arms, put his elbows on Cade's shoulders, and rubbed his hands over his short-cropped hair. He kissed Cade's neck, opened his mouth, sucked the spot where his neck met his shoulder, and bit down lightly. Cade groaned. One of his arms moved up and gripped Braden's hair, holding his head in place where he still bit and licked that sweet spot, and the other arm moved down, gripped Braden's ass and pulled him tighter into his body. Both of them growing hard, Braden's erection rubbed against Cade's, and he started grinding down onto Cade's stiff cock.

Cade's voice was gravelly and made Braden shiver. "Baby, no, you're hurt. We should wait until you're feeling better."

Braden pulled away, enough to look into Cade's gorgeous blue eyes. "Please, don't make me wait. I need to feel you become a part of me. I need you to erase his touch, replace it with your own. I need to feel alive and loved."

Shaking his head, Cade tried again. "Braden, you know I love you, but I don't want…"

Braden interrupted, in panic and desperation. "You don't…" He swallowed and tried again. "You don't want me? After…"

Cade's eyes popped wide, he shoved his hands into Braden's hair and held him in place. His face morphed into anger, his whisper menacing. "Don't you *ever* insult yourself, or me, like that again! Do you *really* think anything could *ever* happen to make you undesirable to me? Am I so fickle I'd just change my mind because some deranged motherfucker kidnapped you and laid his hands on you?"

Braden felt Cade's anger down to his bones and a deep well of shame filled him. He'd done it again. He'd hurt Cade and insulted him. He attempted to look away, but Cade's grip was tight in Braden's hair, and Cade forced his head back up to look him in the eyes, waiting for an answer.

Braden's whole body started to shake and Cade, looking disgusted with himself, took several deep breaths and let go of Braden's hair, wrapping his arms around him, pulling him close, and using his palm to gently press Braden's face to his neck. "Fuck, I shouldn't have gotten angry at you. You're so scared you're shaking like a leaf. I'm sorry, baby. I was trying to say I don't want to hurt you. I just don't want to fucking hurt you any more than you're already hurt."

Braden shook his head. "You didn't scare me. I know it's not in you to hurt me. I'm just… I'm breaking apart. I feel so dirty, even after I showered. I feel like I can't get him off me, I can't get clean. I just wanted you to help me feel like me again, to help make me clean."

Cade pulled back and Braden looked up at him. Cade took a deep breath in and let it out in a whoosh, but then nodded his head. "Are you sure?"

Braden's breath quickened, and tears pooled in his eyes that he quickly blinked away. "Positive."

Cade slid his fingers into Braden's hair. "Do you want to top? I don't mind. Baby, the last thing I want is to scare you or overwhelm you."

Braden shook his head and closed his eyes. When he opened them again, he saw the love and concern etched across Cade's face and he smiled, tentatively. "No. I need you to do what you did our first time together. I've never felt like that before and I want, I need, to feel it again. Take control, own my pleasure."

Cade raised his brows. "Are you sure you're ready for that?"

Braden nodded. "Yes, please, I… I need to let everything go. I need to forget. Make me forget, Z. Please."

Cade's jaw clenched. "I'll make you forget, Bray, but you need to promise me if it gets too intense or you change your mind you'll tell me to stop. Don't let me keep going. Promise me."

Braden nodded, almost desperate now. "I promise. Z, please."

Cade nipped along his jawline and whispered in his ear, before biting down. "Shhh, baby, just feel."

Goosebumps broke out over his arms and legs, and shivers raced up Braden's spine. Cade reached over to the nightstand and pulled out his slick. He set it on the bed beside them and slowly raised the shirt Braden was wearing up his chest. He gently pulled one of Braden's arms through then, even more carefully, pulled his casted arm through. He stretched the neck out a bit and slowly pulled the shirt off, avoiding the damage done to his head. He tossed the shirt to the floor and pulled Braden's face to his for a slow, but deep, kiss.

Cade pulled away and looked him in the eyes. He leaned forward and kissed the damage Eric did to his temple and eye. He pulled back again and placed his open palm over Braden's chest. His heart was beating fast and his breathing was faster as well. Cade kissed his nose. "What has your heart beating so fast, baby? Is it me? Do I do this to you?"

Braden nodded and Cade lifted Braden's right hand and placed it over his own heart. "You do the same to me. Feel that, Braden? It beats for you."

He pulled Braden's hand off his chest and brought his fingers to his lips. One by one, he kissed Braden's fingers, sucked one into his mouth, and looked into Braden's eyes. He bit that finger and soothed it with his tongue. Cade lifted Braden off his lap, laid him on the bed, and straddled his thighs. He ran his fingers softly down Braden's neck and over his chest. He spent a little time on both nipples; licking, sucking, and nibbling. He loved the feeling of Braden softly rubbing his hands over his head as he did it. He leaned down and kissed Braden's bruised ribs, kissing down his stomach to his belly button where he dipped in with his tongue and swirled it in a circle around the outside. Braden squirmed and whimpered. Cade grinned. "I love that, so sensitive."

Cade planted open-mouthed kisses from his belly button down to the waistband of his boxer briefs and licked just above it, across his belly. He pulled them down, slowly, scooting back as he went; Braden's hard cock, finally released, pointed up toward his chest. Cade growled in approval. "You're beautiful when you're hard for me."

Cade bent Braden's legs up and sat at his feet, his knees split on either side of them, and slid the boxer briefs off. He stood on the bed and shucked his own boxer briefs in seconds before he was back down on his knees. He pulled one of Braden's ankles up to his lips and took a bite of his heel, licked up his instep, and then sucked on his big toe. He heard Braden gasp and moan and he repeatedly sucked on his toe until Braden whimpered and the muscles in his leg shook. He chuckled. "So responsive, so fucking sexy. Your body will only ever respond like this to me. I'll make sure of that. Only my touch, Braden."

Braden moaned at the continued assault on his senses, but he responded, helpless to do otherwise. "Only your touch, Z. Only yours."

Cade hummed his appreciation. "That's right, baby."

Cade saw Braden's hand move to grip his hard shaft, and he moved up Braden's body and loomed over Braden, looking into his eyes. He looked down at Braden's cock and back up, his own eyes narrowed in challenge. "What did you just say, not ten seconds ago?"

Braden's eyes flared big, and he let his cock go in a rush. Cade saw a blush work its way from Braden's chest to his cheeks. Fuck, he loved that blush. He'd have to figure out a way to make it happen more often. Braden's eyes twinkled, and he pulled his lips into his mouth like he was trying not to laugh. Cade narrowed his eyes at him. "Cheeky. Don't do it again."

Braden shook his head, acknowledging Cade's order and when Cade made his way back down to his feet again and continued using teeth and tongue, Braden let out his pent-up breath in a whoosh.

Cade began to kiss, lick, and bite his way up Braden's leg until he was at his inner thigh. He spent some time there, licking and sucking the juncture between his thigh and groin. He lightly traced his tongue up and down the crease, thoroughly enjoying making his boy squirm until he came to Braden's hip bone where he bit then kissed and licked across to his other side and bit there as well. Feeling Braden undulate and hearing him moan caused Cade's voice to deepen to a guttural rumble. "Listen to you, gasping, moaning, so ready. Tell me what you need, baby."

That demand must have thrown Braden as his breath grew shaky and he threw his forearm over his eyes. "You. I need you. Anything, everything. I just need you so much."

Cade leaned up and removed Braden's arm. "Don't ever be embarrassed or ashamed you need and want everything from me. I'll give you that and more."

Cade saw the internal struggle play across Braden's features. He knew something else was going on in Braden's mind as he watched Braden close his eyes, gather his courage, and open them again. It hit Cade then; Braden didn't just need his touch and his love to feel clean, he needed his strength and his courage to restore his confidence. The anger at what had been done to his boy flared again, but he pushed it aside. He was careful to keep his voice gentle as he drove his point home. "It's just you and me, baby. I'll give you all I have. Until you're strong enough, you take what you need from me. There's no shame in that."

Braden sucked in a breath, a single tear escaping down into his hairline as he stared up into Cade's eyes. "How do you always know?"

Cade kissed along the trail the tear had left, toward Braden's ear. "You're a part of me, just as I'm a part of you. That's how it works between us."

Braden nodded, another tear trickling down the side of his face as he told Cade he loved him, over and over, and clasped his face firmly, pulling him down for a deep, passionate kiss. Braden poured so much emotion into the kiss Cade felt it to his toes. He slid his hand under Braden and gripped the back of his neck, giving Braden what he needed.

When they finally parted, Cade smiled. "I love you too, baby. So much."

Braden traced Cade's lips with his fingers. "Show me."

Cade stared into the depths of Braden's eyes and saw what he needed to see. Much of the fear and pain that had, moments ago, been etched over Braden's face was smoothed away, replaced by a trust that humbled Cade. It was exactly what he needed to see to continue showing Braden how much he was loved.

He bent to lave his tongue down Braden's neck to his chest where he kissed and bit one of Braden's nipples while he pinched and tugged on the other. Braden groaned and skimmed his hand over the back of Cade's head, begging for more without words. He continued until Braden's erection, which had flagged, came to life again. He gently rubbed his lips over his damaged ribs and his stomach and nipped his hip again. He buried his nose in the curls at the base of Braden's shaft and breathed him in. He smelled fresh, like soap, but also of pure Braden, that smell he always had that drove Cade crazy. "I'm gonna taste every bit of you, and you're gonna beg me for more."

He trailed his tongue to the other side and hugged Braden's thigh to the side of his face as he sucked on his skin there. His free hand gripped Braden's cock and gave it a tight stroke with a twist at the top and down again where he held it in a firm grip as he laved his way over to Braden's balls. He palmed them, squeezed gently, and reveled in the quick inhale the move garnered from Braden. Keeping his grip light, he lifted them and bent to lick his taint in a circular motion, causing Braden to suck in another sharp breath between clenched teeth and his hips to rise involuntarily. "Lift your legs. That's it. God, you're gorgeous spread open for me."

Cade moved lower, placing an open-mouthed kiss on Braden's smooth, perfectly round cheek. He nibbled and bit lightly on both sides, and thoroughly enjoyed the little catches of Braden's breath and whimpers he let out. He kissed and licked his way toward Braden's center, used both hands to spread him wide open, and rimmed him with his tongue. Braden cut off a groan. "Holy fuck! Mmm, please, more."

Cade chuckled. "Like that, baby?"

All he got was a strangled moan as Braden bucked underneath him. Cade took his time, but finally moved back up to his taint, licked his sack, and traced his tongue all the way up along the underside of Braden's stiff cock until he could take the head in his mouth and flick it with his tongue.

He felt Braden grip his head and hold it in place while pumping his hips up to try to get more of his cock in Cade's mouth. Cade growled in response, making Braden squirm from the vibrations. He released Braden's cock with a pop, looked up at him, and waited until Braden made eye contact.

Braden looked down, confused, panting. Cade raised a brow. "Who did you give control to?"

Braden groaned. "You."

"Did you change your mind?"

Braden whimpered. "God, no. Please."

Cade kissed and licked the juncture of Braden's thigh, making Braden writhe within his tight grip. When he looked back up at his boy, Braden's eyes were heavy lidded, pupils blown. "Passing control to me means giving up your own. If it's too soon, baby, you need to tell me to stop. Do you want me to stop?"

Braden shook his head. "No, no, no. Please, don't stop."

"If you get scared, if you panic, if it doesn't feel right, you say stop. Understood?"

Braden eyes widened, but he managed to nod.

Cade continued to look him in the eye until Braden realized what he expected and cleared his throat. "Yes. Understood."

Cade nodded. "Put your hands above your head and keep them there."

Braden moved to comply, his right hand gripping the cast on his left wrist. He maintained eye contact with Cade throughout, as his breathing became faster and his cock dripped precum.

Cade reached over and grabbed the slick, squeezing some on his fingers. He tossed the tube down and began to massage the slick into Braden's ass, slowly massaging outside and in, taking his time, reveling in Braden's undulating body that was seeking more.

He raised his other hand to Braden's sparse happy trail, lightly tickling there, which had Braden making a startled little "eeep" noise and trying to squirm away from his fingers. Cade smiled, filed that information away for later, and slowly slid his hand up to play with Braden's nipples. He took the tip of Braden's cock into his mouth, swirled his tongue around it then took it deep, to the back of his throat. Up and down, up and down, over and over again.

Cade's fingers explored Braden's ass, two in, then three, loosening him up. Fuck, he was tight. He swallowed when Braden's cock hit the back of his throat again and Braden cried out and began to babble incoherently. Cade swallowed down again and pressed upwards with his fingers and hit Braden's prostate, nudging it several times. When he felt the change in Braden's movements, he pulled off, gripped the base of Braden's cock tightly to stop the impending orgasm and gently eased his fingers out of his tight hole. "No, you don't. Not yet."

Braden groaned and choked out, "You're killing me."

Chuckling, Cade sat up on his knees and looked down at his boy. "You're so damn gorgeous, laid out before me like that, following orders so beautifully."

Cade leaned and grabbed the slick, squeezing some more onto his palm. He gripped his cock, stroking it several times, all while looking into Braden's eyes. He caught the slight hesitation and saw Braden glance down and back up. He shook his head. "Don't tense up. You were made for me, don't you know that by now? We're a perfect fit, Bray."

That brought Braden's eyes back up to his, a gorgeous smile gradually making its way across his face. Cade slowly breathed in, his heart beating faster. "God, I'm so fucking grateful I found you. You're so damn strong, baby, even in your surrender to me, so strong."

Cade leaned over Braden, gripped his cock, and very slowly slid deep inside of Braden. As he'd promised, they were a perfect fit. Cade squeezed his eyes shut and groaned. When he opened them, he saw the look of pleasure on Braden's face, making his heart skip a beat. "So tight. God... you're so... perfectly... tight," he whispered while he slid in and out on each word.

He opened his eyes and leaned down on his forearms, bracketing Braden's arms within his, above Braden's head. His heavy-lidded gaze met Braden's before they kissed. Cade's hips moved in a steady, undulating rhythm without pause. "You're mine, Braden. All of you, mine. Nothing will ever change that. Feel confident in that now, in us."

Braden nodded his head, but when he closed his eyes, Cade tugged on his hair until he opened them again. He forced Braden's eyes to his again, needing Braden to understand his words, to feel them deep inside. He continued driving relentlessly into Braden, hitting his prostate on every go, his heavy-lidded gaze never wavering. "Your happiness is mine. Your pain is mine. Your pleasure…" Cade felt Braden clench down on him and he groaned and he sped up his thrusts. "Oh god, your pleasure is mine."

He reached down between them and gripped Braden's cock in his firm hand and began to pump in pace with his thrusts. He broke eye contact to suck, kiss, and lick on Braden's neck, on his favorite spot. He continued his assault on Braden's neck, bringing goosebumps to Braden's skin and whispered repeatedly, "Mine."

He began to move faster, breathe heavier, and then he whispered once more in Braden's ear. "Come for me."

Cade bit down on that sweet spot on Braden's neck. Braden whimpered and complied immediately, shooting ropes of cum between them, his ass squeezing down on Cade's cock. The vise-like grip on his cock caused Cade to let go as well, coming deep within Braden. They both moaned in pleasure, riding out their orgasms, their panting breaths the only sound left in the room. Keeping himself from collapsing on Braden, he gripped Braden's ass to keep them together and gently flipped them over. Braden settled on top of him and laid his head on Cade's chest. Cade wrapped his arms around him when he felt the last remaining shudders run through Braden.

They both drifted in sated bliss for a while, until Cade's erection finally softened and slipped from Braden. They both moaned at the separation. Cade turned Braden on his side while he got out of bed. He got a warm, wet cloth to clean them both and tossed it into the hamper. When he returned to Braden's side, he noticed immediately something was wrong. "Baby, what is it?"

Braden shook his head and smiled sleepily over at him. "Nothing."

Cade waited him out, and Braden finally admitted, "Head and ribs hurt. I'll be fine."

Cade swore under his breath and got Braden some of his pain meds. "I'm sorry. We should have waited."

"No! Don't say that. I'd do it again in a second."

Braden popped the pills before lying back down facing Cade and reached out, beckoning him. Cade laid down next to him, drew the covers up and wrapped himself around Braden, careful not to hurt him. He frowned, whispered he was sorry again and Braden shook his head. "Don't."

Cade narrowed his eyes. "Don't what?"

"Feel guilty. Please."

Cade sighed and kissed Braden tenderly. "Did I give you what you needed?"

Braden's eyes drooped, and he hummed. "That and more."

"Good. Sleep now," Cade ordered gruffly, his arms wrapped protectively around Braden.

Braden slept soundly for several hours, but nightmares interrupted their sleep sporadically throughout the remainder of the night. Every time, Cade was able to stave them off with his touch and his voice. Cade had a tough time getting back to sleep afterward and spent a lot of time thinking about how to help Braden get past his fears. A few ideas took root in his mind, and he drifted off to sleep, hopeful.

Chapter 4

BRADEN

Braden woke alone in bed and felt the stirrings of panic. He looked frantically around before he realized the bathroom door was open and the shower was going. He got out of bed, took his pain meds, and headed in to join Cade but heard the water shut off. Leaning against the bathroom door, he grinned as his gorgeous giant pushed the glass door open and stepped out, steam following him. His face and hair were covered with the towel, unaware of Braden's perusal. Braden almost laughed when he realized his regular-sized towel looked like a hand towel for Cade.

He smiled at his lover. "You're beautiful, you know that?"

Cade lifted his head at that comment, dragging the towel one last time over his hair before he lowered it to his chest to rub the remaining water from his torso. He tilted his head in that questioning way he had. "You're the beautiful one, Bray. I'm too scarred up to be beautiful."

"That's where you're wrong. Those scars just add to the whole package. They just show you're a survivor."

Cade approached, a hungry look in his eyes, making a shiver run the length of Braden's spine. He wrapped his arms around Braden, pulling him close. "Sorry I didn't wait to shower with you. I was awake for a while and watched you sleep, but you were so out I didn't want to wake you. Mmm, you're so fucking gorgeous when you're all tousled and rumpled from sleep. I just want to devour you."

Braden looked up at Cade, letting him see his desire. "So, devour me."

"Baby, you're hurting, and as amazing as it was, we're not repeating last night's adventures when you ended up in pain."

Braden made a disgruntled noise in the back of his throat, and Cade chuckled. "I let my family know you were out of the hospital yesterday. My mom texted to ask if you'd like to come to their house for dinner tonight to meet them. Think about it, and we can talk about it later. If it's too soon, we'll do it another time, no pressure. Do you want to check your levels and take a quick shower while I finish getting ready?"

Braden sighed at the missed opportunity for another ravishing, smiled at Cade and agreed. He stripped, knowing no one would blame him for the show he put on while doing it. Cade growled, leaned over and spanked him on the ass. "Stop being bad and get your sexy ass moving."

Braden blushed and realized that spank took his arousal from happy morning wood to DEFCON 1 and tried to turn away before his reaction was apparent. He realized he was too late when Cade's heated and hungry stare consumed him, and he found himself unable to move in any direction, held immobile by Cade's gaze.

Cade hungrily stalked to Braden, pulled him gently against his aroused body, and kissed him senseless. He nipped Braden's bottom lip and pulled away to get the plastic baggie and some waterproof medical tape. He wrapped Braden's casted hand, pulled Braden flush to his body once again, and growled as he grabbed Braden's ass cheeks in his big hands. "You can bet your sweet round ass I'll remember that reaction in the near future, and we'll explore it thoroughly. Until then, stop teasing me and get a move on."

Braden blushed then smirked sexily and pulled Cade's head down, so he could whisper in his ear. "Yes, sir."

Cade gripped Braden's hips, not allowing him to move away. Cade's serious expression did little to disguise his arousal. His gritty voice lowered. "One day, you're gonna say that to me and mean it."

Cade watched as Braden's pupils blew at the combination of his words and his voice, his boy's breathing hitched. "Promise?"

Braden smirked when Cade narrowed his eyes. He turned and walked into the shower stall, tossing a flirtatious smile and a wink over his shoulder at his man, loving the thrill it gave him when Cade rubbed his hand over his mouth and said, "Fuck me sideways, you're gonna be the death of me, boy."

Braden heard Cade's comment and heat spread through him. Cade had never called him boy before, and though he probably would have hated it in any other context, something about the way he said it during their playful sexual banter revved his engines, and he hoped to hear it again. He turned the water on and got under the spray when it heated up.

He was just as surprised at his reaction to that spank as Cade was, especially considering what he'd recently been through. He didn't want to second guess anything he felt for Cade and was a bit giddy, knowing if he could be feeling this way right now, he was going to get through this fucked up situation and come out on the other side stronger.

He hurried through his shower, his levity short lived as his anxiety forced a rush job to get him back to Cade. He put on his glasses and was just finishing with his insulin when he saw Cade sit down on the bed and slip some socks on before he tugged on his beat-up leather combat boots. Braden went to the closet and took a few minutes to calm his racing heart, not wanting Cade to know he was feeling so apprehensive.

He took some deep breaths and focused on what he should wear. He wasn't going to be working, and he might be meeting Cade's family. He decided to dress up a bit, but not overly, so he didn't come off as trying too hard. He felt a completely different nervous flutter in his stomach at the thought of meeting them at their house.

He sat down next to Cade and finished dressing. He was about to stand to get his watch when he realized the last time he saw it was when he placed it on the counter before he started baking the day he left with Eric. He tried to take a deep breath, but it caught in his throat, and he slouched then winced at his sore ribs, his casted palm lying on top of his empty right wrist where he wanted to put his watch. He was frustrated with his emotional reactions; they were going to do him in. He felt like he was up high one second then down low the next. It was exhausting.

Braden sighed, discouraged more than was probably warranted. He turned his head and looked up when Cade slid his hand into his hair.

Braden blinked back his tears, annoyed they'd gathered at all. He opened his mouth to speak, but Cade covered his lips with a finger and shook his head. "We're not gonna let the little things bother us. You've got a new watch now and I removed several of the links, so it just might fit. If not, I'll take another few out. We'll get another leather band made for it, as well. It's as simple as that."

Braden felt a weight drop from his shoulders, and he smiled up at Cade. "Yeah, that would be great. Can I try it on?"

Cade lay back and reached for the watch that was sitting on the nightstand on his side of the bed. He sat back up and put the new watch around Braden's wrist, and it fit nicely. He saw some color return to Braden's cheeks. "I'll upload your data from the old watch, so you won't lose any of your reminders or anything else you've coded in."

Cade grinned when he saw that perked Braden right up, and he pulled him close for a kiss. He pressed his forehead gently to Braden's and they sat there for a few minutes. "I'm hungry. Let's fix something for breakfast then we need to talk. I heard Nana several hours ago when she went over to the café, so that's being handled."

Braden looked over at Cade and decided it was now or never. He needed to know what he was facing when he met Cade's family. "Can I ask you something?"

"You can ask me anything, anytime, Bray."

Braden rubbed his hands against his thighs back and forth several times before Cade rested his own hand on Braden's, stopping the nervous gesture. Braden took in a deep breath. "Do they hate me for what I put you through by going with Eric? I just want to know what I'm facing when I meet them tonight."

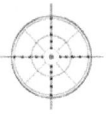

Cade

Cade eyes widened incredulously. "My family?"

Braden kept his head down and nodded. Cade got down off the bed and onto the floor in front of Braden. Knees spread on either side of Braden's feet, he whispered gruffly, "Braden, look at me."

Braden tucked his hair behind his ears and raised his eyes to look at Cade. The emotion, the love on Cade's face relaxed him immediately, even before Cade's words. "What you're facing tonight at my parents' house is your new family, Braden. You're going to walk into a home where you're already considered a son. You're going to gain a mom and a dad, and whether you want them or not, you're going to gain three brothers and a sister."

The disbelieving look on Braden's face made Cade smile. "Braden, my mom will want to hug you, happy you're okay. If that makes you uneasy, I'll take care of that, so don't worry. My sister is going to try to keep it together, but she'll probably end up teary as well. My brother, Finn, the doctor, is going to pepper you with questions about your health and how you're feeling, and my older brother, Gideon, is going to pepper *me* with questions about the case and what we've got on Eric. My other brother, Aiden, is a SEAL and is deployed overseas, so you won't meet him tonight. Braden, you have nothing, absolutely nothing, to be concerned about. I promise you, baby."

Cade stood and pulled Braden up with him. Braden smiled and finally let the worry leave him. "A new family, huh?"

"If I'm stuck with them, you're stuck with them."

Braden grinned, reaching out and lightly rubbing the backs of his fingers on Cade's abs. Braden was about to say something when his stomach made its hunger known. Cade grinned. "Come on, let's eat something then get on with the day."

They went to the kitchen where Cade cooked an omelet for them both. They sat eating their breakfast and Braden geared up for the conversation that was to come. They chatted about inconsequential things while they ate and, once finished, sat on the couch facing each other. Cade reached out and ran his hand over Braden's thigh. "Cooper is the one handling the search for Eric right now. Do you want me to relay the information to him that you tell me, or would it be all right for him to be here? I don't want to pressure you if you're uncomfortable talking with him here."

"No, it's fine. He can come over. But I have to warn you, I wasn't conscious for most of it. I don't think I'll have much to tell you. But, before he comes over, I want you to know something. I never spoke a word to him."

Cade stared at him, dumbfounded. "You…What?"

Braden seemed uncomfortable, facing away from him and playing with his watch. Cade slipped his palm around the back of Braden's neck, gently turning his head to face him. "We don't hide from each other. That's not how this works. I need to understand what you mean, and I need you to look in my eyes when you tell me."

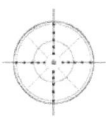

Braden

Braden huffed and was just about to explain when Cade patted his lap. Braden's skin betrayed him when it flamed red. He couldn't help but remember their date night, which felt so long ago now, and how Cade had first had him sit on his lap. He couldn't keep a relieved sigh from escaping as some of the chaos deep within him calmed. He got up, straddled Cade's lap, and settled down, feeling much more self-assured than the first time around. Cade rubbed his thighs and stayed silent, letting Braden gather his thoughts.

Braden couldn't help but lean forward and kiss Cade quickly on the lips before he explained himself, eyes on Cade's. "When I got in the car, he looked so smug. It hit me then he always had that look when he'd won. His ploy worked to get me there, but that didn't mean I was going to participate. As soon as I saw that look on his face, I ignored him."

Braden looked down at Cade's large hands on his thighs. He traced his fingers along the veins on the back of Cade's hands, gathered his courage, and looked up into his eyes again. "I know it's pathetic and childish, my attempt at sticking up for myself was silence. But, I remembered how much he loved it when I was scared, angry, and sad. How happy it made him when I cried, argued, begged, and fought back. I just decided not to react. It felt good, but boy, did it piss him off."

Pride evident in his eyes, Cade pulled Braden to his chest, wrapping his strong arms around him and holding him close. "You're so fucking brave. Don't belittle your actions by calling them childish and pathetic. You knew you couldn't beat him physically, but man, you could fuck with his head, and you did. That takes an incredible amount of guts, especially when I'm sure most of the injuries you have are a direct result of your actions. Am I right?"

Cade released him, and Braden looked into his eyes. He blushed at the admiration he saw there and began to feel some measure of pride in himself again. He nodded his head. "Yeah."

"He was probably shocked as hell nothing went according to plan. As much as I want to admonish you for it, I can't—it gives me too much satisfaction. Let me text Cooper to come and listen while you walk us through what happened. Detective Miller will ask you many of the same questions, so you'll have to go through it all again, but we need to see what you know for our own investigation first."

Cooper came over, and they had Braden walk through his account of what happened from the time he got the text to the time he woke up in the hospital. He talked about what he could remember about the house and remembered the last thing he saw that he recognized was a street sign for Twin Peaks Blvd, right before Eric had lost control and repeatedly slammed his head into the window. When he told Cooper and Cade about the bedroom setup, it almost made Cade lose his shit, not to mention the handcuffs and unnecessary violence. By the time he was done, Cade was pacing with his hands curled into tight fists.

Braden stood, and instead of heeding Cooper's silent warning to stay back, he approached Cade from behind and placed a hand between his shoulder blades. Cade immediately stilled and turned slowly. Braden could see him struggling to keep his temper, so he reached up and pulled Cade down and kissed him until he relaxed and wrapped his arms around Braden's body to pull him closer. Cooper cleared his throat after several long moments and brought them both back to reality.

Braden broke the kiss. "We have too much shit going on today and no time for Vaughn's big bag so that will have to do." Braden smirked, knowing both men would fall for it.

Cooper and Cade let out identical aggrieved huffs. "Heavy bag."

Braden chuckled. "Whatever the fuck."

Cade, knowing he'd been had, did his best to hide his smile and replace it with a menacing look. "Are you trying to manage me, Braden?"

Braden bit his lip and couldn't keep his own smile off his face. "How am I doing?"

"Remarkably well, actually."

Braden nodded, turning serious. "Good. I know hearing that stuff makes you crazy. But I need you with me right now."

Cade sighed deeply, his smile gone. "You're right. I'm sorry, baby."

There was a knock at the door and Cooper stood to answer it. "Detective Miller. I'll bring him in."

Braden spoke up. "Bring him into the kitchen. I need to bake, so he can ask me whatever he wants to ask me while I keep myself busy."

"Braden, you're not supposed to be…."

Braden glanced back, interrupting Cade. "Z, a stranger is going to be asking me for a bunch of information I don't want to share. Not to mention, I'm not meeting my new family for the first time without baking something for them."

Braden saw the softening of Cade's expression and the moment he relented about him taking it easy. Braden gathered ingredients, greeted the detective while avoiding his handshake, and warned him he'd be working in the kitchen while he answered the questions. He washed his hands and busied himself with baking. He answered all the questions but barely made eye contact with the cop. He couldn't find it in himself to do so. What that said about him, he wasn't sure, but as he was hanging on by a very thin thread and recounting everything he'd been through yet again, he wasn't too worried about it.

When the conversation was drawing to an end and it sounded like Detective Miller was almost done with his questions, Braden surprised them all with his emphatic statement, "I want to press charges."

At Cade's audible indrawn breath, Braden focused on his work. He didn't want to second guess his instincts. "From what I understand, there's

DNA evidence from the latest situation that occurred. There's also a rape kit at the same hospital from over a year ago. He raped me and beat me when I was trying to leave him. I also have that on videotape."

"Wait, what? You never mentioned anything except him beating you. You were raped and there's a rape kit with DNA evidence that you never used against him? What exactly do you have on videotape, and why the hell didn't you use it to press charges a year ago?"

Braden turned around quickly, surprised by the judgement flying out of the cop's mouth. One look at Cade, whose body had been a tightly drawn bow-string during Braden's recounting of the facts, had him reassessing his desire to jump to his own defense; it looked like he didn't need to deal with the stress of that particular chore.

Braden watched as Cade sat up slowly, loose limbed now, no longer tense; a stance Braden could only call ready. Ready for what, Braden didn't know, but he was sure the cop had no idea what he'd just gotten himself into. Braden was glad the deadly look in Cade's eyes wasn't aimed at him. He glanced at Cooper and saw he'd changed his stance as well, but where he'd previously been relaxed, he now looked tense. He was no less ready than Cade was, and Braden had to marvel at their opposing reactions.

He turned back around and kept working, waiting for the inevitable. He didn't have to wait long, and a chill raced up his spine when he realized this was Cade's other persona, the one he'd only heard about, never seen, and had actually doubted. He shook his head, almost feeling sorry for the cop. Almost.

Cade's voice at that moment, the one Braden would be happy to never hear again, was very deep, strangely calm, and reflected absolutely none of the anger he knew was bubbling under the surface. "Detective, you seem to be operating under the false assumption it's your right to be conducting this interview, questioning Braden, and performing your duties on this case. Let me be very clear with you, regarding your reality. I am allowing you to perform your duties on this case."

When the detective went to speak, Cade stopped him by raising his hand, stripping him of his rank. "Miller, you would be wise to understand your place and keep your mouth shut until you're fully cognizant of your situation. Until today, you've been very professional. You've treated

Braden with respect and you've performed your job duties admirably. I specifically didn't ask for a more senior detective because of the way you've worked with us so far. Please understand it would take a simple phone call to have you removed from this case, or any case for that matter."

Cade leaned back in his seat, appearing almost bored. "This has turned into a big case, one that could make or break your career. Do not make the mistake of thinking I'm bluffing and try to push my boundaries. You will remain on this case as long as it is handled according to my needs and the needs of my partner, Braden. The second you deviate or try to circumvent my requirements, it will be too late for you on this case, and perhaps in your career. Contrary to what you may be thinking, I don't enjoy throwing my weight around, considerable as it may be."

He paused, and Braden turned to look at him. As they made eye contact, Cade continued, seemingly ignoring the detective and talking to Braden. "Braden has a videotape of his rape and beating, but it will not be used until it appears it's the *only* way to get a conviction. You will not see this video. The only person privy to the video, should it be needed, will be the lawyer I will hire to try the case."

Braden nodded, and Cade turned his attention back to the detective who was practically vibrating with indignation. "You can't tell me what will and won't be used as evidence! Who the hell do you think you are?"

Cade tilted his head as if pondering the question. "If you don't know who I am, that's on you. Due diligence, Detective Miller. If this story goes to the press, as I assume it will in order to help you capture Mr. Pollard, you will keep Braden's name out of the headlines. Sexual assault victims have that right. If his name is released, you will be out of a job. We're done here."

Cade glanced at Cooper and spoke in Dari. "Get this joker out of my face."

Cooper responded in kind. "He won't be making any more mistakes on this case, Cade. I'll make sure of it."

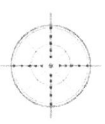

Cooper

Cade nodded and approached Braden, effectively cutting off any further contact with the detective. Cooper escorted him out the front door and armed the security system on his way out. He was just about to speak, but the detective beat him to it. "Look, I'm sorry. I was out of line, but he can't just–"

Cooper shook his head and took a deep breath and interrupted the detective before he had a chance to go on. This guy needed to understand Cade was never one to make empty threats. "Miller, do you think his anger is unwarranted? You went at Braden for making a personal choice that was his to make. You know damn good and well treating rape survivors like that heaps guilt on them for the simple fact they got assaulted. And it's significantly worse for male victims because there's a huge stigma attached to male rape."

Miller's shoulders slumped, and he sighed and muttered, "He had enough evidence though. He could have avoided all this..."

"You're victim blaming, and you know better. Be careful what you say. That right there would have been career ending, telling Cade's partner he's at fault for being raped and stalked. I know you were trained on how to treat survivors. You wouldn't be here otherwise. If you want to keep your job, you'll listen to what I'm saying. And do your homework, man. His name isn't Zavier Cade, it's Zavier McCade. Huge difference. If that name doesn't ring any bells, then you've had your head in the sand."

"McCade, as in…."

Cooper nodded his head. "Now you're getting it."

Miller let out a shaky breath and rubbed a hand over his mouth. "Shit."

"That about covers it. But, I gotta say, regardless of who Cade is, you shouldn't be treating survivors of assault the way you just treated Braden."

Miller nodded and rubbed his hands over his face. "Fuck. I know. I'm sorry. I just hate that these assholes constantly get away with what they do. It feels like my job is a losing battle."

Cooper regarded the detective. "I get it. I do. Listen, Cade specifically kept you on this case because he was impressed with your maturity and the way you were handling everything. The day you first showed up, he could have easily made a phone call and gotten a more seasoned detective on the case. He did you a solid. All he wants in return is for you to do your job the way you were trained to do it."

Miller nodded. "I know. I fucked up." He sighed, looked away, then met his eyes with what looked like curiosity lifting his brows. "Could he really just make a call and…"

Cooper huffed out a laugh. "Yeah. Cade calls the Chief of Police uncle, and his family is friends with the mayor. He doesn't make idle threats."

Miller's mouth gaped until he realized it and closed it with a snap. "Jesus, that's crazy. Look, I know he doesn't want to see me right now, but pass along that I'm sorry, all right? I'll say it next time I see them. I just fucking hate seeing repeat offenders not get the punishment they deserve, but I shouldn't have treated Braden that way or gotten so defensive."

Cooper crossed his arms over his broad chest. "I'll pass along your apology. If you behave appropriately and professionally, everything will be fine." Cooper gave the detective a sardonic smile. "Cade's an easy-going guy, but if you fuck up, you do not want to be on the tail end of that shit storm, I can assure you."

Miller laughed uncomfortably. "Yeah, that's becoming clear. We'll have no further issues. I promise you."

Cooper watched as the detective walked to his car and got in, sitting there for several minutes before he gave a perfunctory wave and slowly pulled out of his spot and drove away. Cooper headed into Maya's place to update the team on what he'd learned in the last few hours. He wasn't sure what would help with apprehending Eric, but he needed to be looking at this data with the rest of the guys and make sure they did everything within their power to track this asshole down.

Chapter 5

CADE

Cade waited until Cooper ushered the detective out the door before turning Braden into his arms. "I'm so sorry you had to go through recounting everything again and then have him come at you like that. If I knew he was going to react that way, I would have insisted upon relaying the information on your behalf. It won't happen again. Are you okay?"

Braden's eyes popped wide. "Am *I* okay? What about you? You seem more upset than his mouthing off probably warrants. Did you need to threaten his job? At first, I was pissed at him, but after that tongue lashing, I'm feeling kinda sorry for the guy."

Cade kissed him on top of the head. "Don't. He'll handle this properly going forward. He had no right to judge you for the decisions you made in the past. They were your decisions to make and it was completely unprofessional of him to berate your choices. I won't have him, or anyone else for that matter, treating you poorly. Not if I'm in a position to prevent it."

"I just hate you had to get stressed out over it."

Cade rubbed his back in soothing circles. "The only thing that stresses me out is if someone I love is in pain, mentally or physically. Frankly, I wasn't even mad at the guy. That was an emotional outburst from him, so there's probably a reason behind it on his end. However, that doesn't mean I'll allow it, and if he pushes things, he'll wish he hadn't."

"But can you really do the things you threatened?"

Cade pulled back and looked down at Braden, his face serious. "I would never lie in a situation that involves your well-being. I wouldn't put you at risk like that."

Braden nodded, his expression solemn, voice grave. "I have a serious question for you."

Cade looked concerned. "What is it, baby?"

Braden can't help but let a grin slip across his face. "Does my new family like chocolate?"

Cade narrowed his eyes. "Yes, everyone likes chocolate. You know, you're getting awfully cheeky with me lately. There must be some form of punishment out there to suit my needs."

Braden's smile lit up his face. "Punish me later, in bed. For now, I need to make some chocolate ganache to dip these cream puffs into."

"Jesus, baby, you can't say shit like that to me, you know it stirs me up. I think you're angling to explore some domination and submission and push your boundaries. Are you really ready for that?"

Braden blushed. "Well, I figure you dominate me in bed already, why not push it a little further while you're at it?"

Cade's expression remained serious. "It's one thing for you to ask me to take control and for me to ask you to put your hands above your head and not move them, but anything further needs to be discussed thoroughly between us. I'm not interested in forcing submission on you, Braden. I never want you cowed."

Braden took a deep breath before explaining what he'd just discovered for himself. "Everything you do feels perfect to me. It's like you have a direct line to all my hot buttons. I think from a personality standpoint, you're more dominant and I'm more submissive. I think that's just how we are, intrinsically, both in and out of bed."

Cade nodded. "I don't ever want to skirt that edge with you without having discussed it thoroughly. I don't ever want you to compare me to him because of the way I treat you, in or out of bed. That would kill me, Bray."

"You would never. He was abusive, period. What you do is take control in such a way I feel safe and loved, taken care of. You make me feel more desired and more satisfied than anyone I've ever been with."

"Yeah?"

Braden grinned up at Cade. "Yeah."

"Good. That's what I want for you when we're together. We'll have to talk about the other stuff later, and believe me, I'll be bringing it up because you've got me thinking of so many possibilities."

Braden was still smiling as he began to make the ganache. Cade came up behind him and told him he had to use the restroom. He watched Braden's reaction to ensure he was going to be all right in the kitchen on his own. Braden tensed but nodded.

When he came back in with his iPad, ready to get some work done, he was surprised to hear Braden's playlist coming through the small set of speakers on top of the refrigerator. Braden looked relaxed and when Cade approached him, he looked over his shoulder, smiled, and nodded he was indeed okay. A weight lifted off Cade; it was a start. He looked up from his work when a plate carrying a rather large cream puff dipped in chocolate was placed in front of him.

He smiled up at Braden and was just about to dig in when his phone rang. He looked at the screen to see who it was but didn't know the number. He glanced at Braden, gave him a reassuring smile and put the call on speakerphone. He had a feeling it was regarding Detective Miller, so he relaxed into his seat and answered.

"Hello?"

"Mr. McCade?"

"Who's asking?"

"Sir, this is Lieutenant Peterson. I'm calling about one of my guys you've been working with, Detective Miller."

"Yes."

There was a pause on the other end of the line, perhaps the lieutenant was surprised to not be getting much of a reaction from him. He wasn't about to make this situation easier on anyone, so he waited. The lieutenant cleared his throat. "Mr. McCade, I'd like to apologize on behalf of Detective Miller. He's a good cop, and at the end of the day, all he wants to do is get the bad guys.

I'm sorry for the way he went about it today, and he understands he fucked up. I assure you, sir, Mr. Cross's case will be handled as you requested, and Mr. Cross himself will be treated with the utmost respect going forward."

"You realize we shouldn't even be having this conversation, correct? He should have the training to know how to treat survivors of sexual assault, or frankly, survivors of any type of violence. Treating the survivor like they are the guilty party should be number one on your 'shit not to do' training list. So, I'll ignore most of what you just said and take away two things: Braden's case will be handled as I've specified, and he will be treated with respect, going forward. Is that correct, Lieutenant?"

"Yes, sir. Everything you said is true, and Detective Miller has taken the required training courses. I will make sure he gets further training going forward. Can I be frank with you, sir?"

Cade sighed. "I would hope so, Lieutenant. Otherwise, what the hell is the point of this conversation?"

"Right, sir. Well, I just wanted to let you know I believe what happened today was a result of something much more personal to Detective Miller. I am unable to provide any details, but I believe that is what happened. I will be working with him to rectify the situation. In the end, the why doesn't matter. He handled Mr. Cross poorly, and for that I apologize again on behalf of Detective Miller and the SFPD. I assure you, it won't happen again."

Cade snuck a glance at Braden to see how he was handling everything. "Lieutenant, it's your responsibility to see he gets the help he needs to be successful at his job. As I told the detective, he can continue managing this case, as long as it's handled properly. If something in his past causes him to behave in this manner, perhaps working in the SVU may be too much of a trigger for him, and you may be inadvertently setting him up for failure. That's just my two cents."

"Yes, sir. We'll work with him going forward and perhaps moving him to another unit would be best for him. That's something we'll deal with internally. I also wanted to ask if you both had time tomorrow afternoon, say around two p.m., for one of our sketch artists to come by and get a composite drawing of what Mr. Pollard looks like today. All of the pictures we have of him are old."

Cade glanced up to see Braden nodding. "I believe that time will work for us as long as it doesn't take much more than an hour."

"An hour should be enough time. I'll schedule it right now with our composite artist. Thank you for your time, Mr. McCade."

"You're welcome, Lieutenant."

Cade hung up the phone and sat for a minute, looking at it. He glanced up at Braden and saw a look he didn't understand. "What is it, Bray?"

Braden smiled at him and shook his head. "Nothing. I love you. Now eat your puff. I need to head across the street to get a pastry box."

Cade gave Braden an amused look but wasn't deterred from his warning. "Braden, no working."

"I know, I know. I just want to check in on how things are going with Nana. She hasn't worked in years. I just want to be sure she isn't tiring herself out."

Cade quickly ate his puff and told Braden he was going over with him, so he wasn't tempted to do something he shouldn't. When they got there Braden looked shocked. Nana was in her element and looked to be handling things extremely well. She had something in the oven, dough rising on the counter, and ingredients set out for whatever it was she was going to make next.

When they walked in, she washed her hands and approached them. Cade leaned down to give her a hug. She hesitated when she faced Braden and Cade could tell by his expression he was feeling awful about being uncomfortable with anyone else touching him. His heart hurt for both of them when he saw Braden brace for it and then open his arms. The hug she gave him was gentle and she didn't linger, likely knowing how hard it was for her grandson. When they pulled apart, she wiped a tear away, but her smile was a mile wide.

He chatted with Nana while keeping an eye on Braden as he walked down the hallway towards the office. He came back a couple seconds later and went up front. Cade was about to follow him so he wasn't out of sight, but he needn't have bothered because not even ten seconds later, Braden was back in the kitchen, standing still as a statue.

Cade realized his stance was one of terror. He could tell Braden's breathing was erratic and something had triggered a panic attack. He held up his hand to quiet Nana when she asked if Braden was all right. He pulled out his SIG and kept it lowered at his side.

He passed Braden, hating to leave him in a panic, but unwilling to take any chances with Braden's safety. He pushed through the swinging door and kept his body canted so no one could see he was carrying. He scanned the front and relaxed when he realized there was no one that remotely looked like Eric. Maya turned and saw him, a shocked look on her face. He shook his head and walked back in the kitchen.

He tucked his gun back in its holster at the small of his back, heard Maya follow him back, but approached Braden. Only a few moments had passed, but Braden still had a glassy look in his eyes and wasn't making eye contact. His breathing was still erratic, and Cade's heart broke a little at seeing him like that. He stood in front of him and clasped Braden's face in his hand. He tilted his face up toward him. "Braden listen to me, you're having a panic attack. We have to slow your breathing down."

He took Braden's hand in his and placed it open-palmed to his chest. "Feel my breathing. Slow your breathing down to match mine. Deep, slow breaths, Braden. Slower. Slower, baby. That's it. You're doing better. Look at me now."

He slid his fingers into Braden's hair, rubbed his thumbs across Braden's cheeks, and willed Braden's eyes to his. "Look at me, Braden. I need you to focus on me, focus on my breathing. That's it. You're doing great. Slow your breathing a bit more, that's right. Focus your eyes on mine. There you go. He's not out there, Bray. I checked. He's not there. You're safe with me. You're safe. Do you understand, Braden? You're safe."

He saw Braden swallow then he nodded his head. Cade relaxed a bit. "That's good. You're doing great. Keep breathing deeply, slowly. Good. You're safe. He's not here. I'm here, and you're safe."

"I'm safe."

"That's right, you're safe. Come here." Cade pulled him in for a tight embrace and rocked him as he continued to murmur he was safe. Braden's adrenaline was crashing now, and his whole body was shaking. They stood there for several minutes, no one said a word. The ladies watched as Cade reassured Braden.

Braden finally pulled away, and instead of the tears Cade thought he might face, a thrill shot through Cade when what he saw was anger. This he could work with. Braden looked up at him. "I hate him for turning me into a fucking coward. I can't live my life like this. I can't get scared to be in public or to be more than fifteen feet from you. This isn't okay, Zavier!"

"First of all, don't ever call yourself a fucking coward. You've been through hell, and he's the cause of it. Give yourself a break and realize you're doing better every day. You're feeling better, and you did great today when I wasn't with you. Things are improving, but it doesn't happen overnight. We will deal with this together. You are not alone in this, Braden."

Braden nodded but looked dejected. He put on a brave front and told Nana and Maya he had wanted to check in and see how everything was going. They chatted for a few minutes, neither of them wanting to stress Braden out, and for that, Cade was grateful. Braden went over to the closet of supplies and pulled out a large pastry box. While he was doing that, Cade hugged Maya and Nana and assured them both he would make sure Braden was all right.

They walked back to Braden's place, and Braden said he wanted to rest a bit before they went to dinner. Cade watched while Braden got undressed down to his boxers and crawled, exhausted, into bed. He did the same and tucked Braden against him. "I think you're feeling like things are out of control and you don't know what to do or how to make things better. Does that sound about right?"

Braden sighed against his chest and nodded. "That's about it, yeah."

"I have a couple of suggestions, and if you don't like either of them, I'll think of others."

He looked down as Braden looked up at him and smiled, clearly amused he was, yet again, trying to fix things. "Shoot."

"Cooper let me know he's teaching one of Vaughn's pro-bono self-defense classes tomorrow night. Why don't we both attend? You won't be able to do all the moves with your broken wrist, but you can learn a lot. Later in the week, I'll take the other class if Vaughn still needs a teacher, and you can attend again and learn more."

Braden's face scrunched up and he made a funny noise in the back of his throat. "I dunno if I'm coordinated enough or strong enough for that."

He kissed the top of Braden's head and rubbed his back. "You absolutely are. You're extremely athletic. We can go to his gym anytime and practice together as well. I'll teach you how to defend yourself, against Eric, or any other attacker. It may not feel like much, but I think you'll feel like you're taking your control back."

Braden gazed back up at him. "Do you really think I could ever defend myself against someone as big as him?"

"Braden, he's not that big. He just seems big because he's constantly done his best to intimidate you. But the answer is yes. I can teach you to defend yourself against someone as big as me, and I have confidence you'll be damn good at it, the perfect student."

"Okay, yeah. I think I'd really like that. I think, even if I can't do much for the first several weeks, I still want to push myself to learn as much as I can. Just thinking about it makes me feel better. What was the other suggestion?"

"To make an appointment with the psychologist Dr. Himmel suggested, or one of your choosing. My guess is you're suffering from PTSD. I think it might help you learn some coping mechanisms I can't provide. I don't want to push you into anything, but I think it's important."

"You're trying to figure out a way to make things better for me which I appreciate. I can't wrap my mind around my own reactions to things ever since I woke from the coma, let alone focus on figuring out what steps I need to take to be myself again. I think it's probably a good idea."

They chatted for a few minutes until Braden's eyes began to droop and he fell asleep. Cade left Braden to rest and headed to the living room to get some work done. He dug through his old and new mail, double checking to ensure he hadn't missed anything. There was nothing pressing from a client standpoint and from what he could tell, everything in his inbox was currently being managed by the guys back at headquarters.

He sent several emails, asking anyone who needed help to contact him directly and if everything that had come in during the last several weeks had been dealt with. He got several responses everything was being handled, and a couple of his people even asked for an update on Braden.

They'd obviously been informed of his relationship, which was fine with him. It was going to greatly impact their headquarters very soon, so he responded, providing updates and some more information that might clue them in to what was to come.

He opened the reports from his local crew regarding the real estate report he'd had them check on and read through each of their extremely thorough findings. The last several lines of text from each of them was precisely what he needed to hear: 'they are exactly what we need for a seamless transition,' 'it's a go,' and 'perfect for our needs.' He got Cooper on the line and asked him to get things started with the realtor. There was no reason for any type of delay and the sooner they got started, the better.

He spent about thirty minutes getting in a high-intensity interval training workout and then headed back into Braden's room just as he was rubbing the sleep from his eyes. He sat down beside him and smoothed the hair from his face. Braden gave him a sleepy smile. "Mmm, you're all sweaty and sexy. HIIT workout?"

Cade murmured an affirmative and kissed his temple. Braden yawned then groaned. "God, will I be able to get through a day soon without taking a nap? I feel like I'm eighty."

Cade chuckled and shook his head. "Give yourself a break. You were kidnapped, beat to shit, and just came out of a coma less than seventy-two hours ago. I think rest is exactly what you need."

Braden smiled softly, clasped Cade's hand, and started fiddling with it, tracing the scars. "You're so good to me, and I'm lucky to have you. But, what about what you need? It seems to always be about what I need. I feel like I don't know you as well as I should in order to know what you need. I see how you treat me and how you treat others. I've heard your men talk about you, tell stories about serving under you."

"Exaggerations."

"Bullshit, Z. You didn't think I was listening to them when they were talking about you after the break-in, telling stories about your unit. I was listening to every word. You're so quiet about your service to your country, about your job. It's like you don't want that part of you to touch me, but I want to know those things. I think it's important I know them."

Cade shook his head. "You don't need that kinda shit in your head."

Braden tilted his head. "That kinda shit is what you've lived. You know practically everything there is to know about me. Not only because of everything that's going on, but because you demand to know everything about me, so you can understand my needs. You think I don't know that? I do. But I want that from you as well."

Cade got up to pace. "I just don't want the things I've done to color your perception of me. I've done some awful shit. Yes, it's been part of my job, and orders were passed down, but at the end of the day, I did the worst of it, so my men didn't have to. I was proud to serve my country, but I wasn't always proud of the things I had to do as a result."

Braden shook his head. "But there's not much of a choice for you as a soldier, right? I mean, admittedly, I don't know anything about being in the military, but I know a lot of it is following orders. Don't carry that burden. I've seen your capacity to care for others, not just me. You are different with me than you are with your men, but that doesn't mean you don't love them."

Cade sighed. "With my men, it's different. I served with them, and they're my brothers in every way but blood. But in past relationships, I wasn't like this. I never cared enough to let my own guard down and give myself fully to anyone and expect the same in return. I can guarantee you won't always like seeing the other side of me when it does happen. I'm sure I made you a bit uneasy today when I talked to Miller, and I wasn't even mad at the guy."

"You didn't make me uneasy at all, but I was glad I wasn't on the receiving end of it."

Cade gave a rueful smile. "Never, baby. He wasn't going to get by treating you like that."

Braden held his hand out for Cade to come back and sit beside him. "I turned around to stick up for myself, but one look at you and I knew I wouldn't have to stress out about defending my choices. I was happy I finally got to see a side of you that you rarely let me see. It doesn't bother me that you behave differently with me, but it will bother me if you keep from sharing the other side of you. What if I was keeping you from knowing the real me?"

Cade looked at him, an irritable scowl on his face. "That would kill me."

Braden raised a brow then gave him a sad smile. "Right?"

Cade heaved a heavy sigh and rubbed his hands over his face. "Okay, Bray. You can ask me anything. I won't try to hide that portion of my life from you, but I won't share everything with you either. There are some things I can't talk about, with anyone."

"I understand that. Thank you."

"There's not much I won't do for you, but we'll have to talk about it later. It's getting late, and we've got about an hour before we need to be at my parents' house. I need to take a shower and get ready."

Braden nodded and rubbed his hands over his thighs. "I'll get dressed and put the pastries in the box."

"Braden…."

"What?"

"Don't be nervous."

"I'm not."

"You are. But you don't need to be. They already love you."

"They couldn't possibly. They don't know me."

"They know that I'm deeply in love with you. That's enough."

Cade could see Braden relax with those words. After Braden pulled him down for a mouthwatering kiss, Cade watched him as he took some pain medication and started looking for his clothes. Cade turned to go to the shower satisfied that he'd calmed Braden down enough. Once they got to his parents' house, Braden would realize all this worry was for nothing, but until then, he was happy to reassure him.

Chapter 6

BRADEN

The drive to Cade's parents' house took nearly thirty minutes. When Braden realized which area they were driving toward, he got even more nervous if that was possible. These people were out of his league. "Your parents live in Sea Cliff, don't they?"

"Braden, you make it sound appalling. I promise you, my family members are not pretentious douchebags."

"I feel out of my element. This is so beyond what I'm used to, Zavier."

Cade smirked at him. "You're really feeling *that* uncomfortable? Enough to use my full name?"

"Stop teasing me. Seriously, am I even going to use the right fork?"

Cade laughed in disbelief. "The right fork? What is this, *Pretty Woman*? I promise there isn't a dour majordomo named Jeeves waiting to open their door or a French chef named Pierre cooking a seven-course meal with five forks. It's a simple family meal."

Braden snickered, he couldn't help it. "You've seen *Pretty Woman*?"

Cade heaved a put-upon sigh. "Who hasn't? I have a sister, don't I?"

"Ugh, fine! But if I embarrass you or something, don't blame me!"

"Braden, I love you. I'm going to assume you're teasing me right now, because if you're seriously thinking that you could *ever* embarrass me, you're going to piss me the fuck off, and I don't want you to meet my family when I'm feeling angry."

Braden made a frustrated sound and turned in his seat to face Cade. "I'm sorry. I know I'm being ridiculous. I don't know why I'm so nervous. I just feel like you're my forever, and if I don't make a good impression on your family tonight, I could lose you."

Cade had pulled into his parents' driveway, and Braden, so caught up in his confession, didn't realize they were there. He put the car in park and turned in his seat toward Braden. "Baby, I'm your forever, just as you're mine. That's the only thing they're concerned about. I promise they aren't the type of people to pass judgement like that. Now, are you ready to do this?"

"Ready as I'll ever be, I suppose."

"Good. Brace yourself."

Braden looked alarmed then jumped in his seat when his door was opened behind his back. He turned around to see a gorgeous brunette with long, wavy hair and Cade's blue eyes smiling at him. Her smile was so big and genuine he had to smile in return. She winked at him and pouted at Cade. "Zavier, you can't keep him to yourself all night! Hi, Braden, I'm Rowan, Ro for short. I've been dying to meet you! Come on, let's go inside. We've been waiting on you guys forever."

Rowan grabbed his hand and practically tugged him from the car. Braden stepped out of his seat, glanced back at Cade with a look of horror, his voice rising in panic. "Are we late?"

Rowan laughed. "No, Zavier doesn't do late. You're right on time, a few minutes early in fact, but mom has been fretting and acting all nervous like she's meeting a celebrity or the president or something."

He breathed a sigh of relief and realized he already felt less anxious now that he'd met Rowan and she'd said that her mom was nervous. Maybe this night wouldn't be as bad as he thought it would. Braden was so swept up in her enthusiasm he almost forgot the dessert and his testing kit. He quickly leaned in to grab his kit and balanced it on top of the pastry box, barely managing to keep them from toppling. He turned toward Rowan, who was still holding his other hand. She gasped dramatically, dropped his hand, and grabbed them from him. "Did you bake us something yummy? I shouldn't indulge, but oh, I love sweets. Is there chocolate? Tell me you baked something with chocolate!"

Cade rounded the car, took the pastry box and kit from his sister before she could lift the lid, and led Braden toward the house with a hand at his lower back. Rowan, having clasped his hand in hers again, continued asking about the dessert he'd brought, but before Braden could answer any of her questions, Cade spoke up. "Cream puffs. You'll think you've died and gone to heaven. Don't worry, you don't want any, I'll eat yours."

Rowan turned to glare at Cade. "Don't even think about it. I'll just have to work out that much harder to burn off the extra calories."

Cade rolled his eyes at his sister. "You're ridiculous."

Rowan returned Cade's eye roll with one of her own. "Says the guy that can eat anything and everything and not gain a friggin pound! All I'll have to do is *look* at one of those cream puffs and I'll gain five pounds. And that's five pounds my hips and ass can't afford to gain."

Cade growled, and Braden looked at her in shock. "That's absurd! You're stunning! All Sophia Loren gorgeous curves, alabaster skin, thick, wavy dark hair, beautiful blue eyes!"

Rowan clasped her hands together in supplication. "Oh, Zavier, I love him. Can I keep him?"

Cade smirked and shook his head. "No, squirt, I'm keeping him."

Rowan pouted prettily at her brother, something Braden knew she must do often, and probably with a high success rate at getting what she wanted. Braden smiled at them both, knowing just from their back and forth banter they loved each other dearly. They walked up the steps to the front door of Cade's parents' beautiful home and walked in. Braden still held onto Rowan's hand, as she seemed rather intent on getting them inside quickly and didn't relinquish her hold until they were through the door.

The house had a rather large foyer that welcomed visitors with a ceiling that was two full stories and a huge wrought iron chandelier that more closely resembled a piece of beautiful artwork than a light fixture. The curving staircase leading upstairs on the left side of the entryway displayed the same wrought iron artistry, capped by a dark wood handrail that matched the variegated dark hardwoods of the foyer floor. Braden was in awe of the beautiful foyer and would have kept gawking had he not heard footsteps. He turned toward the back of the house to see an older version of Cade coming toward them from the hallway underneath the balcony. He had a welcoming smile that Braden returned and held his hand out. "Braden, so nice to finally meet you. Welcome to our home, son. I'm Duncan, Zavier's dad."

Braden's hand was fully engulfed by Duncan's, and he smiled at the familiar feeling. "It's a pleasure to meet you, sir."

"Oh, we don't stand on ceremony around here. Please, call me Duncan for now, Dad when you're comfortable."

"You're ruining my strategy of convincing Braden we're condescending elitists. I already told him that our majordomo and French chef have the night off."

Duncan's eyes sparkled with humor. "Ah, yes, Jeeves and Pierre. We're on our own tonight, such a trial."

Braden chuckled and shook his head. He realized that Cade's sense of humor was a family trait. Duncan turned toward the back of the house and called out, "Siobhan?"

Braden couldn't help but smile when he heard a woman react like she'd been poked. "Oh! Are they here? Where's my boy?"

Cade chuckled and set the pastry box down on the ornate console table in the foyer. "I'm here, Ma."

A beautiful, older version of Rowan came from where Duncan had only moments before. She wore an apron and wiped her hands on it. She rushed toward them and gave Cade a quick hug and kiss. "Hello, sweetheart, it's nice to see you, but I was talking about Braden."

Cade smirked and shook his head. "So that's how it is, relegated to second fiddle."

She pinched his stomach. "Oh hush, you know I love you."

Braden braced himself for the hug Cade said he'd receive. He wasn't about to reject it, but his heart rate spiked just thinking about it. She turned to Braden and, with teary eyes, clasped his hands. "Oh, my boy. I want to hug you, but there's plenty of time for that when you're feeling more comfortable. You are so brave. Protecting your loved ones that way. I'm so glad you're safe. We were all so worried about you. How are you feeling, darling?"

She released her hold on him and Braden smiled, seeing her desire to wrap him up in a hug and fawn all over him. He glanced over and saw Rowan swiping a tear away with her finger while smiling at him. Braden was practically holding his breath, not wanting to ruin the moment in any way. He felt warmth flood him when he realized Cade had been exactly right. His family already loved him, and he knew it wouldn't take much for him to love them back.

He smiled. "I'm doing fine, ma'am. Better every day."

"No, no. That won't do. You're family. Call me Siobhan, and eventually, when you feel comfortable, Mom."

Braden blushed; he could hardly believe her generosity and warmth. He smiled, nodding shyly. "Siobhan. It's a beautiful name."

"Oh, aren't you sweet. My goodness, it's so great to finally meet you. I feel like I've known you for years after working at your café, helping Maya and Clara."

"You... What?"

Just then there was a commotion from the back of the house and they all turned. Braden heard some shouted cussing. "Buckley get back here!"

Suddenly, the biggest dog Braden had ever seen came running from the back of the house, nails clicking on the hardwoods. He showed no signs of stopping and Braden braced himself, sure that he'd be flat on his back with a canine atop him in seconds, but at the last moment, he veered off, and Braden turned in time to see Cade on his knees being hugged—seriously, hugged—by the dog. He made the cutest happy whiney noises, and his tail wagged a mile a minute. He hopped down, ran in circles in front of Cade, and jumped up on him again. Braden watched the whole scene with shocked amusement then laughed when Cade's voice took on a baby-talk pitch. "Who's my big boy? That's right, you are. You're my big boy."

Braden chuckled in surprise, but his attention was turned when he heard a deep, guttural voice, rather like Cade's, but harsher, from the hallway the dog had run through, "Christ, Zavier. He never misbehaves, then you come in the house and he's a little puppy again, knocking shit over to get to you."

Cade smirked, continued to pet the huge dog, and rubbed his belly when he flipped over. "I can't help it if he loves me most."

The man looked remarkably like Cade, they could possibly pass for twins, but he seemed more intense; perhaps more self-contained and serious. He was an inch or so shorter, which still put him at a ridiculous six-foot-five or so and had the same scruffy beard and dark hair as Cade did, though his was a bit longer. He was just as muscular, perhaps even more so. He approached, hand outstretched. "Braden, it's nice to meet you, man. I'm Gideon, the older brother. We're glad to have you back with Zavier. He was a bear to deal with when you were in danger. I think he needs you to keep him human."

Braden released Gideon's hand. He felt at once at ease and tense in Cade's brother's presence and the combination of the two felt disarming. He had no earthly idea why, but he felt that somehow Gideon was genuine with his words, but they didn't come easily to him. Like just the act of having a conversation was forced. Braden was about to respond when another man came from the back of the house, wearing an apron that read, 'I turn grills *on.*' He was the same height as Gideon, but not nearly as bulky. His hair was longer than Cade's and a bit on the tousled side, perhaps from product, but more likely from fingers running through it. His face was leaner and his eyes a bit grayer than the blue of Cade's. "The steaks are ready. They're on the serving platter on the island."

He stepped forward and shook Braden's hand. "Braden, glad you're up and about. I'm Finn, one of Zavier's younger brothers. I know he's so glad to have you home in one piece. Hopefully, Dr. Himmel treated you well after we got you processed into the ICU. How is your wrist doing, any trouble with it? Anything else bothering you since you were released?"

Braden blushed at the attention; everyone seemed very interested in his answer. He decided to be honest—glossing over his pain wouldn't be believed here, he knew that much. "My wrist aches, and I'm pretty much sore from head to toe and find that I get tired easily, but basically I'm doing pretty well."

Braden calmed when Finn smiled sympathetically. "Good to hear. Ma, anything else you need help with?"

With that, almost everyone filtered into the back of the house and chatted about dinner preparation. Duncan lingered, hands in his pockets.

"Come on back when you boys are ready. If you'd like to show Braden around the house first, you've got time."

Cade shook his dad's hand, pulled him into a one-armed hug, and thanked him. He also passed the pastry box to him and told him Braden had baked for them. A huge smile lit up Duncan's face. "Can't wait for dessert. Take your time."

Braden felt like Duncan must know something was amiss and blushed that he was that transparent. He was confused and in a bit of shock from the comments made by Cade's family. Most of them had commented about the time that Braden had been gone, and Braden felt like he was missing something completely.

Once they were alone, Cade turned toward him and pulled him close. "Are you feeling overwhelmed? Everything all right?"

"I don't know, I…. Your mother mentioned working with Nana and Maya. Gideon mentioned you were a bear to deal with when I was missing, and Finn mentioned getting me processed into the ICU, like he was involved. You didn't mention any of this. I'm just… I'm confused as to what happened."

Cade clasped his hand and walked toward the beautiful sitting room to the right of the foyer. "Here, come sit with me."

Braden glanced back toward where the others had gone. "We shouldn't. You can tell me later. We should probably go in there. I don't want to keep them waiting."

"Bray, you heard my dad. They're fine. They're putting the finishing touches on dinner. We have time. Right now, you're feeling anxious and confused, so that's what I need to take care of. If dinner needs to wait, it will wait."

Cade looked at him sternly, and Braden nodded. "Okay, then, can you tell me what I'm missing?"

Cade sighed, as if annoyed with himself. "I'm sorry, baby, I guess I didn't make it clear how much my family was involved in helping while you were in trouble. I called Finn immediately after I realized you'd left without your testing kit. He's a doctor, and I needed to understand the implications and know what we were up against. He asked what was going on and if I needed help. They dropped everything and were there in an hour."

Braden nodded. He knew Nana and Maya would do the same for him and he'd do the same for them. He was just surprised to hear they'd all been at the café the whole time.

While he was contemplating that reality, Cade continued. "They stayed until you were safely admitted to the hospital. When we located you, Finn and Cooper came with me in the car, and they were both there in the ER when you were admitted. Finn was part of the medical team that treated you when you arrived. Everyone did everything they could do to help get you back to me."

Cade went on to explain more of what happened while he was gone. The voicemail he left Eric and the texts. He told him about the text he received the morning they found him, where they'd found him, and who came to visit him in the hospital while he was in a coma. The picture Cade painted was one of so much love and concern for Braden that he found himself shocked and more grateful than he could ever express. Cade just reiterated how much he was loved, and how many people were worried about him and involved in bringing him home.

He found himself getting mad all over again for putting everyone through it but even more angry with Eric for manipulating the whole scenario. Cade could see his thoughts churning and brought him back to the present. He reassured Braden and had him visit the bathroom to have a moment to himself. He tested his blood and calmed himself down. He felt much better and so happy to be there, so he could thank his new family face to face for all they'd done for him and Cade while he'd been missing. Cade was waiting for him in the entryway when he came out of the powder room. The dog was leaning against his leg like he might fall over if Cade moved.

Braden put out his hand and the dog looked up at Cade. Cade rubbed his head. "Go on."

The dog ambled over and sniffed Braden's hand. Braden bent over a little, though it wasn't much since the dog was massive, and scratched behind his ears. Cade smiled. "Buckley's a bullmastiff and a sucker for anyone who does exactly what you're doing."

He petted Buckley for another minute or so to ensure he had a new friend for life then Cade took him on a tour of the gorgeous house. He thought he would be intimidated and feel out of his element, but the house was a home and every room was inviting and comfortable. He felt even more at ease after the tour, and Cade ushered him toward the back of the house where they heard the noise of the family as they got dinner ready. The kitchen was probably the most gorgeous one Braden had ever seen and he said as much to Siobhan, who responded that he could come over and use it whenever he wished, if he left some baked goods. The room was massive, and it seemed they'd forgone a formal dining room to combine the dining room and kitchen into an enormous space that included a fireplace and a wall of folding glass doors that opened out onto the patio with the most beautiful view of the Golden Gate Bridge in the distance.

Rowan pulled out the counter stool beside her and patted it, so he sat by her and was immediately drawn into a conversation she was having with Finn. It was chaotic, and everyone talked over each other and laughed, a lot. Cade stayed by his side, always touching him in some way. Several times he caught one of Cade's family members glancing their way, seeing their closeness and Cade's possessiveness, his proprietary touches and the frequent kisses he placed on Braden's head. He waited for any type of judgement, anything that would let Braden know they weren't happy for Cade, but all he saw were genuine smiles and some light-hearted ribbing, making Braden blush.

When they all sat down for dinner, Duncan proposed a toast and eloquently expressed how happy they all were to meet Braden and accept him into their family. Everyone raised their glasses in heartfelt cheers, and Braden felt this was the perfect moment for him to thank them all. He cleared his throat, looked around at the faces of Cade's family then up at Cade. "I was scared to come here tonight. I didn't know what to expect, and I was sure you'd all feel angry that I put him through what I did, mostly because I'm angry at myself. I didn't know you'd all been a part of bringing me home safely. I'll be forever grateful for that. For helping me, of course, but mostly for being there to help him, when I couldn't. He has a wonderful family in you all, and I'm so grateful to be so warmly welcomed into it."

Braden glanced over at Cade and rubbed his hand up and down Cade's thigh. He was captivated by Cade's intense gaze, unable to look away. Cade reached over and slid his hand into Braden's hair at the nape of his neck, his thumb rubbing his cheek. They looked into each other's eyes for a few seconds before Cade leaned down and kissed him then whispered in his ear. "You're amazing. I love you so much, baby."

Braden looked around the table when Cade released him and blushed when he realized they were still the center of attention. Gideon raised his glass. "To Zavier and Braden." Everyone raised their glasses again and drank then started passing around the food, and Braden's discomfort ended. They enjoyed a wonderful meal and Braden ate entirely too much but wouldn't change it for anything. He'd taken part in the dinner conversations and truly felt a part of everything. At the end of the meal, he smiled at his new family. "I made some cream puffs for dessert, but if you already have something else, you can easily freeze them for some other time. Please don't feel obligated to have them tonight."

Braden laughed when Finn spoke up. "I want cream puffs." Siobhan stood and gathered a few plates and Braden stood as well, to do the same. She tried to shoo him away, and Cade clasped his hand. "You're our guest, please, you don't have to clean up."

Braden frowned. "Did they mean it, when they said I was welcomed to the family?"

Cade looked taken aback. "Of course, Bray."

Braden smiled wide and kissed Cade on the forehead as he stood again. "Good, then I'm not a guest at all, am I?"

He grinned when Cade narrowed his eyes. Braden asked Siobhan if she was sure he wasn't ruining her dessert plans. She laughed and told him she'd just made a little fruit salad and it could wait. He told her that was nonsense, opened the fridge and pulled out the fruit salad and what appeared to be a creamy sauce to go with it. She began to wash dishes at the main sink as everyone made quick work of cleaning off the table. He washed his hands as best he could with his cast at the small prep sink on the island and searched around for dessert plates. He pulled them out and began to load each one with a chocolate cream puff and some fruit salad. When that was complete, he stuck a finger into the sauce and tasted. He realized it was a very nice vanilla cream sauce and proceeded to drizzle each helping of fruit with the sauce.

After he plated the dessert, he turned and saw a French press coffee maker and an electric kettle. He filled it up, ground some beans and started a fresh pot for anyone who wanted some. While he was doing that, Duncan helped with the dishes, and their kids wrapped up the leftover food and wiped down the kitchen counters and tables. He loved that everyone pitched in, and he could tell by how natural it was that it was a common occurrence and not put on for his benefit. Finn pulled down some mugs for the coffee, and Gideon got the cream and sugar. Everyone started to take dessert and coffee fixings to the table.

Before everyone dove into their desserts, Duncan spoke to Braden. "Son, we wanted to make sure that you had a leather band for your new watch, as the old band you had wouldn't fit the Imperator. We have your old band and watch that we'll return to you, as well. We had them copy the same style and even the same markings, so that it was as close as possible to your other watch band. We hope you enjoy it."

Braden didn't know what you say. They'd gone above and beyond tonight, accepting him, making him feel at home with all of them, and here they were giving him another gift. He watched as Duncan passed it to Gideon and Gideon reached across the table and gave Braden the box with an almost imperceptible nod.

When he opened it, he found his old watch and band, and beside that, the new band. Cade reached over and took off the Imperator on his wrist, took the new leather band out of the box and set about putting the watch face on the new band. Once he had it back on his wrist, he grinned and looked at Duncan and then the rest of the family and said a heartfelt thank you.

When everyone had gotten themselves their coffee, they all began to dig into the dessert and there were some happy murmurs and some outright groans when they tried the cream puffs. Braden laughed and ate a tiny portion of his dessert, more intent on savoring the coffee and the company. Cade slid his arm behind Braden's back and pulled him in closer to lean back against him. He switched their plates and began to eat the remainder of his uneaten dessert while Braden sipped his coffee and snuggled into Cade's side.

Rowan admonished her brother. "Hey, don't eat his dessert!"

Cade smirked. "He's done. You're just jealous cause you want seconds!"

Rowan looked at Braden to see if Cade was telling the truth and he nodded. "I only filled up my plate because, inevitably, he eats what I don't want. I don't eat much of what I bake. Strangely enough, even before the diabetes, I wasn't a huge fan of sweets; or at least, sweets in abundance. A little goes a long way for me, so I tend to taste everything in small amounts, but never finish anything. There's more though. I brought enough for everyone to have a couple, so you can have another, or you can put them in the fridge for tomorrow or the freezer for later."

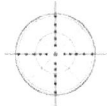

Cade

Cade looked down at Braden, seeing his eyes drooping a bit. Cade glanced up at Gideon who was watching him with interest, perhaps curiosity, or maybe even amusement. It was always hard, sometimes nearly impossible, to read Gideon; he hated playing poker with the guy because he had no tells. Finally, his oldest brother asked about the case against Eric. He answered several questions from Gideon and his dad then Finn asked how Braden was really doing.

Confused why his brother would ask that, Cade looked down at Braden and saw he'd fallen asleep. Cade answered truthfully, knowing everyone in his family was concerned. "He's struggling a bit, having nightmares and not sleeping well, which is probably a big reason why he's asleep right now. He'd never fall asleep like this if he wasn't going through so much. I know you don't care and aren't bothered by it, but when he wakes, he'll feel bad that he fell asleep."

His dad shook his head. "Zavier, your boy needs his rest and if he feels safe enough sitting here by you and with all of us at the table, then that says something about his comfort level here, I'd say."

Cade smiled and nodded. "He told me today he never spoke a word to Eric. He got in Eric's car and let the asshole take him—in his mind, to save us—but he said he knew he'd made a mistake immediately and wasn't going to give the asshole the satisfaction of reacting to him in any way. So, he ignored him, even while Eric terrorized him and beat the shit out of him."

His mom looked close to tears. "He's so brave and strong, handling this as well as he is. He's also gentle and kind, funny and smart. I couldn't ask for a better man for you. I see a happiness in you that I've never seen before. He softens your hard edges. I'm starting to see parts of that carefree young man you used to be, and I can't tell you how happy that makes me."

His sister, on the other side of Braden, spoke softly so as not to wake him. "He's such a great fit, not just for you, but here, with us. I can't wait to get to know him better."

Cade looked at his sister then down at Braden who slept soundly. "I'm so glad you guys have taken to him because whether you had or not, he's it for me. It means a lot that you all have been accepting of him so quickly."

Duncan smiled. "I'm happy to have another son in the family, and I think you're good for each other."

Cade nodded and thanked his dad and was surprised when Gideon spoke up. "I always thought I'd have to make sure the one you chose was worthy of you. With Braden, I find myself hoping that you're worthy of *him*. I look forward to getting to know him better."

Cade smiled at that, not in the least insulted, as he wondered the same thing. Frankly, his brother had spoken more tonight than Cade had heard from him in forever. If Braden brought that side out of Gideon, Cade was grateful for it.

Finn finally joined in. "He's what you need, and you're what he needs. It's as simple as that."

Cade nodded, knowing it was true. He had known his family would accept Braden with open arms but hearing it from each of them and knowing their words were truly heartfelt, meant a great deal to him, and he said as much. They chatted for several more minutes then his family cleared the table, making as little noise as possible. When they were done, Cade rubbed Braden's arm to wake him.

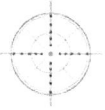

Braden

Braden had been enjoying the cadence of the men's voices and the rhythm of the women's. The next thing he knew, Cade was waking him. His face was aflame, and he apologized.

Finn smiled, and Braden relaxed under his watchful gaze. "You're gonna get tired pretty easily for the next week or so, is my guess. Your body is getting over some significant trauma, not only from the concussion but also the coma. Please pay attention to it for the next week or so, and your recovery will go much smoother."

Siobhan patted him on the shoulder. "Honey, please don't worry about it. We pushed you too soon to come and meet us. That's my fault. I begged Zavier to bring you."

Braden smiled at Siobhan and thanked her. Cade's voice was a quiet murmur in his ear. "The only reason I woke you is so I could get you home to bed."

Braden had leaned into Cade and tipped his head toward him to hear his quiet words. He nodded and looked up at Cade, who bent down again to kiss him softly. They stood and headed into the foyer. Rowan approached him first and clasped her hands tightly in front of her, he could practically feel her desire to give him a hug but neither of them stepped forward. Finally, she reached towards him and grabbed his hands, whispering that she was so happy to meet him and telling him she'd stop by the bakery in a week or so to see him and Maya again. She squeezed his hands as they grinned at each other. Braden knew he had a new friend in Rowan, and he couldn't be happier. Siobhan stepped forward and gently rubbed his shoulder. He braced for a hug, but she clasped his hands as well and squeezed. He let out a relieved sigh, knowing they understood he wasn't ready for much human contact yet. She gave his hands a little shake and said, "Don't be a stranger, darling. Please come and see us in the next few weeks."

Braden nodded and smiled as Duncan approached. They shook hands, Duncan clasping the back of his with his other, patting it and letting him go. "It was great to finally meet you, son. You're welcome here anytime."

Gideon approached and gave him a very manly handshake, and Braden grinned, forgetting to be intimidated by Cade's taciturn older brother. When Braden went to pull his hand away from him, Gideon whispered loudly, "You're perfect for my younger brother, Braden. Let me know if he doesn't treat you well. I have a feeling I could do better."

Braden's eyes popped wide then he covered his mouth and chuckled when he saw the twinkle in Gideon's eyes. The comment hit its mark, and Cade growled menacingly, attacking Gideon from behind with a chokehold. Braden would have started to get nervous if he didn't see Gideon wink at him before he did a few quick movements to get himself free and get Cade on the floor.

Braden, mouth agape, looked at the two grown men wrestling on the foyer floor and was startled when he felt hands on his shoulders pulling him out of the way. He looked back and saw Finn shaking his head at them. "They never could help themselves. It used to get bloody when Aiden would join in. Just don't get caught in the fray."

Braden watched Rowan delicately step in the middle of powerful arms and legs, and strangely enough, the fighting stopped immediately. The brothers pulled apart from each other, careful of their little sister as they got up.

Siobhan grinned. "She's my secret weapon. To this day, she's the only one that can get them to stop fighting."

Braden laughed and couldn't help but be a little impressed with her. After Cade and Gideon were done with the good-natured ribbing that followed their scuffle, Braden said his last goodbyes to Finn. Finn patted his shoulder. "Take care of yourself for the next few weeks. Give yourself a break and allow yourself to heal."

Braden promised he would and watched curiously as both Finn and Gideon followed them out and Duncan kept his arms around his wife and daughter at the door. He turned and waved at them as Cade led him down the front steps toward the driveway. When he turned back, he realized that Gideon had already gotten to their car and was checking the area around the front of the house. Finn brought up the rear, following them. Braden's stomach dropped and he crossed his arms over his chest to ward off a chill that he was sure wasn't in the air. Cade leaned toward him. "Just a precaution, Bray. I didn't ask it of them, they're just making sure you're safe and that the rest of my family is safe."

Braden's moaned, covered his face with his hands. "Jesus, you'd think I would have learned my lesson when we took Nana out to lunch. We should have waited to come here until he was caught."

Gideon heard him and shook his head. "Everyone is perfectly safe, we're just being careful. You're one of us now, and we protect what's ours."

Braden looked at Cade curiously, but Cade nodded and the look on his face let Braden know in no uncertain terms that Gideon was being completely serious about being protective of him. An overwhelming sense of security settled over Braden. Cade's family was more than he ever could have hoped for.

He didn't stop to think of his actions, he just walked to Gideon hugged him quickly and pulled away before Gideon had a chance to reciprocate. He wasn't quite ready for that yet. He had a tough time meeting Gideon's eyes, a bit embarrassed that he'd been so overcome, not to mention he felt awful that he might have inadvertently put them in danger by coming to see them. He moved back to Cade who brought him in close a happy smile on his face.

Cade helped him into his seat, latched his seatbelt as he kissed him, and then gave his brothers each a hug before folding himself into the driver's seat. Both of them let him know that if he needed help with anything at all, to give them a call. Feeling great about how the evening went, he placed his hand on Cade's thigh as he backed out of the driveway and waved to Cade's family as they pulled out.

"Why weren't you worried about Rowan when she came out to greet us?"

"A couple of reasons: one, Jackson and Sawyer were in their car following us to my parents' house, and if anything had happened, they would have been there to help us, and two, Cooper pulled out ahead of us and beat us there and checked out the surrounding area before we arrived. I promise you, my family is not in danger because of Eric, I'm just as overly cautious with them as I am with you."

Braden nodded and was about to ask Cade a question, but he needn't have worried. "My guys are staying on until Eric is behind bars. Maya and Nana will be safe, Braden."

Braden leaned toward him and rubbed his leg with his casted hand. "Thank you."

He relaxed into his seat and asked Cade to tell him more about his siblings. For the rest of the ride home, Cade did. Braden learned all of them were trained in martial arts of some form or another, and they all knew how to handle firearms from an early age, as their father was career military and wanted them all to know how to take care of themselves and others, should it be needed. Finn was the resident genius of the family who graduated high school at sixteen and went to Johns Hopkins University for medical school. Cade told him about the sibling he hadn't met, Aiden, his youngest brother and an active duty Navy SEAL who, when he retired from the Navy, would be groomed to become the new CEO of McCade Military Watches, taking over for their father. When he spoke of his sister, he called her brilliant and a proud smile spread over his face when he talked about her career as a highly sought-after computer engineer. Finally, there was Gideon who he said was a former Navy SEAL.

"What does Gideon do now that he's no longer in the military?"

He turned to look at Cade when he heard a funny sound and realized he was rubbing his face and his short, scruffy beard caused the noise. Braden looked away and blushed, thinking that a simple move like that shouldn't be getting him worked up. He couldn't help sneaking another glance, because really, his man was hot. Cade rubbed his hand over his mouth one more time and looked rather uncomfortable. "His official line is that he's retired. But the reality is, he could tell us, but then he'd have to kill us. So, we just don't ask."

Braden whipped his head to look at Cade and laughed at the absurd use of that line. "He.... Wait, what?"

He watched Cade for signs of amusement, a clue that he was teasing him, anything. There was nothing. No sign of amusement, no eye contact. Cade kept his gaze on the road. "Gideon isn't like the rest of us, not really. Even when he was younger, he was set apart. I mean, we're similar in that we all excelled in school and sports, but instead of those traits drawing people near, it set him apart. He became a SEAL, and he was in his element."

Braden listened with rapt attention, not wanting to interrupt Cade for fear that he'd stop talking about himself and his family.

"For a while, we could tell he was happier than he'd ever been. Not that he chatted a lot, but he seemed settled. Something bad occurred late in his SEAL career, just before he left the teams. He won't talk about it. Whatever it was, it took that glimpse of the settled, happy Gideon away from us, and he's been different, even more closed off, ever since."

Braden frowned. "Did you ask him directly?"

Cade nodded. "Yeah. Once he left the SEAL teams, he became more withdrawn. I tried to get information out of him, but the more I did, the less he came around, so I stopped. For a while, he was employed with a government organization—that much we know. I don't think that's the case any longer. I think he's working on something locally because he hasn't been going on many trips lately, according to my parents. Other than that, like I said, we don't ask."

Braden gaped. Surprised didn't even cover it. This was the stuff of movies, not real life. "You're being serious."

"Very."

"So, I should avoid asking him personal questions?"

Cade shrugged. "It's up to you. He liked you, and I don't know many people I can say that about. Who knows what he'd tell you."

Bewildered that the conversation had ended this way, he sat in silence the rest of the trip. He tried to picture Gideon as some top secret spy operative. As much as he wanted to be able to laugh it off and ignore Cade's comments, he could see it. If it wasn't for Cade's admission, Braden would have just thought that Gideon was quiet, one of those brooders, a complete introvert. While that may be true, he didn't doubt Cade's words.

When they got back to his place, Braden realized Nana was already in bed and left her a note in case he didn't see her in the morning. He tested his blood, and they wasted no time getting ready for bed. Braden was exhausted and as much as he wanted to make love with Cade, he didn't have the energy. Cade must have noticed how tired he was because once they got into the bed, he simply wrapped his arms around him and held him as he fell asleep.

Chapter 7

BRADEN

Something wasn't right. Braden felt it deep in his gut and that, if nothing else, was what woke him from a deep sleep. He heard the hardwood floor creak out in the foyer and knew they weren't alone in the house. Did they set the alarm last night? Eric had gotten in, somehow, he'd gotten in, and he was coming for Braden. He reached his arm out to Cade to wake him as quietly as he could, not wanting to give away to Eric that he was awake. He shook Cade's arm and got no response. Now was not the time for his soldier partner to sleep soundly. He turned to Cade to shake him a little harder, using his good hand instead, but what he saw made his breath catch and his stomach roil.

Blood, so much blood, everywhere. Where was it coming from? And then he saw it, Cade's throat had been slit open, blood spreading out from the wound as he watched. Braden cried out in agony. He pushed himself off Cade's chest, backing himself toward the edge of the bed. His legs got caught in the blanket, causing him to sprawl backward onto the floor. He heard a shout and realized it must have been his as everything went black.

"Braden, can you hear me? Open your eyes, Bray. Come on."

Braden heard Cade's voice, and his heartbeat accelerated. Cade was sitting next to him, looking at him with concern. How was that possible? He looked at Cade's shirt. "Blood. Where's the blood?"

"Braden, what blood? I woke up when you were thrashing around then you cried out. You're not bleeding."

"No, you... You were bleeding. Your throat. He...."

"Baby, no. Look at me, I'm fine. You yelled out in your sleep. I woke you up. That's all. I'm fine, look, no blood."

Cade pulled him up to sit across his lap while Braden's body convulsed in uncontrollable shivers, as if he was freezing. "He killed you. He slit your throat and there was blood everywhere. Oh god, I thought you were dead."

Cade held him tight and rocked him. "I'm fine. I'm all right, Braden."

That's where they were when Nana came to check that everything was all right. She stayed quiet, but her offer of help was clear on her face. Cade shook his head and pulled Braden tighter to his chest. She nodded and left as quickly as she came, giving them privacy, a concerned look in her eyes.

Cade sat there patiently, stroking Braden's back and hair. When Braden looked up at him, the color was drained from his cheeks. "You can't die on me like that. I couldn't handle it."

"Bray, stop. Listen to me. Eric will not kill me, and he'd have to, in order to kill you. That's not going to happen. He will be handled. I promise you that."

Braden just clung to him. He didn't say anything further. Whether he was convinced or not, Cade didn't know. "Talk to me, Braden. Do you honestly feel that I'm going to die and he's going to get to you and kill you? Do you think I'm going to let that happen to you?"

Braden was quiet for several beats too long for Cade's peace of mind. He was about to say as much when Braden finally spoke. "No. It's just that I'm having all of these nightmares. Some are of my time with him in the past, some my most recent time with him. Tonight's dream was so real. I had your blood on my hands, and I heard him out in the hallway. He's messing with my head, and he isn't even here. I'm so angry at him and at myself for letting him get to me this way."

Cade pulled him closer, held him tighter. "Braden, PTSD isn't something you can just fix by snapping your fingers. It's going to stay with you for some time, which is why we need to get you in to see someone. There is nothing wrong with you. Getting upset with yourself isn't going to help matters. You need to talk to a professional."

Braden nodded. "Yeah, all right."

"We're gonna call in the morning and make you an appointment with the psychologist that Dr. Himmel suggested. Later in the day, we're going to go to the self-defense class. I know you're feeling vulnerable and I think that's where the dreams are coming from. We're going to take care of this together. You aren't alone."

Braden nodded and hugged him back. "I'm not going to be able to sleep for a while. If you need to rest, go ahead. I can read or get up and watch TV in the front room."

"I'm awake as well. I'd rather be up with you, anyway. What would you like to do?"

Braden peered up into Cade's eyes. "Can we just stay in bed and talk?"

Cade nodded. "Yeah, we can do that."

Braden reached up to touch Cade's tags. "Will you tell me more about your past? Why you still wear your dog tags? What made you leave the military?"

"I'll tell you anything you want to know, as long as it's not classified. Do you want to ask me questions or do you just want me to lay everything out?"

"Just talk about your past, about some of the things you went through. I don't care if the stories are in order, or if you have to keep most of the specific details to yourself, I just want to know more about you."

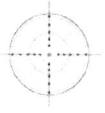

Cade

Cade reluctantly agreed. He didn't want Braden tainted by his past; it wasn't pretty. He knew Braden felt like he didn't know him which baffled Cade. Braden knew him like no one else did. He set his personal feelings aside for the time being and decided he would tell him everything he was able to tell him.

Braden had bared his soul to him; the least he could do was return the favor. He cleared his throat and addressed the easy question. "We call them ID tags, not dog tags. My dad still wears his, and so does Gideon. Ironically, I never wore them while on missions. In fact, for most of my career they were kept stateside. We wouldn't ever wear something that could identify our name and rank because about seventy five percent of our military career was spent overseas in hostile territory."

"You wear them under your clothes. I never noticed them until I saw you in a tank top."

"I don't wear them if they will be visible in public. People who do that aren't wearing them for the right reasons. They're not worn for adornment. I wear them out of respect for my service to my country and as a daily reminder of the men I lost under my command. I'll be impacted by those deaths for the rest of my life."

"But you don't wear them as punishment, right?"

Cade smiled. "Not punishment, no. When the deaths were fresh, when I was in the middle of an op and carrying a fallen soldier over my shoulder, there was guilt, and then later, a million different thoughts about what I could have done differently. I was trained, and trained well, to plan the safest and most strategic ops for each situation, and I was very good at what I did. But I'm human, and of course, there's second guessing and remorse."

Braden gripped his hand. "How did you deal with it?"

"I became an expert at compartmentalizing, because I couldn't have continued to do my job, and do it well, day in and day out if it wasn't for that. But when I was discharged, it was like all the years of delaying those feelings came crashing back. I went through some dark days when I first got out. I was finally honest enough with myself to know that I needed help, so I went through a shit ton of therapy."

"You sound annoyed."

Cade shook his head. "I waited too long. I should have done it immediately. I don't know anyone who served on the front lines who didn't have a tough time when they returned to civilian life. I had a great therapist, and I'm in a place now that I know I'm not infallible and I did everything in my power to protect my men. That doesn't mean I don't regret their deaths every day, and the hole those deaths created in the lives of their families."

Braden did his best to soothe him with his touch, and Cade found himself talking. Cade explained most of his scars came from a particular explosion that had riddled his body with shrapnel and killed two members of another team. When he returned stateside and everything had healed, he'd covered them with ink.

He told Braden of the mission where he was captured and tortured. Cooper and his team found him using the GPS on his watch which one of his captors had stolen. He'd been in bad shape but had considered himself lucky as there were others there that hadn't made it.

There had been good ops where they were able to rescue the people they were tasked with extracting. He'd been on unconventional warfare missions where they trained foreign troops in some of their methods. He smiled when he recounted a few of their search and rescue missions where they were able to help small villages near combat zones that had been nearly destroyed. He talked about the failed missions that resulted in a death on their team. And finally, the last mission, the one that solidified his desire to get out of the military while he could still make a difference by choosing the types of jobs his team went on.

Braden hugged him tighter and Cade rubbed a soothing hand down Braden's back, which he supposed was for them both. He hated every minute of this conversation so far and knew it wouldn't get any better until it was over. All he could do was hope that Braden's feelings for him wouldn't change as a result of the recounting of his past. His memories, so vivid, came back to him in technicolor.

The final straw was the last op and it was fucked from the word go.

The intel came in last minute from an unverified source which, strangely enough, wasn't that uncommon. The plan was to head into enemy territory where there was a team of al Qaeda extremists holed up before crossing the border to find sanctuary in the next country over. Cade felt uneasy about everything from the source to the mission itself. He knew it was an op that could go FUBAR, but it had been handed down from the upper echelons and their team was chosen. Though it was their mission, it was his job to ensure they did it in the safest way possible, which is why he made a change at the last minute.

Instead of heading out late the next day and being dropped into friendly territory as he'd logged, he arranged for his team to hitch a ride in a MH-47G Chinook Helicopter that was on its way to another base. He followed his gut and kept the plans mostly to himself, only telling his senior team members, Cooper, Sawyer, and Jackson.

He was honest with them, admitting he was uneasy, but that the mission was still a go. Jackson stared hard at Sawyer who was rubbing the back of his neck and then spoke to him using sign language. They signed back and forth for several minutes. Cade knew to let them finish their conversation before asking questions; they'd picked up a lot of ASL, having worked with Jackson for so long, but when Sawyer and Jackson got going, the speed in which they could communicate was well beyond what he could understand.

Sawyer finally looked at Cade. "I don't have a good feeling about it."

Cade looked at Sawyer, head tilted, waiting. Jackson kicked Sawyer's foot and signed something, to which Sawyer sighed, heavily. "You know me—I have a sixth sense about these things. That day isn't good. Can't that be enough? It always has been in the past. You know my hunches are spot on."

Again, Cade didn't say a word. He waited and glanced at Jackson who put his hands out, palms up, his fingers wiggling, signing to give Sawyer a minute. Cade sat back and stared Sawyer down until he was pacing and rubbing his hands over his head in frustration. Cade finally relented a bit. "I don't feel like that day is a good day either. I trust your instincts, Sawyer, but I think you need to talk to me about what's going on. It's not as simple as you're making it out to be, is it?"

Sawyer paced back toward Jackson and sat down very close to him, and for the first time Cade thought maybe they were more than just best friends, but he let it pass without comment. He saw Jackson lean down, elbows on his knees, and turn his face toward Sawyer, who looked back at him.

Sawyer sighed as he looked up at Cade. "It's more than a sixth sense. Sometimes it's flashes, sometimes I see full scenes of something to come, other times it's just a niggling sense that something bad is going to happen, and I have to react immediately, like when I pulled Cooper away from the land mine two years ago."

Cooper nodded. "You said you saw the mine."

Sawyer shook his head. "I told you guys I saw it, but I didn't. Something, some kind of innate sense of impending disaster, comes over me and nudges me in the right direction. I knew something was going to happen to Coop, so I yanked him out of the way, and the bomb experts were called in to dismantle it."

Cade knew immediately he had to change their plans. "Did you see a scene for tomorrow, a flash, or was it a niggling sense?"

Sawyer rubbed the back of his neck. "A flash of some outbuildings, and at least one of us gunned down, but I can't see who it is. When I look down, there's blood all over my hands. That's it, but it was enough to tell me that shit is going to go down if we stick to the plan."

Cade nodded, got up, and left without a word. He returned hours later to brief the team that they were moving their mission up and would leave on the Chinook today at nineteen-hundred hours. He told everyone to hit the rack and get some shut eye, and he'd provide mission details once they were airborne. The two newbies grumbled as everyone moved to follow orders. He made eye contact with each offender, a silent warning that they'd be having a discussion later, and things quieted down immediately.

Cade saw Cooper move to get up, but he signed 'don't ask' and walked out of the room; the less everyone knew, the better. What he was doing was against regs, regardless of the fact he was responsible for their team and all the decisions fell to him. Special Forces teams don't operate under the authority of ground command, they answer to a combatant command that directs military forces within a set geographical boundary, regardless of service branch.

Their mission was to get in, kill the leader, and get out, while taking as many of the extremists out as possible. Cade was highly suspicious of their intel, so as far as he was concerned, they were going in blind. He spent the flight outlining their objectives, assigning specific duties to his team, and going over alternate plans. He tasked himself with getting in, killing the leader who was supposedly a highly valued member of the extremist militia, and getting back out, with Cooper as his back up. They'd drop in a small town close to the border and would have to hoof it five klicks to their intended location which was an old abandoned security checkpoint and *other outbuildings, temporarily being used as an al Qaeda hideout according to their intel.*

Their insertion occurred without incident, but instead of making Cade feel better, it made the hairs on the back of his neck stand at attention. He shared a look with Sawyer who merely shook his head. Under the cover of night, they made it to their destination, an outcropping of rocks just outside of the checkpoint, and began reconnaissance.

The tangos were packing up, readying their camp to move out, most likely with the dawn. There was a harried and frenetic energy about them. Cade had his team stand down, to wait and watch for his signal. Explosives were being set with trip wires all over the makeshift camp. Either someone had let them know they would have company the next day, or they just happened to be getting ready to leave at precisely the right moment. Cade didn't believe in coincidences.

His team was dressed in local garb, so it would be easy for them to get in and out once things settled down for the night. Ironically, the tangos' actions made things much easier for them. Cade quickly explained that they'd be rewiring all those explosives to detonate once Cade had completed his task and they were free and clear of the security checkpoint.

They waited for nearly two hours until people took to their makeshift sleeping quarters. Cade had the group disperse to take care of their individual assignments, and he walked quietly into the interior of the camp with Cooper beside him. Those that were worth the least would be around the outer edges of the base; those that were worth the most would be tucked further inside for the added protection and what few luxuries there were at such a desolate and abandoned set of buildings.

They followed along the path of improving conditions using their night vision goggles. Dispatching the two sentries at the rear entrance of the main building didn't take much effort. Both were smoking and talking, paying little attention to their surroundings. They dragged them inside and one of Cade's new guys took their place, standing guard. They passed through the building slowly, checking the few rooms, all empty save one.

Cade and Cooper knew who they were looking for, so there would be no mistaking his identity. They made it to the room that most likely would house the leader and entered swiftly and quietly. There was a man on a pallet on the floor who appeared asleep, however, when they got closer, he moved to sit up and talk to them, obviously thinking they were his soldiers. He spoke quietly in Arabic, asking if everything was completed.

Cade replied with a staccato affirmative in the same tongue, avoiding inflection and the man seemed satisfied enough to lie back down on his pallet. When Cade continued to draw closer to him, he sat up again and asked what was wrong. Cade got a good look at him then and saw that he was, in fact, their target. He realized too late that Cade wasn't one of his men. As he began to yell, Cade swiftly and silently sliced his blade across the target's throat, nearly severing his head.

Cade turned toward Cooper, saw the man at his feet, and realized someone must have come in to check on their target. Cooper held up his finger to signal quiet. Cade flanked the other side of the door, waiting for the person coming swiftly down the hallway. When the tango ran through the door, Cade caught him from behind, snapping his neck quickly then gently placing him on the floor.

What Cade saw on the floor next to the guy's hand made his blood run cold. He tapped Cooper on the shin and showed him the knife on the floor that was covered in blood. Cooper's eyes narrowed in acknowledgement and he nodded, but they continued on with their plan. When they were sure the hallway was clear, they both left the room in opposite directions to check that the tasks of the others were completed, and everyone had gotten out safely.

He was just turning the first corner when he came to a body in the hallway. Though he'd half expected it, he still couldn't believe what he was seeing. Chaz, the newbie they'd left at the back entrance, was inside the building where he had no business being, dead by the tango's knife wound to his throat.

He hadn't yet had time to truly get to know the kid, and now, he never would. The guilt threatened to swamp him. Losing one of his men, regardless of how well he knew him, was something he always had a difficult time with, and this time was no different. The fact that this young man had disobeyed direct orders and placed himself in danger didn't seem to matter in the grand scheme of things. This mission was fucked. He'd known it from the word go, and he knew it was going to get worse before it got better.

He knew he had to get his team the fuck out of dodge, so he leaned down and hauled his man up into a fireman's carry across his shoulders. Cade held on to Chaz's arm and leg with his left hand, so that his right hand was free to hold his sidearm. He got Cooper on coms and, speaking in Dari, quickly and quietly told him what had happened and that he'd give the go ahead to detonate the bombs once he was far enough away with Chaz. He was outside and was rounding a corner of one of the outbuildings when he heard a noise behind him and turned just in time to see a tango raise his gun.

As much as he didn't want to shoot anyone and wake up the rest of the camp, he didn't have much of a choice. He raised his gun and was about to shoot when his attacker got one off first, hitting him high on the right side. He nearly dropped his man but was able to keep hold and get a shot off at the tango, taking him down with a shot to the head, and started hoofing it out of there. He got Cooper on coms again and explained the gunshot had been his and they didn't have much time before every tango in the fucking place would be falling out to attack.

Cooper validated that everyone else had gotten out, and they were at their rendezvous point. Cade heard movement behind him and sped up, turning a corner and seeing freedom ahead. He ran as fast as he could from the camp and told Cooper to blow it sky high. He thought he was far enough away to avoid getting any backlash, but true to this fucked up mission, he wasn't quite there. He caught a bit of shrapnel on his back and legs but kept going. Once he got to his men, Cooper came forward along with Jackson and Sawyer and relieved him of his cargo with some angry mutters and several questions about why the kid had been where he'd been.

He admitted he had no fucking clue why the kid had gone against orders, but kept his mouth closed about his own injuries. As long as the other men traded carrying the body of their fallen soldier, he'd suffer through the five-kilometer trek to the landing zone and get the fuck out of dodge. As team leader, he always protected their six, and this mission was no different, as they made their trek to the LZ. Strangely enough, they had no further troubles that night and just as his energy flagged and he began slowing his men down, drawing curious looks from them, they arrived at the LZ with only seconds to spare. They were extracted without delay and flown back to base.

His men didn't find out he was injured until they boarded the helicopter, and Cooper asked him what was really going on. When he admitted he was shot and had some shrapnel wounds, his men got to working on him immediately. Only when the adrenaline ebbed did he realize he was in worse shape than he'd thought. When they arrived back to base, he was taken immediately to the clinic where he was treated and stabilized enough to travel. He was then flown to Germany for surgery and continued treatment then home to recover completely.

"And that brings us to the creation of Custos Securities which you already know all about." Cade sighed and continued, "I don't think I missed anything big, but if there's anything else I can think of, I'll share it with you."

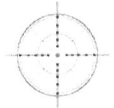

Braden

Braden sat, calmly caressing Cade's arms that were now locked around him from behind. He was leaning back against Cade's chest, and this time he had the feeling he was facing away from him for Cade's benefit, not his own. He could feel the tension radiating through Cade's whole body. He didn't feel bad for wanting-no, needing-to know more of Cade's past; however, Braden felt horrible it was at such a cost to him.

He turned to the side so he was leaning across Cade's belly, propped his head up with his hand, and gazed at Cade in consternation. He used the fingertips of his casted hand and softly ran them down the side of Cade's cheek. He felt Cade's clenched jaw and felt a sick sort of dread in the pit of his stomach. He pulled his hand away and slowly sat up and moved back. He pulled his legs into his chest and held them there with his arms around them, his chin on his knees. He pulled away from Cade physically, but he knew Cade had pulled away from him mentally, and he felt bereft at the loss.

"Do you…" Braden swallowed and tried again, "Do you resent me for wanting to know you better, for asking this of you?"

Cade took in a deep breath and let it out slowly. He closed his eyes and brought his hands up to rub his face then entwined his fingers behind his head and squeezed his eyes shut. Braden was awed at the strength of those huge, tatted arms and the muscles contained within. He'd be willing to bet they were almost as big as his own thighs. Thinking about how much strength ran through Cade's body, and how he'd used that body for most of his life to protect others, had him yearning to reach out to him. But the longer Cade took to answer, the more panicked Braden felt. If he'd known this was going to be Cade's reaction to talking, to telling him about his military career, would he still have asked? Braden knew that in the end, the answer would be yes.

Braden was amazed at everything Cade had done in the Special Forces, and he was so damn proud of him. His partner was a fucking hero. He was so remarkable, and Braden had a niggling feeling that Cade wouldn't agree with that assessment. Braden didn't want Cade to have to compartmentalize his work life from his life with him. He didn't think that was fair to either one of them.

Maybe Cade needed some time alone after talking about his past. As much as he didn't want to leave him alone when he was in pain, and Braden knew that's exactly what was going on, maybe that's what Cade needed. Braden didn't want to push and didn't want to mess up their relationship in any way. He looked at Cade who had tilted his head back and was now focused on the ceiling. Feeling a bit defeated, he released his legs. He scooted to the edge of the bed to get up and give Cade space. He went to stand up then sucked in a startled breath when he was hauled back onto Cade's legs, sitting sideways across his lap, gaping up at him in surprise. Cade looked deep into his eyes. "Don't walk away from me right now. I'm holding on by a very thin thread, and you walking away would tip me over the edge."

"I was gonna give you some time alone. You weren't responding to my question, and I just thought you didn't want me around while you were feeling so vulnerable. I didn't want to pressure you."

Cade rubbed his hand back and forth over his short hair and sighed. "I was trying to figure out *how* to answer you. First, let me say that I could never resent you for wanting to know me better, Braden. That's not…"

Cade shook his head and closed his eyes again. Braden sat patiently and reached up to feather his fingers over Cade's eyebrow and down to his cheek. Cade cleared his throat and tried again, "That's not the case at all. I'm not proud of some of the things I've done. I'd rather you didn't know everything I just told you, and there's more that I can't share with you that's worse. I had to do some pretty fucked up shit, and I've had some pretty fucked up shit done to me."

Braden's brow furrowed. "And you think I've lost respect for you, knowing this?"

Cade shrugged. "I don't know, Bray. Yeah, maybe. Active duty Special Forces isn't pretty. It isn't glamorous. All that shit people read, hyping us up, it's just so much bullshit. I've killed a lot of people, Braden. I don't want my violent history bleeding over into our life, making you afraid of me. I couldn't handle you looking at me like I'm a monster, thinking of me differently. And I realized I wouldn't even blame you if you did."

Braden slowly moved out of Cade's arms and maneuvered himself back onto his lap, straddling his waist. He got as close to Cade as he could and looked him in the eyes. "You know what? I do look at you differently, Zavier."

Pain etched itself across Cade's face as he looked down as if he was ashamed. The sight of it broke Braden's heart. He tilted Cade's face back up toward his and whispered brokenly, "Before tonight, I thought of you as my protector, but you're a fucking hero, Zavier. How dare you think of yourself as a monster or belittle the things you've done serving our country. Do you think I'm so naïve I had no idea you had killed people?"

Cade shook his head. "I just—"

Braden put his hand over Cade's lips and shook his head. "And how could you think I'd look at you with fear? You'd kill yourself before you ever touched me in anger. I'm so proud of what you've done and what you continue to do to help people. God, your family must be so proud to have a son like you. Can't you understand how amazing your achievements are? It would kill me to know you aren't proud of yourself."

Cade looked at him for several long moments then Braden could literally feel the stress leaving his body when he heaved a deep sigh. Cade smiled sadly. "I am proud of a lot of what I've done, but sometimes I feel the terrible things I did while active duty will never be eclipsed by the good that was done. It's the biggest reason I got out when I did."

Braden looked deep into Cade's eyes. "I don't see it that way. I think you had to have known you'd be ordered to do some gruesome things in that line of work, and deep down, you know it was for the greater good. You have a career you can be proud of. I've never been more in love with you, never felt more attraction to you than I do right now."

That gorgeous smile Braden knew he had finally showed up on Cade's face. "Yeah?"

"Yeah. Want me to show you?"

Cade whispered gruffly, "What kind of a question is that?"

Braden smiled. "I'm going to show you how crazy in love with you I am. I'm going to prove to you that everything you just told me only made me fall more deeply for you."

Chapter 8

BRADEN

Braden leaned the scant few inches needed to capture Cade's lips with his. He reached between them and lightly cupped Cade's jaw in his hands, tilting his own head for a better angle. He could feel Cade's breath quicken against his skin as they kissed. He began to roll his hips into Cade's. His hips were tightly encased in Cade's large hands as he helping to guide them. Braden kissed his way across Cade's jaw. "Will you take your shirt off?"

Cade's breath caught, and he leaned forward, reaching behind him and grabbing his t-shirt behind his neck to yank it over his head. Braden had no fucking clue why the way Cade removed his shirt like that made his stomach flip with arousal, but it did. Cade made to grab Braden's hips again, but he scooted back toward Cade's knees. "Can I take your boxer briefs off?"

Cade smirked, tilting his head, as if taking Braden's measure. He licked his bottom lip then planted his palms on the bed and lifted his hips, raising an eyebrow, silently challenging Braden. Braden smiled and got to his knees. He leaned forward and slid his fingertips into the sides of Cade's boxer briefs and slowly pulled the tight material from Cade's hips. As he did so, Cade's hard cock emerged from the waistband, and when they were lowered to his upper thighs, his cock rested on his lower abdomen, right between the v line made by his muscular abs. Leaving his boxer briefs where they were, Braden leaned down and licked each line creating that gorgeous v. He then took Cade's cock in his fist and squeezed and was rewarded with several drops of precum sliding down the side of the fat mushroom head. Braden licked it up, taking the head into his mouth and sucking. He heard Cade's quick inhale then his hand was in Braden's hair pulling it back from his face and holding it tightly in his fist.

Braden kept his cock in his mouth but managed to angle his head to look up into Cade's eyes. The desire he saw there took his breath away. He made a last lick at Cade's cock and moved back, getting a tortured groan from Cade in response. He pulled Cade's boxer briefs the rest of the way off and continued to ask for what he wanted. "Will you turn over and lie face down?"

Once Cade complied, he removed his own boxers and t-shirt quickly, and put his hair up in his leather thong he swiped from the nightstand while straddling Cade's lower back. He then lay down on top of Cade so his lips were right next to Cade's ear. He licked the edge of that ear and down his neck where he nipped at the juncture of his neck and shoulder. He leaned up a bit and whispered, "I'm going to kiss and lick every single scar on your body, worship every single inch of you that's been damaged. See, I don't see them as shameful reminders, I see them as badges of honor. They're proof that you've used your body to protect others your whole adult life."

Cade groaned loudly and buried his head in his pillow. Braden began licking and kissing his way along his left arm and then his right. He would lick and kiss each scar then sometimes bite the tattooed area surrounding it. Cade hissed. "Your hair, why don't I feel it?"

"I pulled it back."

Cade turned his head to look over his shoulder at Braden. "Take it down. I need to feel it, baby. I've been waiting to feel it touch my skin when you kiss my body."

Emotion swamped Braden. "Really?"

Cade gently turned over. He sat up and clasped Braden's face in his hands. "Fuck, yes. I love that I can grab onto it, tug on it." He did so, pulling on Braden's tied back hair. "I've been looking forward to feeling it trail along and tickle my skin when you kiss me, when you suck my cock."

Braden yanked out the thong, shook his head to loosen the silky strands and tossed the thong back where he'd gotten it. He smiled at Cade as his long fingers sifted through his now loose hair and tugged at it again. "I'll never pull it back again when we're making love."

Cade slid his hands from Braden's hair and skated them down over Braden's shoulders. Continuing down, he gripped Braden's forearms, looked at him sternly and when he spoke, his voice was deeper, raspy. "Don't pull it back unless you're at work or running."

Braden could do nothing but nod as shivers slid over his skin at Cade's tone. He glanced down to his arms where Cade held him firmly and saw the goosebumps there. Cade followed his eyes, saw them for himself, and ran his hands up and down Braden's arms. When he glanced back up, satisfaction gleamed in his gaze. "Now, finish what you started, baby."

With that, Cade lay back down, turned over, and moved his hands to his sides. When Braden scooted up to sit on Cade's upper thighs, Cade palmed the sides of Braden's calves, almost like he was grounding himself, getting himself ready for the onslaught of sensation to come. Braden kissed his shoulder blades, no longer worried about his hair getting in the way. Now that he knew how Cade felt about it, he'd use that to his advantage.

As he kissed and licked down Cade's back, making sure to use his fingers to find every single dip and ridge resulting from Cade's many scars, he felt Cade tremble below him. The fact that his kisses and the simple touch of his hair on Cade's skin undid him, was remarkable to Braden. He loved that he could affect his lover so completely.

Braden thought about how much it turned him on when Cade talked dirty to him. He blushed just thinking about it, but he wanted to see if it made Cade react in the same way, if it made his body hum. He bolstered his courage, drew in a quiet breath, and whispered, "I've never seen anything as beautiful as your body. You're like a Greek sculpture."

He trailed his tongue along Cade's ass cheeks, moving down to lick, kiss, and bite his upper thighs. "You're my protector, my warrior. So damn strong."

He slid his knee between Cade's legs, spreading his thighs open. He trailed his lips along the backs of his inner thighs. Cade let out a shaky breath. "Oh god, I knew your hair would feel good, but I had no idea, no fucking clue. You're going to be the death of me, Bray."

Braden chuckled and continued, massaging Cade's thighs while he ran his lips over Cade's calves, his hands reaching to knead the rounded globes of Cade's ass cheeks. He couldn't stay away any longer, so he made his way back up Cade's ridiculously long legs. He sank his teeth into Cade's round muscular ass, receiving a grunt in response, and felt his body undulate underneath him. He took his palms and placed them on either ass cheek and slowly spread them open. "Oh, Z, look at you, so gorgeous."

Braden leaned down and licked from Cade's taint to the top of his ass and then back down to his center. He concentrated on drawing as much pleasure from Cade as possible. He laved and sucked his hole, something he'd never really enjoyed in the past but was enjoying immensely with Cade. He felt Cade's whole body tense, and he moaned loudly as Braden speared his tongue against his pucker. Cade nearly unseated him when he bucked up against Braden, his voice guttural. "Oh *fuck*, Braden!"

Once Cade relaxed enough for him to slide his tongue inside, Braden held his cheeks as wide as he could get them and dove in. He gave Cade the rimming of his life, eliciting groans and grunts and Cade's hips pushing back to meet Braden's eager tongue. Once he had Cade on the fine edge of losing control, he pulled away. "Someday, if you give me permission, I'll slide my cock deep inside of you. But tonight, I'm going to ask permission for something else."

Braden moved up, sliding his cock in the crease of Cade's ass and lay down on his back, kissing and sucking his neck. He gripped Cade's hands with his own and moved rhythmically back and forth. He was going insane with lust and could have come just from the friction alone, but he wasn't done. He leaned up to Cade's ear and bit down on his lobe. "Will you let me ride your cock?"

Cade groaned and clenched his fingers around Braden's, his voice shaky. "Fuck yes, baby."

"Will you turn over for me? I want to explore the rest of you."

Once Cade turned over onto his back, Braden straddled his waist again, leaning forward to kiss Cade's full lips. He moved on to Cade's arms and kissed every scar. There was a particularly long one that slashed lengthwise up his inner forearm and then curved off to the side. He kissed and licked it from one end to the other. "How bad was this one? You glossed over it, when you told me it was a defensive wound."

"Bray…"

"How bad, Z?"

"Jackson had to apply a CAT above my—"

"What's a CAT?"

"A combat application tourniquet."

"Jesus," Braden drew a breath in, sat back on his heels, and rested his forehead to Cade's sternum. He took a few deep breaths; all the while Cade's hands were caressing softly up and down his back. "I'm fine now. I can't hide my past, it's written itself all over my body, but that time in my life is over. Come on. Come on now, I need you with me."

Cade's fingers in his hair, pulling him up so he could look in his eyes, were exactly what Braden needed to bring him back to the present. They looked at each other for long moments, each lost in their own thoughts, but communicating such love to the other. He sat up, bracing himself on Cade's chest with his hands, before leaning over and opening his nightstand drawer to pull out his slick. He squeezed some on his fingers and reached around to ready himself. He got more lube then reached further back to get Cade's cock slicked up. Suddenly desperate, he didn't take time to prepare himself for Cade's size. He pushed back and guided Cade's cock to his entrance.

He heard Cade say, "Braden, I need to--" But it was too late. Once Braden pushed Cade's cockhead in, he sank back and impaled himself on Cade's cock. Braden squeezed his eyes tight at the intrusion. It was painful, but he felt so deliciously full and alive, he reveled in the discomfort. He sat still for a moment, enjoying Cade's caresses that started at his shoulders and made their way down to his hips. He left no inch of Braden's skin untouched and Braden's body was on fire for him. He knew this was what they both needed, this life-affirming action. He couldn't think of a more perfect way to celebrate the fact that they were both alive and desperately in love. Once his body adjusted to the intrusion, he began to slowly move his hips.

"That's it, ride my cock, Bray. Fuck, you feel amazing."

Braden hit his stride and was moving at a steady pace on top of Cade. His hands had finally stopped their exploration and settled on Braden's hips. Fingers gripped Braden's round ass cheeks, squeezing at the same tempo as his thrusts. Cade suddenly gripped his hips on an upward stroke, so he had to pause his movements. With his knees bent for leverage, Cade began lifting his own body, thrusting in and out of Braden at a fast pace. Braden was in sensory overload, having never felt anything like it.

Cade was relentless and continued to hold Braden in place and pistoned his hips so hard and fast Braden could only grip Cade's biceps and hold on for the ride. Just when he was sure Cade couldn't continue much longer, he growled between clenched teeth and picked up the pace, giving Braden the pounding of his life, pegging his prostate with every thrust. He felt a tingling in the base of his spine, muscles clenching as he felt his orgasm build.

He hadn't realized his eyes were closed and he was making noise until Cade ground out, "Look at me. Keep your eyes on me when I'm fucking you. Mmm, I love those little noises."

Braden's eyes popped open as he moaned, Cade's thrusts continuing. "Please. Can I—"

Cade's forehead was sweaty, his jaw clenched. He glanced down as Braden's hand reached for his cock. "Oh fuck, yes. Jerk it."

Braden gripped his cock in his fist and began pumping it in time with Cade's thrusts. He was so close to orgasm his moans turned to whimpers. He braced his other hand on Cade's chest while he quickened his pace. He let out a strangled plea, and Cade's eyes met his. "Yes. Come for me, baby. Come all over me!"

Braden had no fucking clue what it was about that deep, guttural voice Cade used when issuing those sexy commands, but he shot off the biggest load he ever had, and he moaned and whimpered as it just kept coming. Cade grunted as the first stream of Braden's cum hit his chest, and Braden felt Cade shoot his own load deep in his ass at the same time. He could feel each pulse as he was held in place and Cade's pace slowed. Their combined orgasm was something Braden knew he would never forget. As the last streams of their cum left their bodies, Braden nearly toppled forward; his energy was spent.

Cade caught hold of him and gently settled him down on his chest. He groaned when the new position moved Cade's cock within him, cum leaking from his body as Cade's cock continued to impale him. Loving how slick Cade's cum made him, he sighed, boneless, not caring a bit that he was lying in his own cum on Cade's chest; only caring that Cade's arms were wrapped around him so tightly, he almost lost his breath. They lay there for a while, recovering, unable or unwilling to voice their thoughts and intrude upon this moment.

Braden woke to Cade smoothing his hands up and down his back and whispering in his ear. "Baby, I'm gonna go and get a washcloth to clean us up."

It wasn't until then that Braden realized he'd drifted off and Cade was no longer hard and inside of him. He groaned when he pushed himself slowly off Cade onto his side and whispered, "Sorry. I'm honestly not sure if I fell asleep or I blacked out."

Cade chuckled and leaned over to kiss Braden senseless. "You and me both. Give me a second. I'll clean you up and make you comfortable so you can get some sleep."

Braden smiled sleepily up at Cade and turned over onto his back. He whispered, almost too quietly for Cade to hear, "Always taking care of me."

Braden smiled dreamily at Cade's response. "Always, love."

Braden woke when he felt the warm, wet washcloth glide over his skin and was just about to drift off again when Cade brushed his hand across his cheek. "Baby, can you sit up? I have your testing kit."

That woke him right up. He reached for the kit, shaking his head. "Wow, you sexed me into a stupor. I would have forgotten completely."

As Braden got out the supplies, Cade asked, "Can you show me what to do?"

Braden's head popped up and he looked wide-eyed at Cade. "You wanna learn how to give me my insulin?"

"I do."

Braden blushed and smiled. Oddly pleased that Cade would want to learn enough to be able to administer it for him. He couldn't keep the smile off his face as he walked Cade through the process of testing his blood. Braden handed Cade the syringe, told him what dose was needed and pinched some skin on his stomach while Cade dialed the dose he required. He explained what Cade needed to do and watched intently as Cade inserted the needle and slowly pushed down on the plunger.

As Cade waited the few moments needed before pulling out the needle, they gazed at each other, the look they shared filled with a burning intensity. Cade glanced back down, gently eased the needle out and handed it back to Braden. Cade rubbed Braden's stomach, as he'd seen Braden do himself, many times. Braden smiled again as he placed everything back in the kit except the needle, which he'd extracted. He walked to the bathroom to dispose of it properly in the container he kept below the sink and walked back to bed, where Cade waited for him, holding back the covers.

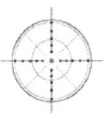

Cade

Braden crawled in, looking exhausted from the night's events. As he scooted closer, Cade pulled him nearly on top of him, needing Braden's weight to ground him in the here and now. Braden settled himself, getting comfortable, and let out a contented sigh that filled Cade with satisfaction and relief after the night they'd had.

Cade didn't want to think about how uneasy he was feeling about Braden's nightmares and panic attacks. It was already morning, but he set his mental alarm clock for a couple hours so he'd feel rested for the day. He'd let Braden rest as long as he needed to, waking him only to test his blood and eat. As soon as working hours rolled around, he needed to be on the phone making appointments for Braden and for himself.

He woke Braden at nine a.m., so he could test his blood. He brought him breakfast in bed and his testing kit. They ate together in relative silence, Cade thinking and Braden still half asleep. He took their dishes back to the kitchen when they were done, happy that he hadn't seen a hint of panic as he headed toward the door. After cleaning up the kitchen, he walked back into their bedroom as Braden was coming out of the bathroom. "You still look tired. Why don't you continue resting? You could use it after the last few days, but especially after last night."

Braden looked up at him with a small smile that didn't hide his apprehension as he glanced at the door. Cade understood immediately and put him at ease. "I have some work to do. I'll sit in your reading chair in here with you."

Braden blushed. "Thanks. I'm sorry I'm such a mess."

"None of that, Bray. We're handling this together."

Braden nodded and got back in bed. Cade left the room to get his laptop, and he was able to get several hours' worth of work done. When he was sure Braden was not going to wake up for some time, he went out into the living room to make a few calls. He called the psychologist's office and made an appointment for Wednesday afternoon, giving Braden a couple days before the session. Then he called Cooper to let him know that he was needed to sign some paperwork that afternoon and where to meet him. He also let him know they'd be attending his training session at Vaughn's that evening. He quickly placed a call to Brody.

"Boss man, how is Braden holding up?"

"He's doing all right. It's been tough, but he's hanging in. Thanks for asking, Brody. I just thought of something a minute ago. Did you ever search for a gun permit for Eric?"

"No, I didn't think of it, but I should have. Sorry about that."

"No, don't be, I just thought of it myself. Listen, maybe do a check from the time he got tossed from his job. Or better yet, do a check from back when Braden left him and see if he got himself a gun. Check under his name, but also check for any permits made locally within that time frame in case he's got a fake ID. He's holed up somewhere, and I figure if we can find a request for a gun permit, we might catch him with a fake ID and find out where he's renting if the owners do background checks. You can relay any info to Cooper. We've got a composite artist coming over here this afternoon. When I have Braden's depiction of what Eric looks like today, I'll send it to you guys."

"Sounds good. Do you want me to let you know if I come up with anything for the permit?"

"At this point, no. I can't have my focus split, and Cooper is leading the search for him. I would have called him about this, but I know he's out getting a run in with Maya right now, and I didn't want to forget it while it was fresh in my mind."

He finished the call and fixed them both some lunch. He woke Braden a few minutes later and let him know about the composite artist. They both ate then Braden got ready for the day while Cade got a HIIT workout in and showered. When the artist arrived at two p.m., he checked the security camera, and he wasn't surprised to see Detective Miller standing next to a shorter, much slighter man.

He opened the door and ushered them into Braden's home. He extended his hand to the man he figured was the artist. He was built along the lines of Braden, but even thinner, with beautiful amber colored eyes surrounded by the longest eyelashes he'd ever seen. He had a bit of a swollen purplish bruise on his cheek, below his eye that his long bangs helped to conceal, when he nonchalantly, but intentionally tipped his head just so.

"I'm Zavier McCade. You must be the composite artist."

They clasped hands, and the man slowly gazed up at him with those startling eyes, a bit of a shocked look crossing his face. "Uhm, yes, I'm Sebastian Phillips, it's nice to meet you. You're.... Wow. You're really.... There's a lot of you."

Cade laughed at that and lost a bit of the tension he was carrying for having to put Braden through this. "I guess there is."

He seemed nervous, was unable to hold Cade's gaze for long, and looked down at his feet. Sebastian was a beautiful man, bruise or no bruise. His eyes took up a good portion of his face and his lips were lush and full. He had a scruffy dark beard that seemed a bit out of place on his face but lent an air of hipster to his looks that he'd have lacked otherwise, perhaps aging him a bit, which might have been the goal.

Braden stepped forward, smiling widely at the turn the conversation had taken. He rubbed his hands on his pants a few times in a nervous gesture. He was getting much better at being touched by people other than Cade, but he still had to prepare himself for it. He held out his hand to

Sebastian while Cade slid his big palm under Braden's hair to softly grip his neck. "I'm Braden Cross," Braden looked up at Cade then back at Sebastian. "He is quite something, isn't he?"

"Um, yeah."

Cade watched them grin at each other; they seemed to click immediately. Sebastian looked at Cade's proprietary grip on Braden's neck and put on an affected sigh. "He's all yours, I'm assuming?"

"Every last inch," Braden responded.

Sebastian ignored Cade and completely focused on Braden. "Does he have any brothers?"

Braden chuckled. "Three, actually, and they all look remarkably alike."

Sebastian's face went utterly slack, his mouth gaped in comical disbelief, and both of the smaller men laughed and grinned at each other then looked up at him again. Sebastian lowered his gaze immediately, his grin still in place, a blush suffusing his cheeks. Cade found himself in a situation he'd never been in before, at a loss for words. He looked at Detective Miller with a plea written all over his face. "Get me outta this, detective."

Detective Miller lost some of the stiffness in his shoulders and chuckled. "I got nothing, man."

Cade shook his head as if he was crushed the cop wasn't going to be any help. He ushered them all into Braden's living room and asked if anyone wanted anything to drink. No one did, and they all sat; the visitors in the chairs and Braden next to Cade on the couch. They sat for a moment in silence until Sebastian cleared his throat. "Can I drag the ottoman over and sit a bit closer to you while I work?"

Cade watched as a smile spread over Braden's face as he nodded. "Yes, of course."

Sebastian slowly pulled over the ottoman and seemed to struggle a little with the effort. He got closer to Braden, who'd grown tense as the seconds ticked by. He pulled out his sketchpad and pencils then looked at Cade, saying deadpan, "Okay, I'm going to need you to take your clothes off now."

It was Cade's turn for a gaping mouth. "What? This is for a composite sketch of Eric Pollard!"

Sebastian grinned a ridiculously gorgeous grin, completely unrepentant. "Oh, I know, I just wanted to see you naked."

Braden looked at Cade's incredulous expression and laughed so hard he had to clutch his ribs. Cade hadn't heard Braden laugh that hard, probably ever, and took a quick look at Sebastian and realized the artist was a genius who knew exactly what he was doing. Flirting outrageously with Cade had relaxed Braden.

Cade kept his eyes on Sebastian and saw just when the artist thought no one was looking any longer, the wattage of his smile dimmed, and his continued laugh seemed more forced. He gripped his pencils tighter, took a deep breath, and squared his shoulders. He continued to banter with Braden about Cade's good looks and enormous size, but Cade could see this behavior wasn't natural for Sebastian.

The act he was putting on was a good one, but it was taking its toll on him. Cade could see sadness lurking in his eyes, which, strangely enough, seemed to be coupled with fatigue. He was curious about a man that hid so much behind silly flirtatiousness in order to make people around him feel at ease. Cade smiled in response to the quick, surreptitious, though contrived, wink Sebastian tossed his way while Braden continued to laugh, and he played along. "I have it on good authority that I am a fine male specimen."

Sebastian nodded his head, all mock seriousness. "Oh, honey, you are. You really are."

Braden laughed as everyone settled in for the task at hand. Sebastian began asking questions of Braden that Cade never would have thought helpful. Even watching the face take shape upside down, he could see Sebastian was immensely talented at what he did. Braden had gripped his hand as soon as the discussion of Eric began, and Cade did his best to help Braden remain calm. The drawing was completed about fifty minutes later, and Cade took a picture of the sketch, texting it to his local guys and to Brody.

Sebastian got up to leave and let them know he'd put some finishing touches on it and have it on Detective Miller's desk by the end of the day, so it could be used on the six o'clock news. Cade and Braden both got up to walk him to the door, thanked him for his help, and shut the door behind him. Braden frowned and looked up at Cade. "Did he look sad to you? Even when he was joking, he still looked sad to me."

Cade smiled down at Braden, pulling him close, not even remotely surprised that Braden had seen some of what he'd seen in the young artist. "Yeah, baby, I saw it too."

Detective Miller waited until they came back in from walking Sebastian to the door. "I'd like to apologize to you both for my behavior yesterday. Braden, I was insensitive and rude to you regarding your personal choices. I didn't mean to place blame on you, that was not my intention."

Cade was about to interrupt, but Braden beat him to it. "It may not have been your goal, but even now, you're judging me for my choices. I can see that much, plain as day, written all over your face."

The detective sighed. "My sister died years ago at the hand of her rapist. She was left for dead in an alley behind a bar after being raped and badly beaten. Once she was released from the hospital, she went to get her credit card at the bar. The rapist followed her and raped her again and killed her in her home."

Braden shook his head. "That's awful for you, and I'm sorry. This may sound harsh, but that should have no bearing on how you run your investigations."

Miller took a defensive stance by crossing his arms over his chest. "She admitted to me in the hospital that she knew who'd done it and she refused to use the information she had to bring charges against him. She could be alive today if she'd done that. So, I always have a tough time not getting frustrated with others when they have the information that's needed to put people away for their crimes."

Braden sighed and shook his head again. "I made the decision that was right for me at the time, and I don't regret it. For one, I didn't, and I still don't, want to have to testify against him. I don't want to relive everything that he did to me in front of strangers and be cross-examined and attacked on the stand. And two, without the circumstances being as they were, I wouldn't have met Zavier."

Detective Miller nodded his head and was about to speak when Cade interjected. "Detective, if it's so easy for you to fly off the handle and come at people like you did Braden, perhaps you're in the wrong line of work, or at least the wrong department."

Miller gritted his teeth. "Now listen, that's unfair. I'm a good cop."

Cade narrowed his eyes, staring the man down. "I didn't suggest otherwise. You wouldn't be on this case at all if it weren't for the instincts I see that you possess."

Miller tried to interject but Cade cut him off. "I'm not finished, Detective. You have an enormous responsibility to the people you are trying to help. You're doing them and yourself a great disservice if you stay in a position that you aren't suited for."

Miller practically growled. "Who are you to tell me I'm not suited for this job! Who better than someone who has had it happen to someone in their family?"

Cade shook his head sadly. "That's exactly my point, Detective. You're unable to remain unemotional. If you can so easily shift blame and fall back into your personal feelings, you can't do your job effectively. Frankly, I'm surprised you're still in the department."

Miller threw up his hands. "I don't have to stay here for this bullshit. I've had enough."

Cade shrugged. "You walk out that door, you're done with this case and most likely the SVU. Shut your ego down for a minute and just listen to me."

Miller crossed his arms over his chest. "Say what you're gonna say. I can't stop you."

Cade huffed out a laugh. "Man, I'm trying to help you. Don't you get that? I think you could go from good cop to extraordinary cop if you didn't have this albatross hanging so heavily around your neck. To be effective at what you do, you need to be able to remain objective and detached. You have to learn how to compartmentalize."

Cade could see that Miller was finally hearing him. His stance wasn't so defensive, and his face had relaxed. He was about to say something, but Cade didn't let him. "I think if you were in a different department, you'd move up the ranks quickly and you'd be much happier in the long run. I'm not trying to lecture. You're gonna do what you're gonna do. Regarding Braden's situation, you can continue to manage this case. I'm sure you'll proceed as we have discussed."

The detective nodded. "Yeah. I'll handle it." He glanced over at Braden. "I really didn't mean to blame you. The decision was yours to make. I'm sorry for handling it the way I did."

Braden smiled. "Apology accepted. I just want him to be found so I can move on."

"I get that. I'll do my best to make sure he's apprehended. Thanks."

Cade stepped forward and shook his hand. Braden followed suit and they headed to the front door to show him out. After he shut the door, Cade pulled Braden in for a tight hug. "You okay?"

Braden nodded his head and squeezed Cade around the waist. Cade kissed the top of his head. "I have several things I'd like to do before we go to Vaughn's. You want to get your bag ready for the gym then we can head out? Also, before I forget to tell you, I made an appointment for you at the psychologist's office on Wednesday afternoon."

Braden nodded and thanked him, and they both went into Braden's room to gather some workout gear. They grabbed a few snacks for later and were on the road quickly thereafter. When they pulled up to an office building, Braden saw Cooper come out and approach the car. Cade leaned over. "Cooper's gonna keep an eye on you for a few minutes, if that's all right. I have some papers to sign. I shouldn't be more than ten minutes, as Cooper has done most of the work. Will you be okay without me for that long?"

Braden blushed, humiliated that he had to be asked that, but still grateful that he had been. "Yes, I'll be fine."

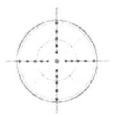

Braden

Cade leaned over and kissed him soundly then got out while Cooper got in. He knew Cooper had heard their exchange, and he was still blushing and had a difficult time meeting Cooper's eyes. "Braden, you have nothing to be embarrassed about. PTSD fucks with people's heads. You have *no* control over how your body and mind are reacting to the trauma. If Cade is your lifeline right now, you fucking hold on to him and keep him near until you no longer need that lifeline."

Braden nodded, grateful Cooper understood. "It's just so humiliating. I've never been dependent on anyone like this, so I feel stupid."

Cooper reached over and put his hand on Braden's shoulder. "No one is judging you, especially not all the former military guys on your detail right now. We know what PTSD can do to people. You're lucky you have that lifeline. Many people don't. Tonight, I'll do my best to show you some new ways to defend yourself, and I'm positive Cade will work with you and continue those lessons."

Braden was overwhelmed with gratitude. "Thanks. I don't like feeling out of control. Being off my schedule and being terrified of my fucking shadow is taking its toll. I'm sure the classes with you and Z will help."

They chatted for several minutes after that, and Braden tried to ignore the increasing panic making him fidget in the passenger seat. His hands were beginning to sweat when Cade finally came through the doors with a smile on his face. Braden looked at Cooper and saw his answering grin and looked at him quizzically. Cooper turned to him, his grin still in place. "Braden, I think you'll be a very happy man in the next thirty minutes. I'll see you at Vaughn's later. Maya's coming, and I know she's been missing you."

Braden thanked Cooper again. He suddenly felt sad when he realized he'd been missing her and hadn't been making an effort to see her since he'd been released from the hospital. Maybe they could all grab dinner together after class. In fact, liking that idea more and more, he suggested it when Cade got to the car and switched places with Cooper. They both agreed, and they were off, Cade watching his mirrors carefully for anyone following them.

"Where are we going?"

Cade smiled. "You'll see. I hope you'll like it."

Chapter 9

BRADEN

Cade drove for another fifteen minutes and ended up down in the more industrialized area of town. He parked in front of a warehouse which took up a full city block and ushered Braden out of the car. Holding his hand, Cade unlocked the door and led them into the building, leaving Braden completely confused as they took the elevator to the fourth floor.

The place was bare of anything and everything making it usable and was absolutely huge. He stopped at one of the dirty windows and Cade took a handkerchief from his pocket, wiping the window clean. Braden looked out and decided at least it was in a cool looking part of town and the surrounding buildings, all fairly similar, were kept up.

He faced Cade with a bemused expression on his face. "So, what's this?"

"This is one of our new office buildings."

Braden's breath caught. "What?"

Cade smiled down at Braden. "This is one of two identical, side by side warehouses that we're going to renovate immediately to turn them into the new Custos Securities headquarters. We actually start renovations two weeks from today. I wanted to wait until everything was finalized before I told you."

Braden, bewildered, couldn't help but repeat himself. "What?"

Cade chuckled and clasped his hand. "One of the reasons we came to San Francisco, besides seeing our families and taking care of a job, was to scope out a new location here for our headquarters."

Braden's hand flew up to his mouth and his eyes were teary. "It's really.... You're moving your business here? You're really not leaving?"

"Baby, I told you all you had to do was say the words. And what did you do?"

Braden blinked, and tears fell. "I said the words."

Cade stepped forward and brushed the tears away, smiling. "You did. So, here's the result. We came here to check out several locations. We weren't sure if we were going to move here, because of family, or somewhere closer to the military bases in southern California, but I knew fairly quickly after meeting you that if things worked out, I wanted to be where you were."

Cade leaned forward and kissed Braden's lips tenderly. Braden drew in a deep breath when they pulled apart. "I don't even know what to say. I'm literally at a loss for words."

Cade chuckled a bit, clasped Braden's hand, and brought it to his lips. "How about I just talk about it a bit, and you can think about what you want to say?"

Cade grinned down at Braden when all he could manage was a wide-eyed nod. "Okay, so we're actually standing on my personal floor. I've been wondering if I should buy a house or keep myself close to the business. In the future, we'll buy a home together, but in the meantime, I've been removed from the business for a while now, and I'd like to get back to being closely involved in the day to day activities."

Braden brow furrowed with worry. "I'm sorry."

Cade shook his head and closed his eyes. "Baby, that's not what I meant. There's no need for you to be sorry. I wouldn't change a thing, and while I've been away from the office for this case, that's not what I was talking about. You are now my top priority and if this case takes a long time and it came down to it, I'd hire someone to replace me until this case was dealt with. All right?"

"But—"

Cade gripped his chin, forcing Braden's eyes to his. "No buts. Let me explain."

When Braden nodded his head, Cade continued, "Cooper and I feel that we are much more present for our employees when we are on site. Cooper has been the one on site in Colorado Springs, and I want to give him a break from that. We run the business as a twenty-four-seven operation, obviously. There are always people working at any given time, depending on the job and the needs of the business, so it helps to have one of the owners on site, should the need arise."

Braden's shoulders relaxed. "So, you're going to make this floor your living quarters?"

Cade wandered away a bit, turned in a circle, taking in the space. "Yes, I'm going to renovate it, open up most of the outside walls to be surrounded by windows. I don't know yet if I want to close in the space with rooms or leave the whole thing open. My mind doesn't work that way, so I'm at a loss. What do you think?"

Braden looked around the space again with new eyes. "I think, to take advantage of the space, you'll want to leave almost everything open concept, apart from maybe the bedrooms and the bathrooms."

Cade prowled slowly back toward him and pulled Braden into his arms. "What else would you do?"

Warmth surged through Braden when he saw real interest from Cade about what he would do in the space. He pulled away from Cade but continued to hold his hand as he walked around the empty floor, envisioning renovations that would make it perfect for Cade. "I'd keep the bedrooms fairly small, maybe only two of them, at most three and only use them for sleeping, for the most part. Everything else out here should be made for convenience and completely open. Your people will come see you and inevitably you'll bring work home with you. You'll want your own workspace and dining area and kitchen and living room area, but no walls, just sectioned off areas. If needed, half walls, maybe to help separate the spaces if you wanted, but other than that, let the light in with surrounding windows. Or, you could…."

Braden stopped when he looked up at Cade and saw his avid interest had turned into something more predatory. Braden blushed again, damn his skin, and swallowed past the lump in his throat. Cade prodded, "I could what?"

Braden ran his hand through his hair and held it back from his face. He turned toward the center of the room and then back to Cade. "This isn't too much? Too many opinions? I don't want to overstep."

"There's no overstepping with us, Braden. I really want to know, if you had unlimited funds and could make this space into anything, what would you do?"

Braden nodded, letting go of his hair. "Uh, well, it's the top floor in this building, right? So, the exposed beams up there are probably structural, but maybe not all of them are. The ceiling is high, so you might be able to create a loft space. I mean, keep the bottom floor completely open concept, and create a lofted second floor that could have all of the bedrooms and bathrooms and private living quarters."

Cade smiled and urged him on. "Okay, but how would that work?"

Braden started getting into it, his arms gesturing while he continued to describe his vision. "I mean, it's an industrial space, right? So, you could have everything be industrial, but comfortable. Make it all livable but keep with the aesthetics of the building. I mean, if that's something you'd like?"

When Cade nodded, he continued, "So put in some industrial metal stairs and railings to a second-floor lofted space. It could either take up half of the area or the whole area, depending on privacy needed and number of rooms. Instead of full walls on the bedrooms that face the lower level, put sliding frosted glass doors that open the rooms up to allow some of the light from down there into the upper rooms."

Cade grinned at Braden as he continued to express his ideas, his excitement growing. "The rest of the downstairs could be completely open with a gorgeous kitchen and a huge island and a big dining table to feed as many guests as you think you'd have. If you wanted an office upstairs you could do that, for privacy, or have one downstairs."

Braden ran out of steam and realized he'd been babbling for some time about how he saw the living space working out. He turned around to face Cade and walked back over toward him. "Just some ideas for how it could work out for your space."

"What if it wasn't my space?"

Braden's brow furrowed in confusion. "What do you mean?"

"What if it was *our* space?"

"You want us to live together permanently?"

Cade nodded. "Yes. I wouldn't want to be in the same town and live apart. But, I want to give Cooper some time away from the office. He's been living on site since the beginning, and I feel like it's my turn to do so. I know it's not ideal."

"No, it makes sense."

Cade continued, unsure of what Braden was thinking. "You probably love living across the street from the café, and I know it's asking a lot to even think about it, but I guess that's exactly what I'm doing. If you really don't want to leave your space, Cooper's already said he's fine with continuing to live on site."

"My place is convenient--"

Cade nodded. "I understand. I'm happy to live there with you, if that's okay with you."

Braden smiled. "You didn't let me finish."

"I'm sorry, Bray. Go ahead."

Braden rubbed his hands up and down Cade's upper arms. "My place is convenient, but I'm not extremely attached to it. You're moving your business here. Moving in with you isn't a lot to ask at all. I think I'd really love it."

Cade swallowed Braden up in a bear hug that lifted him off his feet. He tilted his head back to look down at Braden and grinned at him. "That makes me really fucking happy. And now, I'm going to ask a huge favor, and if it stresses you out or you don't want to do it, I'm okay with that."

Braden was bemused when Cade continued to hold him off the ground. "What is it?"

"Would you be willing to oversee our living space, while Cooper and I focus on our work space? We have an architecture firm we're working with that says they can handle both. We'll be working with a couple of architects for the business side and you'll be working with a different one for the living space."

Braden grinned. "Seriously?"

Cade grinned back and nodded. "Seriously. You'd have carte blanche, spare no expense. I want you to choose anything and everything you would want for your dream home, especially your kitchen. Hire an interior decorator too—the space is too big to deal with on your own. I don't know how many years we'll live here, or rather, how many years you'll be happy living here, before you'll want our own home for us."

Braden was finally put down on his feet. He tilted his head at Cade in confusion. "But this *would* be our own home for us."

"I just mean away from my business. Eventually you'll want us to have our own home, I'd imagine, space for kids, a yard with some grass, that kind of thing."

Braden tilted his head, confused. "Are you under the impression that I feel like I'm compromising by agreeing to this, to living here?"

"Wouldn't you be?"

"No. I'd be living with the man I love and creating the home of my dreams. I'd still be downtown, which is where I have always lived and always want to live. This isn't a compromise, Z, this is…. This is everything. I'm really excited about this."

Surprised etched itself across Cade's face. "Seriously?"

Braden chuckled, shaking his head at Cade's incredulous expression. "Hell yes, seriously! I'm excited to work with the architect and interior designer to choose what I want for our space. Are you kidding me? You've just put a kid in a candy store."

Cade gathered Braden up in his arms, lifted him off his feet yet again, and kissed him senseless. He leaned back down to reconnect Braden's feet with the floor and looked into his eyes. "Thank fuck! God, I was so worried you wouldn't want to live here in some old warehouse directly over my offices. I was a bit panicked."

"I just want to be with you, wherever that may be. You're home to me."

"God, Braden, the things you say to me."

Cade leaned down again and kissed him so softly and sweetly that Braden's heart swelled in his chest. A feeling of such happiness came over him he thought he might need to pinch himself to be sure it was real.

Reality intruded several minutes later as they made their way to the car. Braden remembered where they were going and why. For the brief time that they'd been in the warehouse, Braden had completely forgotten about

Eric. His stress levels climbed up a few notches, but he was grateful to Cade for giving him that feeling of normalcy, even if just for a short amount of time. He was bound and determined to take all the steps needed to make sure they had the future that Cade had just shown him was possible.

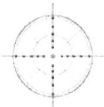

They arrived at Vaughn's and were met by the man himself at the security desk. He pulled them aside, looking tense. "Look, Cade, I know I always make you put your gun in my lockbox, but I know that having Braden here is a unique circumstance. You can keep it on you, but please keep it covered up. You'll be in a class with women, some of whom have been the victims of violent crimes. You're menacing enough as it is with your size and your tattoos."

Cade nodded, grateful. "Understood."

Vaughn gestured behind him. "I'm going to go into the class tonight to introduce both you and Cooper. If you could head toward the corner opposite the door, the women will feel more at ease and less confined."

Cade nodded and ushered Braden to the locker room. They changed and went back out to meet Vaughn. He led them to a classroom that had a door that opened directly into the lobby and saw that Cooper was already there chatting with Maya. There were several other women chatting toward the front of the room.

When Maya saw him, she jogged his way and stopped when she got to him, not knowing if she was welcome to touch. He opened his arms wide for her and his heart lurched as she got teary-eyed and walked into his arms, wrapping her own around his neck. He gave her a bear hug, lifting her off the floor and she wrapped her legs around his waist and held on for dear life. The pain in his ribs was ignored as he comforted his best friend, knowing she needed him as much as he needed her.

She nuzzled her face into his neck, which always tickled him, and kissed him there. When she finally pulled a bit away from him, he set her down and she swiped at her eyes. "I've missed you. I'm so sorry I haven't made more of an effort to come see you. It's been so busy at the café, and I'm doing my best to keep an eye on Nana, so she doesn't overdo."

"My, it goes both ways. I haven't made the effort either. Things have been hectic for us both. Did Coop tell you about dinner tonight?"

"Yeah, I asked Coop to make us a reservation at Lers Ros."

Braden's mouth watered at the thought of the best Thai food in town. They both grinned at each other like loons and hugged again. He whispered in her ear that he'd missed her, and she squeezed his waist harder before stepping away. He glanced around and realized that there were a lot more women in the room and they were getting mostly curious, but some wary glances. They moved apart, and Braden gravitated toward Cade when Vaughn went to the front of the room. "We've got a new instructor tonight, everyone. Actually, two of them, as the instructor for Thursday's class is also here."

He walked over toward their group and stood between Cooper and Cade. He nodded toward Cooper. "This is Cooper, he's former Special Forces and highly skilled at hand to hand combat. He's half of a partnership at a company called Custos Securities that is based out of Colorado Springs. Their office headquarters has several classes in self-defense, just like this one, so they are well versed in training not only soldiers, but civilians in self-defense techniques."

Cooper raised his hand in a wave. "Hi, ladies. I'm looking forward to helping you learn a few things tonight."

Vaughn nodded toward Cade. "The second half of that partnership is Cade, and he will be instructing the class on Thursday. He is also former Special Forces and he is one of the only men that has ever truly bested me in a cage fight outside of my career fights. He can be vicious, and he fights dirty, which is what you all need to learn to do."

Braden glanced at Cade and knew he was doing his best not to look intimidating. Unfortunately for him, that was impossible. He smiled and raised his hand in a wave of his own. Braden saw unease still reflected at both men. He understood how intimidating they both could look and was sad that just the fact that they were big men made these women nervous.

Vaughn continued to speak to the women. "From a personal standpoint,

I trust these men with my life and with my daughter's life. They are the ones that brought Mikayla back to me when she was kidnapped which was one of the biggest reasons I started these classes to begin with."

At that, the group of women reacted. Some of them covered their mouths with their hands, holding in gasps. Others looked at Cade and Cooper with more interest and much more trust than before. And Braden smiled to see several of them had blushed and sent them flirtatious glances. Braden knew they'd get nowhere with Cade and they wouldn't fare any better with Cooper, as he'd never try to pick up women in a setting like this one. However, Cooper was definitely swoon-worthy, and that fact was made even more apparent when he grinned at the attendees. "Ladies, I've invited my sister Maya here to kick my ass."

The women laughed, just like he wanted them to, and from that point on, the class was putty in his hands. He talked to the class about his take on self-defense. "Why don't you all have a seat for a few minutes while I chat with you a bit? After that, we'll all get up and practice some techniques. I want you to speak up if you have questions, if something doesn't make sense, or you want me to show you something specific. Some of what I say may be a repeat of the classes you've had before, so bear with me, as I know some of you are new, and others have attended before."

Everyone sat, and Cooper had a rapt audience. He made eye contact with everyone there as he continued to talk. "I think one of the best weapons you have in your artillery is your voice. Women are taught from an early age to be quiet and unobtrusive. Get that lesson out of your head. Your attacker doesn't want to hear you and he sure as shit doesn't want anyone else to hear you. If you're in a situation that makes you uncomfortable, say someone gets too close, speak loudly when you tell them to back off."

He asked everyone to stand up and pair off. As they did so, he asked one of them to get in the other's space and have the other tell them loudly to back off. He demonstrated by exaggeratedly walking up to Maya and getting into her space. She blasted him loudly, starting off the class's practice of using their voices. A few times, Cooper approached the pairs, asking them to talk louder. When that exercise was done, everyone remained standing as he continued.

"If you think someone is following you, turn around, face them, and yell for all to hear, 'Stop following me!' Talking to someone loudly not only shows them that things aren't going to go as easily as planned for them, but it brings attention to what's going on for anyone around you, and it may be the first step toward making them back off and leave you alone."

Again, the group practiced yelling at their "attacker." There was some laughter and the group seemed to relax even more. Cooper asked them to sit again. "Using your voice, though a very effective tool, obviously isn't going to save everyone all of the time. So, there are some things that you should keep in mind when you're in a situation that you feel is out of control. You want to keep things easy, you want to be able to do those things quickly, and you want to keep them simple."

He went on to explain that their best bet was to always go for the soft tissue areas of the body; the center of the throat just below the Adam's apple, the eyes, the nose, the mouth, the ears, the groin, and the stomach. He said the soft tissue was where you get the most bang for your buck and the places that are the easiest to find.

Cooper explained that he was going to show them how to do small, fast moves, moves that could debilitate the assailant long enough to allow the victim to get away. He warned them about trying to perform complex moves because adrenaline would be high, and the mind clicks to fight or flight mode where complicated moves would be forgotten. If practiced, the things he was going to teach would become instinctual.

The rest of the session was filled with learning several moves that were quick and could do a lot of damage in a short amount of time. Braden ended up being able to physically do quite a bit of what Cooper was teaching, using Cade as his partner. None of it was full contact, just practicing the simple moves over and over. Cooper worked with Maya to demonstrate the exercises and then walked around, checking on everyone's stance as they practiced. Cade had to correct him several times, and he was incredibly sexy when he was being so completely serious. Braden got a kick out of it and loved the fact that Cade had the confidence in him to learn the techniques and later use them, if needed.

Cooper wrapped up the class discussing what Thursday's class would entail. Apparently, Maya would be joining the class to 'kick Cade's ass' as well. When he was about to wind down, he looked at Maya and grinned devilishly. "You ready?"

Maya raised an eyebrow but kept a straight face. "You got your cup on?"

Cooper threw his head back and laughed, along with everyone else in the room. "With you as my practice partner? Always! Mom didn't raise any dummies."

With that, Cooper turned toward the class. "Ladies, it's been great working with all of you. We're gonna close with me attacking my sister here. She doesn't know what I'm going to do, or how I'm going to come at her, but I've drilled these lessons into her, so she better make me proud. Keep in mind that she's had a lot of practice, but also remember that I'm holding back, and she will be as well. Our aim isn't to hurt each other, just to show you some of the moves we did today. If you have any questions after class ends, you can come up and ask me, Cade, or even Maya, if that makes you more comfortable."

With that, he turned toward Maya. "You ready, little girl?"

"Hell yeah, pretty boy, do your worst!"

They faced each other then Maya turned around and began to walk away from Cooper. Braden jumped when Cooper went in for the attack and put her in a chokehold from behind. He moved so fast and so quietly, Braden didn't expect it and seeing Cooper like that was eye-opening. Braden thought for sure he had her. Suddenly, she swiveled her hips, hooking her left foot behind his right one, twisting her torso the opposite way. When he went to step back, his foot caught on the one she'd planted behind his and he went over.

Braden was so impressed with her, he almost missed what happened next. Cooper recovered and reached forward to grab one of her ankles. She fell and scrambled to her back and he moved in between her spread legs. Braden thought for sure that she was done at that point, but as Cooper wedged his knees by her hips and her feet were on either side of his hips, he leaned down over her and she caught his shoulders in a locked arm grip and he couldn't push down any further. He brought his hands up to her throat and at that point, Braden covered his mouth as he watched Cooper move to choke his sister.

It didn't seem to faze her though as she did a series of moves which ended in her arms crossed and gripped over his. She lifted her hips as leverage, brought them back down and curled herself toward him, somehow breaking his chokehold. She swiveled her hips, managed to wedge both feet against him and pushed herself a leg's length away. Gripping his wrists, she started mock kicking him in the face. He blocked her feet, which allowed her to hop up and make her escape.

The class was silent for a second, all of them shocked at just how fast it all happened and how quickly Maya had reacted. Then collectively everyone started clapping and hooting and congratulating her. She laughed and did a curtsy and Cooper gave in, laughing and clapping for her as well. Braden was so proud of her. He'd definitely be talking to her later. He'd had no idea she could do all that and was surprised she'd never told him.

Class was over and already Braden was looking forward to the next one. He showered in the locker room with Cooper and Cade, working quickly to get done and dressed again for dinner, his routine taking a little longer due to the cast. They walked toward Maya in the lobby. Braden took one look at her and grinned. She had rosy cheeks and she was fidgeting with her workout bag, all while talking to Vaughn. Well, well, well, his Maya was being flirted with, and by the look of things, she was enjoying it. She glanced their way and Braden could see her take a deep, relieved breath. Interesting. He'd have to talk to her about it later.

Vaughn realized she was glancing behind him and turned to greet them all. He thanked Cooper for helping with the class then at the last minute, leaned in and kissed Maya on the cheek and told her thanks again for the help. Maya's rosy cheeks turned into flaming red cheeks as she murmured back that it was no problem. Braden gave her a 'we'll discuss this later' look and she turned and walked out the door. Cooper, eyebrow raised at her quick escape, jogged out the door after her and tossed back over his shoulder that they'd see them at the restaurant.

They reconvened at Lers Ros and chatted about the warehouses. Maya was as excited as Braden at the prospect of working with the architect and interior decorator. After teasing Braden that she'd never be able to get over him not living right across the hall, Maya said she'd be with him to help every step of the way. Cooper even made a few comments about taking over Braden's side of the house. Maya warned him that if that happened, he'd need to learn how to mind his own business and stay out of her life. Cade and Braden just laughed at the siblings as they railed at each other about the rules that they'd have to set if they were going to share the building.

Braden was feeling a little bit more like himself and attributed much of that to the company at dinner, but also the earlier class. When they arrived back home, Cade turned on the TV to catch the eleven o'clock news. Braden was brushing his teeth when Cade called him in from the bathroom. Braden lost the strength in his legs and sat down on the bed as he watched the newscaster continue her story. "He is wanted for the alleged kidnapping and assault of a local man he has been suspected of stalking for the last six months. The identity of the victim is being withheld at this time. If you have seen this man, or if you know of his whereabouts, please contact the number on the screen. Do not attempt to confront this man, as he is considered armed and dangerous."

Braden watched as an older, but very clear picture of Eric came on the screen, alongside the drawing that Sebastian had done earlier that day. He'd known it was coming, so he wasn't altogether sure why he was so surprised to see it. Only when Cade stood in front of him, blocking the TV, did Braden realize that a commercial was running. Cade crouched down to his eye level. "You all right?"

With his mouth full of toothpaste, all Braden could do was nod slowly, not convincing Cade at all. He held up a glass of water and Braden tossed it back, swished, and then spit it back into the cup. Cade handed him the face towel he had slung across his shoulder and he wiped his mouth. He placed the towel down on the dresser and the toothbrush and glass on top of it and kneeled at Braden's feet, his knees spread to surround Braden. He started to rub Braden's upper thighs and Braden blinked and then focused once more on Cade's face. "I'm fine. Really. It was just a shock. I wasn't expecting it then there he was. But I'm good. I feel somewhat relieved that it's done and it's out there. Hopefully something will come of it, or he'll make a mistake as a result and be caught."

"Until that time, or until we find him ourselves, I'll be with you, every step of the way. We're in this together."

Braden smiled, loving his man for repeating that to him, sometimes several times a day. He knew it to be true, but it was nice to hear it, regardless. He looked down at their joined hands in his lap and nodded. "Together."

Braden checked his levels and they finished getting ready for bed, both equally exhausted. They whispered their 'I love yous' and were both asleep in minutes. Braden woke with a nightmare again that night, but nothing nearly as terrifying as the night before. He was able to get back to sleep almost immediately after Cade brought him some water and pulled him onto his chest.

Tuesday was a restful day, and Braden found himself sleeping much of it away again. When he voiced his frustration, Cade reminded him he was being ridiculous, and he was doing exactly what the doctor had asked of him. Later that night, they went to Vaughn's and used a private room for Braden to learn some more self-defense moves, but mostly to try to make sure he retained and repeated Monday's teachings.

Later, as they ate dinner with Nana, she said something to Cade about Jackson and Sawyer and Braden looked up at him in question. Cade caught his look. "I've got Jackson and Sawyer splitting up the duties, but they're keeping an eye on Nana. One of them is with her from the moment she steps out of your front door until she is back here at night."

Braden was about to ask about Maya when Cade smiled at him and said, "Cooper is with his sister, doing the same. We're not taking his threats lightly. If I need to bring more people here for this, I will, but for now, I think we're all right. I don't believe he'd go after Nana or Maya. He's too obsessed with you. But I wanted them covered."

Braden walked to him and pulled him down for a kiss then hugged him as tight as he could. "Thank you. I love you so much. This means the world to me."

Cade held him for several minutes, and when they pulled apart, Nana gave them both a beatific smile and started telling them all about her day. They all spent some time chatting then relaxing in front of the TV for an hour before they went to bed. Braden woke to another nightmare but didn't want to wake Cade. He lay awake for several hours and finally drifted back to sleep around five a.m. Cade woke him for his insulin, but he dozed back to sleep until close to noon. When he finally got himself up, he got ready for the day and his therapy session. He was looking forward to the appointment because he truly hoped it would help him come to grips with everything that had happened, but he was also nervous to let himself be vulnerable with a complete stranger.

Chapter 10

BRADEN

The doctor's office was warm and inviting. There was huge, ornate dark hardwood reception desk, behind which was a gorgeous, voluptuous African American woman with a riot of beautiful curls and a dress of vibrant fuchsia. She looked up as they entered and smiled a mile wide. "Good afternoon, gentlemen. How can I help you?"

Braden stepped forward and smiled. "Hello, my name is Braden Cross. I have a two p.m. appointment with Dr. Gabriel Price."

"Braden, welcome. I have a bit of paperwork for you to fill out. Can I get a copy of your insurance card? Also, would either of you like anything to drink?"

Braden told her that they didn't need anything and handed her his insurance card and quickly filled out the paperwork. When he was done, he handed her the clipboard and went to sit next to Cade on a brown leather loveseat. They faced a beautiful, built in saltwater fish tank that brought brightness and color to the room. He leaned forward, forearms on his knees, and watched the fish for several minutes. He found himself relaxing bit by bit, which probably could also be attributed to Cade's hand rubbing in slow circles on his back. He heard a chime go off and the receptionist stood and opened the door behind and to the right of her desk. "Braden, you can head on back to the first room on your left. It'll be the only door open at this time. Dr. Price will be with you in just a few minutes."

Braden stood. "Can I bring my partner back with me? I'd like him to attend the session."

She smiled. "Of course."

Cade placed his hand on Braden's lower back and guided him through the door. Braden smiled as he walked into the beautifully appointed office with sunlight streaming through the blinds. The ceiling and one wall were painted a striking pear green. The wall opposite was taken up by an enormous bay window, with three sections. In front of each of those three sections were three unique, large bonsai trees. They sat on the butter soft, mahogany brown leather couch that backed up to the green wall, behind which was a stunning abstract tree of life triptych in bright colors all swirled together in a somewhat *Starry Night* reminiscent fusion of greens, blues, reds, oranges, and yellows.

They were just getting comfortable when a man about Braden's size knocked on the door frame and came into the office. He was dressed in what Braden would call casual chic, a button up light blue shirt with a cable knit camel-colored toggle sweater over it, navy pinstripe trousers, and a pair of the most beautiful Louis Vuitton double monk strap brown leather dress shoes Braden had ever seen. For some reason, the fact that Braden appreciated the man's sense of style immediately had him feeling slightly more at ease.

The handsome man smiled at them both. They stood as he walked toward them with his hand extended. They shook hands as he introduced himself. "Hi there, I'm Dr. Gabriel Price, but I prefer to be called Gabe. You must be Braden Cross."

Braden released Gabe's hand. "Yes, I'm Braden and this is my partner, Zavier McCade."

Gabe gestured to the sofa they'd been sitting on and sat in the matching leather chair adjacent to them as they resumed their seats. "I nearly mistook you for Gideon McCade, who I'm assuming is your brother, and I see the resemblance to Dr. Finnegan McCade as well."

Cade raised a brow. "Yes, Gideon's my older brother and Finn's my younger brother."

Gabe nodded but shared nothing more on the subject. "So, Mr. Cross and Mr. McCade, what would you prefer to be called?"

"You can call me Braden."

"Cade." He leaned back, making it clear that this session was for Braden.

"All right, so Braden, I'm assuming you want Cade to attend this session and possibly future sessions with you, is that correct?"

"Yes, it makes me more comfortable. He's my partner, but he's also my guard, and at this point, we both don't deal well with being separated. I have panic attacks if he's not fairly close to me."

Gabe's eyebrows rose in surprise. "Okay, I think we'll definitely be coming back to that in a few minutes. If you feel the need for Cade to stay here during our sessions, it's all right with me. I don't have much information, but Dr. Himmel's records indicate that he believes you may be suffering from PTSD because of an abduction and physical attack. I'm assuming it's a very recent attack as evidenced by your casted wrist and visible head wounds."

Braden raised his casted hand to the wound on his temple, gently pulling his hair over the damage. Grateful when he felt Cade's hand squeeze his neck, he settled back into the crook of his shoulder. "Yes. I left willingly with my stalker after receiving threats to the life of my grandmother, best friend, and partner. The damage you see is a small portion of what occurred while I was with him."

Gabe steepled his fingers together, elbows resting on the arms of the chair. "I'm sorry to hear that, Braden. We'll go into that in detail, but for right now, let me tell you about my own therapy philosophies. We can then discuss how we can approach your therapy together. All right?"

Braden sat forward, leaning his elbows on his needs and nodded. "Yeah, that sounds good."

"This session, as it's our first, will be two hours. I do this so that we can discuss our therapy options and I can get a better understanding of what you want to get out of the sessions. As a lot of the first hour will be me talking to you, your insurance will be billed for one hour, as all future sessions will be. How does that feel to you?"

Braden smiled and told Gabe that everything he said was good with him. He relaxed into the crook of Cade's shoulder again, feeling much more at ease with the doctor's calm demeanor. He listened as the doctor explained some of his treatment options for PTSD patients. The more he spoke; the more Braden knew that he could trust this man. He then asked Braden to walk him through what happened.

Braden decided to start at the beginning, which meant telling Gabe about his relationship with Eric and how it ended. After that, he began talking about the stalking, about Cade coming into his life, Eric's escalation, and his subsequent kidnapping. He finally ended with a discussion of his injuries and the impact they were still having on him. "The doctor told me I can't work for six days and I can't run for ten days."

"You run?"

"Yes, I began running when I was in Junior High. I had been diagnosed with Type 1 Diabetes before going into seventh grade. I joined the track and field team, running cross country, to help regulate my glucose levels. I've been running ever since—mostly regular marathons, some ultramarathons when I can fit them in."

Gabe laughed incredulously. "When you can fit them in? You say that like you're scheduling a stroll in the park. Braden, I've run a couple marathons myself, and I can tell you that I nearly didn't finish both times. I can't even fathom what an ultramarathon would be like. That's huge!" He looked at Cade, who had been completely silent since he was last asked a question. "Does he downplay stuff like this a lot?"

Cade looked down at Braden as Braden turned to look up at him, brow furrowed. He smiled and kissed Braden's head and turned back to Gabe. "He thinks of his running as a way to reduce stress, which then helps his glucose levels and keeps him from getting migraines. He doesn't see each marathon or ultramarathon as a huge accomplishment in itself. He also never mentions he's been written up in several newspaper articles and multiple foodie magazines for his baking at the Sugar n' Spice Café, where he's part owner."

Gabe's eyes popped, and he grinned. "That's you? Your little, uh, what are they called, chocolate croissants?"

"Pain au chocolat."

"Yes, those. I can't get enough of them."

Braden smiled and thanked him then shrugged. "I like to run, and it benefits my health. I love to bake, so I'm doing what I love. That's how I see it."

Gabe looked at Braden like he could see through him. He did it for several, long, drawn out moments, making Braden fidget. "We'll discuss more about that going forward. For now, our time is almost up, and I have some homework for you. I want you to write down all the things, big or small, that scare you the most about what's going on with Eric. Keep track of what wakes you up each night in a cold sweat, those things that make it hard for you to function if Cade is away from you for any length of time. Bring them in next time, so that we can discuss them."

Braden rubbed his hands up and down his thighs, a nervous gesture that brought Cade's hand to his neck, calming him immediately. He swallowed and nodded. "Yeah, all right. I can do that."

Gabe glanced at Cade's large hand encircling the back of Braden's neck and smiled. "In addition to that, I have a running assignment for you. I want you to contact your local animal shelter, or if you don't have one in mind, you can go to the San Francisco SPCA. I want you to arrange to volunteer to exercise their dogs by taking one with you on your runs at least twice a week."

Braden grinned. "Seriously?"

Gabe smiled in response. "Seriously. If you work with the SPCA, you can tell them that I sent you. They know me well. They'll be able to match you up with larger dogs that can keep up with you."

Braden loved this particular homework assignment. He'd never thought of volunteering to exercise shelter dogs. He'd had a dog when he was younger, but after she'd died, he didn't have the heart to try to replace her. He was excited that he'd be able to help make a difference by volunteering this way. He said as much to Gabe and was given another writing assignment to keep a journal of his thoughts and feelings during the experience. That portion of the homework didn't excite him much, but he knew they weren't just idle requests, so he'd do it, regardless of his feelings about it.

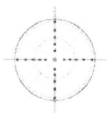

Four weeks had passed. Braden was feeling like his old self more and more every day. Today, he was immersed in one of his favorite pastimes, baking at the Sugar n' Spice Café. He busied himself with several recipes at once and thought back over the last several weeks. Therapy was going great. He was making strides at putting the kidnapping behind him and could go longer and longer stretches of time without being in the same vicinity as Cade, though he was never far, as he was still being guarded. His nightmares had almost completely stopped.

He was enjoying the time running with the shelter dogs. He'd had a tough time when his favorite dog was adopted. The Belgian Malinois was the first dog he'd run with and he was so big and beautiful. He'd obeyed every command he and Cade had given him, and he had a sweet and protective nature. After he'd been adopted out, Braden had been immensely sad, but he'd kept volunteering to exercise the dogs to help the animal shelter and to continue to help himself.

He didn't understand at first why Gabe had asked him to run with the dogs. He enjoyed it, so he continued doing it and writing down how it made him feel. He had been doing it for more than a week before it finally clicked that helping someone or something else such as the dogs put him in a completely different headspace. He was the nurturer in this instance. He was taking care of someone or something else besides himself. He was able to get out of his head and stop worrying every second what would happen with Eric. Once he figured that out and talked to Gabe about it, he'd known he was right when Gabe smiled at him and nodded his head. They'd discussed it for the rest of that session and into the next.

The other thing they'd uncovered was that Braden was much more apprehensive about what was going to happen to his loved ones than he was about what would happen to himself. His deepest fears stemmed from Eric doing something to hurt Cade, Nana, and Maya. He wasn't necessarily afraid that if Cade left him alone, Eric would come to get him again. He was more afraid Eric would go after Cade because of who and what Cade had become to him. He was afraid Eric would get him again and hurt or kill him, but more because of what that would do to his people than the fact that he'd be hurt again or die.

Once those things became clear during his therapy sessions, some of the stress of the past several weeks left him. His shoulders felt considerably lighter and his mood was improving greatly. Maya was being watched by Cooper, much to her dismay. Nana, though no longer working full time at the bakery, had decided to stay with him until the Eric situation was sorted out and he was captured. She was working several days during the week and would often just stop in to help him out in the kitchen, so she could spend time with him and give him a rest.

His cast was still on his wrist, but all his other injuries had healed nicely. He was going into the doctor's office in two weeks to get the cast removed, and as far as he was concerned, it couldn't happen soon enough. Nana was enjoying being back in the city again, closer to some of her old friends. She was being her regular social self and meeting friends several times a week. When she wasn't home, Jackson or Sawyer would watch over her and she reveled in it, saying it made her feel like a celebrity, which amused them all.

On the days Nana would come in and bake for him, he and Maya would both take off to the warehouses with Cooper in tow and work with the architects and the designers to get his and Cade's new home renovated. They were focused on the building that they'd be living in first, so they could move in as soon as possible. So far, everything he wanted to incorporate was working, and they were able to have a loft area that lent itself to three bedrooms and an office.

A master suite with an office attached ran the width of the building, and two bedrooms that shared a Jack n Jill bathroom ran down the length of the building beside the office. The rooms opened to a walkway looking down over the open floor below. Each room was fronted with what Braden called 'magic glass' walls and sliding doors that would let in the light from the windows on the bottom floor, but with the touch of a button, they'd turn opaque to block out the light.

The walkway would be lined with a glass railing system, framed by beautiful dark wood, a theme that would continue down the stairs as well, again, allowing the natural light from the windows into the bedrooms. When Braden had first envisioned the space, he'd thought that he would want to have the space be more industrial, but the more he worked with the architects and designers, the more he realized he wanted something warmer for their home and decided to use more dark woods rather than cold metal.

Braden couldn't quite fathom how much the architects and the construction crews were being paid for this job. The work was being done at a ridiculously fast pace, and he was practically tripping over workers every time he entered the building. They were everywhere, working on everything. Every time Braden mentioned something that might be nice, he received new plans the next day, incorporating his ideas. He had some surprises up his sleeve and had sworn the architects and designers to secrecy. At first, they'd seemed uneasy when he'd ask that of them, until he explained what he wanted then everyone was in on it.

He didn't want Cade feeling like this wasn't a home that could offer everything that any other home in the Bay Area could offer. He didn't want his future husband worrying that he was going to want to up and move in two years' time. He wanted this to be their home for years to come, and he figured he just had to make Cade understand that's what he wanted by incorporating aspects of their possible future, which included kids, into their new home. He got more and more excited every day.

He was keeping Cade away from their floor, telling him he wanted it all to be a surprise. It wasn't an easy task, as Cade had to keep him protected, but Cooper had agreed, if Maya was with Braden, he'd be happy to be the one keeping tabs on them both. As a result, Cade had been able to focus on his work with the architects for the business portion of the building, and Cooper was with them, and therefore, in the know regarding Braden's surprise plans.

Braden was happy with the progress of their new home and in running back and forth between the café and there, he'd realized that the drive was actually very short. He could run it no problem, if he chose to do so, once they moved in. He left so early in the morning to get to the café, he would miss traffic and get there in his car in about ten minutes. He knew the change in their lives, once the building was done, would be immense, but he felt ready to take it on.

Cooper had let him know he was serious about renting or buying the condo from Braden once he moved into their converted warehouse. The only outstanding issue was Eric. He was more hopeful every day that the APB for his arrest had frightened him off and had him running scared, right out of town. He'd bet his next batch of scones that Cade was in the office talking to Cooper about Eric at this very moment.

Braden didn't speak about it with Cade much, as he knew his optimism wasn't shared. He could see the issue was bothering him, even though Cade was showing no outward signs of stress. It was in the grim line of his lips, the tightening of his jaw, the strong grip of his hand when he held Braden's, especially when they were outside, in the open. Otherwise there were no other signs that Cade was at all impacted by the situation. They were immeasurably happy with one another, and Cade's strength and protection was like a balm to Braden's frayed nerves.

However, it seemed that the better Braden felt about things, the worse Cade felt about them. He knew they were going to have to talk about it.

Cade was happiest when Braden was feeling secure and safe, so he doubted Cade would discuss how he was truly feeling about Eric. Cade wouldn't want to worry him. He made a mental note to discuss the issue with Cade that evening, so they could get things out in the open.

Chapter 11

CADE

"He's much smarter than I would have given him credit for. He pegged the little old lady he rented that house from as a potential threat and was moved out of the place before the cops could get there. At least they were able to search the place thoroughly and forensics found traces of Braden's DNA on the carpet and in the bathroom—more evidence to convict him. We gotta assume that he's holed up somewhere else with a new go phone and another stolen vehicle. The fucker has gotten really adept at hiding and boosting cars."

Cade growled. "He's still in town, Coop."

"Oh, hell yeah, he's still here. The psych profile you got from Gabe reflects that he isn't one to give up. He's here and he's dug himself in for the duration until he sees his moment, his chance to grab Braden again. I know how uneasy you're feeling. How is Braden doing, really?"

Cade sighed. "Much better and feeling more self-assured. I don't want to fuck with his new-found confidence, but I also don't want him thinking that he's out of harm's way either. I'm gonna have to talk to him. I don't want any of us getting complacent. That's exactly what Eric is waiting for."

"Agreed. So, when Killian gets back from the training with Thor, we'll keep him around, until Eric is dealt with."

"Yeah, I think that's probably for the best. He's the only one that could do it right now, as everyone else is tied up with cases. He can help, and I know Thor will be a big help as well."

Cooper stood and stretched. "It will also be good to have him around for the construction of the warehouses. I know he'll have some ideas about the basements and the tunnels that we found during the inspection."

Cade stood as well, slipping his phone in his pocket. "Go check on Maya, I'm gonna go see if Braden is done for the day. We can head to Vaughn's together if you're both ready to go."

Both men walked toward the kitchen and stopped at the sight before them. Their expressions went from grave to astonished grins when they came upon a hip-shaking Braden, arms raised and dancing next to a hip-bumping Zoe, having a very good time together. What made the whole thing funnier is that they were attached to each other by Braden's ear buds, each wearing one, so they couldn't dance unless they were right up on each other, which they were, oh, they were.

Neither of them knew they had an audience. The grinding they were doing had both former Special Forces men leaning up against the countertop enjoying the show, which finally tuned the dancing duo into the fact that they had an audience. Braden gasped, blushed, and covered his face with his hands, laughing. All the while, Zoe kept her hips moving and just smiled at them as she danced around Braden, shamelessly unaffected by her audience.

Cade approached Braden, grinning at him. He pulled out the ear bud, handing it and the attached phone to Zoe who continued to shake her fine ass all over the kitchen, much to Cooper's delight. He gathered Braden into his embrace, bent him back with one hell of a kiss, causing Braden to grip Cade's triceps to keep balance. When Cade finally eased him back up, Braden's lips were swollen and red and he was blinking up at Cade with a stunned expression on his face. "I do love a man who can shake his ass and shake it well."

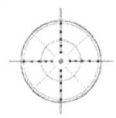

Braden

Braden snickered, butting his forehead up against Cade's sternum, fighting his embarrassment at being caught shaking his ass like he was at some club, not in his own kitchen at the café. Cade tucked his finger below Braden's chin and tilted his face up, leaned down and kissed him again. "You ready to go to self-defense? I know you've had a long day. Are you up for the class tonight?"

Braden smiled up at him and nodded, pulling off his apron and setting it on the counter. Cade's mobile rang, and he frowned at what Braden assumed was an unknown number but answered the phone. "McCade."

Braden could hear someone speaking quickly on the other end. "Yes, Mike. Of course, I remember you. Mmm hmm. Did you call an ambulance?"

After several long seconds of the other person talking on the other line, Cade's brow creased, and he shook his head. "Where are you, Mike? All right, listen to me now, I need you to get back to your friend and stay with him until the ambulance arrives. What's his last name? All right, thanks. I'm gonna send someone your way to pick you up, so after he's taken, stay where you are."

Cade paused again and rubbed his hand over the scruff of his beard. "Mike, I know you're worried, but you need to stay calm for your friend. I'm not sure who will be coming to get you, but whoever it is will call you by name and tell you mine, all right? Hang tight."

Everything had gotten quiet in the kitchen. Zoe had long since stopped dancing. Maya, Cooper, and Layla had come from the front when everything had been shut down for the day, and everyone had been listening to Cade's side of the conversation. They continued to watch as Cade got off the phone and called his brother. "Finn are you doing anything that you can't get out of?"

Cade looked relieved and nodded. "Good. There are a couple homeless vets I met several weeks ago. Something happened to one of them and the other called an ambulance. I want to make sure the one that's hurt gets the help he needs and isn't treated poorly because he's homeless. I'd like to help them both get back on their feet. Yeah, the VA Hospital. The one that's hurt is named John Davis, his friend is named Mike. Yeah, okay, thanks."

He ended the call then dialed again. "Sawyer, who's with Nana? Good, I need you to pick someone up over at Peet's Coffee on Mission and 3rd Street. Yeah, across from St. Regis. His name is Mike. Give him my name and take him to the VA Hospital. His friend is being taken by ambulance, and I'd like to get them both help. I'll have you work with Olivia on getting someone there to help you with them."

Braden watched his man work, knowing he was unaware he had an audience. Cade called his office manager. "Olivia, hey, did you leave the office already? Good, I'm gonna need some help, if you're up for it, and a healthy bonus on your next check?"

Cade chuckled. "I figured. So, we have a bit of a situation here with a couple of homeless vets. I'm going to need you to work your magic with Valery at Veterans Affairs. We need someone that can help us with a vet that's sick and headed to the VA Hospital here. If we could have someone meet Sawyer there or get in touch with him that would be good. Yeah. Yeah, that's great. Thanks."

Cooper approached Cade. "Do you need anything? I can see if Vaughn can get a sub in to take the class?"

Cade shook his head. "Nah, man, let's keep that commitment. Vaughn needs the help, and Braden needs the practice."

Cooper nodded and asked if Maya was ready to go. She nodded, and they headed out. Cade looked Braden's way. "Ready to go?"

Braden nodded, and they were on their way as well.

The class dragged on for Braden. He could tell Cade was distracted and wanted to get updates on John. After they showered and dressed, Braden couldn't take anymore. "Let's go to the hospital and check on John."

Cade turned his head toward Braden, a surprised look on his face. Braden rubbed a hand up and down Cade's back. "You've been distracted ever since you got the call. Talking to Sawyer or Finn won't be enough for you, so let's go."

Cade narrowed his eyes at Braden. "Let me talk to Cooper. You can head home with them. I'll come get you when I get back."

"Would I be in the way if I came with you?"

"Do you want to come with me?"

Braden crossed his arms over his chest and shrugged. "Well, yeah, but if I'll be in the way and you'd prefer I didn't come, I can go home with Cooper and Maya."

Cade rubbed his hands up and down Braden's arms and leaned down to give him a sweet kiss. "I always want you with me, Bray. I just figured you'd prefer to spend some time with Maya, rather than come with me to the hospital to check on a virtual stranger."

"Stranger or not, you're invested in his welfare, so that means I'm invested as well."

Cade looked into his eyes so long Braden wasn't sure what was going through his head. He crowded Braden back against one of the walls of lockers, slipping his fingers into his hair, and gripping his head, tilting it up for a bruising kiss. When he pulled away, he was grinning down at Braden. "I love the shit out of you."

A surprised laugh burst from Braden before he could stop it. He waved his hand near his face and feigned being overheated. "Sweet nothings whispered with such reverence. I'm swooning."

Cade snorted and started pulling him from the locker room. "Oh, I'll whisper some stuff in your ear later that'll make you lose your mind, baby."

Braden let himself be led out of the locker room and toward the exit. He did his best to avoid making eye contact with anyone on his way out. He didn't want anyone seeing the blush suffusing his skin.

The lighthearted feeling slipped quickly away once they were outside and Cade swept the area with his gaze and hurried them to the car. As they pulled out of the parking spot, Cade got on the phone with Sawyer to figure out where to meet him.

They spent the remainder of the trip in silence, Cade seemingly deep in thought. When they finally pulled up to the hospital's valet parking, they got out, and Cade dealt with the car while Braden waited close by.

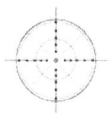

Cade

Cade clasped Braden's hand as they walked inside. He texted someone, and a second later, his phone rang. Apparently, John had suffered a mild stroke earlier and a bigger one had hit immediately upon his arrival. He was still in surgery, and Finn wasn't sure how long it might take. While they waited, he assured Cade that Mike would be able to stay in John's room as a visitor overnight. Cade made sure that Sawyer would work with Olivia to find him a place to stay after that, and they'd do what they could to get both men back on their feet.

After three hours had passed, during which time they'd eaten dinner in the hospital cafeteria then gathered in the waiting room, the neurosurgeon approached Finn. Everyone except Braden, who was asleep on the sofa, stood to hear the news about John. He made it through surgery and they were able to stop the bleed in the brain, however, they wouldn't know how bad he was impacted by both strokes until he woke.

As Cade was about to wake Braden to go home, Sawyer caught his eye and nodded to the hallway. When he got out there, Sawyer was rubbing the back of his neck and just seeing the gesture put Cade on alert. "I'm getting a bad feeling right now. I think you need to get Braden home."

Cade crossed his arms over his chest, his tension mounting. "Did you-_?"

Sawyer shook his head. "No, I didn't see anything. Just got the sense that this isn't a good place for him right now. I'll follow you guys home to cover you."

Cade reached in his pocket and pulled out his valet ticket. "Take this down to the valet and get both your car and mine pulled around. I'll bring Braden along in a few minutes. I'll have Finn walk us down."

Sawyer headed downstairs and Cade got Finn's attention, pulling him out into the hallway. He filled him in, and he readily agreed to walk them downstairs to give Cade some backup. Cade let Mike know he was taking Braden home, gave him Sawyer's number for him to call the next morning and headed toward a still sleeping Braden.

Cade crouched down and nudged Braden gently to wake him up, asking if he'd be all right to walk to the car or if he wanted to be carried. Cade managed a smile as Braden sat bolt upright and got to his feet to avoid being carried out of the hospital like an invalid. He asked about John and Cade told him what the doctor had said.

Finn made his presence seem like an info-sharing session, and Cade was glad Braden didn't pick up on their combined tension as Finn explained to Braden what had occurred during John's surgery. They made it to the entrance without incident, and Finn chatted with Sawyer while they both kept an eye on the surrounding area as Cade helped Braden into the car. Braden was still groggy, and Cade was grateful he didn't have to explain what was going on. He just wanted to be able to focus on getting him home safe, and he didn't want to worry Braden unnecessarily. Once they were in the car with Sawyer at their six in his rental, he felt much more at ease.

Cade glanced over when Braden spoke into the quiet. "I should have gone with Maya and Cooper. Sorry I fell asleep. I didn't exactly help any. I know I never met him, but can we come visit him tomorrow?"

"I wanted you there, and I'm glad you got a little rest. These types of things might happen occasionally. You are always welcome to come with me to do anything, unless I'm on active assignment or it poses a safety risk for you. And yes, we can come visit him tomorrow after work. How does that sound?"

Braden smiled. "I'd like that. Can I ask you something about them?"

"Mike and John? Yeah, of course."

"When we were on our date and you talked to them, you seemed to have gift cards for them already and a roll of quarters."

More tension left his body as he kept his eyes on the road. "I keep a roll of quarters and gift cards to places like Target and Walmart. I stop when I see people who need help and give them one of my cards with our office number and a toll-free number for Veterans Affairs written on the back. They can use the quarters to call if they need help. I give them gift cards to buy food or clothing, toiletries, that kind of thing."

Braden watched out the window as they turned onto his street. "Sometimes I think that you're way too good for me. I don't know that I deserve you."

Cade pulled into a spot close to Braden's home and turned the car off.

He surreptitiously watched Sawyer find a spot further down, hurry out of the car, and head their way to make sure they got inside. He glanced at Braden, frustration clear in his gaze. "Let's get you inside and continue this conversation once we've gotten you secure."

He got out of the car and came around to Braden's side, opened his door, and led them inside, nodding once to Sawyer in thanks. He disengaged then rearmed the security system, feeling as if they'd somehow had a narrow escape.

He led Braden into his bedroom, turned and gathered him close, a serious expression on his face. "First of all, you know as much of my story as I'm able to tell you. You know damn well that I've done a lot of fucked up shit. I try to do what I can to make up for that, to balance the scales. And second, do you think I could love you as deeply as I love you if you weren't worthy of me? We're together now because you were made for me."

The look in Cade's eyes brooked no argument and Braden smiled up at him. "I was made for you."

Cade smiled in return and smacked Braden's ass. "That's right, now come on, we're both exhausted. Let's get ready for bed and get some sleep."

They brushed their teeth, Braden took his insulin, and they crawled in bed. They were both too drained to do much but whisper their love for each other and cuddle before they drifted off, with the agreement they both needed an extra-long run in the morning to make up for their unproductive self-defense class that evening.

Cade made a mental note to have a discussion with Braden regarding his thoughts on Eric and the scare they'd had that night. He knew Braden wouldn't like that he'd been kept in the dark, but there was nothing to be done about it now. Braden was already asleep in his arms and for that he could only be grateful.

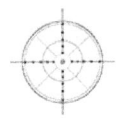

Braden

They awoke late the next morning and barely had time to shower before heading over to the café. After their long day yesterday, they were both feeling a bit off. When several batches of pastries were completed, they got ready for a run, hoping it would get them back in gear. Pounding pavement, searching for calm was clearing Braden's head incrementally, but his mind was still churning. He glanced over at Cade and saw his eyes searching their surroundings. Braden thought that constant vigilance must be exhausting, always on high alert, always ready. He wanted this bullshit with Eric to be over, needed it to be over. He felt like their lives were on hold, stagnant.

He finally broached the subject with Cade, not really wanting to talk about it at all, but he knew they had to. He couldn't wait another second. "You don't think he's given up, do you? I thought maybe he'd seen his face on TV, gotten scared, and bolted, but that's not what you think is it?"

Cade tried to avoid the conversation. He felt it was best to wait until they could be face to face. "Why don't we talk about this when we get back?"

Braden's stride faltered. He knew that tone of voice. That was Cade's, 'this brooks no argument' voice, but he didn't care, he wasn't going to be kept in the dark. "No. I want to talk about it now. I deserve to know what's going on. If he's gonna come at me, I need to be prepared for that, not off in la la land, completely unaware that I'm about to get swiped."

"Braden…"

"Zavier, I can give you a lot of leeway when it comes to most things, but I can't be kept in the dark, not about this."

Cade knew he was right, but he didn't like that they were having this conversation when he couldn't gauge Braden's reaction. With one last look around them, Cade finally glanced his way. "Sawyer was really uneasy last night at the hospital, had a hunch that it wasn't a good place for you to be. He followed us home to make sure we didn't have issues getting you home safe."

Braden scowled. "Why didn't you tell me?"

Cade glanced around, keeping vigilant. "He told me right as we were getting ready to leave and I didn't want to worry you. I figured today was good enough. You were exhausted, and so was I."

"Please don't do that again."

"Braden—"

"Please, Zavier. You have to trust that I'll deal with whatever comes. I need to know what's going on. Please."

"He hasn't given up. I got a psych profile from Gabe. He's obsessive and you're his obsession. He'd sooner die than leave things as they are with you. He dropped you off into my care because at the time, he didn't want you to die. Maybe, in his head, he truly wanted you back, thinking eventually you'd come around, see it his way, and want him back as well."

Braden's pace slowed at the insinuation in Cade's voice. "So, you think he wants me to die now?"

Cade met his eyes briefly then looked ahead. "I think, now that the stakes are higher and his whole life is fucked, he isn't so concerned about you living. I think he's changed his goal. It isn't to get you back any longer, but to take you and punish you until you come around to his way of thinking or your body gives out."

Braden's breath hitched and his pace slowed some more. "You think—"

Cade barreled on. "I think he sees the downhill slide his life has taken, and he blames you for everything. I think a switch was flipped when the cops started looking for him, and we're past the point of thinking he will ever be stopped. That won't happen until he's behind bars, or six feet under."

Braden stopped at that, just flat out stopped running and bent over, hands on his knees, his breath coming out in pants. He hadn't expected that answer, though what the fuck he thought he'd hear, he had no clue. Maybe he should have expected it—hell, he'd pushed and pushed, and he finally learned what Cade had been thinking—but for reasons unknown to him, he hadn't expected it at all. "You must think I'm so stupid and naïve, thinking maybe it was over, maybe he was done. I thought the last several weeks with no notes, no threats, no break-ins or vandalism were good things. No wonder you've been so fucking stressed. God, and to think I thought you were overreacting."

Cade glanced at him then quickly away, keeping his eyes moving, looking for threats. "I don't think you're stupid, nor do I think you're naïve. You made the assumption most people would, given the circumstances. Because what sane person would keep coming at you after everything that's gone down? But that's just the point, Braden, he's not sane. He most likely lost what little sanity he may have had after seeing the reports of him as a wanted man."

Braden tried to say something but didn't seem able to get anything out. He felt anxiety begin to take over, and he wasn't sure he could hear anymore, but that wasn't an option either. He couldn't keep still. As Cade continued, he crossed his arms over his chest and began to pace. It was all too much.

"In his mind, losing his job was a challenge. He wasn't listed as having been fired, and he could easily move to another state and get another job without much hassle. All he needed, to do that, was you to be with him."

Braden stopped and stared at Cade, frantically shaking his head. He didn't want to hear anymore, but Cade was keeping his eyes on their surroundings and didn't see him. "Now he's backed into a corner with limited options. He no longer has that picture in his head of an easy transition to another location and fitting into a new job and city with little to no difficulty. Now, he has his face plastered all over every news channel, listing his crimes. Every single time he sees those reports, he also sees you as the one to blame for everything, his downfall, and he's angrier than he's ever been before."

Braden looked at Cade in horror as his words sank in. He felt the color drain from his face, and he felt sick. His hands shook, and his palms began to sweat. It was his worst nightmare, and he knew without a doubt that everything Cade said was true and terror like he'd never felt seized him. He had to get away, that was all he knew. Before he could process what his feet were doing, he was off like a shot, running full tilt to get away from the truth, to get away from what he knew he'd never survive. He couldn't have stopped himself if he wanted to.

His vision tunneled, the edges of his vision blurry, showing clearly his escape route ahead and nothing else. He ran, not hearing Cade calling out his name or his heavy footfalls as he chased after him.

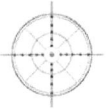

Cade

Cade saw the fear grab hold of Braden, and he braced himself for the panic attack to follow. What he didn't expect was for him to run and run faster than he'd ever seen anyone run. He was so caught off guard that it took several drawn-out seconds to process what was happening. He yelled Braden's name several times as he chased after him. He knew he had a very short amount of time to catch him. He couldn't maintain the speed Braden was running for very long, so he knew if he was going to catch him, he had to do it fast.

Panic seized his chest as he saw Braden running for an intersection without slowing. He saw a car driving their way, and he knew Braden wasn't seeing anything or anyone around him. He had to get to him, he had to get him out of the way, or Braden was going be run over by that fucking car.

He put on a burst of speed; the only thing on his side at that point was adrenaline. He reached the intersection seconds before the car did and shoved Braden out of the way so hard he went flying. The only thing he could do to prepare for the inevitable was turn his back to the car. If he could lessen the impact, he might be able to walk away.

His calves hit the fender, his back, the hood of the car then he was rolling. He tucked his body into something resembling a ball, trying to protect his head with his arms. He felt the impact of the windshield against his arms and his head, and then he was rolling off the roof of the car and landing in a heap on the ground. The only thing he heard before everything went black was the screech of tires as the car finally braked to a stop.

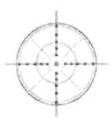

Braden

Braden felt hands on his back, shoving him, and suddenly he was hurtling through the air. He hit the ground with a bone-jarring thud. Disoriented, he looked behind himself to see who had pushed him. The last few seconds of Cade's free fall from the top of the car would be forever etched in his brain. He had no more thought of fleeing. Seeing Cade crumpled on the ground after being struck by a car was the wake-up call he needed to get himself together.

Fear suffused his whole body when he realized Cade wasn't moving. He went to get up and realized his own trip through the air had left him with more than a couple aches and pains. He'd have to take stock of his newest injuries later; for now, he just had to get to Cade.

Finally getting to his feet, he made his way over to Cade's side as quickly as he could. He knew enough not to try to move him, so he got down on his hands and knees and touched Cade's arm tentatively. He called out his name and squeezed Cade's hand. Still no reaction. He felt something hit his foot and turned around. He saw booted feet, but when he looked to see who'd kicked him, he was only able to see a fist flying at his face, faster than he could deflect. He sucked in a breath as pain exploded through his jaw before the blackness overtook him.

Chapter 12

ERIC

Eric's face spread into a sinister smile as he drew back his fist and let one fly, catching Braden on the jaw with a solid right hook. Goddamn, that felt good. He'd been waiting to knock some sense into Braden, and he loved the rush of adrenaline that coursed through his body. He dragged Braden unceremoniously to his car. He was about to put him in the backseat when he heard bystanders approaching. Several of them were holding up cell phones, like they were recording everything. He even heard someone shout, "Hey!" He pulled his gun from his waistband, waved it in their general direction, and took mild satisfaction in seeing them all duck for cover. He hefted his prize into the backseat and was in the car speeding off before that fucking brute of a man had even moved. He hoped the bastard was dead, but if he wasn't, he'd never be able to find them.

If he was honest with himself, he knew he'd never win if it came to a fight between him and McCade. He'd taken his advice after listening to that voicemail on his phone repeatedly. He'd googled his name and what he had read had sent him into a deep-seated panic. The shit that was online about him was unbelievable. He knew that there was no way all of it was true, but if even half of it was, the man wasn't someone he wanted to come face to face with, ever. The only thing saving him was the fact that McCade couldn't possibly find him now. He'd been very careful. He'd gotten out of that house he'd been renting the second he saw himself on TV, knowing that old bitch would turn him in.

He'd cut and dyed his hair and grown and dyed his beard. He'd even managed to find a man that looked enough like him and snagged his wallet, complete with driver's license. He was now renting a shittier house in a shittier neighborhood, but along with that shittier address came neighbors that turned a blind eye and minded their own business. That was what was going to keep his ass safe from that Special Forces asshole.

Said asshole was pissing him off, more and more each day. He'd varied Braden's schedule and changed his running routes. In the past, he'd been able to sit and wait Braden out because he'd known his routines so well. All he'd had to do was sit in a coffee shop or some other business on his route and inevitably Braden would jog by. Now, he never ran the same route twice and he was Never. Fucking. Alone. Braden wasn't stupid enough to fall for the same scheme twice, so he knew nabbing him again was going to require luck, and a shitload of patience. It had finally paid off. Big time.

After a lot of frustration with Braden's new and unpredictable schedule, he'd given up on trying to follow him everywhere he went. In the end, he admitted to himself that he'd have more luck being a bit unpredictable himself. He had a new look and a different stolen car so he'd drive through Braden's neighborhood side streets, usually once, sometimes twice a day, on the off chance he'd get lucky. Frustration was mounting, but all he could think about was getting Braden's traitorous ass back where it belonged, so he could figure out how best to punish him for his transgressions.

After several weeks, his plan didn't seem to be working out, but last evening he happened to be driving by when Braden and his asshole keeper were pulling out. He'd followed them to the hospital of all places, but after doing his level best to figure out a way to nab Braden that night, he'd admitted it was too risky. There were too many people there that looked capable enough to get in his way. He'd left, frustrated that he'd let an opportunity pass, but unable to manipulate the situation in his favor.

Frankly, he didn't think the time would ever come when he'd be able to get him. There hadn't been a break in the security on Braden for one second since he'd left him unconscious in that car what felt like forever ago. He'd been waiting and waiting for an opening and had been elated that he'd seen them yesterday, thinking his luck had changed and he was angrier the day after, knowing he'd failed and feeling as if he'd never get another chance.

He'd forced himself back into his stolen beater that morning knowing it would probably be a fruitless trip but unwilling to become lax in his plan. And wouldn't you know it, his little reconnaissance mission of the neighborhood had turned unexpectedly in his favor a second time, when he saw them jogging up ahead of him, and then slow down.

He couldn't believe his luck when a parking spot had opened up and he'd been able to pull over to watch their discussion. He'd then seen Braden take off like a bat out of hell. It was pure good fortune Braden took that intersection at that exact moment. Eric didn't second guess himself. As soon as he'd seen Braden take off, he'd pulled out of his spot and picked up speed. He honestly didn't care which one of them he hit, he was armed either way.

The "accident" couldn't have worked more in his favor. Just thinking about it made him laugh. He should have shot McCade while he'd had the chance, however, he wasn't stupid, and he knew having that many witnesses, especially with cameras rolling, would have been an idiotic move. Retrieving his property while being watched by half a dozen strangers was one thing; murder in cold blood on video, another altogether. And Braden was his property, of that there was no doubt, and everyone would know it.

It was too late for McCade. He'd have to live with the fact that he couldn't save Braden. He didn't know what he was going to do with the little fucker. It was almost too good to be true. He knew he'd be beating a few lessons into him very soon, but after that, he wasn't sure. He'd waited long enough to have his tight little ass again, so that was also on the agenda. He was not feeling generous, so he wasn't going to be gentle by any stretch of the imagination. In fact, he couldn't remember ever feeling this angry. It was a living, breathing thing inside of him.

He'd seen red when he had watched his own face come up on the six o'clock news weeks ago and then again and again on each local newscast. If Braden had been there at that moment, he wouldn't have been able to stop himself from snapping his fucking neck. He'd had time to calm down since then, but the fact that he was now living in a hovel and hiding from the cops on bogus charges was enough to make sure Braden never forgot the lesson he was soon to learn. As long as Braden dropped the charges and explained to the cops that it had all been a big misunderstanding, and that Braden was, in fact, his for the taking, everything should be fine.

If he decided he *was* feeling generous, he might keep Braden around. They'd have to work out some rules for him to abide by; otherwise, he had no further use for him. He smiled at that last thought, knowing how easy it would be to just let Braden lapse into another coma and walk away when he was done with him.

Chapter 13

CADE

Cade could feel someone nudging his shoulder. They spoke, but the words weren't clear, almost as though they were far, far away. "Hey man, are you okay? Wake up, buddy."

His return to consciousness was a slow process and he realized his head was killing him. When he opened his eyes and brought a hand to his head to feel the huge lump that had formed there. He looked up into a stranger's eyes in confusion. He wondered what the hell had happened when a stranger leaned over him. "Man, that crazy bastard ran right into you and then kidnapped the guy you pushed out of the way!"

Cade sat bolt upright and ignored the screaming pain that thumped through his skull. He looked around to be sure. "The man I was running with was kidnapped?"

"Yeah, man! The driver slammed his fist into the little dude's jaw, dragged him into the back of his car and took off."

Cade threw himself back, clutching the sides of his head and screamed, "FUCK!"

The stranger's eyes widened, and he backed up a bit. "The cops have been called. They should be able to help you soon."

Cade realized he didn't have time to spare. He'd probably only been out for a couple minutes or so and his head was killing him, but he needed to get his ass in gear and track Braden. He reached for his phone on his arm band and realized it wasn't there. He searched around for it and found it about a foot away. Reaching for it, he saw the shattered screen immediately but tried to use it anyway, cussing like a sailor when he realized it was totaled. He tucked it in his pocket and looked for the guy he'd been talking to. "Can I use your phone?"

The guy nodded, pulled out an old flip phone and handed it over. Cade opened it and dialed Cooper as he walked away from his would-be helper. When Cooper answered, he didn't waste time on pleasantries and spoke low. "Coop, he got Braden while we were out running. I need you to pick me up. Bring the emergency go bag and some clothes for me. Oh, and Braden's testing kit. My phone is dead, use my tracer to track me. I gotta get away from the scene so I don't get delayed by the cops. Once you're off the phone with me, call Brody and get all of Braden's tracers activated and searching."

He hung up, not waiting for a reply. He knew it would be a bit before Cooper was able to get there, not only because of everything he had to bring, but because traffic was starting in earnest. He handed the guy back his phone. He was about to tell the guy that he was going to leave and to contact Detective Miller, but it was too much to explain, and he heard the sirens approaching, so he thanked him for the use of his phone then turned and ran toward where Cooper would be coming from and away from the sound of the sirens. He heard the guy call out to him, but he ignored it. He'd have to call Detective Miller as soon as he was picked up.

By the time Cooper had finally pulled up alongside him, he'd gotten himself in the right headspace, put all the other shit aside for now, including the pain in his body and head, and flipped his internal switch for the battle to come. Cade noticed Jackson and Sawyer sitting in the backseat, ready to go, and he was grateful. He hopped in the SUV and gave them all a very short explanation of what happened while he stripped down completely and redressed. He began filling the pockets of his cargos with another ammo clip, several knives, and a few other things that Cooper had brought with him.

He felt some nausea threaten the meager contents of his stomach, most likely due to his head injury, and if he had to guess, he was probably covered from head to toe with bruises and scrapes. None of that mattered. He had to swallow down the nausea and ignore the pain. As soon as Braden was safe, he'd let his body react as it needed. He couldn't believe he'd fucked up. If anything happened to Braden, it would be on his head.

His men didn't ask any questions or push further for information. Cooper silently handed over his own phone, knowing Cade would want to make calls. He pulled out his broken phone and tossed it in the cup holder knowing it would be trashed properly, later. Cade was in the zone. He dialed Brody and put it on speaker. "Do you have him?"

"Yeah, I've got him. He's in the Bayview, Hunters Point area. Not a good part of town, so we know Eric's options are limited at this point. It's a really rough neighborhood, which will keep people from calling the cops if they hear anything from him, but most likely anything from you guys as well. I'll keep eyes on him to make sure his location doesn't change. When you get to Bayview, call me, and I'll direct you to his latest location."

Cade hung up with Brody and sat, running through scenarios in his head. He remembered he had to call the detective, so he pulled up the contact on Cooper's phone and dialed. "Detective, this is Cade. I'm calling to let you know that he's taken Braden again. I was hit with his car while we were running and when I came to, Braden was gone. A witness told me Eric punched him in the jaw then dragged into the car. I left the scene of the accident, so you'll need to smooth it over with the cops. I wasn't going to be delayed in my search for him by a bunch of beat cops asking a million questions—"

Cade rubbed his head where it had hit the windshield and looked at his bloody palm. "I don't much care about procedure at this point, deal with the fall out. I'm out in search for him now, just so you know. The only info I have from the accident is that he was driving another beat up Honda, white, at least ten years old, but I have no idea what model. I was too busy being thrown through the air by the impact to notice. Once you get the witness statements from the cops at the scene, let me know if there is any further information regarding the car. I didn't even see him, so I have no idea if he's changed his appearance again. My phone died when I hit the pavement, so call me at this number if you learn anything new."

He hung up the phone without waiting for a reply, knowing that the detective was pissed, but unable to care. He wanted to hit something, he was filled with so much rage, most of it at himself. He was being swamped by guilt. They'd both been exhausted last night and getting up so early to get to the café had been the last thing either of them had wanted to do. He should have insisted someone run with them. Sawyer felt uneasy, and Cade just assumed they'd gotten home and were safe after the hospital scare, but he should have been more diligent.

The day had felt off from the get go. He hadn't been at the top of his game, and Braden would be hurt, again, because of it.

Cooper interrupted his thoughts. "We're coming into the Bayview area, should hit Hunters Point soon."

Cade got his head back in the game, looked out the window to the seedy area they drove through. He felt adrenaline course through his veins, readying his body for the fight to come. He dialed Brody, and he picked up before it rang a second time. He gave them the address and told them good luck. He plugged it into the phone's GPS. They were still several miles out. Traffic had thinned in this part of town.

He hooked in his earpiece and tested it out, speaking quietly, outlining his plan. Sawyer and Jackson were to stay outside guarding the front and back exits, in case he made a run for it. Cooper was to go in the front, while he took the back. He received affirmatives from all three, validating that all ear pieces were functional.

They'd spend a couple minutes surveilling the house and surrounding areas first. He wasn't about to bust into the place without doing his best to figure out what the hell they were going into, but he wasn't about to waste any time when Braden could be getting hurt as they scoped out the place.

What he did know is that they had the element of surprise on their side. Braden would never tell Eric about the tracers, and he was positive it would never occur to him. At this point, Eric was riding high and feeling quite smug that he'd managed to get to Braden again.

What worried Cade the most was the amount of anger Eric would be carrying for Braden. He also knew from the psychological profile that Eric would most likely keep Braden around for a while to torture; his need for revenge had to be satisfied before he did anything final. He was a sadistic bastard and a rapist, so he could do all manner of things, and he'd had him at the house for nearly an hour now. Though that didn't seem so long, it was long enough to do a lot of fucking damage. Cade knew he needed to find it in himself to stay above the emotions of the situation. It would kill him to see this whole scenario as just another battle, but he had to be able to distance himself somewhat from Braden to be able to focus on bringing Eric down.

They rounded the corner of the closest side street and pulled over. Before they got out, Cade gave them a few brief instructions. That's all that was needed for his men to fall into their familiar pattern of surveillance. All four men got out, armed and ready to go, and hoofed it the rest of the way. They separated and began spreading out between the houses to get to their destination.

The houses were all in extreme need of repair. Several of the homes were boarded up and covered in graffiti. Cade was about to exit the street into an alleyway, when a blond-haired woman with a black eye and track marks on the arm that was holding onto a little girl's hand came toward him. They both paused, startled, and looked at him. The woman was savvy enough to know that she needed to forget she saw him, immediately. She averted her eyes automatically, jerked her daughter's arm to pull her away, and they both scurried across the street to get away as fast as they could.

Cade saw Sawyer silently slip over the chain link fence at the back of the house. There wasn't much back there but a copse of thick blackberry bushes, behind which he was able to take cover. Cade stayed back, out of sight of the house, for another few minutes then approached behind Sawyer who gave him several hand gestures: no movement, no sound, all clear to approach. Cade gave an imperceptible nod and approached the steps up to the dilapidated back porch, gun drawn.

He closed in on the back door and stood to the side of it, listening for anything. Hearing nothing, he expected the worst, and his stomach dropped. He pulled his tools from his pocket and picked the back door lock. He gave the signal to Sawyer that he was on his way in, and heard Sawyer speak into his ear, telling the others. He then heard Jackson's roughened voice say the same about Cooper.

He opened the door, unable to keep it from squeaking as it opened. He paused, waiting for any reaction in the house, but heard nothing. He was in the kitchen and approached the front of the house. Entering the front room, Cooper signaled that he was going upstairs. Cade nodded, indicating he was headed to the basement.

They split again, and Cade approached what he assumed was the basement door. He opened it up and was thankful that it made no noise. There was a door at the bottom of the stairs with light coming from underneath, so his approach wouldn't be noticed. He placed his foot onto the dingy carpeted step and it was then that he heard several thumps and grunts. He got to the bottom of the stairs quickly and quietly, needing to make sure he had the element of surprise.

He opened the door and again was thankful it was silent, as he was able to enter the basement without being heard. It was a finished basement, but like the rest of the house, it had seen much better days. It was grimy and smelled of mildew, hinting of water leaks. It was sparsely furnished with a nineteen-seventies style sofa that was threadbare and a few low slung, circular chairs facing a twenty-five inch TV that was at least fifteen years old. His quick scan told him that no one was there. The sound of a gunshot made terror freeze the blood in his veins. He ran toward the closed door to his right, dimly aware that Cooper's pounding feet signaled his approach from upstairs. Gun drawn, he pushed the door open.

If he lived to be a hundred, he'd never forget the image he saw next. Braden was lying, half sprawled on the floor, half slouched against the bloody wall, holding his stomach with his hands, blood seeping through his fingers. Eric, still holding the gun, stood several feet away, looking at the gun in his own hand like he was surprised it was there. Cade eased his way toward Braden.

Braden's eyes, one of which was nearly swollen shut, swung his way, a desperate plea in them. Eric's gaze soon followed, widening so much that Cade could see more of the whites of his eyes than anything. Gun trained at Eric's head, he growled out, "Drop it! Raise your fucking hands, or I'll shoot you between the eyes."

Eric immediately tossed the gun down and raised both of his hands. Cade didn't react when Cooper threw the door open more fully and ran toward Braden. "You keep him alive, Coop."

Cooper ripped off his shirt and fell to his knees beside Braden. He placed his shirt over the gunshot wound, applying pressure. He updated their men, just in case they hadn't called it in yet. "Sawyer, Braden's been shot. Call nine-one-one and get an ambulance here. And call Detective Miller and get him here as well."

Cade moved further into the room, advancing toward his target. He realized, with great satisfaction, that Eric looked extremely roughed up. He had a bloody lip, blood coming from his broken nose and his swollen cheek had a large bruise. Eric saw the look in his eyes and scrambled backwards, falling in his panic. He flipped over and pushed himself to his feet, trying to put distance between himself and Cade, but the room was small, with only a stained mattress on the floor and one exit, which was behind Cade.

Cade stalked his prey, tucking his gun in its holster at the small of his back, narrowing the distance between them. Eric backed himself up against the wall and glanced to the right, seeking any means of escape. Cade could see by the look in his eyes that he knew he couldn't get away. The last vestiges of control left Cade and he growled like an animal as he lunged.

Eric did his best to slither out of the way, but nothing was going to stop Cade at that point. He caught Eric by the throat and slammed his head against the wall. Pressing his neck into the wall and lifting him nearly off his feet. "You like exerting your power over those who are smaller than you? How does this feel, since you like abuse so much?"

Eric flailed wildly and did his best to kick, punch, and scratch Cade's hand, but the efforts were ineffectual at best. Cade let up enough to allow him to breathe and reveled in the great gulps of air he sucked in, followed by several coughs and wheezes. Eric gathered up his strength again and took a swing at Cade. It glanced off Cade's cheek, not even causing his head to jerk back. Cade looked at him and smiled. He let go of Eric's throat, slamming his fist into his gut, doubling him over immediately. Cade brought his knee up into Eric's face. The man squealed like a pig, and he was on the ground a second later, nearly knocked out.

Cade followed him down, his adrenaline spiking, a fever spreading through his body. He was finally going to be able to punish the man who had terrorized Braden. His vision bled ruby red and all he saw was a man he needed to destroy. He straddled Eric's hips and began raining blows down on his head, his chest, anywhere he could reach. He'd never lost himself in his anger, he'd always kept himself in check, but this man had reduced him to a killer. His fists were streaked red from Eric's blood.

He lost touch with reality and had zeroed in on inflicting pain. Strangely enough, he made no noise. All that could be heard in the room was the wet thump of flesh meeting flesh, and he'd have told anyone that would listen that nothing could have stopped him from killing Eric, slowly, with his fists.

He was barely aware of strong arms coming around him, trying to hold him back and stop him. But Cooper had miscalculated his rage and he was able to wrench himself free and continue the beating. What he wouldn't have counted on stopping him was a simple whispered plea, slamming his internal breaks and stopping him mid-punch.

"Z, no."

Braden's tortured whisper did what nothing else could have done. It brought him back to the present. He looked down at Eric's battered and torn body. He was surprised it didn't look worse. He realized with a sick twist of his stomach that he'd held himself back. Somehow in that angry haze, he'd held himself back. He'd kept some modicum of control over the power of his punches, but instead of feeling better with this knowledge, he felt worse.

The reason he'd held back wasn't so that he wouldn't kill Eric; oh no, it was so that he could prolong the torture, prolong the fight, and prolong the pain that Eric would feel before death. He'd been the cat, Eric the mouse. He wrenched himself away from the bloodied, unconscious man. He crawled his way over to Braden who was now on his side, reaching his arm out beseechingly to him. Cooper had returned to Braden's side and resumed applying pressure to his wound and was now easing Braden onto his back. When he had Braden's hand in his, he raised it to his lips. "Hang on, baby, help's on the way. I'm so sorry, Braden. He never should have been able to get to you."

Cade heard the sirens outside and prayed they'd be fast enough to save him. Braden was looking very pale, his eyes a bit glassy. His head fell to the side and just as his eyes were about to close, they flared to life as he gasped. Cade threw himself to the floor, his body blocking Braden's, as he reached for his gun. Just as the cops and paramedics came through the door a bullet hit Cade in his left side, and two bullets found their mark dead center of Eric's forehead.

The lead cop yelled, "Drop your weapons! Get your hands in the air!"

Cooper set down his weapon and raised his hands. Cade set his gun down as well but ignored their demand completely and turned to help Braden. Detective Miller entered. "Lower your weapons, officers. These men aren't our perp."

Cade resumed putting pressure on the wound. Braden was now unconscious and as pale as he'd ever seen anyone. Panic was a living, breathing thing inside him as he yelled, "We need a paramedic over here, now!"

Several paramedics approached and began to work on Braden. One of them approached Cade, who had shuffled back on his knees by Braden's head, bowed over him protectively, gently caressing his forehead. At the pat on his shoulder, he whipped his head up, ready to take the person's head off. The paramedic said something about his bullet wound and he shook his head. "I'm fine. Just help him. Everyone needs to be helping him. He's dying. I'm fine."

One of the paramedic's working over Braden looked up. "Sir, you have to back up, we need to place him on the stretcher."

Cade nodded and stood, watching as they put Braden on the stretcher and rolled him toward the door. He got up to follow and the same paramedic as before approached him again, putting his hand on his shoulder to stop him going forward. Cooper approached immediately and pulled the paramedic's hand off Cade's shoulder before Cade could lose his shit.

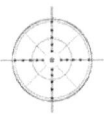

Cooper

Cade ran to catch up to the stretcher carrying Braden and Cooper held the paramedic back. "You need to back off. I know you're only trying to do your job and help him, but he's had bullet wounds before. This one isn't going to kill him, and he won't have anyone working on him when they could be working on Braden. Either go help with the other man they just took out on the stretcher or get out of his line of sight."

The paramedic raised his eyebrows at Cooper, but Cooper only asked which hospital they'd take him to and then turned away from him. Jackson entered the room and walked toward him just as Detective Miller approached him from the other direction, but he held up his hand to them both as he dialed his phone. "Maya, he's been shot and so has Cade. They're going back to the same hospital. Head over there now and I'll find you both when you get there. I don't know how bad it is, just get there."

Detective Miller started talking and he held his hand up again to silence him as he dialed another number. "Finn, Braden's been shot in the stomach and lost a lot of blood. Cade's been shot in the side, doesn't look too bad, but he'll need to be seen. We're headed back to the same hospital he was in before."

Cooper rubbed his shaking hands over his mouth as he listened to Finn, the adrenaline fading fast. "No, he won't let anyone work on him. He'll be all right until he reaches the hospital, but he'll need to get sewn up and checked out to be sure of the damage. Not to mention, Eric hit him with his car and he was thrown and hit his head, so he's most likely got a concussion."

Cooper glanced up when the detective made his impatience known. Cooper continued to ignore him. "He's gonna want you in that surgical room with Braden. He lost a lot of blood, it didn't look good. You're going to have to find a way to be in there keeping an eye on him, but you gotta get Cade to promise you he'll get medical attention while you're seeing to Braden. You need to get there…"

"You're already there? Thank fuck. He lost consciousness and looked extremely pale, gunshot to the abdomen, exit wound in the back. I'll deal with the cops here then I'm on my way."

Cooper turned to Detective Miller and cut him off before he even got started. "Detective, I don't know if you were here for the gunshots, but you have witnesses. The police and the paramedics that were here saw Eric shoot Cade before we both shot him in the head. You can come to the hospital to get our statements or anything else you need from us."

Miller followed them as Cooper and Jackson headed toward the stairs. "How did you know he was here?"

"Braden was wearing tracers."

"Why the fuck didn't you give us that information?"

"Don't even try to convince me there wouldn't have been some kind of delay for bullshit bureaucracy or waiting for backup."

"What you did isn't…"

"What we did was skip all the crap you have to wade through. You couldn't have gotten here as fast as we did, and I can't even imagine what would have happened if you'd have tried to negotiate hostage terms or some such bullshit. We did what we needed to do because we weren't willing to risk Braden's life on the off chance you could have gotten here in time. We did what we needed to do, end of story. We'll be at the hospital."

Cooper strode with Jackson to the car that Sawyer had brought and they drove to the hospital. Cooper checked with Sawyer. "Did you see them get into the ambulance?"

"Yeah, the paramedics kept trying to help Cade, but he wasn't having it. They finally gave up and let him ride with them. Do we need to contact his family?"

Cooper shook his head. "No, I already called Finn. He's at the hospital already, paving the way to be in on the surgery for Braden. He'll make sure Cade gets treated. He'll most likely call his family while he's waiting for them to arrive. If they have questions they can't get answers to, they'll call me. All we can do now is wait."

Chapter 14

CADE

Cade was hit by an overwhelming sense of déjà vu as he climbed into the ambulance. He sat toward the back, as close to Braden as he could get without being in the way of the paramedics. They checked on Braden's vitals again, one of the paramedics running an IV and talking to the ER using medical jargon that he ignored for his own peace of mind. As they sped through the city, the siren was on full tilt.

The paramedic speaking with the ER was administering a drug into the IV. The other one was monitoring Braden closely and applying pressure to the wound. He glanced over at Cade and nodded toward Cade's injury. "You don't want us to help you, so I'm assuming you're not a stranger to gunshot wounds?"

Cade shook his head. "Not in my line of work."

"Which is?"

"Former military, security. You don't have to distract me from what you're doing. I'm fine, just help him."

The paramedic's brows rose. "Just be aware that infection is a real possibility. You've got holes in your shirt and I'd imagine pieces of it inside of the wound. You'll want to get it seen to as soon as you get to the hospital."

"I'll get it seen to as soon as I know Braden is taken care of."

The paramedic shrugged his shoulders, finally giving up on getting through to Cade. He remembered he needed to signal his family that they were needed and tapped his watch to get to the correct screen, hit several icons then put his hand on Braden's head, threading his fingers into his hair. A second later, Braden's watch sent out the alarm code he'd just sent to his family, and the paramedics all glanced at the watch on Braden's wrist.

Ignoring anything but Braden, he leaned farther forward in his seat, elbows on his knees and his other hand pushing into his own hair, ignoring the twinge of pain in his side. He waited like that until they pulled into the emergency bay at the hospital where he was more grateful than he could even comprehend to see Finn in his scrubs, ready to manage Braden's care.

The paramedics pushed Braden out of the ambulance and were met by Finn and another man, along with several nurses. As they listened to the pass-down on his vitals, Cade leaned down and whispered to Braden, telling him he loved him, and he'd be waiting on him to get out of surgery. They began to rush him inside toward an operating theater. Finn walking brusquely to keep up, Cade by his side. "Zavier, this is Dr. Brown, he'll be performing Braden's--"

"You're Braden's surgeon, Finn. He can assist."

"Zavier..."

"Finn, Braden is my life. He's the very fucking air I breathe. No one but you will know how important his life is. No one. And I won't trust another surgeon with his life but the best."

Dr. Brown finally spoke, "Dr. McCade, I'll assist if you're willing to perform the surgery."

Finn nodded at Dr. Brown, and the man followed the nurses through the operating room doors. Finn stopped just outside of the OR, knowing they didn't have time to waste. He reached out and pulled Cade's shirt up to look at the wound. "I'll perform the surgery if you agree to have this taken care of, right now. Not to mention the head wound from Eric's car taking a go at you. Go back to where we came in, tell an ER nurse that I sent you back there to find Dr. Nisha Patel to stitch you up when she's free. Deal?"

Cade let out a breath he hadn't known he'd been holding and nodded. "Yeah, deal."

Cade watched his brother hurry into the OR and just stood there, staring at the door for several minutes before he reluctantly went back the way he'd come. He passed an ER nurse on his way through. "Dr. McCade asked me to head back this way to get a Dr. Patel to stitch me up when she was free. Is she here now?"

The nurse looked up at him startled and just stared. Cade's brow rose, and he prompted again, "Dr. Patel?"

The nurse nodded her head. "Uh, yep. Yes. She's...." She looked around the ER in search of the doctor and then pointed to a woman across the room. She was dressed in a bright purple surgical cap and black scrubs with bright purple skulls on them, covered with the typical white doctor's coat. She was a beautiful woman, tiny, and from what he could tell, without a scrap of makeup. She was standing at one of the desks, looking at a patient's chart. He thanked the nurse and walked her way. "Excuse me, Dr. Patel?"

Dr. Patel looked up and then up some more. "Good god, how many of you are there?"

"Pardon me?"

"McCades. How many McCades are there?"

He gave her a half-hearted smile. "Several."

She raised an eyebrow and looked him up and down. She must have noticed the hole in his bloody shirt because she set the chart aside and straightened, her eyes popping open wide. "Shot?"

"Yes, Doctor. Finn told me to come see you and get fixed up."

"He did, did he?"

"Yeah. My partner was brought in and is in surgery. I need to get stitched up and get back to him. I also got hit by a car earlier and was tossed ass over end, hit my head then ended up on the pavement."

She glanced at him, a look of shocked amusement on her face. "So, you were hit by a car, where your head got injured, flew through the air and landed on the street. Then you were in some kind of fight from the look of those swollen bloody knuckles, and to cap it all off, you were shot. Did I miss anything?"

Cade mentally ran the events of the day through his head and then shook it. "Nope. I think that covers it."

She raised a brow at him, realizing he was seriously answering the question she had posed half as a joke then shook her head. "And you're still standing."

She walked him to an ER surgical room and had him sit on the bed. A nurse came in and asked him for his info, and they got him into the system before Dr. Patel started working on him. She then pumped him with a round of antibiotics before she numbed the area. He refused to be put out, not wanting to delay getting back to Braden. She cleaned out the wound, muttering that he was lucky the shot missed his intestines and only passed right through muscle on its way back out as she sewed him back up.

She told him not to shower for forty-eight hours, to come back in if there was any sign of infection, and to take it easy, nothing strenuous for two weeks. After checking in with the OR nurses and verifying Braden was still in surgery, she cleaned his head wound. She then sent him to get a CT scan, confirming the concussion, and plied him with a large dose of acetaminophen. She cleaned up his knuckles, and while there was some bruising and a scrape he remembered he'd gotten from Eric's teeth, the blood on them seemed to all belong to Eric. Finally, she warned him she had to report the GSW to the police, and he gave her Detective Miller's number, informing her that the police were well aware of the incident. He was on his feet again and headed to the OR waiting room.

As soon as he entered the room, he realized he should have expected to see everyone, but he was caught off guard. His whole family was there, including Aiden, who approached him immediately and hauled him in for a bear hug. Cade hugged him back fiercely, aware that he'd needed the contact. Nana and Maya were there, as well as his men. They all gathered around him, asking for details. His mom pulled up his shirt and looked at his dressing, her face losing all color. He hugged her and addressed everyone. "Have any of you heard anything?"

Everyone shook their heads, and he was relieved there wasn't bad news. His mom didn't want to let go. "Are you going to be all right?"

"I'm fine, Ma. It was a clean shot that only passed through muscle in my side, in and out. It's not me we need to worry about. Braden's in the

OR right now. I made Finn promise to perform the surgery. He demanded I get stitched. It's been two hours since we brought him in, so I don't know how he's doing. He was unconscious when the EMTs got to him, gunshot wound to the abdomen with a lot of blood loss. I'm sorry, I need to go try to find out more, I can't just sit here."

He turned as a harried woman in green scrubs approached and called out, "McCade?"

The whole group turned, and Cade jogged toward her. "I'm Zavier McCade. Dr. McCade is in performing surgery on my partner."

"He's approved you, and only you, to be led to the operating theater's observation room. Please follow me."

He turned to everyone gathered. "I'll do my best to keep you informed."

He walked with the nurse toward the observation room. She showed him the monitor that was showing the surgery that was taking place in the theater. He took several deep breaths and focused on the close up of his brother's hands holding medical instruments that were probing Braden's abdomen, along with a pile of what Cade dreaded was intestines, covered by some kind of gauze. Before she left the room, the nurse got his attention again. "When he speaks, you'll hear him on the video monitor. You can also look down on the theater to watch that way, but you won't see the details as well. If he speaks to you, and you need to respond, press the button on the intercom there to your right and hold it down while you talk."

With that, she left, presumably to return to the room below. His brother paused, hands still inside of Braden's abdominal cavity. Cade looked down into the room to see what had caused him to stop what he was doing. Finn's back was facing the windows, but Cade heard him say, "Zavier, are you patched up?"

He pushed the button down and held it while he talked. "Yes. Tell me."

Finn shook his head, resumed working. "The bullet missed his spine, so that's good news, but I'm afraid the good news stops there. He's in bad shape, Zavier. Before we even went in, we typed his blood and shot him full of antibiotics. The wound perforated his small bowel. He's lost a lot of blood and we've already given him a transfusion. The fact that he's extremely healthy is a huge part of what's keeping him alive. We've performed an emergency laparotomy, as he presented with major intra-abdominal damage. He had some internal bleeding, which we believe we've stopped. At this point, it's a matter of us finding all of the damage done to the bowel and patching each spot."

"So, under the gauze are his intestines?"

"Yes, they are moistened sterile dressings covering the viscera as we need to keep them damp while they are outside of the abdominal cavity. When they are all sutured, we can place them back into the abdomen."

"His diabetes."

"We're keeping an eye on his levels. We've already given him some insulin, as his blood sugar levels were a bit high. His levels are very healthy right now and we've got that under control. What worries me is the risk of infection. The bullet did a lot of damage to the small bowel. We've got a lot more to suture, but then I think we'll have it all dealt with."

"Finn, is he going to make it?"

"I can't make you any promises, Zavier, except that I'm doing everything I possibly can. A small bowel evisceration causes waste to be released into the abdominal cavity, possibly traveling to other areas. Not to mention the bullet passed through his shirt, so we're trying to keep our eyes out for any fibers. His risk of infection is enormous at this point, and only exacerbated by his diabetes. Like I said earlier, he's been shot with antibiotics, but we don't want to overdo that, either, because then some bacteria may become resistant."

"You don't think the antibiotics will work?"

"We hope they will, but after we finish and patch him back up, he'll need to be under very close watch. I'll be placing him back in the ICU for recovery, but because there is such a strong possibility of hospital associated infections, I'll be monitoring his progress and assigning specific medical and nursing staff. Everyone entering the room will be required to wear a gown, gloves, and a mask. There will be no visitors allowed for at least the first twenty-four hours."

"I need to be able to stay with him."

"I've already got that covered. Once I have him stitched back up, he'll be moved there immediately. I've worked it out so that I'll be able to continue to manage his care in that department. They can always use the help and won't mind me managing the care of one of their patients. When I'm off duty, I will ensure that someone I trust is managing his care, and I will always remain on call. He'll be there at least a week, recovering and being checked often for any sign of infection. I will do everything in my power to ensure he goes home with you when he's well enough."

Cade couldn't talk for a long while. He recognized the hoops his brother had already jumped through for Braden while he was getting his own gunshot wound taken care of. The fact that he was having someone get everything handled with the hospital administrators while he was still performing the surgery on Braden, humbled him. He finally managed, "Thank you, Finn. And while a thank you is not enough, it will never be enough, it's all I have right now."

"It's all you need, brother. He's got a long road of recovery ahead."

"Finn, when he woke from his coma the last time he was here, he was almost immediately assaulted with one of his migraines. They seem to be brought on by both internal and external stressors. Is there a way to give him meds for that now, to avoid it, when he wakes?"

"Possibly. I wasn't aware of that going on last time. Hang on, Zavier."

Finn continued without pause, "Beth, can you please check Braden's file from his last hospital stay less than two months ago and find out all of the meds given to him for migraines. Page Dr. Himmel, I believe he's working today. Either get him to join Zavier in the theater or have him call the OR."

Less than five minutes later, Dr. Himmel entered the theater holding his ever-present iPad, a concerned look in his eyes when he saw Cade. He shook Cade's hand. "Was he attacked again, Cade?"

"Yes. Gunshot wound to the abdomen."

Cade watched as Dr. Himmel pulled up what he assumed was Braden's file on the iPad. The doctor approached the window and pushed the button on the speaker. "Finn, I'm here, how can I help?"

Finn continued with the surgery, suturing Braden's small intestines, all the while talking to them. "You treated him for migraine. Beth found Imitrex was used on him when he woke from his coma. The antibiotics we are using are safe for use with Imitrex, but we'll have to wait in giving it to him until he's out of surgery. We are obviously anticipating his body may react as it did before and produce a migraine, so I'd like to head it off at the pass."

Dr. Himmel flicked through several pages in the file he was looking at and nodded. "You're going to want to give him a standard dose, so that later, if the migraine continues, you are able to give him a repeated dosage, which is what we had to do. It seemed to help him tremendously."

Finn looked toward them. "Did you also administer separate pain meds for his other injuries?"

"We did, but you'll have him on something more powerful, obviously. It shouldn't interfere." Dr. Himmel skimmed down the page he was looking at, scrolling through what appeared to be chart notes, before continuing. "Keep up your dialogue with him though. Once he wakes, keep checking in with him. I had his nurse checking his migraine symptoms along with his glucose testing every few hours. It may seem over the top, but at this point, you're going to be worried about infection, so checking more often than normal is for the best."

Finn nodded. "Thanks, Ed. We'll be moving him directly over to the ICU after surgery, but we'll be using Infection Control Policy with the staff."

"That's exactly what I would do. Will you oversee his care there?"

"Yes. I've already cleared it with them."

"If you need me to spell you and help manage his care while he's there, please let me know. I'm sure I can work it out on the floor."

"I might take you up on that. I'm sure Braden and Zavier would appreciate a familiar face."

Cade looked at Dr. Himmel. "Does that offer include Sam? Braden liked her."

Dr. Himmel smiled. "She's a favorite and would probably enjoy a change and a nice little boost to her resume. Finn, let me know the details and what you feel is needed. I'll work with you on it."

"Thanks again, Ed. Zavier, let me finish up with the lacerations here then I'll sew him back up and we'll get moving with him over to the ICU. You'll need to get cleaned up and wear scrubs and other protective gear when you go into his room. You can't go in there wearing what you're wearing."

Cade shook Dr. Himmel's hand again then backed up and sat when he felt the bench hit the back of his knees. He didn't think he could hold himself up a moment longer, even if he tried. He knew he should feel relieved that Braden would make it through the surgery, but the fact that his risk for infection was so high had him struggling to breathe. Not to mention the guilt for Braden even being in this situation weighing him down. He sat there, trying to gather his inner strength as he watched his brother sew the love of his life back together, piece by piece.

He remembered everyone out in the waiting room and pulled out Cooper's phone. He sent a mass text to everyone waiting there, telling them everything he knew and told them he would be watching the remainder of the surgery and would let them know when they were on the move.

Several long, drawn out minutes went by before the responses began. The phone, muted, continued to vibrate in his pocket. He finally had to pull it out and turn it off. He couldn't deal with everyone's well wishes and questions. He sat, silently watching every move his brother made, so damn grateful Finn was in that operating room, saving Braden's life. And Finn would save his life; of that, Cade was sure. He wasn't out of the woods, not by a long shot, but he couldn't believe that it was too late for them, that he'd ultimately saved him from Eric only to lose him.

It was a full two hours later when Braden was ready to be taken to the ICU. They were bypassing the Post-Anesthesia Care Unit to avoid exposure to other patients. Braden was moved efficiently to a bed from the OR table. Once on the bed, he was covered with sterile sheets and blankets. They removed the ventilator but there were still multiple IVs infusing pain meds, antibiotics, and fluids into his body.

Cade walked quickly beside his brother and Braden who was being rolled down the hallway by a nurse and a few orderlies. When they were about to enter the ICU, a nurse approached them. Finn asked him to go with her to get cleaned up and changed while he saw to Braden. Cade hated leaving Braden when his life was hanging in the balance, but he knew his brother was the best person to leave him with, and he'd neutralized the only other threat to Braden hours earlier.

He was given some scrubs and was pointed toward a locker room. Once he was there, he pulled his shirt over his head and tossed it in the trash. He was about to take his pants off when he remembered everyone was still in the waiting room anxious to hear any news. He quickly dialed Maya, who answered immediately. He explained what happened in the OR and that Braden was not allowed visitors for at least twenty-four hours. He knew she'd pass along all the info to everyone else. He hung up and glanced at his reflection in the mirror. He saw the exhaustion, but he also saw relief.

He got himself back on task and went toward the sink where he was able to wash his face and hands. He leaned over and rinsed his hair of dried blood and sweat. He put on the scrubs which were big enough to fit over his broad shoulders and were short sleeved. The pant legs, however, were about four inches shy of his ankles. He sighed in resignation and tucked them into his combat boots before heading back out to the hallway.

The nurse led him into the ICU and toward Braden's room. At the door he had to put on an isolation gown, gloves and a mask. They even made him put coverings over his boots. When he entered, he realized it was in the exact same layout of the previous hospital room, just painted a different color. He relaxed when he saw Finn monitoring Braden's vitals. He sat and waited for him to finish up.

Cade knew what his brother had arranged for Braden wasn't hospital protocol. He'd made arrangements for Braden's previous doctor and nurse to manage his care when Finn wasn't available. Braden would have a bigger room than was usually provided for Cade to be able to stay with him in isolation.

He was humbled, thinking of everything Finn had done for them so Braden could remain infection free while Cade stayed with him. He knew he was incredibly fortunate to have his brother on his side. His reputation at all the local hospitals was beyond reproach. He was the best trauma surgeon in San Francisco, probably in all of California. He had surgical privileges at all the local hospitals and was asked to consult on cases with other surgeons often.

He glanced at Finn. "Can I touch him?"

Finn nodded. "Yes. You can talk to him, too. With this much trauma, we're keeping him sedated for several hours to keep him immobile."

Cade sat by the hospital bed and gently clasped Braden's hand in both of his as Finn continued. "We've given him an IV dose of his migraine meds. He may be disoriented when he wakes."

Cade nodded up at Finn. "Would you be willing to go out and update the family?"

"Yeah, of course. Zavier, some things I didn't mention because I wanted to be able to talk to you face to face. It looks like Braden was hit in the eye. His past injury to that same eye was broken open again. I had Dr. Brown stitch it back up instead of calling a plastic surgeon because the open wound was mostly in his brow line. He has defensive wounds along his right arm, and we re-casted his left wrist because it was covered with blood that had seeped into the internal bandaging. He has some bruising on his legs as well. It looks like he put up one hell of a fight before he was shot."

Proud of Braden, Cade nodded. "Yeah, Eric was bruised and bloody with a broken nose before I beat him half to death and shot him between the eyes."

Cade heard a shoe scuff behind him and turned to see Dr. Himmel and Sam looking at him, wide-eyed. Sam, looking a little pale, brought her hand up to her chest, and Dr. Himmel placed a comforting hand on her back. Cade shrugged. "Sorry you had to walk in on that, Sam, Dr. Himmel. If it makes you feel any better, he did all this to Braden before I had to kill him."

Sam moved further into the room to stand next to him. "I saw the news reports listing that Eric guy as wanted for Braden's kidnapping. I just wasn't expecting to hear that when I came in. It was just a shock to my system."

She looked up at Finn, a bit of hero worship in her gaze. "Dr. Himmel got me cleared to work with Braden during my shifts if you'd like to make use of my time, Dr. McCade."

Finn nodded. "I was hoping we'd be able to steal you away from your regular rotation. Thank you. We're treating this as we would anyone we admit into the Infection Control Department. If you need to study up on the requirements of patient care and treatment, I can get you the information."

Cade thought he saw a smile reach Sam's eyes. "I'm well versed in their protocols. I've been working with Dr. Himmel to be cross trained in case a position opens up over there."

Dr. Himmel assured, "She'll be exactly what you need and can help you with any other nurse you need to bring on. I'm also available. We'll provide you with our schedules, as we'll need to keep them the same, but that way you can work to cover the times we are not here with you or with other staff."

Finn nodded. "Thank you both for making yourselves available."

Dr. Himmel and Sam left them alone. They continued to talk about Braden's injuries and the care he'd be receiving then they both lapsed into silence. Finn laid down on the sofa under the windows, and Cade leaned back in the reclining chair beside Braden. They both dozed off for several hours, sleeping through Sam's visit to check Braden's vitals, though they both woke when Braden stirred.

"Wha…" Braden cleared his throat and tried again. "What's going on?"

Cade heaved a relieved sigh. "Baby, welcome back."

Braden looked at him, clearly confused, and Cade worried about what Braden remembered. "Z, what happened? Why do you have a mask on?"

Finn sat up on the sofa, staying out of the way. With Braden so recently out of surgery and far from being out of danger with his injuries, Cade was glad his brother wasn't leaving. He pulled his chair closer and brushed Braden's hair away from his face. "Baby, Eric kidnapped you again. You fought him, and he shot you in the abdomen. You've just come out of surgery. Your risk of infection is high, so everyone that comes in your room has to wear protective gear."

A look of terror took over Braden's pale face, and he tried to push himself up but winced in pain and whimpered. His breathing became labored, and he was about to try to talk, but Cade put his hand on his shoulder to keep him down. "Baby, stay calm for me. You're gonna be all right. You never have to worry about him again. Never, do you understand me?"

Tears came to Braden's eyes, and he shook his head and whispered brokenly, "So, he was caught? He'll eventually get out of prison. It'll never be over. I'll never truly be rid of him, will I?"

"Yes, you will. It's over, Bray. Truly over. He's dead, baby. I killed him myself when he tried to shoot you a second time. You never have to worry about him again."

Tears fell down Braden's cheeks, and he raised his hands to cover his face. Cade stood above him, clasped his hands in his, and drew them away. He leaned over to press masked kisses to his forehead, cheeks, and then gently over his lips. Braden choked back a sob. "It's over? It's really over?" Braden watched Cade for confirmation. When he nodded, Braden broke down. "Oh god! Oh my god, I'm so glad. I'm... Oh Jesus, Z. I'm happy he's dead. What does that make me? What kind of person does that make me?"

"Baby, it makes you human. I'm glad he's dead, too. I'm glad we won't have to put you through a trial. I'm glad we won't have to look over our shoulders wondering if Eric has somehow found a way to get to you. I'm glad we can finally start our new life together without fear. We're human, Braden, and you've been through hell because of him. It's completely normal to feel relieved that it's finally over."

Braden nodded, but closed his eyes for several minutes. Cade knew he needed that time to gather himself together, so he sat and simply held Braden's hand. Braden's eyes popped open, and he looked at Cade in concern. "Shit, Z, he hit you with his car! Are you all right?"

"Got a bit of a concussion, but yes, I'm fine. All we need to worry about is you, Bray."

"How bad is it?"

At that, Finn stood and walked back to Braden. He placed his gloved hand on Braden's shoulder. "Braden, you were shot in the abdomen and the bullet perforated your small intestines. There was internal bleeding and lot of damage to the bowel that needed repairing. You've had a few units of blood transfused. We are giving you antibiotics to help fight infection, meds for the pain, and we are monitoring your glucose levels closely. We've also started you on anti-migraine medication."

Braden's eyes were wide with shock, and he looked to Cade for reassurance. "Bray, let him finish and then you can ask all the questions you want."

Braden gripped Cade's hand tighter and nodded for Finn to continue. "Because of the bullet, waste was released into your abdominal cavity. This makes your risk of infection extremely high. That, coupled with your diabetes, means it's a waiting game to see how your body deals with all the trauma. On top of all that, we have to monitor you for postoperative fever, hemorrhaging, and respiratory complications."

Finn pulled a cord, wrapped it around the side bars of the bed, and placed the handle with a button on top of Braden's lap. "Anytime there's abdominal surgery, air gets trapped inside of your abdominal cavity and causes pain, so you'll have that to contend with in addition to the pain from the surgery. You're on a drip that's monitored by an IV pump for continuous pain meds, but you've also got a patient-controlled anesthetic for breakthrough pain. You can hit that button, and if you're allowed a dose of pain meds at that time, it will be automatically administered through your IV. Any questions so far?"

"Did you perform my surgery?"

Finn patted Braden on the shoulder. "Zavier wouldn't have it any other way. I hope that doesn't make you uncomfortable."

Braden reached up and caught Finn's hand with his and squeezed. "Thank you for saving my life."

Finn glanced at Cade then smiled down at Braden. "There was no other option, but you're welcome. You look exhausted. With the pain meds, you'll spend a lot of time resting and healing. Try to get some sleep. We'll be monitoring you closely through the night. We'll be in and out every hour and will also help you change your position. We'll be bringing a bed in here for Zavier tonight. We'll need to be waking him every few hours as well because of the concussion. Sam is on your rotation, so she'll come in and check on you. I'm going to grab a quick bite to eat and bring something back for Zavier. Think you can get some sleep?"

"Yeah, I'm having a tough time keeping my eyes open."

Braden glanced at Cade and held out his hand as Finn left the room. When Cade took his hand in his larger one, he brought it to his lips and kissed it. "Rest and heal, Bray. That's the only thing you need to worry about."

Braden's eyes drooped, and even though he knew he didn't have to ask, he couldn't help himself. "You'll stay?"

Cade stood up to kiss Braden's temple. "Baby, I'm not leaving until you're ready to come home with me."

Braden nodded then his eyes closed, and he was asleep. Cade pulled out Cooper's phone and saw a text from him, via Sawyer's phone, saying that he'd be bringing in some clothing and toiletries for him. Cade asked him to work with Maya to have him bring anything Braden would need or want while he was here for the next week. That done, he picked up the big lounger, brought it as close to Braden's bed as he could, and proceeded to lean back, clasp Braden's hand in his, and fall asleep alongside his partner.

Chapter 15

CADE

The three days following Braden's surgery were, thankfully, uneventful. Detective Miller had come on the second day to take their statements. As the cops and the paramedics were witnesses to the shooting, there wouldn't be any issues with closing the case as a justifiable homicide. Braden had no complications those first few days, and Finn let them know that he was cautiously optimistic.

Braden had a procession of visitors. Cade could see some of the joy that had been slowly seeping out of Braden—because of Eric's terrorization—slipping back in. His smiles were more natural and reached his eyes. He was quick to laugh and even quicker to groan when laughing caused pain. Nana was holding down the fort at the café again. Braden was tired easily, and his visitors never stayed long.

On the fourth day, Braden began to run a fever. He was experiencing more abdominal pain as well as losing his appetite. Finn did an ultrasound but didn't find anything. He ordered a CT scan and before the scan, injected a contrast medium into Braden's IV. Cade followed him up to the floor with the scanner and stayed outside of the room while it was done. The CT scan revealed one of the things Finn had been worried about: an intra-abdominal abscess within the intestines.

When they got Braden back to his room, Finn sat down on the edge of

Braden's bed. "We have two options. I can go in and drain the abscess by needle—we'd use a sedative and local anesthetic—or I could go in surgically to drain it."

Cade spoke up immediately. "Why would we choose the more invasive method? Which one would you recommend?"

"We'd choose the more invasive method because the worry is that draining the abscess won't fix the root cause. My guess is that there's something wrong with one of the sutures in the intestine, but I don't know that for sure. It's a very risky surgery, and we have no idea what we'll find in there. There's no guarantee we can find and fix everything but leaving things as they are isn't an option. It's completely up to you, and I understand if you don't want me to open you back up again."

Braden looked at Cade and then back at Finn. "But you'd recommend the surgery if it was you?"

Finn smiled gently. "Frankly, Braden, I'm recommending the surgery because it's you. I don't want to do the needle aspiration then have you come down with another issue when we could go in there, do some exploring, and find out what's truly causing the abscess and fix it. I don't want to have to do this, but I'm afraid that simply draining it and not fixing the overall problem will just be a stop gap and, in the end, keep you here longer."

Braden worriedly bit his lip and looked at Cade. "Z, what do you think?"

"Baby, ultimately, it's up to you."

Panicked, Braden shook his head. "I can't hear that right now. I can't make this decision by myself. Please, don't put that on me."

"Braden, look at me. Is this a decision you want me to make for you?"

Braden nodded. "Yes. I'm sorry. I know it's weak, but I just…."

"It's not weak. You're feeling overwhelmed, and if this is what you need, it's what I'll provide. The decision is an easy one for me. When Finn recommends something medically, I listen."

Braden took a deep breath, nodded, and squeezed Cade's hand, thanking him without words. He looked at Finn. "Okay, I guess you go back in."

Finn placed his hand on Braden's leg. "All right. We'll have you sign the consent forms then get you prepped and ready. I don't want to wait any longer. We'll give you a dose of antibiotics pre- and post-operation. After surgery, we'll resume all your medications, including your anti-migraine meds. Your glucose levels are within normal range, but we'll continue to closely monitor them. Any questions?"

"You'll be performing the surgery, right?"

Finn smiled. "I don't think Zavier would have it any other way."

Cade didn't smile at that. "I don't trust anyone else with his life, Finn, it's as simple as that."

Finn glanced at his brother. "I'll do everything in my power to ensure that we get to the bottom of this infection and find the abscess."

Braden placed a calming hand on Cade's and looked at Finn. "He knows that, Finn. We both do. I'm sure everything will be fine. Let's get it over with."

Braden called Nana and Maya and told them what was happening. They told him they'd be shutting down the café and heading over right away. Just before they prepped him, Gideon and Cooper came to visit. They entered the room as Finn was coming in to check on Braden one last time before scrubbing in for the surgery. He nodded at the men and suggested to Cade that he not watch the surgery alone, so both men accompanied him to the operating theater.

Cooper and Gideon sat back on the bench, but Cade stood and kept watch through the windows and on the monitor. The volume was up, and Cade could hear Finn speaking to the anesthesiologist and the nurses that were in there with him.

Cade looked down through the windows and spoke to no one in particular. "I don't know that his body can take much more. I failed him again, and he might die today because of it."

He heard booted feet on the floor and then his brothers, one of blood and one of allegiance, were at his back. He felt Gideon's hand land solidly on the back of his neck and Cooper's on his shoulder. He leaned into them, taking some of their strength. Gideon, not much on talking, let alone about feelings, spoke up. "From what I've been told, Braden lost it and ran like a bat out of hell away from you. You gave chase, shoved him out of the way of an oncoming car, and were hit in the process. No one could have known it was his car."

"I shouldn't have talked to him about Eric while we were running. I should have waited until we were at home, safe."

"Would he have waited until you were at home?"

"He didn't want to wait, no."

"So, you asked him to wait?"

Cade sighed. "Yeah. I should have tried harder."

Cooper piped in. "Cade, you can make your boy do a lot of things, but waiting on the truth from you about Eric? No way. He would have pushed, and he wouldn't have stopped until you told him everything. Tell me that's not true."

"He did push, and I caved. I should have pushed back harder."

Cooper shook his head at that. "That wouldn't have worked. That's not how your relationship works, Cade, even I know that. You tell each other the truth, all of it, even when it's not good."

"It doesn't fucking matter now. We're here, and any way I look at it, that's on me."

"And we're saying that's bullshit, Cade, and I bet he told you as much."

"I haven't said anything to him about it. I'm not going to say anything that will stress him out. He doesn't need that."

Cooper continued, on a roll now. "You haven't said anything to him about it because he wouldn't agree with you, and he'd be pissed as hell that you're harboring this much guilt and haven't told him. I do not envy you that conversation. You saved him, Cade. That's the truth and that's what he knows."

"Fuck that. I had to save him because I put him in that situation in the first place!"

"So, you're God now? You're omnipotent? You should have been able to tell the future and known that he'd react like that, or that Eric was in the car that hit you? None of this is anyone's fault but Eric's! Get that through your thick fucking skull."

Cade shook off their hands and was about to respond to Cooper when Finn's voice broke into their heated silence. "Zavier, I've found the abscess.

I'm working to drain it now, but it's in a dangerous spot. This is directly over the spot where he had internal bleeding during the first surgery, so I need to check the entire area for any other signs of infection, in addition to the abscess."

Cade waited and watched Finn's movements as he inserted a needle and drained the abscess. A nurse stepped forward and took the needle from him when he was finished, and Cade watched as he gently moved aside what he assumed was some of Braden's small intestine. He froze when he heard Finn curse under his breath. Gideon and Cooper must have heard it as well, because suddenly, they were beside him, watching the monitor, all of them unsure what they were seeing. Cade's insides froze as he looked at the area Finn was working on and saw blood seeping into the abdominal cavity.

Finn started barking orders. The nurses began moving around, quickly setting things up. One handed Finn a tube that they saw was providing suction. Gauze was being used, and Finn was muttering under his breath. As much as Cade wanted to interrupt and ask what was going on, he didn't want to break his brother's focus.

Finn, who continued to work, finally spoke, "Zavier, he's bleeding internally again, it appears to be coming from the ileocolic artery, which feeds into the intestines. It looks like it has been slowly seeping and feeding into a second abscess, just beginning to form. I have to find the source and patch it up, but it's a mess in here. Things may get worse before they get better. Are Cooper and Gideon there with you?"

Cade pushed the speaker button, held it down, and took a deep, shaky breath. "Yes. Find it and fix it. Whatever it takes, Finn."

Finn continued working, his movements quick and precise. "Whatever it takes. I won't be talking with you while I'm doing it. Keep your shit together up there or have them do it for you. We're shutting the sound off."

"No, I need to..."

"You don't. I'll let you stay up there, but only if you keep yourself under control, Zavier. Are we clear?"

Cade didn't like it, but he wasn't about to lose his chance at being as close as possible to Braden while the worst was happening. Gideon's hand landed heavily on his shoulder. "We're clear."

The sound was clicked off, but the video remained on. He could tell that Finn was barking orders as the nurses started moving again, one of them using the phone. Finn continued to work on Braden the whole time, his concentration never breaking, even while speaking to those in the room with him.

A man quickly entered the room, hands raised after scrubbing in. Nurses approached and put surgical gloves on him immediately. He glanced up at the theater, and Cade saw that it was Dr. Brown from the first surgery. He nodded to Cade and walked to Braden's other side. He had a conversation with Finn, nodded, then his hands were side by side with Finn's, inside of Braden.

Cade had no fucking clue what they were doing. Suddenly, a scalpel was placed into Finn's hand and Braden's intestines were being partially pulled out of his abdominal cavity, as they'd been the last time. Cade tensed, ran his hands over his head and gripped the back of his neck to keep himself steady. He could see a lot of blood and he knew that something awful was coming. His gut twisted, and he turned to Cooper. "Did Sawyer send you both to me?"

He could tell that was what happened by Cooper's reaction to the question. His jaw clenched. "Was it a scene, a flash, or a fucking niggling sense?"

Cooper's body tensed, but he didn't answer. Cade was about to ask again when he saw a flurry of activity down below in the OR that grabbed his attention. Everyone had jerked their gaze toward the electronic monitors Braden was hooked up to which prompted Cade to do the same. He knew from past experience that the monitors connected to Braden were now beeping at those in the OR in warning. Braden's heart was slowing down and, from what Cade could tell, there was entirely too much blood filling up the empty space in his abdomen.

Cade turned partially away from the monitors and snarled at Cooper. "Tell me!"

"It was a flash. He saw this happening then he saw you losing your shit. We don't know what it means, but you've got the best surgeon you could possibly have. We have to trust him, Cade."

Cade turned back to face the windows and the monitor and watched as Braden's heart slowed even more. Finn and Dr. Brown worked feverishly to stem the flow of blood. It wasn't working. Cade watched with a growing sense of panic, as Braden's heart slowed and then, finally, flatlined. He took a step back, unable to assimilate what he'd seen into his reality.

Something in him snapped, just snapped, and he knew he needed to get down there. He needed to get down there with Braden. If Braden was truly dying, or dead, he wasn't going to do it without him being there. He rushed the door and was stopped mid-stride when Cooper grabbed him and did his best to hold him there.

An anger like he'd never felt before clawed its way up his spine, and he lashed out. He sent Cooper sprawling to the floor, staring up at him in disbelief. He ignored him and took another step toward the door but was caught up again in a chokehold from behind. He was turned in the direction of the monitor, and he saw a flash of movement, but all he knew was that he needed to be with Braden. He needed to get down there. A couple moves later and he was out of Gideon's hold as well. They both came at him then, full force, and though he tried with everything he had, he couldn't fight them both. They held him immobile, not allowing him to get to his partner.

He shouted and struggled like he'd never struggled before. He got free of them both and made for the door again, and again he was caught in their chain-like grip. He thrashed and thrashed and, unbeknownst to him, bellowed Braden's name while he continued to struggle to get to him. He saw movement again in the monitor, but this time, it was just the two sets of hands being pulled away from Braden's abdominal cavity. No more movement came after that, and he knew. He knew he'd lost the love of his life, and he hadn't been there with him. He'd failed him, again, in his last moments. He'd failed Braden.

His legs gave out, and the arms that had previously been holding him back, now held him up. His body went rigid, and he roared in his grief, yelling Braden's name, struggling in their firm grip. Wrenching free, he fell to his knees, hands listless at his sides. He had no strength left and would have fallen on his face if it wasn't for Gideon and Cooper surrounding him in his grief, giving him their strength.

His mind had disassociated itself from reality, flashing on scenes with him and Braden: *the first time they'd met, the night when he'd carried him to his bed and stayed there with him, taking care of him; their all day date that ended in the best kiss he'd ever had; sleeping with Braden in his arms; watching Braden doing what he loved most, baking in his kitchen; jogging with him that first time and then later with the shelter dogs; the way Braden touched him; the gentle way Braden clasped his hand in his own, comparing the differences in size; Braden waking up from the coma; Braden smiling and laughing with Maya; Braden dancing with Zoe; Braden hugging Nana; Braden laughing and smiling; the look on Braden's face while they made love and his blissful expression when he came…*

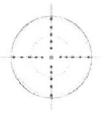

Cooper

Cooper glanced toward Gideon in a panic; nothing they were doing was snapping Cade out of his scary stupor. He saw blood on Gideon's shirt and glanced down at his own, finding blood there as well. His gaze snapped to Cade's side where his gunshot wound was. He lifted Cade's shirt and saw that the dressing was saturated, the tape barely holding it on, the skin underneath torn apart, and the stitches no longer holding the wound together.

He looked toward the windows and was trying to figure out how he could pull Cade out of his own head. He walked to the window and pushed the button on the speaker. "Finn, turn on the fucking sound, man. He doesn't know. He lost it when Braden flatlined, and he doesn't know. Turn on the speakers, so he can hear it."

Cooper saw Finn nod to one of the nurses as he continued to stitch Braden back together. The sound came back on, and if Cooper had to guess, it had been turned up full blast. The sound Cooper knew Cade needed to hear filled the room. Cooper went back to Cade, knelt in front of him and brought his head up with both of his hands. He hated the devastated, vacant look in his eyes. Cade wasn't tracking, so he began to repeat himself over and over, until Cade truly heard him. "Cade, listen to that. Can you hear that? Cade, listen. Can you hear it?"

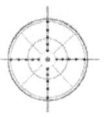

Cade

When the blood in his ears started to diminish and thoughts of Braden slowed, Cade started to calm. As much as he didn't want to come back to reality, he knew he had to. He pushed for it, reached for it with his mind, and finally, he heard Cooper's voice, though it was muffled.

He closed his eyes, concentrating on Cooper's voice. "Cade, can you hear that?

He opened his eyes and focused on Cooper. His image slowly changed from blurry to clear. "That's it. Focus on me. Listen, Cade. What do you hear? What do you hear, Cade?"

Cade listened and at first he didn't hear anything. He looked at Cooper in confusion and Cooper smiled. "Listen."

Cade did as he was told. He closed his eyes, and he listened, pushing back his own thoughts. Ignoring everything else in the room, he listened. That's when he heard it, a solid, repeating, rhythmic beep that could only mean one thing. He shook his head in denial and looked at Cooper. Cooper grinned, nodding. "It's what you think it is. It's exactly what you think it is."

Tears coursed silently down Cade's face and his hands, resting on his thighs, shook. He fisted his hands several times, shook them out then bent over, hands on the floor and let the maelstrom of emotion run through him. He had no control over his body any longer. His arms weakened, and Cooper and Gideon, again, kept him from falling on his face. His whole body shuddered, and he had to just ride it out, letting the tremors pass through him before he could even begin to gather control of himself.

The only thing that kept him grounded was that fucking heartbeat. His whole being was centered around that sound. Other things tried to filter in,

Cooper murmuring to him, Gideon's firm grip on his neck, Finn talking to the other hospital staff in the OR below, but none of it broke through except that steady and strong heartbeat.

He took several deep breaths and sat back on his knees until his control returned, and he made to stand up, with the help of his brothers. He walked on shaky legs over to the window and looked down at Finn still working diligently at sewing Braden back together. A nurse approached and wiped his brow. Cade glanced at the screen to get a closer look and realized that Finn was putting the final few stitches into Braden.

He finally stepped back, hands raised, which is when Cade saw the defibrillator sitting on its stand, right next to Braden. His heart skipped a beat when he realized what had been done to bring Braden back to him. A nurse brought a rolling chair to Finn and pressed him down into it as the others in the room went about finishing with cleaning up after the surgery and putting fresh dressings over Braden's wounds.

It wasn't until that moment that Cade's heart beat a little faster, realizing how much stress he'd put his brother under, asking him to be responsible for Braden's life. He'd have to thank him later, but he'd never be able to apologize for doing the asking, just for the toll it took on him. No one else would have been able to bring him back, no one else was as capable, or had as much incentive or love invested. Cade knew Braden was alive because of Finn. He'd forever be grateful.

He saw his brother lean over, placing his elbows on his knees and taking some deep breaths. His head hung low and he brought a hand up and rubbed his head, nearly dislodging the surgical cap, a true sign he was exhausted. He turned and looked behind him as if he knew Cade was watching and spoke through his facemask. "We got everything, but we'll need to keep a very close eye on him. The abscess is drained, and we found the source of another infection. We stopped the bleed, which had started before we even cut him open, so it's a good thing we went in when we did, or it would have been too late. Hell, it almost was."

Finn shook his head, ripped off the mask, and let it fall between his feet. He rubbed his hands over his face, his exhaustion evident now in every move he made. "They'll be giving him antibiotics in a moment, and that should do the trick, but it will be a long recovery. Two abdominal surgeries in four days is going to slow him down considerably. If he makes it through the next seventy-two hours without any issues, he should hopefully be all right, Zavier."

Cade nodded at Finn, unable to speak or risk losing control again. The nurses began to move Braden which grabbed Finn's attention, and he stood. Another nurse turned off the sound, and Finn looked up and gave him the signal to move out. He left the room with Cooper and Gideon on his heels, walking down the stairs at a fast clip to meet them in the hallway.

He approached Braden's bed and placed a gentle hand on his ankle. He kept moving toward Finn, who was walking behind Braden's bed. He was signing off on something on an iPad. When he handed it back to a nurse, he looked up. Cade took Finn by surprise when he slammed into him, hugging him tightly. Finn's "oomph" made him smile. Finn returned the hug, whispering brokenly, "I thought I'd lost him. Oh fuck, Zavier, I've never been so scared in my life. I knew I couldn't give up. I knew you'd never recover if I did."

Cade's body shuddered, emotion swamping him. "I thought he was dead. I thought he was gone, Finn. I saw him flatline then I saw you and Dr. Brown pull your hands out of him, and I thought you were calling time of death. I lost it. I saw nothing after that. I only got my shit together when Cooper finally got me to listen and I heard his heartbeat."

He gripped Finn tighter and got a grunt for his efforts which made him smile. "God, Finn, I'll forever be grateful. Thank you. Thank you so much. I hate that I had to put it on you, I'm sorry for the toll it took, but you're the only one who could have saved him. I'll never be able to repay you for his life, never."

They finally pulled apart, Cade's hands resting on Finn's shoulders. Finn shook his head. "There's nothing to repay. Do you think I would ever say no to helping in such a way? I never could have lived with myself if someone else had done the work and he was lost to us. There was no other option. Plus, I've always wanted to be the favorite brother."

Cade laughed, pulled him in once more, and slapped him on the back. "Oh, you've earned that title, brother, that's for sure."

Finn pulled away and wiped a hand down the front of his scrub shirt in confusion, then looked at Cade's and yanked his shirt up. "What the hell happened up there?"

Cade looked down with wide eyes then rubbed a hand over his head. "Uh, after he flatlined, I don't remember much until Cooper brought me out of my head. You'd have to ask them."

Finn shook his head. "So, Sawyer was right?"

Cade nodded. "Never been wrong, as long as I've known him."

"Christ, Zavier, let me get you sewn back together."

"You can do that once Braden comes out of anesthesia. I'm not going to have him wake up without being there. We'll have Maya and Nana come in and you can sew me back up. Until then, put another dressing on it, and I'll change my shirt. I don't want Braden waking up and seeing me like this. He doesn't need to be worried and stressed about anything."

Finn rubbed his hands over his face, letting his frustration show, and then nodded. "Yeah, I don't blame you, but not a minute longer. Shit, Zavier, you were four days out. You had to have raised holy hell in there to tear that wound open. Come back into the OR with me quick, so that I can dress it properly."

They went back to the OR, and Finn got a lot of gauze and a big surgical dressing to cover Cade's freshly opened wound. "You ripped it open after it had almost healed. It's gonna leave a pretty thick scar, but I'll do my best to minimize the damage."

Cade shrugged it off, and they both turned toward Braden's room, where the nurses had gotten him situated. Finn told Cade he'd talk to Maya and Nana and walked toward the waiting room.

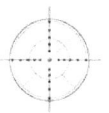

Finn

Finn walked in and saw that Cooper and Gideon were there. Cooper had his head in his hands, elbows on his knees, and Maya was leaning into him, rubbing his back. Gideon, his usual intense and solemn countenance torn away in the wake of what had happened up in that theater, sat with Nana, his hand on her back, speaking to her quietly.

He quickly discussed the surgery and what to expect going forward. He wanted to make sure Braden woke up and was feeling all right before he brought any of them back. They were both relieved and thanked him profusely. Finn caught Gideon's eye and they both went to the hallway. "What the fuck happened in there, Gideon? I've got Zavier's blood on my shirt, and he's still seeping."

Gideon, stoic demeanor back in place, shook his head. "He went to hell and back in the space of a couple minutes. I've never seen that kind of grief manifest itself so viscerally. I don't think we can even fathom the kind of love they have. Hell, I can only hope that I find someone to love even half as much as he loves Braden."

Finn stared, shocked at his brother's admission, before he realized he was staring at Gideon's retreating back. He'd dropped that bomb then immediately turned and walked away, his emotions still too close to the surface for his own comfort, Finn guessed. He shook his head, still in shock, and made a mental note to ask Cooper more about what happened later. He veered off in the direction of the locker room and changed into a fresh scrub shirt and brought another back to Braden's room for Cade. They sat on either side of Braden's bed and waited another thirty minutes for him to wake up.

When he did, he looked around the room in confusion and then settled his eyes on Cade, as if drawn there by some internal compass. They just looked at each other for several long moments. Finn watched as a tear slide down his brother's cheek and his voice was shaky when he spoke. "We almost lost you this time, Bray. No more infections, no more internal bleeding, you've got to get better now. We clear?"

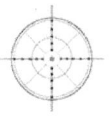

Cade

Braden's bewildered expression, as if he was caught so completely off guard by his tears, nearly made Cade smile. Nearly. He let out a relieved breath when Braden finally nodded and whispered, "We're clear." Braden reached his hand out to him. "What happened?"

Cade gripped his hand. "You died on that table today, baby. I lost my shit completely until I realized that Finn brought you back to me."

Braden paled and looked like he'd be sick. Cade watched as he got control of himself and gazed at Finn. "I don't even know what to say, Finn. Thank you for saving my life. Again."

Finn squeezed Braden's shoulder and stood. "I'd do it again in a heartbeat. I'm gonna go get Nana and Maya so they can spend a few minutes with you before you pass out from exhaustion."

Cade sat gently on the bed beside Braden being sure not to hurt him. He leaned forward and clasped his boy's face in both of his hands and kissed him until they were both breathing heavily. Cade pulled away, told Braden how much he loved him, and leaned his forehead against Braden's. That's how Nana and Maya saw them when they entered the room. Maya lightened the mood. "Aww, you guys are so cute!"

Cade smirked and kissed Braden on the forehead as he pulled away. Finn stood in the doorway. "Zavier come with me. We'll grab some coffee and give them a few moments alone."

Braden smiled at Cade and nodded at Cade's questioning gaze, letting him know he was all right alone with Nana and Maya. He told Braden he'd be back in a few minutes and exited the door behind Finn. "Thanks for that. I didn't want to have to explain why you needed to pull me out of the room. Let's get me stitched back up, so that I can get back to him."

He was gone for thirty minutes and realized Finn hadn't been kidding when he'd said he'd have quite a scar left after all was said and done. The wound looked like raw hamburger after being ripped apart. Cade shrugged it off again when Finn looked at him with apprehension. "Haven't had a new tattoo in a long time."

Finn shook his head. "Your boy is probably about to fall asleep until tomorrow morning. We better get back in there."

When they returned, they found Nana on one side of Braden, Maya on the other. They both had one of Braden's hands in theirs and were sitting quietly. Braden was half asleep already but tried to wake a bit when Cade came back into the room. As a testament to the fact that Braden had told them what happened during the surgery, the ladies stood when the men came in and both women beelined it to Finn, giving him hugs and thanking him for saving Braden. They promised they'd be back to visit the next day and left.

Braden lifted his hand and Cade walked toward him, clasped it in both of his, and sat in one of the vacated chairs. Braden's eyes drooped, and Cade caressed his hand. "Sleep, baby. I won't leave your side. I love you."

Braden sighed. "Love you, too."

Chapter 16

BRADEN

Twelve days after being admitted, Braden was home from the hospital, sans cast, and pushing himself hard to recover in record time. Several days after the second surgery, Cade had finally admitted his feelings of guilt at allowing Braden to be taken again.

Braden had known that something was going on because Cade was having trouble sleeping. As they were sharing his hospital bed most of the time, it was impossible for Cade to keep it a secret. He would sometimes jerk awake in the night, and occasionally, he'd call out Braden's name.

After a particularly brutal nightmare, Braden had looked Cade in the eyes and demanded to know what was going on. Cade hadn't known what to expect from Braden when he told him what he was feeling, but he hadn't expected ridiculously frustrating logic.

Braden had pointed out that if Cade's reasoning was sound, Braden was to blame for being beaten and going into a coma the first time he went with Eric. Braden also pointed out that it was his fault for pushing Cade to talk about it out in public, his fault that he ran off without Cade's protection, and his fault that he ran into the street and almost got hit by Eric's car. No matter Cade's rebuttal, Braden had an equally logical response. The conversation didn't make him feel like he wasn't guilty, but it did go a long way toward making him realize that no one except for Eric was fully responsible for everything that happened. He couldn't fault Braden's logic, much as it pained him.

Their conversation did help some with Cade's nightmares, but Braden insisted they talk to Gabe. They even went so far as to call and have him come to the hospital to have a joint therapy session before Braden was released. The session helped both Cade and Braden, and Gabe asked them to continue their weekly appointments once Braden was released.

Braden had gotten closer with Rowan and Siobhan during his recovery at the hospital. He felt a strong kinship with them and knew the feeling was mutual. He was also happy he got to know Cooper, Sawyer, and Jackson more during his stay. They'd visited daily and had even started joking with him and treating him like one of their own. Finn was a regular because he was still managing his care, but he would often stop by while the other guys were there and challenge them to a game of poker. He'd win every single time, and Braden would do his best to keep from laughing at Jackson's incredulous expressions and Cade's shouts to stop counting cards.

Everyone else had been busy while they'd been stuck in the hospital. Cooper had moved over to Vaughn's place with Jackson and Sawyer. Maya had insisted that Nana come stay with her while she helped cover the baking at the café, so Cade and Braden had some privacy.

Braden couldn't thank Nana enough, and when he was talking with Cade about thanking her properly, he realized he needed to thank everyone in their circle for helping him. They both agreed that in several months, when everything settled down, they'd be sending Nana on an all-expense paid cruise to the Bahamas. He'd also told Cade he wanted to have their friends and family over to thank them for everything they'd done to help him with the stalker situation.

Braden didn't want to wait, so they were doing it on Friday, a mere three days after he was released from the hospital. Cade had pushed back and asked him to delay, but Braden turned imploring eyes up to him and he caved. He didn't want Braden to overtax himself or to push too hard. That was precisely why Cade had made Braden promise not to bake a thing and to let him take care of the details. He'd asked Braden to treat the party like he'd treated their date: to just be there and enjoy it.

At first, Braden hadn't wanted to cooperate. Cade had looked at him sternly and his voice had deepened when he admonished Braden. "Don't fight me on this. You just got out of the hospital. I'm making this decision for you, and you're not going to stress about it."

That voice and those firm words had eased something in him immediately, and he'd acquiesced, knowing that Cade would worry about him overdoing it if he didn't heed Cade's demand.

Cade's whole family was there, along with Cooper, Jackson, Sawyer, and Vaughn. Maya and Nana were obviously there, and Zoe and Layla had also been invited, as well as Gabe, who, even though he was Braden's psychologist, had become a friend as well. The place was packed, and Cade had moved furniture around and made Braden's great room area into the perfect gathering spot.

Once everyone had arrived and had the chance to get some appetizers and a drink, Braden dinged a spoon against his glass. "I'd like to say a few things, but bear with me, as I haven't planned anything specific. So many of you here tonight are new to my life, but I feel as if I've known some of you for years. As much as this experience with Eric has been an awful one, I don't think I'd change the fact that it brought many of you into my life. I feel so fortunate. I don't know how it happened. Whether it was the universe aligning the stars just right, or good karma coming my way, but something out there brought me my very own warrior in Z, to fight for me, protect me, and love me.

"He also did something remarkable. He brought me you, a veritable army standing for me, my own personal band of warriors, protecting me. And whether you've been physically protecting me, emotionally protecting me, or both, the result is the same. I'm here today because of all of you. I don't know if I'm deserving of such an army, but I do know that I am so humbled by your support, generosity, and kindness. I have a long road of recovery ahead of me; physically, emotionally, and psychologically. But I know that with my own band of warriors here to fight with me, I'm not alone in this. So, I'm raising my glass in a toast to all of you for your unfailing support and love. I'm truly blessed to have you all in my life."

Several people called out, "Hear, hear!" and everyone raised their glasses in salute. Cade stepped behind Braden, wrapped his strong arms loosely around Braden's waist, and whispered, "You're deserving, Braden.

I don't think I know anyone who is more deserving than you are. I love you, baby."

Braden turned in his arms. "I love you too, Z."

They kissed, holding each other then broke apart and made their rounds to ensure that everyone was enjoying themselves and getting everything they needed. Braden was hugged many times over. He spent time talking to everyone who had come and enjoyed chatting with his guests and watching them pair up with new acquaintances and mingle together.

After quite a lot of circulating, he made his way over to Aiden, Cade's youngest brother who was on leave from his SEAL team for the next week. He'd come to visit Braden in the hospital a couple times, and Braden had liked him immediately. Of all the McCade siblings, he was closest in age to Aiden. Cade's youngest brother was fun-loving and gregarious.

Aiden turned to face him as he approached. With a huge smile on his face, he pulled Braden into a huge but gentle hug. Braden, reveling in the enthusiasm of it, realized something that made him laugh. Aiden pulled back and looked down at Braden. "What's so funny?"

Braden smiled and shook his head, "Nothing, just amusing myself."

"Nope, not the right answer. Spill it."

Braden blushed. "I love your family, and I love their hugs, but each of you hugs completely differently and it makes me laugh."

Aiden looked confused. "How can we all hug differently?"

"Well, let's see. You hug with a lot of exuberance, which I think is a lot like you are in life, enthusiastic. Your mom hugs with so much love and comfort wrapped up in her embrace that you just want to keep hugging her. Your sister, well, your sister hugs eagerly, but quickly, because she needs to keep talking to you and doesn't want the hug to get in the way of the discussion. Your dad's hugs are automatic, almost perfunctory, but that sounds too cold, which he isn't. I think his hugs are just a part of who he is. He hugs because that's what family does and that's that. And Gideon, hmm, Gideon hugs with restraint. I think Gideon holds a lot back, emotionally and physically, so I always feel like he's keeping himself apart in some way. Finn, now Finn hugs me gingerly, most likely because he's my doctor and doesn't want to hurt me, but also because I think he believes that I'm more fragile than I really am. Does that answer your question?"

Aiden looked dumbfounded and then recovered himself. "And Cade?"

Arms wrapped around his chest from behind and Braden knew without even looking that they were Cade's. Then a low rumble sounded in his ear. "Yeah, what about my hugs?"

Braden avoided the question, asking instead, "You call him Cade? I thought his family all called him Zavier."

"I used to call him Zavier until I joined the SEALS. Turns out he's pretty well-known within military Spec Ops, and his nickname is Cade within their ranks, so I just started calling him what he usually asks people to call him."

Braden nodded and looked behind him, up into Cade's eyes, but Aiden wasn't finished. "So, you never answered me."

Braden turned and looked up at Aiden. "Hmm?"

"What about Cade's hugs?"

Braden blushed and felt Cade's arms tighten around him. "Well, Z's my own personal warrior, so his hugs are full of protection and strength, but what it really comes down to is Z's hugs are like coming home."

Aiden smiled wide and slugged Cade in the arm. "How the hell did you get so lucky to find someone that loves you that much?"

"I don't know, but if I ever figure it out, I'll let you know."

Aiden turned when someone tapped him on the shoulder and Cade whispered in Braden's ear. "You're getting tired of standing, I can see it in the way you're holding yourself. I need you to come sit with me for a bit."

Braden shook his head. "I'm fine. Really."

Cade growled. "You've been on your feet for over an hour and a half, chatting with everyone who's here. You come sit with me, or I tell everyone how tired you are and ask them to leave."

Braden smacked one of Cade's forearms that was holding him against his chest. "You're so bossy. You wouldn't dare."

Cade slowly turned him so that they were facing each other. "Braden, your recovery is the only thing that matters to me right now. Don't push me."

He sighed and relented. "Okay, fine. I'll come sit for a few minutes."

"You'll sit for thirty minutes at least, or I'll have Finn come check on you."

Braden scowled. "There's no need for that. He's much too careful of me."

"He's your doctor and my brother. He's as careful as I need him to be."

"Okay, don't get all growly. I'll come sit."

"You love it when I'm growly."

Braden chuckled. "I really do."

He held Cade's hand and they walked toward the sofa where Vaughn was sitting, chatting with Cooper, who was sitting in the chair opposite. Cade sat a bit away from Vaughn on the couch and pulled Braden down next to him, without an inch to spare. He tucked Braden into the crook of his shoulder and began to talk to Vaughn and Cooper. Braden began to feel the pain in his abdomen increase and knew his pain meds were wearing off, and he'd need to go get another dose soon. Rowan broke into his musings when she sat down on the coffee table in front of him and began to chat as if they'd been in the middle of a conversation, which he loved.

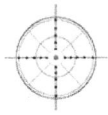

Cade

Cade tucked his left hand under Braden's hip on the couch and gently pulled him closer when he felt him move away while chatting with Rowan. Braden absentmindedly grabbed his hand from under his hip and pulled it around his chest, leaning back into him. A burst of warmth filled Cade's chest when he realized Braden welcomed his possessive grasp.

He continued to chat with Vaughn and Cooper while Braden chatted with Ro, all the while keeping his arm firmly around Braden's chest. He enjoyed the fact that Braden's hand rested on his thigh, stroking it in a soothing, reassuring manner as if he knew Cade was feeling extremely protective. It was as if Braden wanted to send the message that he was all right and understood Cade's over-the-top, territorial behavior.

After they'd chatted for some time about non-business related things,

Cade decided the timing was finally right. "So, you're leasing your building, right? Or do you own it?"

Vaughn groaned a bit. "Leasing and the lease is almost up. The owner is trying to take me for a ride. He knows it's too expensive and a big pain in the ass to have to move the gym. He's an asshole."

"When is the lease over?"

"In about three months."

"Have you thought about moving?"

"It's a good location, and it's so expensive to move all that equipment. If I was to move, there'd be some downtime getting set up in the next location that my customers wouldn't appreciate. I guess I'll go ahead and sign the bastard's paperwork in the next month or so, but the price gouging is really pissing me off."

"Cooper and I have a proposition for you. Let me say first that everything is negotiable. Let me say second that if this is something that you don't want and are not interested in, you can tell us that and we'll have no problems between us."

Vaughn looked taken aback. "Okay, shoot."

"Our employees need a place to work out twenty-four-seven. We will be providing that for them, on site, as part of their benefits package, as it clearly benefits us as well. We want them to have a place to practice their fighting skills in addition to the weapons and tactics training we provide. We want someone we know is the best at what they do. We've purchased two warehouses that we're currently renovating. We've left the first floor of the second warehouse alone until we could talk to you."

Cooper took up where Cade left off. "We're proposing you move your gym into the second warehouse. We would own the building, but the gym would be yours. You would meet with the architect to design the gym's interior. We have a couple of options for payment for you. Option one is you have a lease and pay what you're paying now at your current building. Option two is you have a lease but pay half of what you are currently paying with the stipulation that our employees and their immediate families have free memberships."

Vaughn looked completely astonished that they were even having this conversation. He looked like he was about to say something, but Cade cut him off at the pass. "Keep in mind, we want access to the gym twenty-four-seven because we don't work on a regular schedule. That would mean you'd need to have employees there during off hours, when you haven't before. It would be up to you if you wanted to only keep the gym open twenty-four-seven to our employees, or if you'd keep the gym open twenty-four-seven for the public as well. There would be an internal and external entrance, so either of those options would work."

Cooper continued the tag team business proposition. "We would expect that there would be training classes, which you would provide, for our employees only. We would also expect you to bring in other experts from time to time to provide further training for our people. We would also need to use your facilities to have our own classes where we'd be training them in military fighting techniques. We can negotiate whether those classes would be at an extra cost to us or part of the rental deal."

Cooper looked at Cade, who continued, "We want this to be a lucrative business decision for both Custos and The Knockout. We're not looking to make this arrangement so that it only benefits us. We haven't run the numbers. I've had my hands full and I'm usually the one working with our financial advisors, so that portion of it has been waiting."

Vaughn glanced to Braden, an understanding smile on his face. "Of course. You've been busy with more important matters."

Cade nodded. "We don't know what your gym membership prices are versus the quantity of our employees and their family compared to rental prices. We'll need some information from you to pass to our financial advisors. They can look into what will work best and provide you with a specific proposal with multiple options and financial details outlined. You can then pass the proposal to your own financial advisors and have them run the numbers as well. You can take the time to think about the offer--"

"I don't need to."

Cade's eyebrows popped up. "Vaughn, we'd ensure your business didn't take a hit as a result of--"

"Guys, I trusted you both with my daughter's life, and you brought her back to me. Nothing in my world means more to me than her and you honored that trust. You're two of the most successful men I know, and I consider you both friends. I'd be a complete ass not to take you up on this offer."

Cade grinned and Cooper stood, which prompted Vaughn to stand as well. They shook hands and ended up giving each other a rather enthusiastic bro hug. Cade tilted his head toward Braden, signaling to Vaughn that he wouldn't be getting up. Vaughn clasped Cade's hand in a firm grip and leaned in to hug him one-armed. "I can't tell you how much I appreciate this. I'll be very happy to get out of that lease and give a hearty 'fuck you' to that bastard. I think this is good business for you guys, and it's definitely going to be great business for me."

Cade smiled at Vaughn. "Oh, I think we'll all be happy with the outcome, and we'll ensure the move is as seamless as possible for your customer base."

Cade felt Braden's stare and looked down into his boy's questioning gaze. Braden leaned his head back on Cade's shoulder. "What's got you guys so worked up?"

Cade smiled and kissed him softly. "Just business, baby."

Braden raised an eyebrow and stared at Cade until he smirked and filled him in.

Braden grinned. "That's a brilliant idea!"

Cade nodded, and Vaughn and Cooper took their seats and began to strategize. Cade looked at Braden. "You're still hurting. When can you take more pain meds?"

They'd been sitting there chatting for over an hour. He looked up at Cade guiltily. "I could have taken them a while ago, but I was too comfortable tucked in beside you to move."

Cade narrowed his eyes. "So, I'm going to have to put your pain medication schedule into my watch, in addition to your insulin schedule?"

Braden rolled his eyes at Cade. "No, I'm going to get them now and make myself some tea."

Cade grumbled at that. "Don't roll your eyes when you know I'm right. You don't want to be chasing the pain, Bray. You want to be staying on top of it, so the meds kick in before the pain does. I don't like seeing the strain in your eyes and the fatigue that it brings. Please, for me, take them on time."

Braden leaned up and gently clasped Cade's face in his hands. "I'm sorry. I'll do better, I promise."

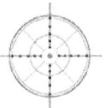

Braden

Braden got up to go to his bedroom. He was waylaid several times and chatted a bit longer than intended before he made it to his bathroom to get his pills. Rather than wait for the tea, he tossed them back in his bathroom, so they'd kick in faster. He then went into the kitchen and turned on the electric kettle. He wanted tea, but he figured others might want some coffee, so he got the grounds ready and his large French press set up. While the water heated, he got out mugs and other coffee fixings and set them on the table.

When the water was ready, he poured some in his mug and poured the rest in the French press. After several minutes he removed his teabag and then pushed the press down on the coffee. He did his best to ignore the pain caused by picking up the kettle and pushing down the press, knowing the pain meds would do their job soon. He saw Cade out of the corner of his eye coming his way, and Braden smiled at how overprotective he was being. He shook his head as Cooper tried to waylay him, and he could see Cade's desire to get to him.

They'd have to have a conversation about that later. Braden didn't want to be treated with kid gloves any longer. He wanted their relationship to be on equal footing as much as possible, as soon as possible As he was setting the coffee carafe on the kitchen table, he saw Finn approach Cade as well. "How's your gunshot wound healing?"

Braden froze, all the color washing from his face, a lead weight settling in his stomach. He wasn't even aware that he'd failed to fully place the coffee carafe on the table. He wasn't aware that it fell and shattered on the tiles of the kitchen floor, burning his legs. He had no idea that his guests had gone completely silent and then en masse started to converge on the kitchen to help him. All he could see and feel were Cade's anguished eyes on his.

Cade got to him first, stopping just shy of physically shoving people out of the way in his haste to get to him. Once there, he began to murmur in soothing tones. Braden's whole body was trembling, and he remained unaware of anything else around him but Cade. "You were shot? How? When?"

"Fuck, baby, I didn't want you to find out like this. Let me get you out of here, you're surrounded by glass and hot coffee. I think your legs got burned."

Cade tried to gather Braden in, but he resisted, pushing back. "No! Tell me what happened. How did you get shot? You were with me in the hospital the whole time! When—"

Cade clasped Braden's face in his hands, pulling his eyes up to meet his. "Please, let's not have this conversation in the middle of this mess and in front of our guests. Can I help you to our bedroom where we can talk and Finn can look at your burns?"

Braden looked down at his coffee stained trousers. "I'm fine."

"You're not fine, you're burned and upset."

"Zavier—"

"Braden, please let me take care of you right now. We'll talk about my gunshot, but let's take care of your burns. Please, baby."

Braden finally nodded, and Cade scooped him up. He did his best to navigate his way through the mess without toppling them on their collective asses and making more of a mess. He made his way through the well-meaning crowd and headed to their room.

Cade kicked the bedroom door shut and set Braden down on the bed. He got down on his knees and took off Braden's shoes and socks, grateful that at least he'd had protection from burns and cuts on his feet. Braden's hands clasped his face so softly Cade had to stop what he was doing and look into Braden's eyes. "Please tell me you're all right."

"Baby, I'm fine. Please, let me take a look at your legs."

"Okay, but promise you'll tell me everything."

"I promise."

Cade rolled up one pant leg and Braden hissed in pain as they both looked at the angry, red skin. Cade strode toward the door and opened it. His shoulders relaxed when he saw Finn coming down the hall with a bowl and several kitchen hand towels in his hands. "Hey, thanks. I was about to come get you."

"Most likely just first-degree burns, but let's have a look. After I assured everyone I'd be checking on you, Nana suggested everyone take their leave, so you had some privacy. Get him some shorts, yeah? Braden, I'm gonna have you take your pants off and put some shorts on. Do you have any aloe for sunburns?"

Braden pointed toward his bathroom as he stood. "Yeah, under the sink, left side."

Finn nodded and headed that way to give Braden some privacy. He found the aloe and a few other things he needed and returned to the bedroom. Braden was leaning back on some pillows, legs stretched out, bright red blotches of skin evident on both legs from knees to ankles. Finn lifted his legs and placed a bath towel under each leg. He went about treating the wounds using the kitchen towels and the bowl of cold water. "They're gonna hurt like a bitch for a few hours, but the pain meds you're already taking should help cut that down. Once the towels warm up, get them cold again. Keep doing that for no more than ten to fifteen minutes, pat dry, and put on the aloe liberally. Keep putting on the aloe for the next several days. You won't blister, but you might peel like a sunburn. Nothing to worry about."

Braden nodded and smiled. "Thanks for your help again, Finn. I'd like to stop needing any sort of medical attention for the next, oh, I don't know, ten years."

Finn laughed. "That's quite a lofty goal. Good luck with that." He looked at them both, regret etched across his face. "I'm so damn sorry, I wasn't thinking."

Cade shook his head. "Don't, Finn. It's my fault. I meant to tell him, I just hadn't gotten around to it yet."

Finn nodded but still looked upset that he'd inadvertently caused the mishap. "Okay, I'm gonna head out. Braden, as I've said, I really want you to be resting over the next week or so. Nothing strenuous."

"Sure thing, Doc."

Finn left, and Braden turned again to face Cade. "Can I see it?"

"Braden…"

"Z, I need to see it to believe that you're all right."

Cade raised his shirt and Braden whimpered and reached out. He touched the still puckered and raw-looking scar. He pushed Cade to turn to find the exit wound. "That's why you kept your shirt and boxers on when they finally allowed me to shower. I thought it was weird that you'd always get up and shower really early then later, only helped me in the shower instead of washing with me."

"I'm sorry, I didn't want you to worry and get stressed out."

Still touching Cade's skin, he asked, "So it didn't hurt anything inside? Why is the wound so big?"

Cade took a deep breath, while Braden sat cross-legged next to him. "It didn't hurt anything inside. It went through muscle and right back out again. They had to clean it up inside because pieces of my shirt were inside the wound, but other than that, all they did was stitch me back together. The wound in the back is the exit wound, which is usually the bigger and uglier of the scars, but I tore open the front wound during your second surgery."

Braden just stared up at him and didn't say a word, so he felt obliged to continue. "You flatlined. I wanted to get to you, to be with you if you passed. Gideon and Cooper wouldn't let me go, and apparently, I didn't like that. I honestly don't remember anything after you flatlined, until Cooper brought me back by listening to your heartbeat on the monitor. I ripped open the wound again during the struggle, and Finn had to sew me back together once you woke up."

Braden's heart beat wildly in his chest just thinking about what could have happened to Cade then hearing about how Cade had lost it when he'd flatlined made it all worse. Eric had taken so much from them. He wondered when it would stop. He wondered if he'd ever feel whole and at peace again.

Braden also worried if Cade's reticence to tell him about the wound wasn't so that he wouldn't worry about him but was more about the fact that Cade thought he was weak now and couldn't handle it. Could Braden even argue against that theory? Could he really convince himself, let alone Cade, that he wasn't weak?

"Don't."

Braden looked up from his lap into Cade's eyes, a question on his face. Cade took both of his hands in his. "Whatever you're thinking, whatever you're telling yourself, don't. Pain is seeping from your pores, Braden. I can practically smell it. Whatever you're telling yourself, it isn't healthy. Talk to me instead. Tell me what you're feeling."

Braden had gotten pretty good at talking about things he didn't want to talk about. He was now rather adept at ignoring his internal alarms when someone, namely Gabe, sometimes Cade, asked him to share his thoughts and feelings and everything in him told him not to do it. He'd realized after the first couple sessions with Gabe that if he was truly going to get anywhere with the therapy, he needed to flay himself open and trust in Gabe's ability to help put him back together, and Cade's ability to love him through it all.

Now Cade was asking that of him and he couldn't deny him, so he gathered his courage. "I'm wondering when Eric's hold on me will end. He's dead. He's fucking dead and he's still got a chokehold on me. I want this fucking PTSD bullshit done, over with. I feel so stupid. I thought… God, I thought since he was dead I'd suddenly be all better. I don't feel all better. I don't want to be weak. I don't like the idea that you thought I was too weak to know you got shot."

"Braden…"

"Please, let me finish."

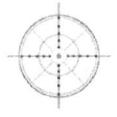

Cade

Cade kept Braden's hands in his, even though he longed to pull him into his arms and onto his lap. Braden was shaking with emotion, as if his entire world was going to shatter and him along with it. Cade wouldn't be able to hold back much longer, but he acquiesced, regardless. "Okay, baby."

"We haven't talked much about what happened once you found out I was gone. I think I need to know. I want to tell you what happened too. I can handle it. I know it's hard for you to believe, but I can handle it. If I know you're going to tell me something that I'm not going to like, I won't lose my shit because I'll be expecting it. I just, I want to be someone you're proud of. You're so fucking brave, so fucking strong. Nothing scares you. I can't compete with that, I wouldn't even try, but that doesn't mean that I don't want you to trust that I can handle myself."

Cade sat expressionless and waited. Finally, Braden smiled sadly. "I'm done. You can talk now."

"Lie down."

"What?"

"You heard me, Braden."

Braden frowned but complied by lying across the bed. No sooner had he stretched out than Cade was on top of him, gently covering him with his much bigger body. He let Braden feel most of his weight and he braced his elbows on either side of Braden's head, so he could look down into his eyes. Cade leaned down and kissed Braden's forehead, his chin, his cheeks, his nose, and finally, his lips. There was nothing sexual about his actions, this was all about getting Braden back into a better mindset, a calmer, less stressful headspace.

Cade noticed that immediately the shivers that had wracked Braden's body just moments ago were dissipating. He felt Braden's breathing slow down and then adapt itself to his. He placed a finger on the pulse in his neck long enough to decipher that his heartbeat was slowing as well. He'd noticed a while back Braden would attune his body to Cade's.

When feeling scared or in need of comfort, Braden would seek Cade out. Sometimes a touch would be all Braden would need to feel reassured, sometimes it was a hug or some whispered words. Cade knew that there was something in him that would calm Braden before he could get worked up into a panic attack.

He felt a moment of regret that he'd been unable to head the most recent attack off at the pass, but at the same time, Braden must have had these feelings for some time. Perhaps this attack was the breakthrough he needed. Cade's job now was to reassure Braden, to convince him that what he was worrying about was completely unfounded.

"Do you remember what Gabe said to you about PTSD and the length of time people have it? He told you that on average, people that have PTSD are usually affected by the symptoms for three to five years."

Braden released a sigh. "But I thought—"

Cade shook his head, silencing Braden. "Some are affected for more time, some less. Some get better faster with therapy or a combination of therapy and meds. You've chosen to forgo the meds, and I don't blame you a bit, but it's the PTSD symptoms that are affecting you. Don't give Eric the power by saying he has you in a chokehold."

"That's what it feels like."

"You're in a healthy relationship. You're running every day. You've got your career, and you're socializing. If you were in a chokehold and couldn't cope with anything, you wouldn't be doing any of those things. And don't call yourself stupid for hoping that when Eric died you'd be fine. You were in a constant state of stress, waiting for him to attack."

Braden nodded, a tear sliding towards his hairline. Cade kissed it away.

"I talked to Cooper and Gideon tonight. They told me what happened when you flatlined. I absolutely lost my fucking mind in there, Braden. I still can't remember it, even after they walked me through it. I fought them both, with all I had, to get to you. It took two big men to subdue me."

Braden's eyes closed, his brow furrowed. When he opened his eyes again, they were full of sorrow. He cradled Cade's face in his hands.

Cade leaned down and kissed Braden's lips, whisper soft. "They tried to reach me, tried to talk to me, but I wasn't there. They were covered in my blood and still I struggled and shouted at them. When I stopped struggling to get to you, when I knew you were dead, they said I just fell to my knees and roared out your name. They said I would have fallen on my face if they hadn't caught me when I collapsed. Am I weak, Braden?"

Another tear slid down Braden's face, and another. Braden shook his head and whispered, "No. No, you're not weak."

"I know you fought him. He had the marks on him to prove it before I even got to him. You fought a fucking monster, Braden. You didn't cower, you didn't sit passively, waiting for a beat down. Do you know how brave that is? You've only been taking self-defense classes for a short time, and yet you fought back with all that you had."

Cade saw a glimmer of pride etch itself across Braden's face and smiled. "I didn't tell you about getting shot because you didn't need that on top of your recovery. I just wanted to get you through the worst of it, and then I was planning on telling you."

Cade, lying on his side now, leg thrown over both of Braden's thighs, leaned over and kissed Braden's lips slowly. "I know when I thought you were dead, I couldn't even fathom going on another day without you. So, let me ask you again, Braden, am I weak?"

Braden quickly shook his head. "No."

Cade raised a brow. "Are you weak?"

"No."

"Do I think you're weak?"

Braden took a deep breath and shook his head. Cade wouldn't stand for that. "Say it."

"No, you don't think I'm weak."

"That's right. You're my fucking warrior, Braden."

Braden's soft smile pulled at Cade's heartstrings. "I'm your fucking warrior."

Cade smiled and nodded. "Yeah you are."

He knew without a smidgen of doubt that Braden would be just fine. It might take some time, but in the end, Braden was too strong not to overcome it. He grinned down at Braden. "Now, do you think there's some food left over? I'm starved."

He got up and pulled Braden gently to his feet. They kissed for several minutes then Cade chuckled when he heard Braden's stomach growl. "Come on. Let me feed you, and we'll get to bed early."

"Z?"

Braden's apprehensive voice caused Cade to turn and face him. "Yeah?"

"How did you know what I needed?"

"That's my job, right? I know what my touch does for you. When you feel uneasy, scared, or upset, you touch me to help ground yourself.

Now that I know that we'll hopefully be able to stave off future panic attacks."

"I love you, Z."

"I know, baby. I know you do. I love you too. Now come on, let's get you fed and to bed."

They grinned at each other and clasped hands as they walked into the kitchen to stuff themselves with Lers Ros catering and Nana's baked goods. They fed each other, laughed, and teased each other, and for the first time since they met, there was no stress or anxiety between them.

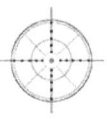

Braden

They cleaned up, got ready for bed, and got under the covers. Braden was still uncomfortable on his side or stomach, so Cade had gotten into the habit of curling his body around him, which Braden not-so-secretly loved. Hell, Braden loved anything and everything having to do with being surrounded by or covered by Cade which was going to make the next several weeks extremely difficult.

They were on a doctor ordered sexual hiatus for at least three weeks. Braden was expressly forbidden to work for at least four weeks, only resuming work on a part time basis for at least two more weeks after that. He was warned that he wouldn't really start feeling back to normal and ready to do all his previous activities, like running, for at least two months.

They were all so thankful that Nana was available to take over for Braden during this time, but he'd already placed an ad in the local paper for a baking assistant. Standing on her feet all day baking was going to take its toll on Nana, regardless of how much enthusiasm she had for the job.

He figured if Nana helped vet the applicants, and he decided on someone he really liked, he'd keep them on after he was able to be back full time, so he could stop working as much as he had been. Maya had suggested they hire someone to assist him years ago. He'd refused at the time, not wanting to have anyone else in his kitchen, but mostly feeling like it was an extravagance that wasn't needed. He'd come to realize he needed more time away from work, not only because of his relationship with Cade, but because he needed time for himself as well.

In the meantime, he was spending a bit of time every day on Cade's laptop writing down the recipes that he had in his head. He knew once he had all of them down in writing, he'd have to test them out ingredient by ingredient to be sure the measurements he listed were accurate. He'd made a lot of them up or had stolen them, with pride, from Nana. When it came to baking, neither of them ever really had to use recipes. However, he had to start keeping them if he was going to have an assistant pastry chef that he would trust to leave the baking to if he was off a couple days a week or if he was on vacation. Just thinking about a vacation away from it all with Cade made his stomach feel all fluttery.

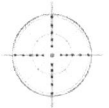

Cade

Cade brought Braden out of his musings. "I'm needed over at the warehouses tomorrow. I'm meeting with the foreman to make sure we're on schedule with warehouse one. They're pushing hard to get our building done with construction in less than four months. They better be, for the amount we're paying them. Warehouse two will be several weeks behind. After that, the interior designers will come in and outfit each floor. I know you took on our home as your project and you wanted to keep it a surprise, but in light of what happened, would you prefer I take over?"

The horror was clear on Braden's face. Cade waved his idea away. "I can see by the look on your face that's not what you want. I was just trying to help minimize the stress for you, that's all."

Braden gazed up at Cade. "Z, creating our home from scratch, choosing things that I think will make you happy and make you feel at home, that's not stressful, that's exciting for me. I want to make a home for you, I want you to walk into our space and feel like you can't imagine living anywhere else."

"I'm sure I'll love it. I'm glad it's not stressful for you."

Braden grinned. "Maya and I are having a blast. Having a business with my best friend has put stress on our friendship. I think we've been pretty good at keeping our friendship strong through it all, but having this extra time with her, doing this project, has really brought us back to where we were in college."

Cade leaned down, pushed Braden's hair back, and kissed him softly. "I'm glad you're enjoying it. I can tell she's happy to be spending time with you as well."

Braden nodded and reached up to rub his hand over Cade's stubbled face. "I'm so grateful to you for handing over the responsibility to me for so many reasons. Being in the hospital for the last two weeks has been hell any way you look at it. I've so been looking forward to getting back to it. Please don't think I'm not up for it, I'll make it work."

Cade smiled. "That's all you need to say. I'll leave you to it. I just wanted to make the offer in case you were feeling overwhelmed."

Braden snuggled down into Cade's arms and nuzzled his neck. Cade kissed the top of his head. "So, what do you think about taking a vacation with me once you're all healed, and once we've gotten the warehouses completed? I'm focused on the construction, and Coop is going to be focused on the move and our people. Once the buildings are done, I've let him know that you and I are going to need some time."

Still tucked into Cade, Braden's voice was muffled. "You did?"

Cade chuckled, kissed his head again. "I did. Actually, your timeline for full recovery coincides with the timeline for the completion of the warehouses, so it's perfect. By then, both you and Nana should have your new employee fully trained. Maybe a week or two somewhere would be possible."

Braden eased himself out from under Cade, so he could look him in the eyes. The smile that lit his face was one Cade hadn't ever seen before, and he knew he'd make it his new mission to see it more often. He smiled back at Braden. "Now that's a smile I want to see every day. Tell me where you'd like me to take us, Braden. We can do anything. Go anywhere. Tell me what you need, and I'll make it happen."

Braden tucked himself back into the protective embrace of his lover and began to talk. They were awake for several more hours as they discussed all the places they wanted to travel together, all the things they wanted to do.

They talked about eventually getting married and having a family. Braden admitted that when they had kids he'd want to continue at the café with a shortened work schedule. That way he could take care of their children, but still maintain his part of the business.

Cade expressed his happiness at Braden's desire to be so involved in their children's daily lives but assured him that he wanted Braden to be able to maintain his independence and the happiness the café brought to his life. They finally fell into an exhausted sleep, feeling excited and hopeful for their future for the first time.

Chapter 17

BRADEN

It had been an eventful four months since Braden had come home from the hospital. He thought about all that had happened since that time, as he did one final walk through of his new home. He collapsed into one of their new, very comfortable, padded leather counter stools lining the back of the enormous kitchen island. Maya slid a glass of wine across the countertop. "Braden indulge with me for a moment, even though you rarely ever drink. I think you could use some liquid courage. Raise your glass with me in a toast to all we've accomplished in the last several months. Everything is perfect."

Braden grinned. "We have accomplished a lot, haven't we?"

Maya lifted her glass and nodded. "I've never seen a more beautiful home. We've done a really fan-fucking-tastic job. He's gonna love it. Cooper told me that he still has no clue that you've already had his things packed up and moved here. Siobhan and Rowan helped you incorporate some of his favorite pieces, and I know that will make him happy. You're turning a page tonight, and I know for a fact that really good things are waiting for you two."

Braden smiled across the island at his best friend. He couldn't agree more. The home that he and Maya had created for the new beginning of his lifetime with Cade was nothing short of perfection. Everything they could think of to make their place a home was incorporated. He wanted it to be beautiful, but mostly he wanted it to be warm and inviting. He didn't want a museum or a modern show place; he wanted dark, warm colors, deep cushions, and soft textures.

He wanted Cade to be able to come home from a long day and collapse into his favorite leather chair that was well loved but still beautiful. He wanted a place where Cade could bring employees and clients alike. He wanted a home that was perfect for entertaining and yet comfortable enough to lounge around in pajamas all day. A place that would transition from a home for two to a home for more, as they welcomed children into their lives. It seemed like an impossible dream, ticking off all those boxes, but with Maya's help and even the help of Rowan, Siobhan and Nana, they'd done it.

Braden was dressed in one of Cade's favorite outfits and smiled when he thought back to the time less than a month ago when he'd come out of their bedroom wearing it and had been dragged right back into it. The result was almost every item of clothing on the floor; glasses removed; his bowtie being used as a makeshift blindfold; the belt wrapped around his wrists, which was then held over his head by Cade as he'd ravished Braden; and their dinner reservations being pushed back a couple of hours.

From their very first time together, Cade had assumed sexual control of Braden. It was an organic need they both had and felt completely natural between them. Braden blushed when thinking about the first time they'd seriously discussed bringing a bit of power exchange into their bedroom.

After their first conversation at the beginning of their relationship about Cade taking control and allowing Braden to break free of the burdens that stress had always heaped upon him, Braden had thought a lot about how he felt about relinquishing control and realized that the more he thought about it and naturally allowed Cade to take that control, the more he needed and craved it.

They'd discussed what they both wanted out of it, and they both knew they'd never be into any type of master/slave relationship, but they were both very interested to see where on the BDSM spectrum they fell. They both figured they'd basically be figuring things out together, slowly, to see what worked for them. Braden wanted to hand over a lot of his control when it came to things that stressed him. He also wanted to be able to let Cade push his boundaries sexually.

Cade had asked him if he'd wanted to take it as far as writing up a contract between them since doing things that way would ensure they covered all of Braden's hard and soft limits and Cade wouldn't push Braden further than he was willing to go. Braden had refused and stated emphatically that the only contract he wanted between them was a marriage contract sometime in their future. Cade's eyes had gotten heated at Braden's admission, and they'd kissed passionately before they'd gotten back to their discussion.

Cade had pushed a bit more, telling him it didn't have to be like a typical contract that those practicing BDSM would use. They could make it up as they went, adding to it, removing things, and making it theirs. Cade wanted to ensure Braden felt safe and secure in the fact that he would always take his limits seriously and keep Braden's safety his number one priority. Braden still refused, stating it didn't feel right for something impersonal like that to be between them. It may be right for some couples, but for them, it didn't feel natural to him.

Cade had acquiesced regarding the contract, but when the subject of safewords came up, Cade was adamant they have something in place for Braden, and when Braden couldn't think of what he'd want to use, Cade suggested the typical green, yellow, and red. Their play was never going to be hardcore, and Cade would never physically hurt Braden, but he would definitely push his boundaries. Both orgasm denial and sensory play could be extremely intense, and Cade knew that Braden may find himself needing to safeword.

When Braden admitted he'd often fantasized about being tied up and blindfolded and then teased, lightly spanked, and thoroughly fucked, Cade expressed his concerns about that being a trigger. He also suggested discussing the issues with Gabe. Braden was embarrassed beyond belief when he'd brought it up at their next session. Though he needn't have been, as strangely enough, Gabe hadn't batted an eye and told them that they should ease into it, but he didn't feel as if it would be an issue as they both had complete trust in each other.

Gabe had suggested before bringing in any type of restraints, they begin with Cade telling Braden to hold onto the headboard and not move. If that presented no issues, they should move on to Cade holding Braden's wrists. From there they could test out some light restraints that Braden could get himself out of if he needed to, and so on. He had also said that until they were at the point where tying Braden up was no issue for him at all, they should stay away from blindfolds. He said that it would be important to keep a visual connection at first so if Braden got nervous or started to panic, he'd be able to look Cade in the eyes and be grounded.

Frankly, the ease of Gabe's suggestions, and the understanding of their dynamic had Cade thinking it wasn't Gabe's first discussion of the BDSM lifestyle. He'd provided them with insightful advice and a breadth of knowledge someone outside of the lifestyle wouldn't have. Braden eventually admitted Cade's suspicion that Gabe was in the lifestyle, and quite possibly a Dom, was probably correct.

Having spoken to Gabe, both of them felt more comfortable that everything they'd been doing and the things they wanted to try together weren't out of the question because of Braden's past. In fact, the results of testing Braden's boundaries had catapulted their love making from amazing to something neither of them could even begin to describe, completely obliterating their preconceived notions of what intimacy between a couple could become.

Cade was able to exercise his need to take control and dominate his lover, and Braden was finally able to allow himself to submit fully to someone he trusted with his life. What they had both been surprised to discover was that instead of Cade's act of restraining Braden making him panic, Braden was able to replace all the bad memories of Eric forcefully restraining him with new ones that involved Braden having the power to choose to willingly and eagerly submit to Cade. Neither of them could have foreseen that being the case, but they were both immensely happy that's how it turned out.

They'd grown immeasurably closer, and Braden was grateful Cade had trusted in his strength enough to bring up the issue of control so early on in their relationship. If Cade hadn't had that insight into Braden and that type of trust in him, and vice versa, he knew they wouldn't be where they were in their relationship today. He looked up from his wine glass, a small smile on his face, and glanced at his best friend.

A knowing look passed over her face. "Where'd you go, just then?"

Braden blushed again. "You really don't want to know."

She laughed at that. "Oh, I don't know, two of the most beautiful men I've ever met, doing naughty things to each other in bed? I seem to be surrounded by sexy as fuck homosexual men. Do you think I haven't read my fair share of M/M romance? Come on!"

Braden's jaw dropped, and he just stared at his best friend in shock. "That's a thing?"

That made her laugh even harder. "Oh, it's a thing all right. But, more on that later, it's almost time for the big reveal."

Braden shook his head. "Nope. No more on that later. No more."

Maya snorted indelicately and tossed back the remainder of her wine. She washed out their glasses, put them into the stainless-steel dishwasher, and headed to the elevator. She hugged Braden like she wouldn't see him for a month, told him she loved him then hit the button. When the elevator arrived, she stepped in and waved goodbye, blowing him kisses as the doors shut, calling out, "Good luck, Bray!"

He started to fidget and unrolled the sleeves of his button up shirt. He then rolled them back up and paced as he waited for Cade to arrive and walk through their new home for the very first time. He looked at his watch and realized he only had a few more minutes. He took another look around, and by the time he was done, he heard the elevator ding. He raced toward the doors, wanting to meet Cade there and see his first reaction.

When the doors opened, Braden was floored. He'd only ever seen Cade in jeans or his sexy tactical pants. His man stood before him in a bespoke suit that screamed sophisticated elegance, and yet, he wasn't wearing a tie and the shirt had the first two buttons undone, revealing one of his tattoos, high on his chest. The jacket fit him like a second skin, and it too was unbuttoned. His hands were in his pockets, causing Braden's gaze to travel down his long frame.

He took in the elegant silver belt buckle with the McCade crest etched into it. His pants were straight legged, flat front, and pinstriped, like the jacket, and ended at the perfect length to show off a pair of Hugo Boss

Chelsea dress boots. He heard a growl and looked up to see Cade devouring him with his eyes. "I can't believe you wore that. Are you trying to kill me? The last time you wore it, you could hardly walk after what I did to you, and we nearly didn't make it to our delayed dinner reservations."

Braden blushed. "I wanted everything to be perfect. Zavier, I've never seen you dressed up before. God, you're the most gorgeous thing I've ever laid eyes on."

They continued to consume each other with their hot gazes. Braden had no clue who stepped forward first, but suddenly, they were in each other's arms and kissing each other like they'd been separated for months, not hours. When they finally broke apart, Cade lowered his forehead to Braden's, and they stood there gazing at each other, breathing heavily. Braden smiled. "Do you want to see our new home, Z?"

"More than anything, baby."

Braden leaned up to kiss Cade one more time then stepped back. He watched as Cade lifted his gaze and took a long look around. The stunned look on his face worried Braden, and his heart started to beat wildly in his chest. Cade put his hand out and Braden grabbed it in his as Cade moved them deeper into their home.

Braden had stayed true to his first suggestion to bring more light in with bigger windows and to keep everything on this lower level open concept. There was only one internal erected wall and it was more of an eight-foot-wide column that went from floor to ceiling to the left of the elevator separating a living room area and a family room area. It contained a double-sided, six-by-six foot fireplace with a gorgeous piece of artwork above it on the living room side and a mammoth flat screen television on the family room side.

The whole place was wired with surround sound, and Custos had outfitted the place with their state of the art security system. Braden was still in awe of the electronics around their home that were all synced to an app they could control on their phones, tablets, or computers. The fact that he could turn on his security system, turn down the heat, turn off the lights, turn on the video cameras, and check the security status of every room from his phone anywhere he may be blew his mind. They walked around to each section of the huge room; living room, family room, dining room, and kitchen.

Cade paused at his favorite chair that Braden had placed in their family room and touched the soft leather. His grip on Braden's hand tightened by a fraction, but that's the only reaction Braden could decipher. He led them toward the kitchen and admitted to Cade he'd created his dream kitchen so that he could do everything he wanted to be able to do, not only at work, but at home as well.

They moved to the dining area, and Cade seemed to admire the huge dining table he'd had commissioned, big enough to seat everyone in their families. His nerves got the best of him. "Um, we can change anything you don't like. We were able to build in four rooms upstairs in the lofted area. You have an office up there, and there are a couple spare bedrooms, and then our master suite. Do you... Um, do you want to go up and look?"

Cade looked down at him with a very serious expression on his face and nodded. Braden led the way to the switchback staircase that was behind the dining area. Braden had a small guest bathroom added under the staircase as well to minimize the disruption of their open living space on the main floor. Cade still hadn't said a word and Braden's anxiety was spiking as time ticked by. When they reached the top of the stairs, Braden led them to Cade's office that Cooper had outfitted, knowing what he'd need. Braden then led him through the guest bedrooms. "There's space to grow our family here, when the time is right. I thought you'd like that."

Cade raised their joined hands to his lips and kissed Braden's fingers but still said nothing. When they reached their bedroom and Cade had looked at everything there, Braden turned to face him at the foot of their bed. Nearly in tears from anxiety, Braden whispered brokenly, "Say something. Anything. Please. Do you hate it, love it, something in between? Your silence is killing me right now."

Cade sat down in the new chair-and-a-half that Braden had placed in their bedroom. He patted his lap and Braden straddled his man, suit and all. When Braden opened his mouth to speak, Cade placed a finger over his lips, pulled him closer, and kissed him gently. When they pulled apart, he explained that he'd always known one day when he settled down that he'd try to create a space that was like the homes he'd grown up in with his family. He'd lived in so many places around the world, half of which were military barracks, but even when the homes were his, they'd never felt like home.

He hadn't spoken when they'd walked around the loft because he didn't have the right words to express how happy he was. He didn't know how to say how much it meant to him that Braden had created a home for him, but he tried. "It was like you reached into my mind and pulled out exactly what I'd want but wouldn't know how to define. I can't wait until I can wake up with you beside me in our new bed. I can't wait to taste the first pastries you bake for me in your dream kitchen. I can't wait to make love to you here for the first time. I can't wait for us to have everyone over for the holidays."

Braden's grin was contagious. "Yeah?"

Cade nodded. "Yeah. And I want to fill up those two bedrooms with the sound of our children's laughter. You've given all of that to me by creating this home for us, and I have a feeling I'll be thanking you for it for the rest of our lives."

Braden felt a tear spill over his cheek, and Cade wiped it away. "Dammit, I'm sick of crying around you. You can't say romantic, beautiful shit like that. No more of that tonight!"

Cade laughed and pulled Braden closer. "Oh baby, I can't make a promise like that."

Braden huffed out a laugh. "All right fine, but if I cry any more tonight, fair warning, I'll be so mad at you."

Cade kissed him soundly on the lips and smiled. "No, you won't."

Braden narrowed his eyes at him. "Don't test me. So, are you ready for a little something extra? I have one more surprise for you."

Cade's eyebrows went up. "There's more?"

Braden smiled wide, "Oh, hell yeah, there's more."

"Lead on. I can't wait to see it."

Braden hopped off Cade and took his hand. He led him to the main floor and then toward the stairwell entrance that was right next to the elevator. He tugged Cade into the stairwell, and feeling a bit of resistance, he glanced back with a questioning look on his face. "Everything all right?"

Cade cleared his throat. "Uh, yeah."

Braden looked at him curiously, shrugged then led him to the rooftop and stepped aside so that Cade could see what he'd done. Cade walked through the door and stopped abruptly, in shock. Braden was nearly as excited about their rooftop oasis as he was their home down below. "Remember when you were talking about moving into this building for just a couple of years? You said you figured one day I'd eventually want my own home with a yard and a place for the kids to play outside. I didn't want a temporary home, Z, I wanted a permanent one. So, I wondered, how could I have both a place in the middle of the city and an oasis for us to enjoy ourselves and eventually enjoy with our kids? This is what I came up with."

Cade looked at Braden, eyebrow raised. "Is that a pool on my roof?"

Braden grinned. "And a hot tub. I wanted a full-sized pool with the size of this roof, but we had weight restrictions, so I had to get a smaller one, but I think we'll make use of it. The grassy areas are real no-mow grass, not turf. There's an irrigation system, so the plants, trees, and grasses will be maintained all year round. There's a huge grill and bar area built in, more of a mini-kitchen actually, and several tables and chairs for entertaining. All of the decking you see is composite, no wood decking to maintain."

"Braden, this is fucking amazing!"

"You like it?"

"No, Bray, I love it."

"Good, cause I spent an ungodly amount of your hard-earned money doing it."

Cade laughed. "That's what it's there for. I told you to spare no expense, and looking downstairs and up here, I'm so glad you listened."

Cade wrapped his arm around Braden's shoulders. "Show me the rest and tell me you have speakers up here for music."

Braden smiled, pulled his phone out of his pocket and waved it at Cade. He logged in, clicked an app, and hit a few buttons, then placed his phone back into his shirt pocket. The speakers came alive with Ray LaMontagne's "Hold You in My Arms." As the sun was setting, they walked leisurely through the rooftop garden that Braden had created for them.

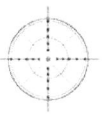

Cade

Cade couldn't believe how perfect it was for them, and he knew they'd both be making use of this spot for years to come: alone, with friends and family, and later, with their children. Braden had high glass walls installed around the perimeter, for safety. He'd had vegetable and fruit gardens planted in hand-crafted raised wooden beds, decorative lanterns hung everywhere and were lit all around, along with candles flickering on every table, and heating lamps glowing near every seating arrangement. He'd thought of everything, and it made what Cade planned even more perfect.

Cade led them back to the door and turned Braden to face him. He drew Braden into an embrace and kissed the top of his head. He began to sway them back and forth, and when Braden looked up at him, his face full of happiness and love, he kept them dancing to the music that was playing for them. He pulled Braden closer and he pulled his head to his chest as they danced. Behind Braden's back, Cade checked his watch and tapped the face a few times, sending a quick message, and continued to dance with the one person who had become everything to him in a matter of months.

Everyone who had been at Braden's last party gathered quietly behind him now. There were a few newcomers there as well, in addition to all their closest family and friends, helping to make this a perfect night for Braden. When Cade saw that everyone was in place, he pulled away from Braden, took the phone from his shirt pocket, and turned off the music. He placed his hands on Braden's shoulders and squeezed, silently asking him to stand where he was. Cade backed up a step and then went down on bended knee.

He looked up at Braden and saw that his beautiful man had tears shimmering in his eyes already and his hands were up covering his mouth in surprise. Cade began speaking from his heart, no words prepared. "Braden, when I got here months ago, it was to get a job done, have a quick visit with my family, and check out a few locations for our new offices. I had no idea that the trip would literally change the course of my life. When Maya mentioned your troubles to Cooper and me, I knew immediately nothing was going to keep me from protecting you with my life and then insinuating you into it." He grinned up at Braden, and his grin was answered with a silent chuckle and a tear slipping from his eye.

"I look back now, and I know that that day is the day I fell. I didn't know it at the time; I thought I'd get to know you, maybe take you out a few times, and we'd see where things went. I think, under all those thoughts, the truth was there for me to see had I really looked. As I guarded you, I got to know you, and the more I knew, the more everything you stand for, everything you give of yourself, became everything I never knew I wanted and needed in my life. You exposed your vulnerabilities to me and in so doing, you proved your strength. I've been surrounded by strong men and women all my life, and I can say without a shred of doubt that you are the strongest of them all. You're always so busy telling me how big and tough I am, how brave. You call me your warrior, but as I explained to you months ago, you're *my* warrior." Cade smiled up at Braden, "Is that how I said it?"

Braden shook his head, his lips tilted up in a tiny smile, which Cade kissed. "Hmmm, how about, 'you're my fucking warrior, Braden.'"

Braden nodded and let out a watery laugh. Cade grinned. "So, I thought, with you being my warrior, and me being yours, we just might have a fighting chance at making this love that we have last for the rest of our lives. And where I come from, a love like ours, though strong all on its own, needs a solid foundation to build upon. So, it's with that in mind that I'm asking you now, tonight, on this beautiful garden oasis that you've created for us; will you take my hand and walk with me toward the life we both want?"

Cade pulled out a ring box and held it up as he continued, "Will you wear my ring as an extension of our love? Will you marry me, Braden Cross?"

Braden moved closer to this man of his that was offering him everything. He sat down on Cade's bended knee, looked at him and smiled. "Yes. Yes, Zavier McCade, I will marry you." He pulled Cade's face closer to his and kissed him then pulled back and looked into his eyes for several long moments. He finally broke their gaze and brought Cade's hand closer to him, so he could pop the lid up on the ring box and he frowned. "Z, it's empty."

Cade feigned surprise. "It is?"

Braden nodded, and Cade raised his voice. "Has anyone seen a ring lying around anywhere?"

Braden sucked in a breath and whipped his head around, taking in all the smiling faces behind him. He raised his hands to cover his mouth again and started laughing and crying at the same time. Everyone converged on them, and Braden made to get up, but Cade held him fast and asked again. "Anyone?"

Everyone shook their heads. "Hmmm, well, I wonder if I can ask someone for a little help."

At that, a deep bark broke through the noise of their well-wishers. Braden's head snapped toward the sound and Cade heard him gasp. "Oh my god. Zavier?"

"Yeah, baby?"

"It's Thor!"

Cade chuckled. "It is."

Braden fell to his knees in the crook of Cade's arms, and suddenly his own arms were full of the dog that he'd fallen in love with months ago. Cade heard Braden laugh. "Hi, baby! Hi, Thor! Did you miss me? I missed you!"

Cade chuckled at the reunion and grinned up at everyone surrounding them. He saw tears in the eyes of the women and genuine happiness on the faces of the men. He looked back down at Braden. "He might have something for you in the pocket of his vest."

Braden turned his questioning gaze to Cade, confused about the "Service Dog" vest, but Cade merely nodded. "Go on. Check."

Braden turned back to the huge bundle of fur in his arms and managed to get his hands on his vest and unzip the pocket. He found it immediately, pulled it out, and gazed down at the stunning ring. "Oh, Z."

Cade grinned. "I had rings made for us with a repeating Celtic warrior symbol around the bands."

Braden slid the extra wide band on and turned to him. He took Cade's face in his hands and leaned up to kiss him. The kiss was so sweet, so full of promise, love, and happiness that Cade was nearly undone by it. As Braden pulled away, Cade cleared his throat. "I also had a little work done this morning. When we make our vows to each other, we'll be forever linked together as one. But I also wanted your mark on me."

Cade began to unbutton his shirt several more buttons and he pulled it open. Braden reached toward his chest and ran his fingers lightly over the Celtic warrior symbol that Cade had had inked onto his chest, over his heart. Braden leaned forward and kissed the ink and Cade lifted Braden's face up to his and kissed him until they were both breathless.

He stood and helped Braden to his feet. While he buttoned his shirt back up, he watched as their loved ones surrounded Braden. He grinned and realized he'd never once in his life been this happy. After countless hugs and congratulations, Braden turned teary eyes on Cade, smiled the most beautiful smile, and waved sweetly. Cade waved back from where he stood and watched, grinning from ear to ear, as Braden talked with their family and friends, showing off his ring and his new dog in equal measure.

After mingling separately and then together, Cade asked Braden to dance again. When they were done, Cade smiled down at Braden. "You mad at me?"

Confused, Braden's eyebrows drew together. "Why would I be mad at you?"

In answer, Cade reached up and wiped away a stray tear, and Braden remembered the conversation they'd had downstairs. He grinned and nodded his head, as he whispered, "*So* mad."

Cade laughed. "Yeah, I can see the anger radiating off of you."

Braden tried to look stern but smiled again and pulled Cade close. Cade kissed his lips sweetly. "You happy, Bray?"

Braden tightened his hold around him. "Oh yeah."

They felt a muzzle trying to pry them apart, and they both laughed and looked down at Thor, the Belgian Malinois that Cade had adopted for Braden months before. Braden crouched down and hugged him again. "He was adopted months ago. Where have you been keeping him?"

"I sent him down to San Diego to one of the country's best dog trainers with Killian, one of my men who is a skilled dog trainer himself, but specifically for military dogs. I wanted Killian to be knowledgeable with other types of dog training, in addition to getting Thor better trained as well."

Braden shook his head. "Where did you get this idea?"

Cade shrugged. "When you were running with Thor, I could tell he had had some training and when I asked to see his information, his file said that his previous owner was a military vet who died of complications from a wound he sustained while in Iraq. He'd put Thor through military dog training, but he never finished and was never certified. He owned Thor outright, so the military didn't come to get him, and I think he got lost in the shuffle."

"That's so sad."

Cade nodded. "The man's parents couldn't care for the dog since they live in a nursing home and didn't know what else to do, so they gave him up. You ran with him the day after he was brought in, and as soon as I saw how he reacted with you and listened to my commands, I looked into his background. I immediately paid his adoption fees but kept him there for another couple of weeks. They allowed him to stay while I arranged for his training."

"But if he's already trained, why did you think he needed more training?"

"I needed him to be trained for you. He's now a certified service dog. He finished his training a couple of days ago. Killian brought him back up here in time for me to give him to you tonight. He's trained in being a guard dog for you, and in the future, our kids, and also helping you with PTSD and with your diabetes."

Braden's mouth dropped open in surprise. "Are you serious?"

Cade nodded and smiled, rubbing Braden's back in soothing circles. "I am. Killian is the big bald guy who's standing with Cooper near the hot tub. He will work with you to understand how Thor can help you navigate any issues you may have with PTSD and managing your diabetes, not that you ever really have issues with your diabetes, but he's fully trained nonetheless."

Braden couldn't help but ask, "But why?"

"Because, I'll be starting a regular work schedule here in the coming weeks when the second warehouse is completed. We'll be spending less time together during the day, and I wanted you to have him with you."

Cade could only stare as his mate's breathing grew a bit shallow and his pupils dilated. He grabbed a handful of Braden's hair at the back of his neck and drew him closer. He growled quietly. "I don't know what the hell just happened, but something I said just turned you the fuck on and I can't do a damn thing about it right now."

Braden, even more turned on by the rough handling and the growling, groaned. "It's not what you said, it's the lengths to which you'll go to ensure that my needs are met. That scared me to death in the beginning, and then later it kind of gave me warm fuzzies to be honest. But now, god, now it just turns me on when you take control."

Cade tilted his head to the side. "That's good, right?"

Braden nodded. "Yeah. It's sexy as hell, and I can't wait to get you downstairs and fuck you senseless."

Cade's grip on his hair tightened. His other hand wrapped around Braden's waist and pulled him in so that Braden was able to feel his arousal. Braden sucked in a breath and Cade ground himself against his fiancé. "You're going to fuck me tonight?"

Braden exhaled raggedly and whispered, "Yes."

Chapter 18

CADE

Cade kept Braden in his arms but loosened them as he looked around to see their guests mingling and eating the food he'd had catered. They'd be here for hours, most likely, and as much as Cade loved everyone, he wasn't about to stay another minute longer. "Everyone, can I have your attention, please? We would like to thank you all for being here tonight to celebrate our engagement. It means the world to us that you're here. Braden and I are going to excuse ourselves, but we'd like you all to stay as long as you'd like. There's food and drink and wonderful company, so please, make use of our beautiful rooftop oasis. Again, thank you all for coming. Goodnight."

Braden looked up at Cade in surprise and then out to their shocked guests. "We can't just..."

"We can."

"But..."

Cade leaned down and hauled Braden over his shoulder in a fireman's carry and walked to the door. Braden, caught off guard, laughed and smacked Cade's back in a futile attempt to get him to see reason. As they drew near the door, Cade, without turning, called out, "Kill?"

Braden looked up and over the crowd of bemused family and friends. Killian, the big, bald, tattooed brute of a man Cade had pointed out to him, raised his bottle of beer in salute and with his other hand, rubbed Thor's head. "I've got him."

Braden began to struggle and tried one more time. "Z, come on!"

In response, Cade smacked his ass and continued. Braden laughed at the absurdity of it all, raised his head one last time and waved with a chagrined smile on his face and then shrugged at their guests, hands in the air, as if to say, 'What are you gonna do?'

Their friends and family were all laughing at this point and a couple had begun to clap then he heard a wolf whistle. Braden muttered under his breath. "You're so going to pay for this."

His blood heated, and the arousal returned when Cade promised, "I look forward to it."

When Cade took the stairs, Braden huffed. "Okay, okay, you can put me down now. I'll come willingly."

Cade chuckled at that. "Oh, you'll come all right, but I'm not putting you down. I kind of like this caveman act I've got going."

Cade continued down the stairs. Just as they hit the landing at the door to their floor, Braden squeaked. "Please, you're pushing on my bladder. You gotta put me down or I'm gonna embarrass us both!"

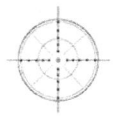

Braden

Cade chuckled and finally put Braden down. "Sorry, baby."

Braden, a naughty gleam in his eye, grinned up at Cade. "Just kidding!"

With that, he dove for the door of their home and laughed when he heard Cade mutter, "Oh, you're in so much trouble!"

Braden let out a startled "eep" when he heard Cade's hard footfalls behind him and bounded for the living room. When he rounded the wall separating living from family room, he realized Cade had anticipated him and was barreling toward him. He hooted and took off again, skirting the coffee table and clambering over the back of the couch. He felt Cade's hand brush his back and he snickered as he put on a burst of speed to get to the kitchen and round the island.

Thinking he had a moment to rest as they could go around and around the island and Cade wouldn't be able to catch him, he looked up, and his eyes nearly popped out of his head when he saw Cade running hell for leather directly toward the island without pausing. He shrieked, which he was sure would mortify him later, and ran toward the dining room as Cade launched himself over the island. "You're just looking to get punished, aren't you?"

"You gotta catch me first!" Braden tossed back over his shoulder, laughing maniacally now, as he dodged the dining table and hauled ass to the stairs. Halfway up, he knew he was in for it when Cade skipped three steps for his two. Reaching the landing, he geared up to beat Cade to their bedroom but was caught around the waist, quickly twisted and tossed, yet again, over Cade's shoulder. His head spinning, all he could do was chuckle, an undignified snort escaping when he couldn't control his breathing any longer.

Cade padded into the bedroom, holding Braden by the upper thighs, occasionally smacking his round ass when he squirmed. He unceremoniously dumped Braden on the bed, where he bounced and broke into uncontrolled laughter when he glanced from Cade's tented pants to his own. They grinned at each other, chests heaving with exertion.

Cade's grin slowly slid away, desire reflected in his gaze. He slowly took off his shirt and tossed it on a chair. Braden briefly thought of his beautiful suit coat and wondered idly where he'd tossed it, when Cade broke into his thoughts. "On your knees, facing me."

And just like that, Braden's body and mind settled into a happy, submissive place. He always melted at the deep tone Cade used on him. He scrambled to obey, a euphoric rush filling him when he complied with Cade's orders. Braden peered up at Cade, his hands itching to take action. "May I undress you?"

Cade raised a brow and shook his head. "You enjoy that too much. This is a punishment."

Braden pouted. He was about to protest but thought better of it and awaited further instruction. He watched as Cade removed his belt and then finished undressing, slowly, Braden nearly drooling as he watched.

"Undress yourself."

Braden stood to follow orders, quickly untying his bowtie. Cade looked around the room. "Since we still need to move our things over here, I'll have to make do with what I have at hand."

"Z?"

Cade lifted a brow and then glanced down to Braden's clothes, which were still on, and then back up to him. "Yes?"

Braden, made swift work of his button up shirt, revealing his undershirt underneath, and blushed. "I purchased a few items that you might want to make use of. May I show you?"

Vaguely amused, Cade gestured to the room at large. "Go ahead."

Braden, shirts having been discarded, unbuckled his belt. He got down on his knees in front of a long, cushioned chest at the foot of the bed and reached under the chest to unlatch it. He flipped the front and top up on its hinge. Braden watched as Cade stepped back, in awe of the piece of furniture he'd had commissioned. Braden proceeded to open several of the drawers, showing some of the items they'd previously purchased together, some new. The rest of the drawers were empty, plenty of room to grow, as it were.

Braden closed the lid, knelt on the cushioned chest and reached behind it, pulling out a pair of black nylon and Velcro under-the-bed restraints. He got up, pulled his pants and boxer briefs off, and made quick work of his socks. When he was naked, he hopped back up on the bed, crawled toward the headboard and reached between the mattress and the headboard, pulling the matching, connected restraints out and laying them at the top of the bed. He turned back around to find a very naked, very aroused Cade. He stopped and just looked his fill, until Cade cleared his throat. He sheepishly met Cade's eyes while he knelt back on his heels, his heart hammering in his chest.

"Turn around, face down on the bed, ass up."

A blush suffused Braden's chest, neck and arms, as he turned around and put his ass up in the air, his face turned to the side, against the bed.

"Knees wide apart."

Braden spread his legs wide open. Cade opened the Velcro of one of the ankle restraints, the noise causing a shiver to race up Braden's spine in anticipation. Once both of his ankles were cuffed, Cade moved to the top of the bed. "Both arms above your head."

Cade cuffed his wrists then walked out of his eyesight. Braden could hear him figuring out the locking mechanism on the new chest at the bottom of the bed, it opening, and him pulling out a couple drawers. A moment later, he was by Braden's side again. He squatted down so that they were eye level. "If it gets to be too much, use your safeword. Understood?"

"Understood, sir."

Cade crawled on the bed beside Braden, removed his glasses, and placed a blindfold over his eyes, causing his heartbeat to spike. Even though it was a punishment, Braden's body thrummed with excitement. From the beginning of their serious discussions regarding Domination and submission, Cade had stated unequivocally that he would never hurt Braden physically, and he'd never use humiliation, publicly or otherwise. He also promised never to punish him by taking away his touch or using the silent treatment. Braden had worried that didn't leave much for Cade to punish him with, but Cade had just laughed at that and warned him that he had many options using different types of sensory deprivation and sensory overload.

"I need something from downstairs, baby. Less than a minute. Are you all right as you are?"

Braden groaned but nodded.

"I need you to say the words, Bray."

"Sorry. Yes, sir."

"Good boy. Count out loud, if it helps."

Braden's love for his man grew. "I'm good, sir. Thank you."

He heard Cade jog down the stairs and then silence until, several drawn out moments later, he heard him bounding back up the stairs.

Next thing Braden knew, he was feeling what must have been one of the peacock feathers they'd purchased, drifting up his back. He knew his punishment for tricking Cade and teasing him into a chase was going to be his own personal version of hell. His whole body was ticklish, something that pleased Cade no end when he'd found out, quite by accident. Braden feared it would be Cade's favorite of his punishments, and Braden's least favorite. He'd almost prefer being shut off from Cade's touch for several hours, rather than endure being tickled, and that was saying something, as Braden needed Cade's touch like he needed his next breath.

The next hour was sheer agony and utter bliss, his muscles straining from the exertion of constantly trying to stay still, rather than flinch away from the next spot Cade decided needed attention. Intermingled with tickle torment were moments of pure ecstasy, being brought nearly to orgasm and then backed off, over and over, and never being allowed to come. All the while, Cade praised him or talked dirty to him. If it wasn't the feather, it was shocking bitter cold in the form of ice torture to his nipples, perineum, cockhead, balls, and asshole. He was whimpering and moaning in equal measure, his body unsure whether it was turned on or off, excited or repelled.

Just when he thought he could take no more and he might have to call a halt to the scene, Cade was releasing him from the cuffs, removing the blindfold, and replacing it with his glasses. He stretched him out on the bed, whispered soothing words while helping him loosen his limbs. Cade had him drink a bottle of water then lay back down for a massage of his sore muscles, all the while praising him.

"You handled your punishment very well, baby."

Curled up now in Cade's arms, buzzing on an aftercare high, he hummed. "Thank you. I thought you were going to take me from behind while I was cuffed."

"Not a chance, love. That's not what was on the agenda for you tonight before you derailed my plans. Remember?"

Braden's stomach did a nervous little dance as he realized, punishment aside, they were going to christen the bed for the first time that night, and he was going to be the one topping. He knew this was a night they'd remember for the rest of their lives and realizing that had him reconsidering. He raised his hands in front of him and realized they were shaking. He looked up into Cade's eyes and saw the gentle understanding reflected there. He ventured, "This is a big night. I don't know what I'm doing. Maybe I shouldn't be the one…"

Cade cut in before he could continue. "You're the perfect one to be doing this, Braden. I've been waiting for you to show interest. I didn't want to push."

Braden looked away. "I've been interested but nervous. You're a tough act to follow. I've never, ever been with anyone who cared so much for my pleasure, even at the expense of your own. I don't want to fuck this up."

"Braden look at me." When he did, Cade continued. "You couldn't possibly fuck this up. Tell me something, what came in the mail for me a few nights ago?"

"Uh, you mean the shoes?"

"The new running shoes, yes. The ones you had your contact track down for me. I mentioned one time that I really liked one of the pair of shoes you run in and you had a pair of them shipped here. Braden, I'm a size sixteen, that couldn't have been an easy task. A couple of weeks before that, what arrived in the mail?"

Braden nuzzled into him. "Your clothes. These are silly questions."

"My clothes from my tailor that you had commissioned for me."

"You needed more pants. You're living out of a friggin army duffle. I called your mom and asked who you used to make your clothing since even your cargo pants are tailor made for Pete's sake. You needed some stuff, and your clothes hadn't arrived yet from your place in Colorado Springs."

"Mmm hmm. And what about the meeting with my people a month ago?"

Braden pulled away and crossed his arms over his chest, frustration and confusion mounting. "What about it?"

"Braden, I mentioned I needed to meet with my people about a potential client whom Cooper had found. Not twenty-four hours later, you had a conference room booked for the meeting for the following day which is something my office manager usually handles. You'd baked more pastries than twenty people could eat, let alone fourteen of us, and had Maya and the girls make us a shit ton of coffee. What about Cooper's car?"

Braden grunted. "What is the point of this?"

Cade raised a brow. "Answer the question, baby."

Braden blushed and huffed. "I know a guy that restores old muscle cars. I made his wedding cake. All I did was put Cooper in touch with him, so he had someone good in the city to work on his Challenger. He loves that car!"

"Sawyer and Jackson's new place?"

"Zavier, you're being ridiculous. I heard them telling you they needed a realtor. I knew Emily would be able to help them."

"Mikayla?"

"Oh my god! Why are you asking me all these questions? She's outgrown her current dance studio. I just recommended a new one. Vaughn took it from there."

"Braden, it was the best dance academy in the area, and it wasn't accepting new students until you made a call."

Braden was embarrassed and uncomfortable. "Well, she's really talented. Look, just tell me, am I sticking my nose where it doesn't belong?"

"What!? *No!* Jesus, Braden, no, that's not what I'm saying at all."

"Well, what are you saying? We're supposed to be making love and celebrating our engagement. I don't understand why you're bringing up all of this stuff."

Cade let out a frustrated breath and rubbed his face. "I'm trying to make a point, and I'm obviously fucking it up. You're worried you won't be able to please me. I'm saying you please me every day. You think I'm the one taking care of you all the time, but you fail to realize you're constantly taking care of me. Not only that but taking care of my people and my family. Strike that: *our* people, *our* family. You're constantly helping people out in little ways, and I'm constantly hearing about it, but never from you."

Braden buried his face in Cade's chest. "It's nothing."

Cade squeezed him tight, "It's everything. Listen, I heard you joking with Maya one day about how grumpy you were with a client who kept changing her mind about what she wanted. You said you hated people and you were just lucky you found a job that allowed you to avoid the public as much as possible. Remember that?"

"Ugh, yes! She was driving me batty."

"Mmm hmm. First of all, for a guy who hates people, you know a shit ton of them. Second of all, you may not like the public, in general, but when you let people into your inner circle, and you have let all of my people into your inner circle, you are utterly selfless."

Braden looked up at Cade, his face skeptical, and made a rude sound in his throat. "I'm far from selfless. Can we change the subject? I don't even know why you're talking about this. It has nothing to do with anything."

Cade shook his head and kissed Braden's lips. "I'm saying that you won't be able to help but please me tonight because that's what you do every single day. It's second nature for you to please me."

Cade held Braden's chin, keeping his focus directly on him. "Braden, what is my job in this relationship?"

"To take care of my needs."

"That's right, I take care of your needs. But you, you take care of my needs as well. You take care of the little details that I can't be bothered with. You said a while ago that you wanted this to be an equal partnership, and I think it already is. We take care of each other's needs, every day. We just go about it differently."

Braden looked up at him, a little shocked. "That's actually pretty insightful and a little bit romantic."

Cade chuckled. "Who knew?"

Braden shook his head then leaned his forehead against Cade's chest. Cade ran his fingers through Braden's hair and tugged it, so Braden was looking up at him. He rubbed his thumb across Braden's cheek, leaned down, and kissed him. "Make love to me, Braden."

Braden looked into his eyes, breathed in deeply, and nodded. He felt some of his own confidence come back when he realized that Cade had so much confidence in him. He reached over to the nightstand and picked up his phone. He used it to dim the lights and turn on some music. He snickered when Cade gave his best Barry White impression. "Setting the mood."

Braden smiled and shook his head. He pushed gently on Cade's chest until he lay back against the pillows. He crawled astride his stomach and looked down at him. He trailed his hands along Cade's tattooed arms and then to his chest, where he paused to really look closely at his new warrior tattoo.

He traced the lines of the shield that was a combination of straight lines and curved edges. It was a beautiful piece of artwork, and the fact that Cade would forever brand his heart with a symbol that he felt represented Braden was tremendously moving. He kissed the spot then traveled a little lower and took one of Cade's nipple rings into his mouth and tugged. The breath that Cade sucked in was gratifying, so he moved over to the other nipple and gave it a tug and a flick with his tongue. He felt hands in his hair, holding him in place and heard, "That's it, just like that."

Braden's eyes nearly crossed, and his erection grew harder. He gave one last tug that would have sent him to his knees had he been on the receiving end and pulled back. He made to take off his glasses, but Cade stayed his hand. "Leave them on. Love you in those glasses. You're my every fantasy come to life."

Braden looked into his eyes and saw the truth there. He got off the bed and asked Cade to stand as he got down on his knees. He bit his lip when Cade cursed, looking down at him with desire burning in his eyes. "Fuck, but you look beautiful down on your knees for me."

Braden wasn't going to make it without embarrassing himself if Cade kept up with the dirty talk. He glanced slowly up Cade's body, taking him all in from one of his favorite positions, and that's when he noticed another new tattoo covering his latest gunshot wound. Braden touched the black star tattoo and then leaned up and licked it. The hairs on his body stood on end when he heard Cade suck in a startled breath through his teeth. He grabbed Braden by the back of his head and growled. "Do that again."

Braden licked it again with the flat of his tongue and then lightly bit it. He looked up at his man and the more he realized how much he was turning Cade on, the more his confidence grew. He lightly trailed the pads of his fingers up the back of Cade's legs. He brought them around to the front and ghosted his hands up those gorgeous, thick, muscular thighs to his hips then reached around and grabbed Cade's ass in his hands, squeezing the firm globes.

Braden leaned in and licked the area where thigh met groin. He hefted Cade's huge cock in his hand and put his nose in the pubic hair above it, Cade's dick against his cheek. He loved the smell of his man. Still holding his cock, he licked up the side and nibbled there using his teeth, lightly teasing, which Cade had professed to love. He gave the same treatment to the other side of Cade's cock and felt his hair being fisted. He looked up and saw Cade's clenched teeth before he opened his mouth and panted. "Stop teasing me and take it in your mouth, nice and slow."

He knew he was going to be topping Cade tonight, but he delighted in the fact that while he was doing it, Cade would continue to be the one in control. Being told what to do, how to do it, and when to do it ticked all the right boxes for Braden and rather than dreading what was to come, he found himself getting more and more eager as time passed. Cade gripped his chin and forced his eyes up. "Are you having a tough time making me your priority right now?"

Braden's eyes popped wide, mortified that he'd gone into his own head and spaced out on Cade. "I'm sorry, Z."

"Don't let it happen again. Take me deep into your mouth, Braden. Focus only on me."

Those words caused a drop of precum to bead on the tip of Braden's cock and slowly drip off. Cade never failed to turn him the fuck on when he was giving orders. He opened his mouth wide and took that massive cock in. He didn't close his lips over it until it had hit the back of his throat. His cheeks hollowed out as he sucked hard, and he moaned when he heard Cade growl, "That's it. Take it deep."

Braden did just that, repeatedly. When it felt like he couldn't take any more, he pushed himself, opened his throat and felt the head slide even further as he swallowed. He'd become adept at holding his breath and repressing his gag reflex, but what he'd learned is that Cade knew how far he could go. Once he took Cade deep, Cade would inevitably hold him still by the hair at the nape of his neck and just when Braden began to panic that he wouldn't be able to hold on another second, Cade would pull him off just in time to gulp some much needed air. The first time they'd done that, Cade had made sure he pulled him off early, so that Braden didn't have a chance to panic. Gradually over time, Braden had learned to trust Cade's instincts, and they'd both enjoyed the hell out of it.

"That mouth of yours is going to make me come if I'm not careful, and I don't want to come until you're deep inside of me." Braden's heartbeat accelerated, and he pulled off him and stood up. He squeezed Cade's hips then trailed the backs of his fingers against Cade's stomach, feeling the ripples of muscle there. He palmed Cade's pecs and squeezed them before he roamed his hands over those broad shoulders to the back of Cade's head and pulled him down so they could share a passionate kiss.

Cade leaned forward and grabbed Braden's ass then the backs of his thighs. It was a familiar move, so Braden braced himself, gripped the back of Cade's neck, and held on. He was pulled up Cade's front until he was able to wrap his legs around him. Cade sat down on the bed and Braden latched onto Cade's neck, sucking and using his teeth while making his way over to the other side. He moved his legs under him so he had better leverage as their mouths clashed in hunger. It was all tongues and lips and teeth, and they couldn't get enough of each other.

Braden moved his hips, grinding them into Cade's, and felt their cocks rub up against one another. He pulled back and looked down, biting his lip as he looked at their cocks. He glanced up into Cade's eyes and down again as he moved his hips, his lip still between his teeth. Cade leaned to the side and grabbed the lube he'd left on the nightstand, righted himself, and squirted some slick on their cocks.

He tossed the lube aside, grabbed Braden's hip with one hand and the back of Braden's neck with the other, and growled, "Grip them in your hand."

Braden groaned and did as he was told, his hand unable to wrap all the way around both cocks at once, but able to hold them together just fine. "That's it. Tighter. There you go. Now lean back on your other hand behind you and pump your hips."

Braden whimpered as he followed orders. The feel of their slicked-up cocks as they rubbed between his tight grip was unbelievable. He continued like that for several minutes until they both panted, and he groaned and let go, unable to take any more without losing it.

He sat back up and kissed his way down Cade's cheek to his neck. He tilted his head back and looked Cade in the eyes. "Will you scoot back and lay down?"

Cade did as he asked, one of his hands tucked behind his head showing off his corded triceps. Braden slid his thighs between Cade's and smiled when they spread for him and allowed him to sit back on his knees between Cade's legs to admire the spectacular view.

He caressed both hands lightly over Cade's thighs as he continued his perusal. His attention was on the vast expanse of inked skin; he devoured it with his eyes and felt deep down to his bones how lucky he was to have this man own him in every way, to have been made for him. He remembered, early on in their relationship, yelling at Cade and saying that he didn't want anyone to ever try to own him again. He had been wrong, so wrong. He wanted to be owned by Cade; needed it, craved it. The silent looks must have gotten to Cade. "Tell me what you're thinking."

Braden licked his lips, looked up into his lover's eyes and answered with blatant honesty. "I was thinking that you're perfect for me, and that you own me in every way possible, and I'm lucky to have been made for you."

Cade sucked in a breath. His eyes had been heavy-lidded and full of sexual promise, but after his words, they changed and flooded with possessiveness. They streaked greedily over his body in turn. "You *were* made for me and owning you is my pleasure and privilege. Every inch of you belongs to me. Do you know the one word I think of every time I see you after we've been separated for any length of time?"

Braden shook his head. "What word?"

Cade sat up swiftly and hugged Braden around the hips. He leaned into Braden and whispered in his ear. "*Mine.*"

Braden groaned at that; every part of him loved how true it was. He wrapped his arms around Cade's broad back and hugged him closer as he whispered, "Yes, yours, only yours."

Cade kept his arms tight around Braden's hips and lay down ever so slowly until Braden was draped over him. Those eyes, half-mast again, reflected blazing heat. He nibbled Braden's ear. "I need you deep inside of me. I want you to slowly make love to me first, and then when we're both delirious with need, I want you to fuck me hard and fast. Can you do that for me, baby?"

He swallowed audibly but nodded, and Cade narrowed his eyes. "Not good enough, Bray. I need to hear the words."

Braden nodded again and cleared his throat. "Yes, I can do that for you."

"That's exactly what I needed to hear. Get the slick, you're going to need to prep me really well. It's been years."

Braden's heart hammered in his chest just thinking about it, and as much as he was nervous to take this step, he knew it was what Cade wanted and maybe even what he himself needed. Maybe if he took this step, he'd be that much closer to banishing the hold he still felt Eric had on him.

Eric never would have allowed him to top, would have laughed in his face if he had asked. He would have thought that bottoming for anyone would make him weak, but in Braden's eyes, Cade's desire for him to top only made Cade stronger. Cade knew where his mind had taken him because he clasped Braden's face in his hands. "He doesn't belong here between us. The only thing that belongs here between us is our love for each other. We both need this, Braden."

Braden nodded. He knew Cade was right and something inside of him just clicked. He knew he could do it, knew he'd make Cade come hard and that he'd follow. At that, Braden gave a naughty smile and received a grin in return. He leaned in to kiss Cade, tugged on his bottom lip and received a throaty growl in response. He licked where he'd just bitten and kissed his way over to Cade's ear. "I'm going to lose myself in you. I'm going to come deep inside of you, but only after I pound your tight ass until you lose that famous control."

"Fuck, yes. Make me lose control, baby." Cade groaned as his hands, that had been caressing Braden's ass gripped the round globes, squeezed, and he used his leverage to grind their cocks together again. Braden bit the lobe of his ear and tugged. He moved down Cade's neck, licking and nibbling his way down to his pecs, where he settled in for a little tug of war with both of Cade's nipple rings. He flicked and pulled on those rings with his teeth, tongue and lips until Cade was pulling his hips down against his upward thrusts with every tug. They both moaned, and Braden took pity on him and continued his downward momentum. He licked his way along those inked lines and circled his navel with his tongue, continuing on a leisurely trip down his sparse happy trail as his fingers did the same to his v line.

He kissed his way up Cade's cock but never took it in his mouth.

Instead, he gripped it with his hand and began to work on Cade's balls. He sucked them in, one at a time, and the moans coming from Cade were music to his ears. He pulled on the skin of his sack with his lips, sucking it in then catching it between his teeth, eliciting a string of muttered curses that caused him to smile even while he tugged lightly on that sensitive skin then dove back in for more. He spent several minutes there until he finally lifted Cade's balls and licked down the center line until he reached his taint. His hand, already grasping Cade's cock, squeezed tighter and began a slow and steady pumping motion while he lightly licked Cade's perineum.

He moved his way slowly down to Cade's ass, pushed his legs up to spread him wide, and trailed his tongue down his cleft. He nibbled on each cheek and nipped his way back to his center where he licked and then blew on Cade's entrance. Braden watched as the skin contracted and reveled in Cade's moans. He repeated that several times then fluttered his tongue over his hole, up and down, until he couldn't control himself and he flexed his tongue and speared it inside. Cade shouted out a string of curses, but Braden was relentless and continued his sensual assault until he heard Cade growl his name and pull his hair. He stopped the torture and lowered his legs. "Fuck, you're too good at that. Don't want to come yet."

Braden grabbed the lube, slicked his fingers up quickly, and hunkered back down. He turned his head to the side and bit Cade on the inner thigh, soothing it with his tongue. He leaned his head against that thigh as he spread the lube over Cade's asshole and watched as it contracted at his touch. Cade raised his legs, knees up in the air, and again, gave more access to Braden. Braden hooked his other hand around Cade's outer thigh and lightly skimmed his hand up along his firm abs to his left nipple and played with his nipple ring as he pressed his finger against Cade's entrance and met resistance. He looked up, meeting Cade's gaze. "Z, will you let me in?"

Cade smiled with satisfaction. "You ask for permission so beautifully."

Braden sucked in a breath when he realized he'd done so without even meaning to, as if his autopilot was already set to submit without conscious thought. His cock got harder at the approval in Cade's voice and harder still as his finger was allowed in, causing a drip of precum to fall on the bed. He whimpered, "Thank you," and continued to slip his lubed finger deep into

Cade. He brought his other hand down Cade's chest, grabbed his cock, and slid it deep into his mouth. He wasn't sure if he'd ever be able to deep-throat the whole thing, but he'd work on it for the rest of his life.

As he slid a second finger in, Cade grunted, and Braden tasted the precum that dripped on his tongue. He began to move his head in the same rhythm as his fingers and was thrilled when Cade's hips began to jut up to meet his thrusts. He slipped a third finger in and began to thrust and then scissor them for several minutes. Finally, he curled them up and tapped Cade's prostate which elicited a "Holy Fuck!"

More precum coated Braden's tongue and he knew Cade was ready for him. He pulled his fingers out, got up on his knees between Cade's legs and grabbed the bottle of lube again. He slicked up his cock and looked into his lover's eyes. "May I make love to you now?"

Cade's eyes closed at his words. "God. Yes, baby, make love to me."

With permission granted, he leaned forward and braced his hand beside Cade's chest on the bed, pressed the head of his cock up against Cade's hole, and was slowly allowed entrance. Holy fuck, he'd never felt anything so warm and snug around the head of his cock. He eased in a bit more, groaned and exhaled. "Oh damn, Z, you're so hot and tight."

"Oh fuck, baby, keep going, I need more of you, all of you." Braden obeyed and slowly slid home. They both moaned, and Braden held still as he waited for Cade to adjust to the intrusion. Suddenly, he felt Cade's muscles clamp down on him, and he looked from where they were joined up into Cade's eyes. What he saw there was an overwhelming hunger. He waited another few seconds and finally got what he needed. "Move for me, Braden. Move for me, now."

A shiver started at his spine and worked its way outward. He began to slowly pump his hips, almost pulling all the way out before he slid back in full tilt. He kept his eyes on Cade's as he did this, wanting to see the pleasure Cade was receiving from their joining. The moment was exceptionally intense as their eyes locked and held, and Braden continued to slide slowly in and out of his fiancé, reveling in every groan, curse, and moan. He'd never felt anything like it, and he realized that he did feel a sense of power, a sense of control that he hadn't been expecting. He felt sweat bead at his temples and realized the amount of energy it was taking him to keep himself composed, to keep himself at a slow and steady pace.

He changed his angle and knew he'd butted up against Cade's prostate by the way his body bowed, and his eyes closed in ecstasy while he moaned deeply. Braden leaned back further and pumped in just a little bit faster. Cade opened his eyes again. "I need you to pound me now, Braden. I need to be fucked hard."

Braden groaned, leaned forward, grabbed the back of Cade's thighs and pushed them back toward him so that his knees were up near his shoulders. He leaned more fully over Cade, pressing his weight onto his thighs for leverage. They made eye contact as he moved deep inside of him, over and over, pounding in and out. He wasn't going to last long at this angle, it felt that good. He leaned down and kissed Cade, who growled as he devoured Braden's lips, fisted one hand in his hair and grabbed Braden's ass with the other to pull him deeper. Cade released his hair and Braden pulled back, silently asking Cade permission. Cade nodded. "Hard, baby."

Braden began a hard pace, his hips moving like a piston. He felt the sweat break out all over his body, and when he looked at Cade's chest, he saw it glistening there as well. He continued his punishing rhythm and loved every grunt he received from Cade as he continued to pound into him. Cade's hands were everywhere which didn't help his control. He knew he was getting close but didn't want to go over before Cade did. He eased back onto his knees and brought Cade's legs up so that his calves rested on his shoulders. "Can I touch you?"

"Fuck, yes. Make me come, Braden." With that, Braden reached around and grabbed Cade's long, thick cock and began to stroke it in the same cadence as his hips. Cade was mindless at that point. Braden loved that Cade could no longer focus on him, his eyes clouded with lust. "Fuck, fuck, fuck, fuck. Yes. Yes, baby. Squeeze it tighter."

Braden did as he was told and continued to pound Cade's ass at the same time. He was out of breath, and the sensations were immense. He couldn't hold on, and when he looked down at Cade, he heard him shout out, "Oh fuck! Oh fuck, Braden, that's it! I'm coming, baby. I'm… Oh god…"

Braden lost it.

Those words, and the tight grip of Cade's ass, clamping down even harder on Braden's cock, a volley of thick white cum spurting out of Cade's cock, tipped Braden over into his own orgasm. He threw back his head and shouted Cade's name as he pumped ropes of cum deep into Cade's ass. The orgasm lasted forever. In the end, his body was a mass of spasms that he was unable to control.

He let go of Cade's legs and collapsed on top of him. Cade wrapped his arms tight around Braden, and they lay like that for what seemed like hours but was probably only a few minutes. Their chests were both heaving, and neither of them were able to form words for what just happened as their minds caught up.

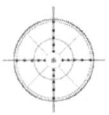

Cade

Cade rolled Braden half underneath him and nuzzled his neck. They lay there, almost dozing, until Cade realized he didn't want them to fall asleep covered in his cum. He moved more fully on top of Braden and kissed him awake. "Wrap your arms and legs around me."

Braden did as he was told, and Cade carried Braden into the bathroom. He turned on the water, and while they waited for it to heat up, he held Braden tightly to him and kissed him slowly. He felt some of Braden's cum slide down his leg and stepped into the shower just in time. He gently put Braden back on his feet. They showered languidly, touching and kissing without haste. They enjoyed each other's bodies, touched every inch of skin.

After they were both clean, Cade clasped onto Braden's hands and wound them around his neck. He lifted Braden up to wrap his legs around his waist again. He leaned him against the wall and pressed him there with his body. The shower heads continued to rain water down on them from all angles as he gazed into Braden's eyes and moved the hair out of his face. He watched droplets of water slide down his face and licked and kissed them away. He whispered, barely loud enough to be heard over the water. "You made me the happiest man alive when you said yes. I'm going to spend the rest of my life ensuring that I make you as happy as you make me. I love you, baby."

"I love you too, Z."

"Let me get us out and dried off."

Cade stepped out onto the bath mat, took a new folded towel and set it on the counter, and then put Braden on top of it. He turned to get another towel and began to dry him from head to toe. He brushed out his hair as he stood between Braden's legs, drying the dripping ends with a towel. Braden checked his blood, and they both crawled back in bed. Cade pulled Braden on top of him and put both of his hands behind his head as Braden got comfortable and laid his chin on his stacked hands on top of Cade's chest, a habit they both loved.

Cade brought a hand down and fiddled with the ring on Braden's finger. He looked into Braden's eyes. "How are you feeling, after what we did?"

Braden took a deep breath. "I think I needed it. I think it was just one more step toward erasing that stain, toward moving on. It felt powerful, being inside of you…amazing."

Cade looked at him for several moments then came at it another way. "How did it feel, emotionally?"

Braden looked at Cade as he patiently tucked a loose lock of Braden's hair behind his ear. Braden shook his head. "I needed it and you wanted it."

"But?"

Braden shored up his courage. "But when you dominate me, I get to just let go and feel and it's, I don't know, liberating? It feels natural when you take such utter control of me when we're in a scene. There's an intense connection when you're deep inside of me, watching me, making me shatter, or edging me until I'm out of my mind and not allowing me to come. I sometimes get this floaty feeling; I don't know, it's like nothing I've ever felt in my life."

Cade smiled. "Yeah, when I can get you into subspace, I can see all of that reflected in your eyes just before you fly. I wanted to give myself to you tonight. You're right about that. I needed to feel you inside of me, to become a part of me, but I also wanted you to be able to feel me that way, in case it was better for you."

Braden reached out and ran a hand over Cade's hair, looking him in the eye. "Nothing is better for me than when we are doing what feels natural for both of us. When I'm in your arms, I feel whole."

Cade pulled him in tighter. "I know, baby. That's how I feel, too."

Braden scratched his short nails over Cade's stubbled jaw. "When you told me that when you look at me you think *'mine,'* it felt right. Being able to tell you that you own me? There's strength in that. There's power in giving myself to you."

"Submitting to someone takes bravery and strength. You're entrusting your mind and your body to me. You can't do that if you don't fully trust me. It took time for us to get to this point."

Braden nodded, and Cade pulled him in for a kiss before he continued, "Remember, if there's ever anything I am not providing you, come to me and ask me for it."

Braden felt a thrill knowing that the rules they'd established together were for his benefit, and whenever Cade reminded him of them, he felt safe and secure. He nodded. "If I need it, I'll ask you for it."

They kissed for several minutes and then Braden grew serious. "There is something I need to ask."

"What is it, Bray?"

"When we get married, can I take... Um, what happens to our names?"

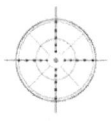

Braden

Cade stopped breathing and didn't say anything for several long moments. He rolled them over so Braden lay pliant beneath him and looked deep into Braden's eyes. Just as Braden was about to explain himself, Cade shifted above him, and he realized that Cade had hardened at his question. A thrill of excitement shot its way through Braden's body and his breath quickened.

Their eyes were fixed on each other and Braden sighed. "I want—"

"I know what you want."

Braden's features softened. "You do?"

Cade nodded. "You'll become Braden McCade." Cade leaned down and whispered exactly what Braden needed to hear. "You're mine, so you'll take my name."

Braden's eyes grew damp, he reached up and held Cade to him and used the words he'd only ever used while they were in a scene, until this moment, when it seemed so much more. "Yes, sir."

Cade's grip on him tightened then he rose up enough to look into Braden's eyes which reflected the truth behind those words. What Braden saw as a result made his body flush hot. Cade gripped Braden's hands in one of his, pulled them up above his head, and wrapped them around the slats on the headboard.

Cade slowly slid his fingers down Braden's inner arm and watched his fiancé's eyes dilate as he shivered. He growled out, "I'm going to fuck you now. It's going to be hard and fast. Don't move your hands from the headboard. Don't come until I give you permission. Do you understand?"

"Yes, sir."

"Fuck, baby, you're going to kill me with that."

Cade reached for the lube, slicked himself up and was about to slide home when Braden whispered, "Z, I need permission for one more thing."

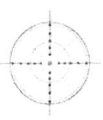

Cade

Cade took a deep breath to calm himself down. When he had himself under control, he opened his eyes. "What is it, Bray?"

"Can I move my hands?"

Cade only nodded, unsure if he could speak at that moment. Braden took his left hand, clasped Cade's hand in his and brought it to his heart. "I want your mark on me. Can I get the same warrior tattoo on my chest, above my heart?"

That was it, Cade lost any semblance of control he'd had. He growled, moved Braden into position, and slid balls deep into his boy. He didn't have the control to prep him, nor did he have the control to slow down. He heard Braden whimper, but when he looked down in concern, satisfaction flowed through his veins when he saw Braden's head thrown back in ecstasy, a flush on his cheeks, bottom lip between his teeth. Braden slid his hand down to Cade's ass and squeezed. Cade knew he was holding on to his control by a very thin thread. As he fucked, he growled. "Hands above your head."

When Braden complied immediately, he ordered, "Open up more for me."

Braden lifted his other leg around Cade's hip and pulled both legs back against his chest. He was splayed open and Cade impaled him deeper. "Eyes on me. Oh, yeah, that's it. You're so good at following my orders."

Suddenly, that tight grip around his cock tightened even further and he knew Braden was squeezing his cock for all he was worth. "You're squeezing yourself so tight around my cock. I can't figure out if you're being bad and trying to tip me over before I'm ready, or if you're being good and trying to please me. Which one is it?"

Braden whispered brokenly, "Please you, Z. I only ever want to please you."

He saw the truth in Braden's eyes, and it sent tremors up his spine. He continued to pump himself deep, so deep into Braden that he saw stars and his voice was a caress in Braden's ear, "You're so good to me. So good, baby."

Cade's heart lodged somewhere in the vicinity of his throat. He couldn't believe he was fortunate enough to find a man that wanted exactly what he wanted for their future. Just thinking about how much effort Braden put into pleasing him made a possessive streak rocket through him. He growled, "You'll wear *our* mark and you'll also wear my family crest."

"Please, yes."

Cade pounded harder and ground out, "By tomorrow night, you'll be branded as mine, permanently."

Braden whispered brokenly, "Oh fuck. Yes, sir."

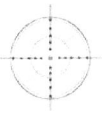

Braden

Cade's pace was unrelenting, and Braden was dying to touch him, dying to grip his ass and pull him in faster, harder, but he wasn't permitted to do so, and as much as that killed him, it also sent a thrill of excitement through his veins that couldn't be ignored. That part of him that wanted, no needed, to submit overrode any other desire he ever had. The complete trust that he handed over to Cade always had a better return than pushing them both for a faster release. Something in Cade recognized exactly what to do for Braden to prolong his orgasms, to build them up into something he never knew he could feel, and he could ride that high for an amazingly long time.

Cade must have slicked up his hand because when he gripped Braden's cock in his tight fist, there was the unmistakable slide of lubed flesh against flesh. He quickly brought Braden to the edge of an orgasm then idled back, softly gripping him, all while fucking him ruthlessly. Once Braden calmed, Cade edged him close to the precipice again then backed away. Braden whimpered, "Please, Z."

"Beg me for it."

Braden moaned and whispered, "Please, can I come? Please, sir."

Cade gripped Braden's cock in his hand again and set a quick, hard rhythm; every stroke ended in a twist. Braden's body tightened, and Cade continued to fuck his ass, deep and hard. He cupped the tip of Braden's cock in his hand and twisted slowly while squeezing and pulling up around the head. He leaned down and whispered, "Come."

As his thumb tapped on Braden's slit, he exploded, his body rocketing off the bed and clenching down on Cade's cock. As Braden's cock shot ribbons of cum on Cade's hand and his own chest, Cade grunted as he came deep inside Braden and growled, "That's it, so beautiful, baby."

Braden's body spasmed once more, then lay replete beneath him, as Cade shuddered, still deep inside of Braden, his body releasing inside of his boy. He rested his head in the crook of Braden's neck, his breath sawing in and out of him. He took his time recovering, knowing Braden preferred he stay deep inside of him as long as possible.

He eventually pulled himself from his lover's body, uncurled Braden's fingers from the headboard slats, pulled his arms down, and rubbed them thoroughly to get the blood pumping back into his cold fingers. He kissed Braden's temple and chuckled when Braden closed his eyes, sighed, and rolled onto his side, hugging Cade's pillow. He headed to the bathroom and was back in minutes, cleaning Braden up, and then himself. He managed to get Braden under the covers, to give up his pillow, and tucked him up against him.

Cade continued to caress his fiancé's gorgeous face and kiss it all over. He ran his hands through his still damp hair. Braden's eyes lazily moved to look at him; he smiled and sighed but didn't say anything and still didn't move. With his leg over Braden's, he used his heel to nudge Braden's leg between his, and he threw his leg over Braden's hip and settled him in close.

Braden snuggled into him, loving the feeling of being surrounded. They lay like that for a long while, and just when Cade was sure that Braden drifted off, he moved his head from under Cade's chin. "I never thanked you for such a beautiful proposal. You're everything to me, Zavier McCade. Everything. And I'm so lucky that you found me."

Cade grinned. "I found you and knew almost immediately that I was going to keep you. We're going to have an incredible life together. I'll make sure of it."

Cade brought his hand from Braden's hip and placed it carefully over Braden's heart. He leaned in, kissed Braden's forehead, and then whispered, "Mine."

Braden leaned forward and kissed Cade's new warrior tattoo and whispered back, "Yours."

Epilogue

BRADEN

~TWO YEARS LATER~

Braden gripped the handle in Cade's Mercedes G-Class and slammed his hand on the dash. If Cade wasn't careful, they were going to be dead before they got to the damned hospital in the first place. He said as much to Cade, and the only response he got was a grunt. He grinned and looked over at his husband as he moved his hand from the dash to Cade's leg. Cade saw his expression and sent him an answering grin in response. Someone honked at them, and Cade's face went from a grin to a comical grimace as he got his eyes back on the road.

Braden snickered. "Really, babe, please don't kill us. It's imperative that we get there in one piece."

"Mr. McCade, are you questioning my driving skills?"

"Yes, Mr. McCade, I am. When I have to grab the 'Oh Shit!' handle and a honk is the only thing reminding you that you need to keep your eyes on the road, it's time for me to step in."

Cade chuckled. "I'll have you know, I am licensed to drive a tank, a Bradley, a Cougar H, a Stryker, any military Humvee, and a Growler."

Braden raised a brow, got out his phone and pretended to type something on it and asked, deadpan, "So, using my real-life translator here, what you're saying is that you're essentially licensed to be a farmer and drive agricultural machinery?"

Cade threw back his head and laughed. "I tell you I can handle almost every heavy artillery military vehicle the army could throw at me, and you liken that to fucking agricultural machinery?"

Braden laughed. "I'll be impressed when you tell me you can fly."

Cade looked over at Braden, raised a brow, and then focused back on the road. "I've flown a helicopter before."

Braden's jaw dropped, and he blushed. "You… Seriously?"

Cade recognized the change in Braden's voice. "Blushing? Shit, baby, how is it that we've been married for more than a year, and I've never known you have a thing for pilots? I think we're going to have to do some role playing until I can get my license."

Braden's eyes widened. "Wait, what? What license?"

Cade grinned as he took a turn too fast and shrugged. "My helicopter pilot's license. We've been talking about buying one for Custos. I wasn't planning on learning to fly it until now."

"You don't have to…"

Cade interrupted, grinning. "Oh, I do. I really do. I like that look in your eyes, and it will be good to have a backup pilot there."

They screeched to a halt in front of the hospital valet parking kiosk and jumped out. Cade dealt with the attendant, jogged around the hood, grabbed Braden's hand in his, and kissed the back of it. They walked toward the automatic doors of the hospital and began to jog through the lobby to the bank of elevators.

They didn't have long to wait for an elevator as it was nearly eight p.m. and not many people were around. Cade pulled Braden into a tight embrace and leaned down to kiss him. "I love you. Don't be scared. She's strong as hell, and we're going to help her through this."

Braden looked up at him suspiciously and stated, "You were distracting me in the car, weren't you?"

Cade smiled softly down at the love of his life. "Did it work?"

Braden scrunched up his face then opened his mouth in exasperation. "Wait, were you lying about getting your pilot's license?"

Cade's face grew serious, and his eyes glittered and narrowed. He clasped Braden's face in his palms. "Have you ever known me to lie to you, about anything?"

Braden sighed and shook his head. "No, Z. I'm sorry."

Cade's face softened, and Braden's body relaxed as Cade kissed his forehead. "You blushed and practically stammered when I told you I'd flown a helo before. Of course, I'm gonna make the most of that reaction, and you know I love a new challenge."

Braden bit his lip, blushed again, and nodded then Cade laughed. "It might have to wait for a bit though, hmm?"

Braden snickered, nodded again, and looked up into Cade's eyes just as the elevator dinged and he huffed. "Dammit, you distracted me again."

Cade chuckled, "You're welcome. Come on, our girl needs us right now."

They jogged down the hallway, stopped at the admissions desk, and gave their names which were checked against a list. They received wristbands for entry and were allowed through the locked doors. They ran to her room and entered into what should have been a quiet, calm, and peaceful room but instead was loud and chaotic as two nurses fiddled with a machine and argued about it, and a third was looking at the computer, all three of them completely ignoring Maya.

From the hospital bed, Maya glanced over at Braden, and the stress in her eyes and on her face sent his heart galloping in his chest. He squeezed Cade's hand in a death grip, looked up at him in panic, and received an answering squeeze in turn and a whispered, "I'll handle it. Go to her."

Braden crossed the room to her and gathered her in a hug. He whispered, "It's going to be fine. Please, don't stress."

He glanced up and was confused to see Vaughn, not to mention the fact that he was holding Maya's hand and she wasn't trying to pull away. Curious. Braden smiled at Vaughn and received a worried look in return. "Did I miss something? She seemed stressed, but I chalked that up to the reason we're here in the first place."

Maya blushed, and Braden looked at her quizzically. "You didn't tell him why you're so anxious?"

When she shook her head, another tear escaped, and he admonished,

"Maya, don't you know enough about him yet to know he'd move mountains for you?"

Her eyes widened, and she looked at Vaughn. "What are you talking about? We're only on our first date for crying out loud! He finally wore me down." She cast a look around the room, and then back to him. "This is too much, Bray. Please."

Braden smiled, sat down in the chair beside her bed, and held her other hand. "Everything is going to be all right."

"But…"

She was interrupted by Cade's deceptively soft, steely voice of command. "Who's in charge in this room?"

A harried woman, hair falling from her ponytail, looked up. "I am, sir."

"Where is her birth plan?"

"Excuse me?"

Cade narrowed his eyes. "Where. Is. Her. Birth. Plan? Is it not hospital policy to pull up a woman's birth plan upon admitting her to the labor and delivery wing and ensuring she is out of immediate danger?"

Her eyes popped wide. "Yes, let me just…"

She hit several keys on the computer and brought up the birth plan. After reading it, she made a distressed noise in the back of her throat. "I'm sorry, sir. I see she wants limited staff in the room, no students. I'm going to go talk to the charge nurse and see if she can get this sorted. We're gonna need a new monitor brought in. This one isn't working properly."

As all three nurses left the room, taking the broken monitor with them, Cade pulled an extra chair up near the foot of Maya's bed to face Braden's, sat and crossed one leg over the other as he relaxed back and placed his forearm along Maya's blanketed leg, resting his hand on her knee, "What else can I do for you?"

At that, Maya burst into tears. "Thank you. I'm so sorry. I was being stupid, but I hate being in the hospital as a patient. I know it's silly, but it was all too much. I couldn't…"

Cade shook his head. "Nothing to be sorry about. You're not to stress. Leave that for me." He rubbed her knee. "Tell me how I can help."

She took a deep breath, tears still coursed their way down her face, "It's already better. Thank you, really."

"Where's your bag? Let's get your music on, at least."

Her tears, which had slowed, began full force again and she wailed. "I was out on a date! What the hell was I thinking? I don't have my bag. I don't have anything. I'm not prepared! It's probably just Braxton Hicks, or something I ate. I haven't had any contractions in a while. I'm so stupid, I probably don't even need to be here."

Cade untucked the blankets from around her feet, pulled her foot closer to him, and began massaging it. Braden knew from a lot of experience how good his hands were. He watched Maya's face relax and heard her sigh as Cade spoke. "Maya, look at me. That's it. Take a deep breath and let it out for me. Is the bag packed in our guest room by the door?"

Maya nodded and indelicately wiped her nose with the back of her hand, causing Vaughn to offer her a handkerchief from his pocket, which she took and played with in her lap. Cade continued to massage her foot with one hand as he pulled out his phone with the other and dialed. "Coop, where are you? Turn around and go back for her bag at our place. I'll have someone bring it down to you, so you don't have to get out. Yeah. Okay. Bye."

He dialed again and waited. "Brody, can you spare a few minutes, or are you working a job right now? Good. I need you to go upstairs to our place. Braden's unlocking the elevator for you right now."

Braden sat up and pulled out his phone to disarm the elevator security and then nodded back to Cade. "Head up to the guest bedroom and grab Maya's go bag. It's right by the door." He pulled the phone away. "Anything else you need, sweetheart?"

Maya sniffled. "My pillow, my Kindle and its charger, and my phone's charger too. Oh, and my slippers that are at the foot of the bed and the robe that's there, too."

Cade smiled and nodded, the phone back at his ear. "Did you catch all that? Yeah, thanks. Take it all down to the front. Cooper is on his way back to get it, and I don't want him to have to get out of the car for it. Yeah. Thanks, man."

He hung up the phone and resumed massaging her foot with both hands. She settled back into her pillow, both her hands held by Vaughn and Braden, and took a relaxed breath that caught the second the door swung open. A tall, extremely handsome, African American man walked in, an iPad in his hand that he was focused on, and a surgical cap covering his head. He looked up and gave them a smile and then tipped his head to the side. "Vaughn."

Vaughn smiled and stood, hand stretched out as the doctor approached. "Hey, Trey, nice to see you, man. I didn't know you were at this hospital. Maya, this is Dr. Trey Woods. He's been a member of the gym for years."

Trey smiled down at Maya. "Maya, how are you feeling?"

"Better, now."

"I hear there's been a misunderstanding about your birth plan?"

Cade stood up, held out his hand. "Zavier McCade, and this is my husband, Braden McCade. It's nice to meet you. Her birth plan was ignored. The nurses that were in here left to talk to the charge nurse."

Trey nodded and smiled. "I've got Sabrina coming in to work with you. She's great, you'll love her. So, Maya, you look beautiful, but how are you feeling? Sounds like you came in with contractions but haven't had any in the last thirty minutes. Is that accurate?"

Maya smiled. "I like you."

"I like you too, gorgeous."

Vaughn grumbled. "Don't even think about it."

Trey laughed, tipping his head toward Braden and Cade. "She's safe from me. I play on their team, not yours."

Vaughn blushed and stammered. "Oh. Fine then. Good."

Trey chuckled and glanced back at Maya. "So, no more contractions?"

Maya sighed. "I'm sorry. No. Maybe it was Braxton Hicks, or something I ate."

"Well, you're here, so why don't we check you out and see?"

Maya nodded. A woman entered their room, a bright smile on her face. "Hey, doc, looks like I'm working with Maya." She turned and grinned at everyone in the room. "Hi everyone, I'm Sabrina. Doc, you want to run some tests?"

"Yeah, let's do that. Thanks, Sabrina."

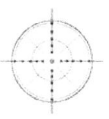

Maya

As they set about getting ready to run their tests, Maya asked to use the restroom and the fetal and heart monitors attached to her were removed. She stood up with the help of Braden and Cade and was headed toward the bathroom when she squeaked as she felt a tiny pop and looked down to see water trickling down her leg and onto the floor. She looked up, a shocked look on her face, just as Cooper walked in with a huge smile and her stuff in his hands. He took one look at her expression, and they both looked down at the floor. His eyes widened comically. "Shit, Sunshine, let's get you back in bed."

She blushed but shook her head. "No. I have to pee." She turned around to face the doctor, who'd come up behind her. "Can I still use the bathroom?"

He smiled. "Yes, of course. Contractions could start any minute, or they could take hours yet, requiring Pitocin to get you going. We'll get this cleaned up, you can get right back in bed, and we'll check and see how you're doing."

Maya blushed again. "I'm sorry for the mess."

Trey laughed. "Gorgeous, that's the least of the mess this room has seen. Don't worry about it. Take your time, and we'll be ready for you when you get back."

She hurried into the bathroom to do her business. When she came back out, she was feeling much better, more herself. She was helped back into the bed and when monitors were placed back on her, she took a deep breath and glanced around. "Where's Sabrina? There's altogether too many penises in this room and not nearly enough vaginas. Cooper, where's Mom? Doc, where's my OB?"

Trey laughed. "Feeling better, I see. Sabrina went to page Dr. Thomas, but she should be here any minute. Do you really want to get rid of me and my penis that badly?"

She laughed despite herself. "No, I quite like you. You can stick around."

Cooper put down his phone. "Dad's parking the car. They should be up here soon."

Maya took a deep breath, happy her parents chose this week for an impromptu visit north. "Okay."

Trey smiled as Sabrina walked back in the room. "Dr. Thomas just arrived. She was at a dinner party, apparently, and needs to change, so she'll be here in a few minutes."

Trey smiled warmly at Maya. "As your contractions haven't started up again, would you like to wait for Dr. Thomas to get here, so that she can check your cervix and run any tests she feels are necessary?"

Maya bit her lip and nodded. "Yeah. I'm sorry."

"No need. She's your OB, and you've been seeing her for the duration of your pregnancy. I'll go check on some other patients and come back to check on you in a bit. Dr. Thomas may pull me in for the birth. Rest easy and ring the call button if she doesn't arrive in the next few minutes and you need anything."

Maya smiled shyly. "Thanks for helping with the nurses."

Trey winked at her and made his way to the door. Braden felt the tension leave her body. He was grateful she'd found a good OB that she felt comfortable with. Cooper and Cade went about setting up her music, got her comfortable in her own slippers and robe, and propped her up on her own pillow. In no time, she was much more at ease.

When her mom flew into the room and gave her a hug, both women got teary-eyed and had a whispered conversation. When Sylvia saw that her daughter's hand was caught up in Vaughn's, she raised her eyebrow at her daughter and made her way around to the other side of the bed and sat by Maya as she extended her hand. "Hello there, I'm Sylvia Sullivan, Maya's mom. Who might you be?"

Vaughn smiled and clasped her tiny hand in his free one. "Mrs. Sullivan, it's an honor to meet you. I'm Vaughn Bowman."

"Please, call me Syl, or if you must, Sylvia. Vaughn, from the gym in Cooper and Cade's building?"

"Yes, ma'am, The Knockout is mine."

Sylvia sighed. "I must look dreadfully old to you."

A mortified expression passed across Vaughn's face. "What? *No!* You're beautiful, ma'am. I can see where Maya gets her good looks."

Sylvia grinned unabashedly. "Oh good, so you won't insult me any longer by calling me ma'am, right?"

Vaughn blushed. "No, ma... Uh, no, Mrs... Sylvia."

Sylvia grinned again and patted the back of his hand. "Good man. So, are you dating my daughter?"

"Yes, I am."

"And you chose now, when she's thirty-five weeks pregnant, to take her out?"

"Technically, no. I began asking her out well over a year ago. I think I just finally wore her down. But now is as good a time as any. And she's never been more beautiful."

Sylvia's smile grew wider, and she looked at Maya who had a shy smile on her face and a nice pink blush on her cheeks. "Darling, I like this one."

Maya narrowed her eyes. "Yeah, he grows on you."

Sylvia laughed at that and hugged her daughter tight. She got up and made her way around to her son. After giving Cooper a hug, she made her way over to Braden and Cade. "How is my favorite couple doing?"

Braden smiled and pulled her into a hug. "We're doing really well, thanks, Syl. Kinda serendipitous that you're here visiting this weekend. Where's Jon?"

"Oh, you know Jon, he doesn't trust anyone with his baby, so he dropped me in front and is parking himself instead of making use of the valet. He's probably parked as high up in the parking structure as he can get, with no cars near Eleanor."

Everyone nodded, as if this was not news. Vaughn spoke up, unable to hide his amusement. "Eleanor?"

Cooper replied, "Oh, yeah! Eleanor is a beauty. She's a mint condition 1969 Mustang. My love of cars comes from my dad."

As if the discussion conjured him up, a man that was the spitting image of Cooper, only with a full head of gorgeous, wavy silver hair, walked in. "How's my baby girl?"

Maya raised both her arms and wiggled her fingers for a hug, happy to see her father. "Hi, Daddy."

"Hey, Sugarplum. How are you? How's the baby? Everything good?"

They hugged while she answered, "Yeah, I think so. My water just broke, so maybe things will get going here soon. No turning back now!"

"That's my girl." He turned and gave his son a hug and then did the same with Braden and Cade. "How are all my boys?"

He got positive responses all around then turned back to Maya, which is when he saw her hand engulfed in Vaughn's much larger one. He narrowed his eyes and tilted his head. "And who are you?"

Maya, exasperated, chastised, "Daddy! Be nice. This is Vaughn. We were on a first date tonight, and I started having contractions, so he brought me right in."

"A first date? Sugarplum, you're about to have a baby, is this really the time to be dating?"

"I wore her down, sir. I've been asking her out for over a year now, damn near the first time I met her through Cade and Cooper."

Jon harrumphed. "How do you know my boys?"

"Your boys rescued my daughter, Mikayla, from her kidnapper and brought her back to me, safe and whole. I'll be forever in their debt."

Cade stepped up to Jon and put an arm around his shoulders. "Jon, this is the man who owns The Knockout, the fighter's gym that's located in our building."

"Wait, you're Vaughn Bowman? The boys have told me a lot about you. I suppose my daughter could do worse."

Vaughn chuckled good naturedly. "I'm sure she could, sir, but I can tell you that I could do no better. Your daughter is one of a kind, and I'm doing my best to win her over."

At that point, Maya blushed furiously, covered her face with her hands. "Please, can we not talk about...." She stopped mid-sentence, curled into herself and grabbed her swollen belly as she groaned in agony. She rode the contraction out, breathing deeply. When it ended, she let out a whoosh and gasped. "Oh, my holy hell. That's much worse than the ones from earlier!"

At that, the door opened yet again and there was Dr. Thomas, right on time. Maya saw her and exclaimed, "Oh, thank god! I'm so glad you're here. My water broke, and I just had a contraction. It was awful, Dr. T. You need to get that anesthesiologist in here, stat! I want drugs. And on top of those drugs, I want more. I want to be floating in bliss and I need you to make that happen."

Dr. Thomas's eyebrows rose, and she smiled at her patient. "Maya, we'll get you an epidural in time. Let's do an exam and see what we're dealing with and get you hooked up to a contraction monitor, in addition to the fetal and heartbeat monitors they've got on you."

Maya grumbled something, and her doctor had to ask her what she'd said. She turned scarlet in embarrassment and whispered, "I'm still leaking."

Dr. Thomas chuckled. "Maya, there's no need to be embarrassed. Your water broke and your body is trying to tell you that it's ready."

A scared look crossed Maya's face. "It shouldn't be ready though. It's too early."

Dr. Thomas shook her head. "We've discussed this. It's a bit early, but we're going to handle it." She looked up at the crowd of family and friends, "If you're here, you know her well enough to know she wants you all up by her head, not down by her feet, while we're examining her or while she's laboring."

At that, everyone moved up toward Maya's head and the doctor did her exam quickly. "Maya you're sixty percent effaced, and five centimeters dilated. I'm going to give you an hour or so and see where we're at, then I'll come and check on you. Technically, you have twenty-four hours before the fact that the water breaks becomes an issue; it's doubtful that'll be the case here, but everyone is different, so I don't know how quickly you'll be ready. If you need anything, don't hesitate to push the button to call the nurse and they can get in touch with me."

Maya took a deep breath, let it out and nodded. As Dr. Thomas left, Sabrina headed back in carrying a pitcher and a cup. "I brought you some water. Also, you don't have to sit. It often helps move things along if you get up and walk around the halls. We have birthing exercise balls as well, if you'd like one of those. I can show you some exercises that you can do on it, if you want. You can shower in your room, even take a bath if you want. We want to make this as comfortable as possible."

Maya nodded, said she'd like to try the ball, and Sabrina left to retrieve one for her. She worked on the ball, took a bath and took a lot of walks, up and down the halls. She'd been having contractions that were spaced pretty far apart for hours and was getting tired. It was another five hours later that her contractions finally started to come faster. She was eighty percent effaced and seven cm dilated when her pain levels increased, and her contractions came closer and closer together. At that point, she finally received the epidural she'd been requesting.

During labor, only four people were allowed in the room. Braden and Cade were there, her mom was there, and Vaughn had refused to leave, which she secretly loved, though she'd huffed and bristled for show when he'd said it. He'd only smiled and kissed her lips, which caused her to grin and relent.

Dr. Thomas handled Maya with care and they all admired the woman for her competence and rapport with her. Maya handled the pushing like a champ, but she was exhausted after an hour and her frustration was showing. Vaughn wiped her forehead. "You're doing great, honey. Keep it up."

"I'm never doing this again! What the hell was I thinking?"

Braden smiled. "You can do this."

Dr. Thomas leaned to the side to make eye contact with Maya. "I need one more big push from you, Maya. I can see the head, so I just need you to last a little bit longer, all right?"

Maya growled, but bore down and Sylvia let out a gasp as the baby was finally pushed out. "It's a girl! Oh, she's beautiful. She's just gorgeous."

Sylvia had her hands over her mouth and tears coursing down her face. They all heard a tiny noise and one of the nurses came and gathered the crying baby and brought her close for everyone to look. Instead of the nurse handing her over, however, Dr. Thomas explained, "Because she came so early, she will need some NICU time. The nurses are going to run some tests before we can let you hold her, to be sure everything is all right."

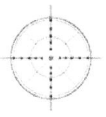

Braden

Suddenly the room felt supercharged. It was as if the fact that Maya was only thirty-five weeks along had been forgotten and the reality of the moment sunk in. Everyone had eyes on the two nurses that were diligently working to clean up the baby and check her vitals. The silence was broken however when, sharing a secret look with Braden and Maya, Dr. Thomas smiled. "I know you're tired, but I think someone else wants to make an appearance. Are you ready to go again?"

Maya smiled tiredly at Braden, who winked at her and leaned over to kiss her on her sweaty forehead. Maya nodded. "Let's do this."

Sylvia's focus went from the baby being worked on back to her daughter. She looked at Maya and Dr. Thomas in consternation. "Wait… What do you mean, go again?"

Cade turned to Braden, a shocked look etched itself over his features. When Braden nodded, tears escaping his eyes, Cade gave an excited whoop, picked his husband up in a crushing hug, and kissed him with more excitement than finesse. Braden had been keeping this secret for months now, and it had been killing him. The bigger Maya's belly had gotten, the more worried he'd become that they wouldn't be able to keep their secret. Much to Maya's chagrin, she'd also gained quite a bit of weight during the pregnancy, so that, combined with the fact that the babies were tiny, kept the questions to a minimum.

Surprise and joy laced his words as Cade whispered, "Twins, baby." And then louder, "Wait, is this why you kept telling me you didn't want to reveal the sex? Every time I went with you two for an ultrasound you had them turn the screen away from us."

Braden chuckled and murmured confirmation. Cade put him back down on his feet but continued to kiss Braden's forehead and his temples and then his lips again; he hugged him one more time and then bent over a grinning and teary-eyed Maya. "Aren't you a sneaky little thing?"

She nodded and chuckled tiredly. "I love you guys."

Cade grinned at her. "Oh sweetheart, you have no idea. We can't even express the love we have for you. This deserves presents. Do you need a new car? New wardrobe? Jewelry?"

Braden piped up. "She needs a new commercial grade espresso machine."

Maya's eyes flew open wide and she shook her head. "No, Braden. I have enough to get it myself. That's not what...."

Cade kissed her forehead. "Shhh, now. Don't insult us. We know damn good and well you didn't carry our babies for nearly nine months for a coffee maker, but that doesn't mean you're not going to get one."

Cade looked over at Braden and he nodded. "It's already ordered and should be here in a couple of weeks, shipping direct from Italy."

Maya gasped. "Oh, Braden, you didn't."

Braden and Cade grinned. "Oh, Maya, I did. Among a few other things you need out front."

Maya narrowed her eyes. "You found my list."

Braden grinned unrepentantly. "I did."

Cade laughed. "You're both pretty good at being sneaky."

Cade and Braden grinned at each other, while Maya scrunched up her face and shook her head. They all turned when they heard the doctor clear her throat. "Maya, you're gonna need to start pushing soon, if you wanna have the other one before the epidural wears off."

Maya made a startled sound then got herself ready. When Dr. Thomas told her to push, she did. It only took three good ones before everyone heard another squall as Baby B made his first appearance. Sylvia, tears still streaming down her face, gasped. "It's a boy! Oh, you guys, he's perfect, he's gorgeous! I can't believe my baby had twins!"

Another nurse wrapped him up and brought him near for everyone to see and then whisked him away toward his sister. Cade and Braden leaned down over Maya, hugged her, kissed her, and told her they loved her. She had tears streaming down her face and she whispered, "I know all that, I do. I love you both. Now go. Go see your babies."

They did as she bade. The nurses were busy weighing the babies and running tests. They got as close as they could and watched as their little ones were wiped clean, poked, and prodded, squalling all the while. They held hands and Braden leaned toward Cade and whispered, "Now you know why I did their bedroom in neutral colors and pretended I didn't want to know the sex. We needed to settle on a name for both a boy and a girl and that was the way I figured I'd keep it from you. I didn't avoid buying clothes for them, like I said I did. They both have a full wardrobe for the first year already. Maya and I went a little crazy. The shoes, Z, the shoes are so adorable and tiny!"

Cade grinned down at his husband and chuckled at that last bit. "Do we still need to buy double everything? You set their room up with one of everything, to keep your sneaky secret. Do we keep them in separate rooms?"

Braden looked horrified by the thought. "No way! They were in the womb together—we can't separate them. All the doubles were kept at Maya's. As soon as we had her move in, when she was having a few complications with the gestational diabetes and we wanted to keep her close, we began putting all the double things at her place. Cooper is the only other person who knows, and that's only because he walked into my kitchen one day and heard us talking. So, we enlisted his help. He has the second car seat in his car. Before we bring the babies home, he'll be bringing over everything for their nursery as well and getting everything set up for us, or at least built, and we can move it where we want."

Braden broke off as he saw Sabrina had approached. "Okay, so I'm gonna hit you with a lot of information all at once. They were born at thirty-five weeks, so hospital policy is to place them in the NICU until they are checked over by a NICU doctor. They are both under six pounds, so we'll want to be sure they are big enough to ride home in your car seats. Most likely they'll just end up being 'growers and feeders,' but the doctor will need to check them for sepsis, which is infection; hyperbilirubinemia, which is jaundice; congenital defects; poor feeding; respiratory distress; and blood sugar instability.

"Those things all sound scary, but your little ones look pretty healthy, just a little small due to their age, so some of these things might take a little time. Their bodies need to learn how to breathe properly, feed properly, and process blood sugars. None of the things I listed are necessarily life threatening and are very common in preemies.

"People fear the NICU, but really, it's a great place for babies to grow and for their bodies to learn how to do these new things on their own that were sprung on them a bit early. And for parents, it's also a great time of learning, as you have doctors and nurses helping you with feeding, learning how to hold them, burp them, swaddle them, and change them."

Cade spoke up. "Can we hold them?"

Sabrina smiled wide. "Oh yeah. They just need to finish up what they're doing right now then you'll be able to hold them. As the babies aren't in distress, you should be able to have a little bonding time before we take them to the NICU. Why don't you take off your shirts and we can have you hold them skin to skin? It helps them stabilize and helps with bonding. Mother's bodies help with temperature control, but because we've got two fathers here, you'll have to be careful not to overheat them. We won't bundle them, but we'll keep a blanket at their backs while you hold their fronts to your chests."

With that, she walked toward the NICU nurses and helped bring them toward their fathers. When the NICU nurses placed them, naked, in both of their arms, the new fathers just held them, rocked them, and looked at them in awe. Braden heard the click of Sylvia's camera, but couldn't tear his eyes away from their little girl. He was finally able to look toward Cade and was so moved to see tears in his husband's eyes that tears came again to his. They moved even closer to each other so that they were, all four of them, touching. They rocked like that for several minutes and then Cade whispered, "Let's switch."

Braden smiled and nodded, and the nurses helped them swap babies. They all settled back into each other again and Braden smiled wide as he heard Syl's camera going wild again. After another few minutes, Sabrina interrupted. "It's about time to get them to the NICU."

Cade spoke up, "Is there a way for family to see the babies right now?"

Sabrina looked toward the NICU nurses who nodded. One of them spoke up. "There is a viewing room you can visit before the doctor sees them. You can sit in a rocker or stand by the window and hold them and your family and friends can come peek through the glass. That will have to do until they're approved for other visitors."

Sabrina smiled and told them she'd head out there and let them know, but Braden shook his head and looked at Cade. "Why don't you go with them into the NICU. Hold the babies by the window and Sabrina can help me lead the family there so that I can talk to them and give them the news."

Cade's brows rose. "You sure?"

Braden nodded and grinned, enjoying the excitement on Cade's face at being able to stay with their babies, knowing his protective instincts were already kicking in. Cade left, a proud new papa, pushing the rolling crib that was holding both of the swaddled babies and following the other nurses to the NICU. Braden turned toward Maya as they were leaving, and saw that she was asleep, and being cared for by Vaughn. He smiled at that turn of events and walked toward the waiting room, to introduce their babies to their new family.

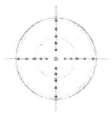

Maya

As Braden and Cade walked toward their babies to meet them for the first time, Maya let out a relieved and tired sigh. Vaughn gathered her close and kissed her softly on the lips, wiping her tears away with his thumbs, making her heart beat faster. While the doctor finished up with her, she gazed into Vaughn's eyes and saw something she hadn't expected from him, tears in his eyes and emotions she couldn't help but see as he promised, "The next time you do this, it's gonna be our baby you're having and you're gonna be Mrs. Bowman."

She gasped, and her eyes flared wide. "What?"

He kissed her soundly before she could say anything more, and when he pulled away, she felt both dazed and hopeful. He murmured, "I don't care how long it takes. I don't care what I have to do to win your heart.

I've waited this long for a first date, I can wait even longer if it means I get to spend the rest of my life with you."

With that, he looked away from her and gazed at her mom who was looking at both of them with hope and a happy grin on her face. Maya watched, bemused, as he grinned right back and winked at her. "Wanna hug your girl?"

Her mom nodded. "I do."

Vaughn stood up and made to move away to give them privacy. But when he did, Maya reached out and squeezed his hand, holding on and keeping him by her side before she could think better of it. The way he looked at her set her heart to racing again. She could see her gesture had moved him and he squeezed her hand gently in his, rubbing his thumb on the back of her hand.

Her mom was at her side, but Maya held on to him even as her mom leaned in to hug her and whisper how proud she was of her and how happy she was that she'd found someone so wonderful. Maya figured it was too early to know if they'd work out, regardless of what he said, but she knew they'd just crossed the barrier she had erected to guard her heart so many years ago.

Thankfully, she was blissfully unaware of the remainder of the birthing process, as the doctor worked fast to finish up. She was soon covered in warm blankets, which was good, as she had been feeling rather cold. Vaughn brought her the water cup and she sipped, and when he kissed her forehead and moved away, she couldn't stop herself from asking, "You're not leaving, are you?"

Vaughn turned back toward her. "No, baby. I'm not going anywhere. Mikayla's at my sister's house and can be there for as long as she needs to stay. I'm not going anywhere until you ask me to leave."

She knew, from the way he said it, that he wasn't just talking about today, he was talking about their future, and something within her shifted. She was scared, but she also felt something for this man that she'd never felt before. They'd become good friends over the last year or so and she had wanted to say yes to him when he first asked her out on a date, but she'd held on to her past and had refused to truly move on.

She wasn't quite sure why she'd finally given in, except maybe it was the family picnic they'd both been to where she'd seen him interacting with his daughter. The sight of the huge, muscle-bound former MMA fighter being so tightly wound around his daughter's little finger was such a wonderful thing to see. She'd started to open up around him more and began to trust that the man she saw was the man he truly was and that he wasn't hiding anything from her. As she drifted off to sleep she felt an overwhelming sense of peace. It was a feeling she couldn't remember ever having felt before. But somehow, she knew she had a bright future ahead of her, with Vaughn by her side.

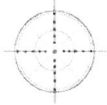

Braden

Braden walked down the hall with Sabrina, heading toward the waiting room. As they entered, Braden could barely believe his eyes. Half of Cade and Cooper's staff from Custos was there, along with Nana and Cade's family and several other friends. He cleared his throat but had to laugh when no one noticed him at all. They were all engrossed in various conversations, mingling together.

He came up behind Nana and wrapped an arm around her. She looked up at him in surprise and let out a gasp, which quieted down the group, for about out a second. As soon as they all saw him, however, they erupted with questions. He held up both of his hands to quiet them down. "Cade is in the NICU—"

There were more gasps and many 'Oh no's.' Again, everyone erupted with questions and he grinned and held up his hands. "Shhh. It's all right. It's not a bad thing. Come on. Maya's nurse, Sabrina, will show us the way and you can see for yourself."

With that, he wrapped his arm around Nana, her expression quizzical. He squeezed her and kissed her head and continued, following Sabrina. As they approached the windows, Cade's back was turned to them and a nurse looked to be handing him a bundle. She nodded behind him and he turned around, holding both babies in his big, strong arms, a mile-wide grin splitting his face. And again, with the comical gasps and gaping mouths as they all realized he was holding two babies instead of one.

Nana approached the window first, tears streaming down her face as she reached up and touched the glass. Cade walked closer to the window, and Braden saw, in the reflection, Nana's hand come up to cover her mouth. She turned toward him, tears streaming down her face and a grin hidden by her hand. She reached up, clasped Braden's cheeks, and kissed each one before turning back to the window.

The hall had grown so quiet he realized Syl had followed them and had kept her camera going. Braden looked at Cade and then back at their family and closest friends and announced quietly, "We'd love for you to meet the newest additions to our family, Harper Addison McCade and her younger brother by seventeen minutes, Hunter Finnegan McCade. Finnegan is for my brother-in-law—without him, I wouldn't be here, and neither would they. Addison is Maya's middle name. Without her, we wouldn't have them."

Sylvia gasped, camera forgotten, and began to cry and Jon gathered her in his arms, a huge smile on his face. Cooper stepped forward and hugged them both, a happy smile on his face.

Braden continued, "Maya did great. She was a trooper. She's recovering right now, resting peacefully. I'm sure she'd love to see some of you, when she feels up to it. The babies were born at thirty-five weeks, so they are considered preemies and will need some time in the NICU. They are healthy, but as you can see, they are quite small and need to have constant supervision, should either of them need a little help with their respiratory system, or possibly some other things that shouldn't be life threatening. As soon as we know more, we'll let you know. We need them to see the NICU doctor as soon as possible, so I'll be joining them right now. Visitors are allowed, but they'll need to see their doctor first before we can figure out a rotation. We'll keep you all informed."

He hugged Nana once again and was then pulled into hugs from the McCades. When he was able to address them again, he smiled. "Thank you all for coming. Each and every one of you mean so much to us and to have you all here, to celebrate this moment, feels right and means the world to us. I know some of you have been here for hours, maybe all of you. We don't know how long it will be before Maya will want to see people or before we will be able to bring visitors back to see the babies. So, since it's the middle of the night, please, everyone, go home and rest. We'll be in contact with you once we know more."

With that, Braden waved and headed toward the NICU doors to join his family.

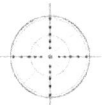

The next eight days passed in a blur of hospital staff and what Cade and Braden had dubbed 'the twin learning curve.' They had made a promise to each other that they wouldn't leave the babies alone while they were in the hospital. However, after the first two days, their family caught on that they'd each been doing alternating twelve hours on, twelve hours off and spending absolutely no time together there as a new family of four, and they were inundated with help during the off hours.

They were finally able to spend some much-needed time together with their newborns. They arrived every morning at eight a.m. and left every evening at ten p.m. Not only did their family and friends pitch in to bring them a late breakfast, a lunch, and a dinner every day and spend time with the babies while they took an hour at each meal time to spend together, but someone was always available to spend the night so their little ones were never alone.

Turned out Harper had a bit of jaundice and they both had trouble with feeding and breathing. They trusted the hospital staff implicitly, but they just couldn't fathom leaving their newborns alone overnight without someone there should something happen. Cooper had jumped right in and built their second crib and set up the rest of their nursery. He was running Custos without Cade, and Braden had his talented new assistant fully trained to manage things on his own while he was away. They'd both taken several months off to be at home with their little ones, so neither of them had to stress about work. Harper's jaundice had cleared up in a few days, but it was another six long days before the twins were both deemed strong and stable enough to be sent home with no complications.

Once home with their precious cargo, they were finally able to introduce Thor to his new brother and sister. The huge dog was immediately protective, and wherever the babies were, Thor was right there, keeping an eye out for them. Neither of the men could quite get over the fact that they were now responsible for not one, but two gorgeous babies. In such a short time, the twins had grown and gotten so much stronger. They were amazed at their progress and so proud to be the parents of such beautiful and tough survivors.

One thing was for sure, they counted their blessings every day, having each other and having been blessed with their two new, beautiful warriors.

The End!

Up next: Saving Sebastian: A Catharsis Novel (Custos Securities Series Book 3) out now!

Author's Note

Thank you for reading *Protecting Braden*. I hope you enjoyed the conclusion of Braden and Zavier's story. I can't wait to continue the Custos Securities Series with Sebastian and Gideon's story, coming soon.

I always appreciate feedback from readers, especially as a new author. If you're so inclined, please take a moment to leave a review.

I love connecting with my readers, as well. You can find me on Facebook; Twitter; Instagram, Pinterest, and Luna David.

Acknowledgements

Husband, husband, husband, what can I say… You and our little monsters are what keep me going every day. When I don't want to write, edit, and edit some more, I just remember what it feels like to hear the words, "I'm proud of you" and I can continue. I couldn't have done any of this without you.

My wonderful family and friends have been exceedingly supportive. I have felt such love and acceptance in this new journey I'm on and I can't thank you enough for that.

Jamie Matthews, damn girl, we did it! Wow! Remember way back when? Back to the time we said, what if? Well here we are, following our dreams! When I get stuck, have questions, want to hash out a scene, or just need to whine about something, you're my go-to girl. You lucky duck, you! I'm proud of you and your perseverance. Hell, I'm proud of us! It's not enough to say thank you, but here it is anyway; thank you, from the bottom of my heart.

To my wonderful beta readers, thank you a million times over! Elizabeth Coffey, Denise Dechene, Jen Barten, Michael Edward McFee, and Becky Ellsworth. You all provided much needed feedback, edits, and suggestions. Each and every one of you had unique ideas that improved my story. I can't thank you all enough.

Kellie Dennis, my wonderful cover artist, thank you. This cover was even better than the first! I was absurdly vague and yet, you somehow read my mind and figured out exactly what I needed. Brilliant, as always.

About the Author

Luna David is a true romantic at heart who was fortunate enough to find and marry her soul mate. Most of the time she considers herself lucky to have been blessed with having g/b twins, but they're giving her a run for her money. She's a stay at home mom and an author, so when she's not begging her little monsters to behave, you'll most likely find her writing.

She loves anything book, coffee or dark chocolate related and can't think of a better way to pass the time than to combine all three. She reads romance novels voraciously and while she prefers contemporary romance with strong Alpha males finding their soul mates, she's a sucker for any well written, romantic story regardless of genre.

She created the Custos Securities Series because she loves to write what she loves to read. Her books feature strong dominant males and the men they would die protecting. Toss in some BDSM and kink and you've got her Catharsis Novel Series and The Boys Club Series. She loves nothing more than making her readers feel a wide range of emotions with her words. And she hopes you enjoy her stories. Happy Reading!

Printed in Great Britain
by Amazon